A COMPLEX, FOUR-SIDED LOVE STORY AND A CIVIL WAR

A COMPLEX, FOUR-SIDED LOVE STORY AND A CIVIL WAR

Adaptation from *KABIL'S SISTER (1994)*
by
Late Kabi Al-Mahmud
Abridged, enriched, and reorganized
by

AZM FAZLUL HOQUE

Email Address: rubinahoque@gmail.com
Author E.Mail: contactazm@yahoo.com
AND/OR azmfazlulhoque2@yahoo.com

Cover Design: AZM FAZLUL HOQUE

Print information available on the last page.

Rev. date: 10/21/2020

To order additional copies of this book, contact:
Xlibris
844-714-8691
www.Xlibris.com
Orders@Xlibris.com
817470

OTHER BOOKS BY THIS AUTHOR:

My Life Through Six Continents (2011)
Memorable Moments (2014)

CONTENTS

ABOUT THIS BOOK

This book is about a complex, intriguing, four-sided love story set in the background of Bangladesh Liberation War against Pakistan in 1971.

The story involves four young people from two different ethnic communities in Bangladesh—two from the local Bengali community and the other two from the refugee immigrant community from India during its partition in 1947, who had settled in the then East Pakistan.

The story revolves around its main character Kabil, a top-ranking student activist who actively participated in the armed struggle for the liberation of Bangladesh from across the border in India. His departure from Dhaka to participate in the nine months-long warfare cost him the love of his life, Rokhi, the daughter of his uncle Ahmed Alam who had earlier married an Urdu-speaking immigrant settler girl in Dhaka. Meanwhile, Rokhi's earlier suitor, Andy (also an orphaned immigrant settler from India), after his love had been rejected by Rokhi, fell in love with Kabil's maternal cousin Momi who herself was dreaming about marrying Kabil from her childhood. However, because Kabil was indifferent to Momi's youthful love and was deeply in love with Rokhi, Momi wanted to love anew and marry Andy. Since the untenable political situation during the liberation war forced Andy and Rohki to leave Bangladesh together for Pakistan, Kabil proposed, after his return from India, to marry

Momi. But Momi being hurt by Kabil's earlier indifference and hurt by Andy's unexpected departure, declined Kabil's proposal.

Kabil then found his unexpected love in a different person who had been his long-time political co-activist, his assistant during cross-border guerrilla warfare from India, and had earlier been married to his close friend Nisar who had been killed by the Pakistani forces on that fateful night of March 25, 1971.

DEDICATION

To my parents, Mr. Abdul Jabbar and Mrs. Azma Khatun,
and to my elder brother, Gazi Mohammad Ekhlas Mian,
in perpetual gratitude
for instilling in me early on a love of reading especially
political and religious history. My father was an avid
reader. Some of his favorites were the translated
Persian epics namely Shah Nama (Book of Kings
and warriors like Rustam and Sohrab) and Kasasal
Ambia (Book of Prophets). These lyrical volumes
were often sources of reading, listening and discussion
in our household during my formative years.

PROLOGUE

This novel is about a complex, four-sided love story based in the background of the Bangladesh Liberation War in the second half of the twentieth century. Civil wars for the liberation of people from the tyranny and exploitation in any country are always brutal, ruthless, senseless, and inhuman. The civil war against the brutalities of the Pakistani military forces leading to Bangladesh's liberation was no exception. There were hundreds of thousands (even millions by some estimate) of lost human lives, and millions of people were displaced internally and externally to India. There were untold numbers of cases of personal sacrifices, sufferings, and human tragedies.

One such tragedy in the Bangladesh Liberation War involved four young lovebirds of a family, which combined people from two ethnically diverse communities who spoke different languages, had different social backgrounds, cultures, and hailed from different provinces of pre-partitioned South Asian subcontinent. These communities were played against each other by the vested interest groups of Pakistani exploiters. In the end, these family members' hopes and dreams, like those of many others, were shattered by the brutalities of the civil war, and the lives of these four young people went in different directions in different countries.

This love story, unlike most others, did not have a happy ending. It was complex and full of intrigue and family trials and tribulations. Momi—an orphaned village girl—was given to believe by her paternal aunty Zakia that when Momi grew up, Zakia would like her son Kabil to marry Momi. Momi grew up with that dream and loved Kabil from her childhood. Kabil, when he left his village home to go to university in Dhaka, met up with his estranged but rich paternal uncle and his daughter Rokhi—a beautiful city girl. Kabil and Rokhi fell in love with each other. Meanwhile, Rokhi's maternal cousin Andy, himself an orphan who worked for Rokhi's parents, was in love with Rokhi ever since she was a teenage girl. But Rokhi never reciprocated Andy's love, especially since she met Kabil. Andy then met Kabil's maternal cousin Momi, fell in love with her, and wanted genuinely to marry her. Since Kabil was courting Rokhi and was in love with her, Momi genuinely reciprocated Andy's love and was willing to marry him.

However, the geopolitical development in the country at that time, over which none of these four young people had any control whatsoever, put their lives upside down. In the end, Rokhi had to leave the country with Andy. Kabil then approached Momi and proposed to marry her. Momi however, heartbroken from Kabil's earlier indifference and Andy's unexpected departure from the country, refused Kabil's belated gesture.

The novel narrates a romantic and presumably platonic love story set in the background of Bangladesh liberation struggle in the 1960s leading to a civil war in the early 1970s. The liberation struggle led by popular mass movement had started in the late 1940s soon after the partition of the South

Asian subcontinent in 1947, leading to the creation of a separate, independent state of Pakistan comprising the Muslim majority areas of the then united India. Pakistan thus consisted of two geographical areas separated by over one thousand kilometers of foreign Indian territory. The eastern part was called East Pakistan and the western part was named West Pakistan. The people of the two parts of Pakistan could hardly be more different from each other ethnically, linguistically, culturally, and in many other ways of their lifestyles. The only commonality between these two peoples was the adherence by the majority of their population to the religion of Islam.

From the very beginning, East Pakistan was subjected to colonial-type economic, social, linguistic, and cultural exploitation by its western counterpart. Even though East Pakistan at that time had numerically more population than West Pakistan had, all economic, corporate, industrial, military, and political power centers including the capital itself of the new country were located in West Pakistan. This was possible because the leadership of the then All India Muslim League Party which ironically was established first in 1905 in Dhaka, Bangladesh and which led the struggle for establishing a separate Muslim majority sovereign country, came from the western part of the subcontinent in the 1940s. This gave West Pakistan a head start in its continued and perpetual dominance over East Pakistan.

Early in 1948, the then leader of the Muslim League Party, who became Pakistan's de facto governor-general and domiciled in West Pakistan made a public announcement in

Dhaka to the effect that the language Urdu of West Pakistan, even with its minority population, would be the state/national language of the whole of Pakistan, ignoring the legitimate right of Bengali spoken by the majority of the population of Pakistan. A young senior student of Dhaka University and then a budding political leader by the name of Sheikh Mujibur Rahman (popularly known as Mujib) was among the first ones to oppose the governor-general's proclamation. That set the stage for a province-wide mass protests and movement which later became known as Mother Language Movement. Years later, the United Nations Education and Scientific Cooperation Office (UNESCO) in recognition of that struggle by the Bengali people declared February 21 as the Universal Mother Language Day honoring the date in 1952 when numbers of students were shot dead in Dhaka by the Pakistani military. That movement led to the subsequent struggles for nearly twenty-five years against the systematic oppression of East Pakistan by its western counterpart. In the 1960s, the struggle was led, among others, by the party of Awami League whose young charismatic leader Sheikh Mujibur Rahman based in East Pakistan was the principal opponent of military dictatorship based in the capital Islamabad in West Pakistan. That struggle culminated in a civil war in East Pakistan in the early 1970s in which the neighboring country India had to intervene in support of the Bangladesh Liberation Forces (Mukti Bahini). India had to intervene because close to ten million refugees from the then East Pakistan had fled to neighboring Indian states because of systematic military crackdown by the Pakistani forces. The culmination of the civil war was the creation of a new independent sovereign country of Bangladesh with its capital in Dhaka.

The love story in this novel is set in the background of this national struggle through the 1960s and the subsequent liberation war in 1971. The story involves two middle-class families in the then East Pakistan. One of the families came from a rural majority Bengali Muslim community and the other from an Urdu-speaking Muslim refugee settler family of communities from various parts of India who had migrated in 1947 to then East Pakistan and settled mostly in Dhaka. In time, these migrant refugee settler communities, patronized by their Urdu-speaking compatriots from West Pakistan, mostly attained the upper hand in government jobs, business and commercial enterprises, and industrial sectors over their fellow local Bengali communities.

The novel narrates the story of an intriguing love quadrangle involving four young members of these two ethnically diverse families. They were closely related to each other. The dreams and hopes of these four young people, as well as that of their parents and other members of both families, were direct victims of one of the cruelest civil wars of the twentieth century which resulted in hundreds of thousands of innocent people being killed and millions being displaced.

I first received an almost torn copy of the novel in 2018 when my younger brother Dr. Abul Kalam Azad sent it to me from Bangladesh through my daughter Dr. Sabrina Hoque. I read the novel with general interest, anticipating that its story would deal with two or more young men and women being in love with each other, and the story would end, after some trials and tribulations, in all of them being with each other and live happily ever after. However, I was intrigued by the twist and turns of the story toward its end. At that stage, I felt that the novel deserved a wider exposure and readership outside the Bengali-speaking readers only. I then decided to abridge, enrich, and reorganize the sequences of events of the story and present it to the wider English-speaking readership.

The novel in original Bengali was titled by its author as *Kabil's Sister*. I couldn't figure out the rationale behind such a title. I could only surmise. Perhaps it was with the hope that most Bengali readers, as I first did when I saw and started reading the Bengali version, would associate and anticipate that the book would deal with the Koranic and Biblical story of Adam and Eve's sons Habil (Abel) and Kabil's (Cain) feud over their respective twin sisters. And that this reference would generate interests in the book among that circle of readers in Bangladesh.

In reading the book, I discovered that the story had nothing to do with that famous Biblical story. I found the story of the book by itself, especially its ending, was intriguing and interesting without any reference to and dependence on that mystical story alluded by the title of the Bengali version of the book on its cover. Moreover, my intention was to provide the interesting story of the book a wider audience among the international English-speaking readers. I also thought that such an international audience might not have as much interests in that Biblical story as the limited Bengali Muslim readers do. I, therefore, thought of a title that would have more relevance to the story narrated in the book itself.

The book tells primarily the story of romantic, broken dreams of its four main characters who were devastated with their love lives by the political and ethnic circumstances of the prime time of their lives. Neither of them had any personal control over these circumstances. They were just victims of such circumstances at that time in the background of which the story was set. But for these circumstances, their lives and the ending of the book's story could easily have been different. The book also narrates the broken dreams of Kabil's father in the story who had great hopes that his younger brother would in time change the economic and social status of his former illustrious, rural family. It also narrates the broken hopes of Kabil's widowed mother Zakia who had brought her orphaned niece Momi (Momena) under her care and raised Momena with her full knowledge that one day she would be married to Kabil when they grew older. In the end, both Zakia and Momena's hopes were also dashed because of the subsequent circumstances. The book further narrates the sad story of a young, uncommon (at that time) female student activist against the Pakistani oppression of her people as her newly married husband was brutally killed, like many others, by the Pakistani military. It is, therefore, the story of broken dreams of not only the main characters of the story but by extension, perhaps of many other similar ones of the time in the country. Hence, I decided to give the book a more relevant title.

My objective in undertaking this work was to expose the story of the book *Kabil's Sister* in its original Bengali version to a wider readership in the international literary arena. As I progressed the work, I felt that the story needed a more attractive beginning other than the scenario of a young man (Kabil), who had grown up in a remote village in Bangladesh, made his maiden trip to the capital city of Dhaka as was the case in the book's Bengali version. I, therefore, composed a relevant scenario based on the political mass movement that led to a civil war in Pakistan in 1971, culminating in East Pakistan being liberated as a new sovereign state of Bangladesh. This was done through a scenario that I created where Mujib was arrested by the Pakistani armed forces on that fateful night of March 25, 1971, which triggered the long-simmering liberation war. This scenario was not included in the Bengali version of the book by its original author. I described at that early stage of the story Kabil's high-profile student leadership in the political movement of Bangladesh by 1971, and his deep involvement in it which led to the tragic ending of the story. This new beginning entitled "Trigger of a Civil War" is incorporated in the first chapter of this adaptation. My rationale for this was that the entire love story was based in the background of that civil war. I also added in this chapter my own composition on a brief description of political, economic, socio-cultural and religious situations in the South Asian sub-continent and the conflict and contradictions in these areas between the two geographically separated parts of the then Pakistan. These background informations which were not included in the Bengali version of the book will provide better understanding to the non-South Asian readers about the root causes of civil war in the then united Pakistan. Then, I presented the author's original version of the beginning of the story by describing Kabil's maiden trip to Dhaka and subsequent events—through the artistic mechanism of his dream on his escape boat on the Megna and the Titas Rivers on his way to the nearest Indian city of Agartala at the midnight of March 26, 1971. These later events then unfolded in the second chapter entitled "A Blossoming Teenage Love" in this adaptation. The adaptation of the original story, therefore, begins mostly in chapter 2 in this English version.

The story was narrated in the 1994 Bengali version of the book "Kabil's Sister" in 40 serialized, untitled chapters. I consolidated these into just four chapters and gave each chapter a relevant, meaningful title. This, I trust, enriches the presentation of the story in this English version of the book with its new title.

For the sake of easy reading by its expected English-speaking readers, I chose to shorten or even slightly change the names of the main characters of the story. Finally, I tried to expedite the progress of events in the story for the ease of today's fast-paced book readers. I did that by reducing the literary descriptions of various natural settings of the story, including those describing the mundane subjects of its heroine's bedroom furnishings and her parents' house and living room settings. I hope by doing that, I did not compromise too much of the literary aspects of the book.

A good portion of the contents of this book is an English adaptation from the Bengali book "Kabil's Sister" (Kabiler Bohn). For that, I am grateful to the soul of its illustrious Bengali author. Finally, I would like to thank my brother Dr. Abul Kalam Azad for sending me the book in Bengali and thank my daughter Dr. Sabrina Hoque Clark for bringing the book to me. I also thank my son Barrister Arman Hoque for bringing some relevant historical facts and Biblical and Koranic beliefs to my attention during my endeavor.

CHAPTER 1

Trigger of a Civil War

March 25/26,1971

Those two days and the night in-between were perhaps the darkest political times in over four thousand year's history of the region of Bengal, the eastern part of which is now known as Bangladesh. Since the partition of the South Asian subcontinent in 1947, the land was named as East Pakistan, forming the eastern part of Pakistan—separated by over a thousand kilometers of Indian territory from its western part—West Pakistan. The two parts of Pakistan not only had two distinctly different geographical, historical, socio-cultural backgrounds, their languages, dress codes, ethnicity, food habits, ways of life, and temperament of the population in the two segments of Pakistan were also distinctly different from each other. The only common link between their two peoples was their adherence to the religion of Islam by the majority of their population in both regions.

For nearly twenty-five years since 1947, the then East Pakistan and its people who formed in those days the majority of Pakistan's total population were subjected to colonial-type political, economic, linguistic, and cultural exploitation by the

1

West Pakistanis who were numerically minorities in Pakistan compared to the East Pakistani Bengalis. This was possible because the political leadership of the Muslim League Party, which successfully fought for a separate Muslim majority nation of Pakistan, though formed first in 1905 in Dhaka, Bangladesh happened to come from West Pakistan in the last days of British Raj in united India in the 1940s. As a result, the capital city of the new nation of Pakistan, its political, military, industrial, and economic power centers were all located in West Pakistan.

Earlier in 1971, the first-ever countrywide fair and free democratic election in Pakistan was held under the tutelage of over a decade-long military-dominated government. In that general election, the Awami League Party with a strong base in East Pakistan then headed by one young, charismatic leader by the name of Sheikh Mujibur Rahman won the majority of parliamentary seats in the National Assembly (also located in Islamabad in West Pakistan). This gave the Awami League the democratic right and legitimacy to form the central government in Islamabad with its leader Sheikh Mujibur Rahman (popularly known as Mujib) as the prime minister of the whole of Pakistan. However, the matter got politically complicated when the leader of the People's Party, Mr. Z. A. Bhutto—with a strong base in West Pakistan and wining majority parliamentary seats in West Pakistan—though numerically fewer than the number of seats won by the Awami League —refused to accept the Awami League as the party winning overall majority seats in the National Assembly and Mujib as the prime minister of the whole of Pakistan. Mr. Bhutto began colluding with the prevailing West Pakistan-based central martial law government under Gen. Yahya Khan and urged the General not to transfer government power to Mujib's Awami League. After weeks and months of political negotiations and horse-trading with Mujib and his associates, General Yahya, in collusion with Bhutto and backed by his West Pakistan-based military and industrial establishments, decided on that fateful night of March 25, 1971, to militarily crackdown and suppress the popular movement in East Pakistan supporting Awami League's legitimate election win and Mujib's right to become prime minister. By then, of course, the popular movement turned into a demand for decentralization of government powers and autonomy for East Pakistan. The political environment in Dhaka on March 25 was as dark and thick as its monsoon heavy clouds. The city was apprehensively waiting for some unforeseen human disaster that was looming on the horizon. There were subdued anger, an undercurrent of fearful waiting in almost every household. Several newspapers that day reported the departure from Dhaka of several prominent West Pakistani political leaders. The reactions to their departure among the Bengali population all over the city were of much fear and apprehension. For them, it meant that the negotiation between Sheikh Mujib and his political and military opponents from West Pakistan for a peaceful transfer of governmental power to the majority seat-winning party of Awami League in the National Assembly had likely broken down. The city was apprehensively waiting for the next move by the martial law government of Gen. Yahya Khan. Dhaka on that day seemed like a city in the Middle Ages whose main gate had been blocked by the enemy, yet the city had not been prepared and equipped for its own defense against the impending onslaught. Being in Dhaka on that day and night felt by its citizens as if they were in ancient Baghdad—then capital of the Islamic Abbasyd dynasty in the thirteenth century, waiting yet unable to resist the possible attack by the Mongol invaders of Halaku Khan. Pedestrians in Dhaka City streets were out and about as if they were indifferent to what might soon happen to them. They seemed like a lifeless current of unarmed people moving on the sidewalks in front of mostly closed shops as if with no definitive purpose.

Among them was Kabil—a high-ranking student leader of Dhaka University and a close associate and confidante of Sheikh Mujib. He was out for a walk on the streets, trying to assess the situation in the city. Kabil was Mujib's chief student representative for explaining Mujib's Six Points Demand manifesto to the public during the recent election campaign. Kabil had been trying since early that morning to contact Mujib by phone with no success. He was told that Mujib had been busy all morning conferring with his senior political associates and was not accepting any phone calls. Kabil was a bit annoyed with the person who rather rudely conveyed the message to him before even Kabil could tell him his name. Kabil knew that Mujib had once given instruction to the people answering the phone for him that whenever Kabil called, they should at least inform him (Mujib) of Kabil's call. Kabil didn't know where and how, if at all, Mujib was negotiating with Yahya and his group on that day. He was not aware of the political agenda for the day of his fellow student leaders as he had not recently spent much time at nights in the student dormitories.

Walking toward the gate of the main building of Dhaka University, Kabil came across several students' protest marches on the streets with female students marching in the front. The protesting students were angry and appeared quite militant. He joined one of the students' marches which he thought had come out from one of the university students' dormitories.

Late that afternoon, Kabil got a message from Sheikh Mujib's office informing him that Mujib would like to see him urgently in his house early that evening. Kabil was relieved that he finally got some news about his leader's whereabouts. Kabil made it on time to Mujib's residence at house number 32 in Dhanmondi-an upper-class residential area in Dhaka. He was quickly ushered into Mujib's office chamber upstairs. There he found Mujib already engaged in serious political discussions with his deputy and close advisor Mr. Tajuddin Ahmed (Mr. T). Kabil paid traditional greetings to them and Mujib motioned him to a chair. Mr. T. picked up the conversation where he had left earlier, "General Yahya had been taking a hard line in our negotiations with him in the last few days. I don't feel he is in a mood to transfer power easily to our party. I'm afraid he might be hatching some drastic military measures to suppress the street protests as early as tonight. In the context of that possibility, I think it will be wise for us, especially for you, Mr. Leader to leave the city as soon as possible and move to some safe zone in the rural areas."

In response, Mujib said,

"I agree with you Taj in your assessment of the overall situation and the risk of our party leaders being arrested. To avoid that risk, I implore both of you and other senior party leaders to leave the city as soon as possible. As for myself, I've decided to stay in the city for as long as I can. Perhaps my presence here may bring some senses to Yahya and his military's madness in killing innocent people. Moreover, I cannot leave my unarmed countrymen and women in the face of imminent danger. But I need the rest of the senior party leaders to leave for safe areas so that you can provide leadership to our movement during my absence . . . dead or alive in Yahya's military prison."

With that, he stood up, hugged Mr. T. and Kabil by turn, and said farewell to them. The eyes of all three of them were about to shed tears as they parted. After both Mr. T. and Kabil had left the house, Mujib had supper with his close family members. He explained to them all the risks and advised them on how to run family affairs during his possible arrest and detention. He explained to his wife that he might be arrested as early as that night and asked her to prepare his routine and often familiar prison kit.

At around eleven o'clock that evening, a convoy of armed military and police Jeeps and vans surrounded Mujib's house. Two senior officers in full military gears in a Jeep appeared and ordered the guard to open the gate. The Jeep stopped at the porch in front of the house. The two officers got down, walked to the front door, and asked for Sheikh Mujib. He was informed of their arrival. As the two officers were waiting, Mujib appeared at the top of the stairs. The two officers stood in *attention* position and gave him a salute as a show of respect and reverence for the man who could and should have been by that time the prime minister of Pakistan. One of the officers said,

"Sir, we have orders direct from the office of the Chief Martial Law Administrator for your arrest." He then showed the arrest warrant to Mujib.

"I'm ready, Officers, as I've been anticipating this since early evening. My only request to you gentlemen is to leave my family members in peace."

"That we will do, sir," replied the other officer as they escorted Mujib to the waiting car in the porch behind their Jeep. The Jeep and the car then drove off.

By the stroke of midnight, the military onslaught on unarmed civilians broke out all over the city. University students' dormitories, prominent private citizens' homes, notable intelligensia were the special targets. Indiscriminate arrests were made; on-the-spot summary executions were carried out. The areas with majority non-Muslim residences and their social and educational institutions like Jagannath

College and the Ram-Krishna Missions were ransacked. There were widespread terrors and mayhem all over Dhaka.

KABIL'S ONLY FAMILY IN Dhaka, his cousin Rokhsana, her Bihari, Urdu-speaking mother Rania (Rownok Jahan), and their cook Halim Meah all woke up in their Bonogram Lane house off Rankin Street by the thunderous sounds of shootings and blasts all around in the neighborhood. They couldn't figure out where the sounds of continuous shootings were coming from. The frequency and the severity of the sounds of the shooting were rapidly increasing. The frequent flashing rays of continuous shootings of rifles, machine guns, and mortars into the sky were temporarily lighting up the city night sky, indicating death and destruction on the ground. There were sounds of horror and fear among people all around. First, Rokhsana poured out the word, "Amma," (mother in Urdu) and jumped out of her bed. She fell on the floor but quickly got up. She opened her bedroom door and ran toward the dining area next to the sitting room. She found the plates, glasses, and souvenirs all falling on the floor by the shaking caused by thunderous sounds of shootings outside. Rokhsana quickly ran to her mother's bedroom and found her lying on the bed facedown. She was invoking God's name (Allah, Allah) mixed with her continuous sobbing. Rokhsana jumped on the bed, embraced her mother, and shouted, "Halim Chacha (uncle in Urdu)! Please bring a jug of water quickly."

Halim had already woken up, got up from his bed on the kitchen floor, sat down inside by the open door, and was shaking by the sounds of shooting. He knew Kabil had not come back home yet because whenever Kabil came home late in the evening, it was usually Halim who would open the front gate. Kabil had left home early that evening to meet Sheikh Mujib in his residence. He told Rokhsana that from there he would go to the university campus to meet with his fellow student leaders and that he would come back home even though it might be late. Halim ran to Rania's bedroom with a jug of water in his hand as soon as he heard Rokhsana's call.

"Has she fainted?" he asked as he entered the room.

"I don't know. You please touch her and see."

Halim leaned on the bed, touched Rania's forehead from the bedside, and realized that she had just fainted but breathing normally. He quickly took a handful of water from the jug and sprayed it over Rania's eyes and face. Rania made an awakening sound. Rokhsana realized her mother recovered from her fainting and put her mother's head back on the pillow.

"What happened, Mom? Are you okay? Are you feeling any pain?" she asked.

Rania didn't respond, looked at Rokhsana with her eyes widely open. Tears were falling from the corners of her eyes. Her lips moved once even though no sound came out. She looked toward the side table where the medicines she usually took as sleeping aid were kept. Rokhsana understood she wanted the medicine. Rokhsana got down from the bed, took a pill from the side table, and gave it with a glass of water to her mother. Rania took the pill, swallowed it with water. As she turned on the bed to the other side, she asked with a shaking voice, "Hasn't Kabil come home yet?"

"Kabil is safe at the home of a friend of his. He called to tell me that," Rokhsana told a blatant lie to reassure her mother. Rania didn't respond and laid down as she had been on the bed looking at the other side. Halim put a light blanket on her body, switched the light off, and both he and Rokhsana came out of the room. Rokhsana came back to her bedroom but didn't dare phone anybody at that hour of the night. She sat down on her bed with her head bowed down to her knees. Suddenly, the telephone rang. She picked up the receiver. Kabil was on the line.

"Listen, Rokhi! I'm speaking from Anjuman's house." Anjuman was a fellow university student activist and wife of Kabil's close friend and classmate Nisar. Anjuman was also a friend of Rokhsana.

Kabil continued, "The military has attacked most of the dormitories of the university students. The students tried to launch counterattacks. In the process many students died. Meanwhile, nobody knows where Nisar is. He went to the dormitory this afternoon for his books and class notes. Before he left, he had told Anjuman that he would spend the night in his room there. I think many students died in the dormitories."

"Where is Anju?" Rokhsana interjected.

"She is lying on the verandah facedown. Listen, Rokhi! It's not safe for me to come back home at this hour. I'll somehow cross the Buriganga River later tonight or tomorrow morning and flee to some safer location. I'll try to take Anju with me as she isn't, as a student activist, safe in town either. Our leader Sheikh Mujib had ordered us to go out of Dhaka by early this evening."

"What about Mujib himself? Have they attacked his house?" Rokhsana asked.

"I don't know, Rokhi. Perhaps they cut telephone lines to his house."

"I hope he is alive."

"I don't know. Listen, tell aunty Rania . . ." Suddenly, the telephone line got cut off. Rokhsana tried to call Kabil back. But the line was dead, and there was no dial tone. Rokhsana laid down on her bed and started crying.

ON THE EARLY MORNING of March 26, another heart-wrenching tragedy took place at Rokshana's house as if all the shooting, massacre, and mayhem of the night before were not shocking enough for Rokhsana and their cook Halim Meah. Halim woke up early that morning and said his morning prayer. He then walked to the front gate, opened it partially, and peeked on the street. He saw a procession of some families, who had lived in this lane for years, walking by with their essential possessions. They were mostly Bengali, poor to middle-class families. The signs of grief, sorrow, sadness, and uncertainty about their fate and future were visible on their faces. He stepped forward a bit into the lane and found that almost all of the shops were closed. He quickly closed the gate and got back inside the house compound. He then entered Rania's bedroom and found that she hadn't woken up yet. He heard her breathing normally and assumed that she was okay. He shut her bedroom door half-closed. At that point, he heard Rokhsana's voice and looked back.

"Halim uncle! Please make a cup of tea for me. Did you go to see my mother?" she asked.

"Yes, your mother is still sleeping. Looks like she survived the first shock of last night. But, I'm afraid, when she wakes up, the first thing she'll do is ask about Kabil".

"You tell her that I talked to Kabil over the phone last night. He left Dhaka last night for his safety and security. He also took sister Anju with him. Anju is also a well-known student activist. Perhaps he took her with him out of Dhaka for her safety."

"Did Kabil call last night?"

"Yes, he called from Anju's house. He also told me that they couldn't get any news about Anju's husband Nisar. Nisar was supposed to have been at his dormitory last night where a lot of students were killed by the military."

Halim kept quiet for a few minutes and then asked,

"They don't have any news of Nisar? You said Nisar was in the dormitory and that a lot of students were killed there.

How could Kabil take Anju out of Dhaka without finding out where Nisar is?"

"What else can he do in this serious situation? He couldn't wait at home for the news about Nisar and take the risk of being captured by the military. Besides, I have a feeling that Kabil knows about Nisar's fate. Nisar had either been captured by the Pakistani military or something even worse might have had happened to him. I could sense from Kabil's voice over the phone last night that something serious had happened to Nisar. But Kabil was hesitant to tell me about it over the phone. Otherwise, why would Kabil go to Anju's house last night in the middle of all those shootings instead of coming home here? And from there why would he leave Dhaka with her? He knew well how my mother and I would fare last night in the middle of all those shootings. I've a feeling that Nisar is already dead." With that Rokhsana broke down in tears.

Shortly after, someone knocked at the front gate of the house. Rokhsana wiped her tears off, fixed her outfit quickly, and ran to the gate while telling Halim, "Okay, I'll go and see who is at the gate. You please go and make some tea for me."

She opened the gate and found Andy (Andaleeb), her other cousin from her mother's side (also Urdu-speaking immigrant refugee) and his domestic help Jubaida (Jubi) standing there. Both were trembling in fear.

"Come inside, brother. Come, Jubi." Rokhsana welcomed them in.

"Tell me first about Kabil," Andy asked with a genuine sense of concern in his voice.

"He telephoned me last night and told me about his plan to leave Dhaka by the end of the night or by early this morning. Perhaps he has already left."

"Thank God. I was worried about his safety last night in the middle of all those shootings. How is my aunty—your mother? Where is she?"

"She fainted last night. She is now sleeping. Perhaps she is okay."

Reassured about his aunty Rania, Andy said,

"On my way here, I noticed the military burned down the office of the Awami League supporting daily Bengali newspaper the *Ittefaq*. Many Bengali people are fleeing out of the city on their way to rural areas. Yahya and Bhutto together really broke Pakistan into two. These two infidels finished off a great nation of Muslims in South Asia."

"The nation can go to hell," Rokhsana responded angrily.

Suddenly at that moment, they heard the unlikely crying sound of cook Halim from Rania's bedroom.

"Rokhi, madam! Please come here soon. Your mother's condition turned for the worse".

Rokhi and Andy rushed to Rania's bedroom and found her lying down on the bed with her head turned on one side on the pillow. A thin stream of blood slid from her nose on her cheek. Andaleeb held one of her hands and called out. "Aunty!"

There was no sign of life or breath in her listless body. Andaleeb realized his aunty had died of heart failure. But her face didn't indicate any sign of death.

AZM FAZLUL HOQUE

Rokhsana abruptly sat down on the rattan stool (mora) by the bedside. For some reason, she could not mourn at that moment. Tears failed to roll down her cheeks. Andaleeb felt frozen for a moment. Only Halim got out of the room, went to the dining area, and began crying with his head on the dining table.

Both Rokhsana and Andaleeb were busy all that day arranging for Rania's funeral and burial. They decided not to take the body to the city's noted graveyard Azimpur. They would rather bury it on the front inside by the wall of their house compound. Once that was decided, Andaleeb went to Anjuman's parents' house to convey to them the news of Rania's death.

Anjuman's father told him, "I'm sorry to hear about your and Rokhsana's great loss at this critical time. Please accept my heartfelt condolences. I will help you find some laborers who will dig the grave. My wife will help in the final body washing of the deceased. Please ask your cook Halim to notify the local Imam to come to lead the final prayer for the deceased late in the afternoon."

Andaleeb felt assured and was about to take leave of Anju's father when he said;

"You are Rokhsana's cousin from her mother's side, aren't you?"

"Yes!" Andaleeb replied.

"You look very tired. Please come and sit for a moment and have a cup of tea."

Andaleeb took a seat and said, "Rokhsana is in a great shock and grief at her mother's death at this critical time. Most of her mother's friends and relatives have fled to Mirpur and Mohammedpur areas where most immigrant refugees are settled. And of course, Rokhsana's only cousin Kabil from her Bengali father's side escaped from your house last night."

"Yes, Kabil left our house well before dawn last night. I'm not sure if they made it to the rural areas as of now. But we feel a bit relieved because he took Anjuman with him. Her mother is grateful to Kabil for his sense of responsibility as one involved in politics at this dangerous time of his political life. We are very sad about the death of Kabil's aunty Rania when Kabil is on the run for his life. Perhaps she died of mental shock."

By that time, Anju's mother appeared on the scene with a tea tray in her hand.

Andaleeb took a sip from his tea cup and hesitantly asked Anju's mother,

"Aunty! Did you get any latest news about Anju's husband Nisar?"

Anju's mother instantly covered her face with the edge of her saree and began sobbing. Anju's father interjected at this moment,

"Perhaps, you didn't get the news about Nisar, our son-in-law. Kabil perhaps didn't have time to inform Rokhi about it either. Nisar was killed by the Pakistani army last night in front of his students' dormitory—S.M.Hall. Kabil didn't disclose the news to Anju either, but he had told me of the sad news before he left. You may pass on the message to Rokhsana later at an appropriate time"

"I think Rokhsana got a sense of the sad news about Nisar from the tone of Kabil's telephone conversation with her last night. Rokhsana also sensed that because Kabil came to your house instead of going to Rokhsana's house last night in the middle of all the shootings. She told me that herself this morning. Now I'm clear what a great loss sister Anju suffered last night. She probably is not aware of her loss yet."

Andaleeb's words made Anju's mother sob even more. Her husband got up and tried to comfort her. He turned to Andaleeb and said, "She'll be okay. You go home now and try to arrange things with cook Halim for the funeral. We'll be in Rokshana's house shortly. Did you manage to send the news of your aunty's death to her friends and relatives?"

"No, sir. Who could I send? I came to your house with much fear and trepidation. From Bonogram Lane to your house, there was no human being on the street. No shop was open. The doors and windows of nearby houses were shut closed. I don't even know where to buy the shroud from, to wrap the deceased's body."

"Okay, you go now. I'll try to arrange for everything as much as I can."

Andaleeb then left Anju's parents' house feeling somewhat relieved.

The funeral services and the burial of deceased Rania were completed shortly after sunset on March 26. Anju's parents went back home soon after with all the people they had brought for burial. Rokhsana had a quick look at her deceased mother's face by requesting Anju's father to do so before the burial of the body. She then retired in her bedroom and hadn't come out since then. Andaleeb was exhausted and had been sleeping in Kabil's bedroom. His domestic help Jubi sat on the sofa in the drawing room all afternoon and finally exhausted, fell asleep on the sofa.

It was now about nine o'clock at night. Only one person in this house and perhaps in this whole neighborhood was still awake. He was their cook Halim. Halim took a shower and then entered the kitchen and started the fire to cook some dinner for four souls who didn't have a good meal all day long. When he finished cooking, he went to wake Andaleeb who woke up by the first knock on his door.

"I'm not asleep, Uncle Halim."

"Okay, dinner has been served on the table. Call Rokhi and Juby and come eat something."

"Okay, I'll wake them up. But I don't feel like eating now."

"Starving yourself will not do any good for you. At a time like this, you have to take care of everything Andaleeb Mian."

"Uncle Halim! There is nothing left to take care of. Staying in this locality, it will be difficult for us immigrant refugee settlers to save our souls. You wait in the dining area. I'll come there soon."

Andaleeb then woke up Rokhsana and Jubi and walked to the dining table. Nobody said a word while they seated themselves, and Halim served them some rice and curry. Rokhsana silently began eating. Andaleeb and Jubi followed her.

Andaleeb broke the silence at one stage,

"Perhaps, there is no non-Bengali family left in this locality, Rokhi! Every family moved to someplace else safer."

"If you are afraid, you can also move somewhere else cousin. Perhaps, you will not mind staying here at least for tonight. Tomorrow morning, you can take Jubi with you and move to the house of someone you know in the refugee settlement area," Rokhsana replied without looking at Andaleeb.

"I didn't mean that, Rokhi," Andaleeb responded quickly. "I am only trying to assess the situation in Dhaka. Where am I going to go leaving you alone here, cousin Rokhi?" he continued.

"I'm also not thinking about anything else and not telling you to move somewhere else. I'm trying to assess the reality. It is not safe for any non-Bengali to stay in this locality. The Bengalis last night have pronounced a declaration of independence from Pakistan. One army major from the Bengal Regiment declared Bangladesh late last night through a clandestine radio, as a sovereign independent country and called upon all Bengalis to join the battle for independence against the oppressive, occupying forces of Pakistan. I heard it on the radio late last night".

"Do you think the people and the students have started a counter- attack on the Pakistani military?"

"Perhaps there are sporadic resistance and even counter-attacks in rural areas."

A COMPLEX, FOUR-SIDED LOVE STORY AND A CIVIL WAR

"Do you think the Pakistani military arrested Sheikh Mujib last night?"

"That is not clear as of now. When Kabil phoned me last night, he said Mujib was likely in his house in Dhanmondi as of that time. But he had advised all Awami League Party leaders and student leaders including Kabil to leave Dhaka as soon as they could."

"What about Mujib himself?"

"I don't think Sheikh Mujib is that kind of a leader who would abandon his people in the face of death and destruction and would flee to a safe place for himself. It is my impression that the military has arrested and taken him into their custody. It will be clear in a day or two whether the military has killed him or took him into their custody. Anything is possible for the murderous forces of General Yahya. For them, Sheikh Mujib is just another dispensable Bengali as thousands of others with no means of protecting themselves. If they had the audacity to kill him, then know that no non-Bengali family is safe in the whole of East Pakistan. The innocent non-Bengali refugee settlers will pay the price for his murder. On the other hand, if the military has only arrested, instead of killing him, then know that even if Pakistan is broken into two separate countries as a result of the barbaric actions last night by Pakistani military, Sheikh Mujib will see to it that no large-scale murder of the refugee settlers will take place because these refugee settlers came from India as a result of the partition of India and creation of Pakistan. Mujib was one of the leaders at the forefront of the struggle for the creation of that Pakistan. Nobody knows better than Mujib under what circumstances these refugees left their homes, properties, and possessions in India during 1947 partition and came almost penniless to take shelter in East Pakistan. Now these same refugee settlers like idiots are opposing Mujib's Six Points Demand for the legitimate rights of East Pakistan. They think the West Pakistanis who largely refused to accept them as refugees in 1947 are now their better friends simply because the West Pakistanis share the same language Urdu with them. Even then, I think they are not opposed to Yahya transferring governmental power to Mujib's Awami League Party at least for keeping the integrity and unity of Pakistan. For they know that their future in this province is intricately linked to East Pakistan remaining as an integral part of Pakistan. That is the reason I'm saying that if the military animals have killed Sheikh Mujib, then refugees like you should think about moving to places where they think they would be safer," Rokhsana concluded.

Rokhsana's words cast a shadow of fear and near panic on both Jubi and Andaleeb. Andaleeb tried to change the subject as if to hide his posture and said,

"I wish we could go somewhere safer in the rural areas for a few days just to get out of the precarious situation in Dhaka."

Rokhsana understood that Andaleeb had been thinking about Momena, Kabil's maternal cousin, and Andaleeb's intended future wife in Montala, Kabil's village home away from Dhaka. She thought it was natural for him. If she hadn't read Momi's previous letter to Kabil a few days ago where

Momena wrote about the communal riot in Montala area and asked not to allow Andaleeb to visit Montala at that critical time, she would herself take the initiative to lock her parents' Dhaka house and go to Momi at Montala for a few days, taking Andaleeb and Jubi with her. She thought how good she would have felt if they could bury her mother Rania next to the grave of her aunty Zakia—Kabil's mother—at Montala. An expression of sudden sadness appeared on Rokhsana's face. To rather hide it, she said, "Brother Andy! I had posted a letter to Momi a few days ago. She probably didn't receive it yet because of this turmoil in the country. When and if she gets my letter, she would probably arrange herself to move to her uncles at Harashpur—Momi's parents' village nearby. You don't worry about Momi, rather think about the danger we all are in here."

In response, Andaleeb said, "Well! Think if we, in the end, do not feel safe in this locality, then will you be willing to move with us to some safer place in Mirpur or Mohammedpur?"

"Why not? You perhaps ask me that question because I've so far considered myself entirely as a Bengali. Until yesterday, I considered that the greatest thing in my life was that my father was a Bengali. But at this moment, seeing your and Jubi's face, I remember my mother's face in earlier days. I remember how sad she had felt whenever she heard of communal riot between the Biharis and the Bengalis. My mother was not a Bengali. Seeing the extreme cruelty of people, I too came to the conclusion that I don't have any other means of survival except being a human being and not a Bihari or a Bengali only. I'm, therefore, neither a Bihari nor a Bengali. I'm simply and above all a human being. The way you think that if East and West Pakistan cease to exist as one united country, then you will not have a country you can call your own. My mother used to think in the same way, I don't know what the future holds for me. But I don't know where I would go, all by myself if you, Jubi and Halim uncle, are not going to be here."

"No, Rokhi! What I'm saying is if we go somewhere else safer temporarily, leaving this locality, will you come with us?"

"Why not? As long as you do not feel safe yourself, I'll stay with you, cousin Andy," Rokhsana said trying hard to assure Andaleeb.

Hearing what Rokhsana had just said, cook Halim rather felt worried and said,

"But leaving this house, I won't find peace of mind anywhere else, Rokhi madam. You have real fear for your lives. Moreover, the mood in this locality is not that good. I'm an old man and am a servant in this house. Who will kill me? No Bihari, Bengali, or military will kill me. I'll stay here, if you allow me, until your cousin Kabil comes back." A sense of fear and sadness was noticeable in Halim's words.

"Uncle Halim! Nothing has happened as of now for us to leave this house. But I just wanted to discuss with Rokhi about the possibilities in the near future. We can never tell," Andaleeb tried to allay Halim's concern. Just at that time, they heard the sounds of a lot of military lorries/ trucks going by on the nearby roads. A curfew has been declared all over the city. The quietness of the city suddenly silenced everybody in Rokhsana's house as well.

Early Morning on March 26

ANJUMAN HAD FAINTED IN her parent's house, where she overheard Kabil telling her parents of her husband Nisar's death in front of his students' dormitory residence. Later that night she regained consciousness although she was still dazed and tired. Yet well before dawn that night, both Kabil and Anjuman left her parents' house since they were both concerned about their safety in the city as active and prominent student leaders. They crossed the Buriganga River, which ran through the city on a rickety boat and made it to Jinjira on the outskirts of Dhaka. There Kabil and Anjuman shared a boat with two other Hindu students of Dhaka University on their way to Bhairav Bazar—a sub-divisional town southeast, some one hundred kilometers away from Dhaka. Kabil and Anjuman were let off the boat at Bhairav Bazar. That evening at a place seven or eight kilometers south of Bhairav Bazar, Kabil and Anjuman rented a boat with a professional row man on the mighty Meghna River in the middle of rain, hail, and heavy winds. Their goal was to reach the confluence of mighty Meghna River's tributary—the Titas River and then sail upstream on the Titas to somewhere near Akhaura railway junction, cross the rail line, and find their way to Agartala, the nearest Indian border town.

It was now getting dark. A storm with rain and heavy wind was brewing on the horizon. Their boat reached the mouth of the Titas River by early evening as the shadow of darkness was falling fast as if to engulf the whole country. Kabil asked the row man to sail slowly upstream on the Titas River. Inside the low-lying cabin of the boat was Anjuman. She was tired, still dazed and soon fell asleep on a mat inside. Kabil sat quietly at the front of the boat outside the covered shelter and tried to reflect on the events of last more than a decade in his life. He thought of how he was born and raised until his mid-teens in a traditional lower-middle-class *Syed* family near Montala Railway Station between Akhaura Railway Junction and Sylhet District town.

He thought about his school teacher father Syed Ahmed Kamal who had died when Kabil was only five or six years old. He recollected his early years' memories of his paternal uncle Syed Ahmed Alam who had gone to Dhaka for his university education, met, fell in love with, and married an Urdu-speaking, non-Bengali girl Rania from a refugee-immigrant family from India. Alam's older brother Kamal (Kabil's father) who had high hopes for Alam's higher education and achievement to restore their family status to its illustrious past was heartbroken at the sudden news of his younger brother's inter-ethnic marriage in Dhaka. That prompted him to cut off all family ties with his younger brother Ahmed Alam for good. Soon after, Kabil's father had died of a sudden heart attack. Kabil was raised by his widowed mother Zakia Banu with their meager family income. Kabil remembered, how after his matriculation, Kabil himself reached out to his estranged uncle Ahmed Alam in Dhaka when he had set out for Dhaka for university education. He also remembered how he had reconnected with his uncle, came to live with him, his wife Rania, and their teenaged daughter Rokhsana, and over the years he slowly fell in love with Rokhsana.

It was now almost midnight on March 26. The row man of Kabil's escape boat was slowly rowing upstream of the Titas River in the quiet of the pitch-dark night with the help of a kerosine lamp. Kabil was exhausted, unsure of where he was heading to and what was in store for his future. Soon he too dozed off, moved inside the canopy of the boat, and fell in deep sleep on one side of the mat. After a period of a short, deep sleep, Kabil's brain phased into a long REM sleep. He then started dreaming about his life's events during the past decade or more. As the row man kept on rowing slowly in the middle of the night, Kabil kept on dreaming.

CHAPTER 2

A Blossoming Teenage Love

Mid-January 1960.

On a dew-covered, cold wintery morning, Kabil, then a young man in his mid-teens, got down from a train at Dhaka Fulbaria Station. He hailed from a small village near Montala Railway Station on the line to Sylhet, close to India-Bangladesh border, not far from Akhaura Railway Junction. The Indian state of Agartala started from the small hills and the red stones close to his village home. Kabil had arrived at Akhaura early previous evening and was waiting there to catch an early morning express train from Sylhet bound for Dhaka because such express trains did not stop at Montala. It was his very first trip to Dhaka. Even though he had arrived at Akhaura early evening before, he did not want to catch a fast-moving express train from Chittagong to Dhaka which generally arrived at Dhaka very early in the morning. He did not want to be in Dhaka that early in the morning and look for his uncle Ahmed Alam's shop in Nawabpur or his house in Bonogram Lane. He decided to take the late-night Sylhet train which arrived at Dhaka at daybreak so that he could walk in daylight and ask people how to get to his uncle's

No.10 Bonogram Lane residence. He had met his uncle only once before in his life. He heard from his widowed mother that his father's own younger brother Ahmed Alam lived in Dhaka. Ahmed Alam had come to attend Dhaka University in 1947. Kabil's father, Syed Ahmed Kamal was a village school teacher. He sold his ancestral land to finance his younger brother Ahmed Alam's university education in Dhaka. During his student days, Alam met and fell in love with Rania, a fellow student.

Ahmed Alam, after his Bachelor of Arts (BA) graduation, married Rania and settled in Dhaka. Rania was the daughter of a perfume merchant who was an Urdu-speaking refugee from India and migrated to Dhaka during the partition in 1947. This broke Ahmed Kamal's heart and the relationship between the two brothers was severed for good.

Ahmed Alam, of course, tried through letters to assure Kabil's father that he would financially and otherwise take care of Kabil's future education and would repay all the loans and other liabilities his older brother had endured for Alam's education. He also urged his older brother to excuse himself from all worldly affairs and prepare himself for a once-in-a-lifetime obligatory pilgrimage to Makkah.

But these letters did not have a soothing effect on older Ahmed Kamal. First, he did not even feel the need to reply to Alam's letters. But later he wrote to Alam that he (Kamal) did not care for any help from his young brother and that he even was not prepared to see his younger brother's face anymore in the future. He told Alam that most of their paternal lands had been sold for Alam's education and that Alam had nothing else in the village to claim for himself as his inheritance. He warned Alam not to visit his paternal home in the future with his Urdu-speaking Bihari wife.

(All refugees to the then East Pakistan were Muslims, and regardless of where in India they had come from, they were referred to as Urdu-speaking Biharis as by far most of them came from the Indian state of Bihar).

Kamal also told Alam not to worry about his son Kabil's education as he (Kamal) as a teacher would take care of Kabil's education. Kamal labeled Alam as an infidel. Ahmed Kamal died of a heart attack only a few days after writing this letter. Alam came to the village after hearing the news of his older brother's death in a letter from Kamal's wife Zakia. Alam tried to convince Zakia that he did not intend to hurt his older brother's feelings. He offered to take care of Zakia and her son Kabil and asked them to move to Dhaka with him. But deceased Kamal's wife Zakia bluntly told Alam that Kamal, in his deathbed, forbade her to keep any contact with Alam and made her promise to that effect. She advised Alam not to pursue the matter any further and go back to his Bihari wife in Dhaka. She herself of course did not consider Alam totally responsible for the sad breakdown in the relationship between the two brothers' families. She knew that Kamal was old fashioned and rigid in his belief about family relationships. Despite that she would not accept any help from Alam as she had promised her husband in his death bed that she would not. She assured Alam that she would manage her six years old son Kabil and her own existence with whatever little assets her husband had left them with albeit with a lot of financial constraints. At that point Alam decided to leave this village for good. That was the end of his relationship with his brother's family and indeed with his paternal village of Montala.

Kabil, after his matriculation had wanted to go to Dhaka to enroll in a pre-university college there. He was pleasantly surprised when his mother agreed for him to go to Dhaka and meet up with his decade-long-estranged uncle Alam. He took his uncle's home address in Dhaka from his mother and set out on this journey to meet with Uncle Alam. His mother knew that she would not be able to support Kabil's higher education and agreed not to stand in the way if his uncle Alam offered to look after him from then on. She told Kabil not to worry about her and to think about his own future from then on. Kabil understood this unlikely transformation in his mother's reaction considering the hardship she had been through for more than a decade to put him through high school. He himself thought that his estranged uncle Alam did not do an unforgivable disservice to his deceased father by marrying a Bihari woman even though he had understood his father's sentiment. Kabil had been, however, a bit disappointed for his uncle did not care about him (Kabil) all these past years even though his mother told Alam not to worry about herself and her minor son.

After getting off the train at Dhaka Fulbaria Station, as Kabil headed for the road outside the station in that thick misty, wintery morning, his mind was racing through this sad story of decade-long separation between him, his parents, and his uncle Alam's family with his Bihari wife, Kabil's erstwhile aunty Rania. He was at a loss which way to go. He did not know in which region of this mega city the Bonogram Lane was, where he was told by his mother that his uncle Alam lived. He neither knew where Nowabpur was where his uncle's business was located. He had seen his uncle only once some ten/eleven years earlier. He remembered Alam was clean-shaven, tall, fair-complexioned with neck-long wavy hair wearing Bihari-style long-coat and narrow/tight dress pajama. Kabil at that age of six was sitting on his uncle's lap when his mother told Alam of their final separation.

He remembered seeing tears rolling down his uncle's cheek as his mother informed him of his father's last wish and her final decision. He also remembered that his mother went through a lot of physical and financial hardship for the last ten/eleven years to put Kabil through his early education in the village school. Kabil had sat for his matriculation examination that year from Montala High School. He expected to matriculate in the first division.

Kabil walked on the road outside the station with all these thoughts racing through his mind and finally stopped in front of a cycle rickshaw who was shouting out calling for passengers wishing to go to Sadaghat, old town Dhaka. Kabil told him he wanted to go to Bonogram Lane and asked how much the fare would be. The rickshaw puller realized by looking at Kabil's face that he was a newcomer in town. "One rupee," he replied. Kabil sat down on the rickshaw without any bargain. As the puller turned the rickshaw, he asked,

"Did you come to Dhaka to look for a job?"

"No, to go to college," replied Kabil.

"Do you have a guardian here?"

"Yes, my uncle," replied Kabil again. Rickshaw puller continued talking almost to himself how he had carried passengers all night and that he lived in Rankin Street near Bonogram Lane and that he now wanted to return home and that was why he offered to carry Kabil to Bonogram Lane for half the normal fare. Kabil did not want to respond to this talk by the rickshaw puller. Kabil pulled out of his pocket an envelope in which his mother had written a letter to his uncle. He looked again at the address on the envelope, No. 10 Bonogram Lane—his uncle's own house. He could not think of any reason why his uncle would move from his own home in these relatively brief few years. He was thinking that if he reached the house early this morning, he would find his uncle at home. Otherwise his Urdu-speaking Bihari aunty might not recognize him. Nor probably, would she be able to read his mother's letter for his uncle that he was carrying with him. He had heard from his mother that his uncle and aunty had a daughter a few years after their marriage. *She must be in her teens by now*, he thought. He wondered if she could speak Bengali at all rather than speaking Urdu.

As the rickshaw puller was plying the early morning Dhaka roads, all these various thoughts were crowding Kabil's mind.

After a while, the rickshaw puller entered the Rankin Street intersection after Tatari Bazar and said to Kabil,

"Get off here. Walk up to Rankin Street. Turn left a little far ahead."

Kabil got down with his small suitcase in his hand. There was a medium-sized crowd in the nearby Bazar. Kabil kept his suitcase at the shade of a banyan tree and ordered a light breakfast from a nearby tea stall. As he was sipping the tea, he was wondering how his uncle, his wife, and daughter would receive him.

Following the road directions from the rickshaw puller, Kabil entered the Bonogram Lane. A short distance onward, he located a tin plate marking No. 10 Bonogram Lane, stuck on an old plasterless brick boundary wall of a house compound. The entrance gate was closed from inside but not locked. As he opened the gate, he noticed an old-style one-story house at the backside of a small garden-type front yard. The front door of the house was closed. There were flower tubs by the front-side railings of the verandah. The verandah in front of the door was four or five steps high from the ground, quite large and clean.

Kabil walked across the small front yard and put down his suitcase on the lowest step of the stairs up to the verandah. The house looked very quiet with no sound of any pet. It appeared that nobody in this house was an early riser. He thought for a moment if he was really in his uncle's house.

After some hesitation, he slightly knocked at one of the doors.

"Wait a second," someone replied in Urdu from inside. Almost immediately a girl of fourteen or fifteen years opened the door. She was wearing light yellow-colored salwar kameez—typical Urdu-speaking Bihari girls of her age normally wore. She had a black scarf covering her head and chest. She was brightly fair-complexioned. Her two big eyes were inquisitive, and she was carrying a toothbrush in her hand. She observed Kabil from top to bottom in one instant curious look.

"Is this the house of Mr. Ahmed Alam?" Kabil asked.

"Yes," the girl politely responded.

"Is Uncle home? My name is Kabil and I came from Montala." Kabil further asked. He then took out his mother's letter to his uncle and extended it to the young girl.

The girl had a look of surprise in her face but readily took the letter and said in mixed Urdu and Bengali, "Come inside please." As she pushed aside the screen of the door, Kabil noticed the large living room inside. He smelled the fragrance of traditional expensive sofa and carpet on the floor. There were many antiques in the room. A cured deer head and tiger skin were fixed on the walls. There was a big chandelier hanging from the ceiling.

"Please take a seat here," the girl invited Kabil. Kabil was not sure where to keep his suitcase. The girl came forward and took the suitcase from his hand and put it on one side on the carpet.

Kabil pointed to the letter he had given to the girl and said, "My mother wrote the letter to my uncle Alam. He will understand everything once he reads the letter. I am his nephew and I came from our village home."

Kabil was not sure who the young girl was. She could be the daughter of Uncle Alam or could be someone else. He had heard from his mother that his Bihari aunty had many relatives in Dhaka. Some of them worked in his uncle's perfume shop and in his spice-grinding factory. The girl realized Kabil's paradox and was mildly smiling in amusement. She said,

"Do not get perplexed. My name is Rokshana. I am your uncle's daughter and therefore your cousin."

Kabil now looked at Rokshana with great affection for a close relative. She was almost as tall as he was.

"How are Uncle and Aunty?" he asked.

"We all are well . . . brother? How is my aunty in the village?" she inquired. "My father often talked about you and my aunty with tears in his eyes. My mother and I often ask him to bring you to our house. But Father says Aunty will not part with you and she is very adamant," Rokshana further added.

"With uncle's permission, you and aunty could have once come to our village to inquire about my mother and me," Kabil said.

"I was quite interested in going. I told my father. He said Aunty would not even recognize us and that she would be upset if we just showed up in the village and that aunty was very angry with Mommy and Daddy. Why is it that, brother?" she asked in Urdu-Bengali mixed language. Kabil did not know how to answer this question from his very simple young cousin whom he had just met for the first time in their lives. He felt quite moved by the feelings of meeting his closest cousin sister. He felt happy and felt a lot of affection for Rokshana. He also wanted to avoid bringing up the old unpleasant memories of what had happened between his parents and uncle after he had married Rokhsana's mother.

"I do not want to remember the old unpleasant things, Rokshana. I want to pay my respect to my uncle and aunty by touching their feet. Would you please call them here?" he asked Rokshana.

"No need to call them here, brother. You are welcome to come to their room," Rokshana replied. She then lightly touched Kabil's hand which moved Kabil with a lot of affection for her. He followed her immediately toward her parents' bedroom. Rokshana knocked at the closed door.

"Who is there?" came a woman's voice in Urdu from inside. Kabil thought it must be aunty's voice. His mind raced back to the distant past. This Urdu-speaking aunty of his was at the center of a psychological and familial dispute between two brothers from a traditional, respectable Bengali family that separated them for over a decade. Kabil's father had sent his younger brother Alam for higher education in Dhaka by selling his landed properties in the village. In the end, when Alam married this Urdu-speaking lady and settled in Dhaka, he was heartbroken. His father with his parochial and provincial attitude toward life could not accept that his educated younger brother could have his choices and likings when it came to matters of love and passion. In the end Kabil's father died heartbroken raising a wall of separation between their two families. Kabil understood his father's attitude but was determined to tear down his father's emotional wall between the two families.

"Please open the door. We have guest," Rokshana replied in Urdu.

A lady from inside opened the door and asked, "Who came?"

"This is brother Kabil. He came from the village," Rokshana replied.

"Brother Kabil?" retorted Rokhsana's mother. Rania was utterly but pleasantly surprised. In that moment of surprise and joy, Kabil knelt and touched Rania's feet as a show of respect. As he did that, a middle-aged man—his uncle Alam—hurriedly got down from the bed.

"You Kabil? My dearest nephew Kabil from Montala?" the man almost shouted.

As Kabil showed his respect to his uncle in the same traditional way, Alam gave him a bear hug and started crying out from joy while pressing Kabil against his chest. Kabil also started crying. Seeing this, Rokshana and Rania also embraced the two men and joined in the crying as a sign of joy in their sudden unexpected reunion.

"Let us settle down now. Let me show brother Kabil his room and let me arrange for his breakfast." Rokshana took the lead in settling all down.

"Wait a minute, Rokhi. Let me first ask him about his mother, my sister-in-law Zakia and about our village home. How is your mother, Kabil?" Alam asked.

"Mother is not keeping very well lately, Uncle," replied Kabil. "She has grown old, can't work hard as she did before. She gets tired even by cooking two times a day," Kabil continued. He then asked Rokshana to give his mother's letter to his uncle which Rokshana did promptly.

"This is your mother's letter?" Alam asked with deep emotions in his voice. "After many years, my sister-in-law cared to write to me Rania," Alam commented, looking at his wife as he opened the letter. He then started to read the letter rather loudly:

"Brother Alam, I pray to God for you and your family. I decided to write you after many years. I think that it would have been better if I could manage without having to write this letter to you. I promised my husband that I would not keep any contact with you after his death. I kept that promise until now. I lived a widow's life, managing my financial life within my limitations and provided for your nephew Kabil's education so far. Kabil is meritorious as you were and sat for matriculation examination this year from our local school. I am confident his exam result will be good. He wanted to go to you in Dhaka before his exam result is out and begged me to allow him to do so. He is aware of the misgivings that took place between you and your brother before his death. Yet Kabil is determined to go to you and restore his loving paternal relationship with you and your family. In the end, I agreed.

Please accept him if you can. Honestly, I have no means to finance him through his college/university education. If you are interested and capable to do so, I will have no objection in it anymore as I once did in previous years.

"I do not expect anything from you for myself. Please ask your wife Rania to forgive me and my late husband if she can do so. I heard a decade ago that you two have a daughter. She must be almost a teenager by now. Please give her my love and best wishes. Please let me know of Kabil's arrival at your place as soon as you can.

Your sister-in-law, Syeda Zakia Banu."

After reading the letter, Alam again started crying covering his face and lying on the bed again.

"Come in, brother Kabil. I will take you to my room where you can have a change of clothes and freshen up. Mother! I am taking my brother with me," Rokshana said. Rania nodded in agreement.

Kabil followed Rokshana to her room which was very well decorated. Everything was nicely arranged. There was a study table with a few books on it next to a single bed. There was a small dressing table on one side with a few makeup items for a growing young girl. There was a traditional, low rattan stool (mora) on one side of an expensive carpet on the floor. The comforter on the bed was disorganized. The heart insignia on the pillow cover was clearly visible. There was a low prayer couch on one side near the window with a copy of the Quran on it near the head. There were a lot of family pictures. There were more salwar kameez compared to sarees on her open wardrobe (alna).

"Brother! you get a change of clothes," Rokshana suggested mildly.

"You show me the place for washing. I would first wash and freshen up and then I will change my outfit," Kabil replied.

Rokshana showed Kabil a rather large-sized family washroom. Water was dripping from a tap on the wall into a metal bucket on the washroom floor. Inside the washroom, there were two latrines on one side. One middle-aged woman, a domestic help, was cleaning the floor of the washroom. There was soap on the soap dish and a few towels. There was toothpaste, razors for shaving, etc. Rokshana suggested that Kabil might wish to take a shower as there might be a shortage of water later in the day,

"Okay, I would rather take a shower now. But please do not worry about me."

"I am very happy to see you, brother," Rokshana replied. She left the washroom after that.

After the shower, Kabil came to the bedroom, opened his suitcase. Inside, there were two shirts, two dress pajamas and two lungi. His mother packed his father's woolen shawl for him in the suitcase. Kabil put on a white shirt and a white dress pajama with his father's woolen shawl as a scarf around his back. While combing his hair in front of the mirror, he noticed Rokshana was behind him with a big smile on her face.

"Daddy and Mommy are waiting to have breakfast with you. Please come," Rokshana said in mixed Urdu and Bengali.

"Rokshana!" Kabil called her with a look of inquisitiveness in his face.

"Yes, brother," Rokshana replied.

"How come you can't speak Bengali clearly and fluently? We are Bengali people. You know that?" Kabil asked.

"Yes, of course," replied Rokshana.

"What grade are you in at the school?" Kabil asked.

"Grade 10," came the reply.

"Do you not learn Bengali at school? Kabil asked.

Rokshana hesitated to respond to this question. Kabil understood Rokshana studied in different language medium.

"That is okay. You will study Bengali with me," Kabil said to lighten the situation.

"You are a Bengali and you must learn your own language," Kabil added.

"I can read Bengali, brother. I took lessons from my dad. But at school, I study in the English medium. I can't speak or write Bengali, because my mother is Urdu-speaking. My mother's family was from Bhopal in India. They all speak Urdu in that family."

"Your father too?" Kabil asked.

"Yes, who would he speak Bengali with? But I speak some Bengali with my friends at school because I am a Bengali."

At that point, Rania moved the curtain on the door and entered the room.

"Listen, my son, I know how to speak Bengali. I learned from your uncle. I will speak in Bengali with you. I learned Bengali with the hope that someday I would write to your mother in your village. But your parents never accepted me as their sister-in-law." Rania narrated with some sense of disappointment. "I would get solace by speaking with you in Bengali. Let's go for breakfast now," she added. Kabil was pleasantly surprised to hear his aunty speak Bengali so easily and clearly.

At the breakfast table, Alam was going through the daily newspaper.

Seeing Kabil, he said, "Come, have a seat."

Kabil sat on a chair next to Alam.

"Your mother noted in her letter that your exams had gone well. I hope you will pass at least in the first division," Alam commented.

"I hope so with your blessing, Uncle," Kabil responded.

"After the result, you get yourself into the Jagannath College. I have friends there. They will take care of you. Take some paratha," Alam further added.

"Okay, son, take some mutton. You will have to finish all these," Rania intervened as Kabil took two Parathas on his plate.

Alam noticed the shawl on Kabil's shoulder and recognized that his older brother used to wear it when he was alive.

"This shawl is still good? My brother used to wear it," Alam commented.

"Yes, Uncle, my mother packed it for me in the suitcase," Kabil replied.

"Do not wear it out. Keep it as your father's memento. You go to New Market today with Rokhi (Rokshana) and buy whatever clothes and other things you need. Buy also some woolen clothes for winter months. Buy some beddings for you. You will sleep in the room next to Rokhi's," Alam continued. Kabil nodded while eating.

"Look, son" Rania intervened. "Rokshana is your sister. Our only child. Your only sister as well. Like, you are your mother's only child, in the same way, Rokshana and you are the only children your uncle and your late father have. You and us will not separate again. You will live with us. You will finish your studies, then both Rokshana and you will take care of your uncle's business."

"Yes, Aunty," Kabil replied politely.

Rokshana was pouring tea for Kabil. She slightly needled Kabil,

"For everything, the answer is just 'yes, Uncle, yes, Aunty.'

Brother! Please say something of your own. Tell us how your mother is, what is going on in your village, etcetera. How did you spend so many years without taking interest in us? Do you understand me?" Rokshana said mostly in Urdu.

"No, I do not understand. Why can't you speak in Bengali as Uncle and I do. We are Bengali," Kabil counter-needled Rokshana. "We are brother and sister. Aunty, please forgive my intransigence," Kabil added. Rania and Rokshana burst into laughter at this. Alam took a sip from his tea cup and added in a low voice.

"Alright, from now on Kabil will teach Rokshana how to speak well in Bengali. Rokhi is a good student even though she studies in the English medium. She has interest in her own language Bengali. You just live with us and have patience." Alam then stood up to leave the table.

Kabil also stood up and said, "Yes, Uncle, I will do. I came to stay."

After breakfast Kabil came back to Rokshana's bedroom. As he took off the shawl from his shoulder to keep it on the clothes' rack, Rokshana said from behind him, "Give it to me. It appears that it is a shawl of much sentimental value."

"How did you realize that?" Kabil asked.

"From your talk with my dad about it," Rokshana replied.

"Yes, it is his older brother's woolen shawl. Uncle recognized it. I will not damage it by wearing it anymore. You better preserve it," Kabil commented.

"Don't worry, brother. I will give you another wrapper. You lie down on my bed and take some rest while I clean and arrange the adjoining room for you."

Rokshana then picked up the wrapper from the bottom of her bed. As soon as Kabil lay on the bed, she put the wrapper on his feet and looked at his body from the corner of her eyes. Kabil looked rather muscular compared to his age. His kinky hair was shiny. His hair was long enough to touch his neck behind. Her look suddenly caught Kabil's eyes, and she swiftly diverted her eyes from his body to his head.

"You need a haircut, brother," she commented. "We will go to a hair salon tomorrow," she said, feeling slightly embarrassed.

With that Rokshana left Kabil in her bed and came out of the room.

During midday Kabil woke up hearing Rokshana talking outside. "Come on for lunch, brother," she said.

Kabil sat up and asked, "What time is it?"

"Two in the afternoon," Rokshana replied.

"Oh, why didn't you wake me up? Are Aunty and Uncle waiting for me?" Kabil asked.

"No, Dad has gone to his factory and mommy has gone to her fashion and tailoring shop. I came back early from school. I am waiting for you to come and join me for lunch," Rokshana replied.

Kabil was surprised to hear that his aunty went to her tailoring shop?

"Is aunty also in business?" Kabil asked in amazement.

"True, brother. Your uncle did not capture my mother for nothing. She is an educated woman, university graduate. Very beautiful also. My uncle, your father, got upset with his brother for no good reason. My mother is a famous tailor master in Dhaka. She is a very good cutter and modern outfitter. Besides, being the daughter of a perfume merchant and the wife of a Bengali man, she is very fashionable. She also earns more than seven thousand rupees per month," Rokshana continued.

"Oh!" Kabil expressed his surprise.

"Would you not fall for such a woman, brother Kabil?" But be careful, if you do that, I will be upset also because I am also Bengali and a niece of your father Syed Ahmed Kamal."

Rokshana was amazed at her own joke and started laughing while sitting on the bed which Kabil just got off from. Kabil understood that Rokshana was not laughing at her joke, but she was expressing somewhat her subtle complaint of the way Kabil's parents had treated her mom and dad.

But he couldn't understand how best he could make up for it. He quietly said, "You go to dining table, Rokshana. I will freshen up and join you there."

Rokshana then quickly left the room. At the dining table, Rokshana asked, "Rice or Roti?"

"I am not used to Roti, Rokshana," Kabil responded.

"Don't worry. Today, rice, fish, and meat, all have been cooked specially for you," Rokshana further commented.

As Kabil started eating a big piece of fish, a young man appeared in front of the dining table. He asked Rokshana in clear Bengali,

"Rokshana, I understand a new brother of yours has appeared, is this him?"

Rokshana did not respond and ignored the questioner. She rather suggested to Kabil, "You finish eating, brother. After a while, we will go to New Market to buy clothes for you."

Later as an afterthought, she added, pointing to the questioner,

"This man is Andaleeb, my maternal uncle's son. He works in my dad's business."

Kabil raised his eyes to have a look at the young man. Kabil excused himself for not exchanging traditional greeting with Andaleeb because he was in the middle of eating, but he invited Andaleeb to join them for lunch.

"I understand you are the nephew of Mr. Ahmed Alam," Andaleeb further added. Kabil nodded in agreement.

"After a very long time, a relative of my aunty Rania in this country suddenly appeared from nowhere. It is a good news," Andaleeb commented with a bit of sarcasm in his tone. "Pass me some food please," he then requested Rokshana.

"Have a seat. You will get your food. But let me and Kabil finish first. After we finish, our cook Halim uncle will treat you properly with your meal," Rokshana responded with a bit of irritation in her voice.

Andaleeb was a little taken aback at Rokshana's tone of voice. He instantly understood that Kabil has to some extent already been able to establish his presence and Rokshana's liking for him in this household and that Rokshana did not like Andaleeb's reference that Kabil had appeared from nowhere. He changed his own tone to lighten the ambiance. He asked Kabil in clear Bengali, "What is your name, brother?"

"Ahmed Kabil. You take a seat please," Kabil responded.

"You are nephew of Ahmed Alam, son of his older brother Ahmed Kamal. My aunty Rania is married to your uncle

Ahmed Alam. In that relationship, I am your older cousin, brother. Rokhi is cousin sister to both you and me."

"Yes, I understand, brother," Kabil commented politely. He again invited Andaleeb to take a seat at the table. Andaleeb was impressed with Kabil's invitation and politeness. He was about to take a seat next to Rokshana but then said, "No, I will not eat right now, brother. I was just kidding, looks like you are getting ready to go out shopping. That is alright. I will come another time to talk to you.".

Hearing Andaleeb speak Bengali clearly, Kabil looked at Rokshana and commented, "Wow! Brother Andaleeb speaks excellent Bengali."

"Yes," Rokshana shot back. "Hearing Andaleeb brother speak in Bengali, you may think he is a saint. But he is a cunningly intelligent man. Sooner or later you will know better," Rokshana continued.

Andaleeb tried to ignore Rokshana's sarcastic remarks about him and said, "No no, Miss Rokhi. Don't think I am that bad."

He then turned to Kabil and said, "Okay, brother. I will see you again later."

AFTER A COUPLE OF months, the School Board announced the results of the matriculation examination. Ahmed Kabil secured the third position in order of merit among all those who were successful in the arts group. His picture was published in all major daily newspapers along with the story of how he was so successful even though he had come from an obscure village. Kabil's uncle Ahmed Alam broke down with joy at the news of Kabil's more than expected result.

Rokshana sent a telegram to Kabil's mother in the village to inform her of Kabil's excellent result. She further informed her that she would soon visit her aunty Zakia in the village along with Kabil.

The following evening, Rania brought home a suit for Kabil as her present on the occasion of his excellent result. She handed the suit over to Kabil and said, "Now, go put on this suit and then come in and join us for dinner."

Kabil accepted the present and paid respect to aunty Rania in the traditional way. At that Rania embraced him and said, "May God bless you, son, and give you the opportunity to be a successful man in future."

At that, Rokshana stood behind her mother and teasingly commented in accented Bengali, "Let me go with you and fix the knot in your tie. You cannot manage that."

Kabil followed Rokshana like a school-aged boy to his room, put on the pant and shirt, then stood in front of Rokshana with the jacket in his hand.

"Okay, fix my tie knot. I am not used to that," Kabil said to Rokshana.

Rokshana had already taken the necktie out from the gift box, fixed the knot, and now put it over Kabil's head and adjusted it around his neck like a noose.

"Okay. Now put on the jacket," Rokshana said. She then helped him put on the jacket from his back.

"How do I look?" Kabil asked.

"Very handsome, like an English prince," Rokshana teased.

She then wanted to pay respect to Kabil by bending herself down to touch Kabil's feet in the traditional way. Kabil immediately stopped that by catching her arms and helping her stand up.

"Hey, Rokhi! What is going on?" he asked affectionately.

"Nothing. Just . . ." Rokshana replied.

"Uncle and Aunty and others are very happy with my result. But you yourself did not say or show anything, Rokhi," Kabil asked with mocking complaint.

"What can I say? I do not know how to dance. Otherwise, I would have shown my pride and pleasure by dancing for you," Rokshana replied with equal tone of mocking.

"Am I asking you to dance?" Kabil asked.

"No, you don't. But I feel like dancing with happiness in my heart," Rokshana replied.

"Rokhi! You look beautiful today as you do always," Kabil commented.

"Come on. Mom and Dad are waiting for us," Rokshana said as she covered her head with the scarf as a sign of modesty. The two of them then walked to the dining area.

At the dining table, Ahmed Alam asked Kabil, "Did you send a telegram to your mother about your result?"

"Rokshana sent, Uncle," Kabil replied.

"Do you want to go and ask for her personal blessing upon your brilliant result?" Alam asked.

"Yes, Uncle, I do," replied Kabil.

"Okay, then go by tomorrow's train," Alam advised.

"Okay, Uncle. Rokshana also wants to go with me," Kabil interjected. At that, both Alam and Rania stared at Rokshana while she was eating.

Rokshana tried to say something in as clear Bengali as she could in response to her parents' stare,

"For the first time in my life, I want to go to my own village. If you two will permit me, I will go with brother Kabil tomorrow morning."

Rania was pleased to hear that from Rokshana and said, "No need for our permission, my sweet daughter. If you want to visit your paternal village with your brother, we will be happy for both of you."

"On the way back, if you can convince your aunty there to come with you to visit us, then we will be happy and think that you are a 'can-do' girl," Rania further added.

"I will try my best, Mother," Rokshana replied.

THE NEXT DAY KABIL and Rokshana took a train to Montala and arrived there shortly before sunset. Montala was a small, not-so busy railway station. As such, there were only a few passengers who got off the Sylhet-bound train at Montala. Kabil put his suitcase down on the platform and stood there momentarily. As he did that, a middle-aged man wearing a black railway turban came to him from the verandah of the station building.

"Wow! Are you not Mr. Kabil?" the man asked. He was the local station master, Mr. Hye.

"Oh yes! Uncle Hye, how are you?" Kabil inquired.

"I am okay. I saw your picture in the newspaper along with the news of your brilliant result," the station master replied.

"God responded to your mother's prayer. Are you coming from Dhaka?" he further asked.

"Yes, Uncle," Kabil responded and then introduced the station master to Rokshana as his well-wisher.

"Who is this young lady with you?" Mr. Hye asked.

"My cousin Rokshana—daughter of my uncle Ahmed Alam," Kabil replied.

Rokshana respectfully greeted the station master who then suggested that they all go to his office for some snack. Kabil respectfully declined the offer, saying that he wanted to go and seek his mother's blessing first. But he promised that he would soon visit Mr. and Mrs. Hye in their residence.

"Well then, you go and give my regards to your mother," Mr. Hye nodded in agreement.

Kabil picked up his suitcase and both he and Rokshana set out on foot to their village home. By then, the sun was just about to set and the local ambiance became rather quiet with no other walkers on the rather lonely village pathway. This was the first time ever in her life Rokshana was walking on a village pathway outside her normal homestead in Dhaka.

She was somewhat mesmerized with the quiet, near-dark surroundings and started following Kabil close by.

"Brother Kabil!" she called out at one point.

"Yes! Rokhi" Kabil responded.

"How far is our village from here?" Rokshana asked.

"Not too far, Rokhi. Once we cross these paddy fields, our homestead is just around the corner," Kabil replied.

"Can you imagine how pleased my mother would be by meeting you?" Kabil asked.

"Yes, brother, I can. She probably will start crying with tears of joy," Rokshana replied.

"I do not know what Mother will say or do. But she would sure be happy. No doubt about it," Kabil added.

"Would she not be upset because of my coming suddenly at this time?" Rokshana asked.

"No, Rokhi," Kabil answered. My mother is a good person. When she meets you, she would regret the way she and my late father had treated my uncle when he had married my aunty. She would think that like I was, you should have been born in this reputable homestead of both your and my same grandparents. But their narrow-minded and egocentric attitude deprived you of that tradition which was rightfully yours. They had differences of opinion over your father's choosing a refugee girl as his wife. But they had no quarrel with you," Kabil elaborated.

"I was not even born at that time," Rokhi commented.

"If you were, my father with the right mentality and affection for you would probably cave in, forgive his brother, and would probably go to Dhaka to see his newborn niece. He probably would not like the idea of his niece—a girl from a traditional conservative Bengali family would grow up in a Bihari dominant environment," Kabil continued. The way Kabil put it, both of them burst into laughter.

"Why did they not like the Biharis?" Rokshana asked innocently.

"I do not know, cousin. There are a number of Bihari families in our Montala Railway Station. I find them very compassionate people. They all used to like me. I do not understand the narrow, silly Bengali-Bihari conflict," Kabil explained.

By that time, they passed the paddy field walkways and reached the threshold of their village.

"My maternal grandparents were not from Bihar," Rokshana commented. "They were from Bhopal in India. But here in this country, all Urdu-speaking people who migrated here from India since 1947 are categorized as Biharis. At the school I am referred to as Bihari even though my father is a Bengali. Very bad, brother," Rokshana explained.

"Don't you object?" Kabil asked.

"I do very much. But who is going to listen? When they hear me speak in Urdu, they conclude that I am a Bihari," Rokshana replied.

From now on, you try to speak in Bengali, Rokshana. Uncle said you can read Bengali. If you can read, you will easily learn how to speak Bengali. When you meet my mother, try to speak to her in Bengali. If you get stuck I will help you out," Kabil advised.

"Okay, brother. I will try to speak in Bengali with my aunty. But if you ridicule me, I will be embarrassed," Rokhi said.

"No, Rokhi. I will not ridicule you. I want you to grow up as a Bengali girl," Kabil assured.

"I am a Bengali girl. Is there any doubt in your mind?" Rokshana forcefully asked.

"No," Kabil replied emphatically. By the time they reached the middle of the village, evening progressed to early night, and it became dark all around. Rokshana felt comfortable walking in these mysterious surroundings along side Kabil. She drew herself closer to Kabil's body. Shortly, they reached the bank of a water-storage pond. On the plastered brick steps on the side of the pond, a group of village women was washing and bathing, taking advantage of the somewhat dark surrounding.

Kabil and Rokshana stopped there for a few minutes.

Seeing Kabil and Rokshana standing on the upper, wider social gathering area of the plastered brick steps, the women washing at the bottom suddenly stopped their work and looked up curiously. Noticing the eagerness and curiosity of the women, Kabil climbed down two steps and introduced himself. "I am Kabil. Kabil from the Sayed family. I have my sister Rokshana with me. We are coming home from Dhaka," Kabil said. At that point, a middle-aged woman from the bottom step walked up, holding her water pitcher on the side of her waist.

"Aren't you the son of brother Kamal?" she asked.

"Yes," Kabil replied politely.

"We heard that you did very well in your last exam. There were pictures of you in the newspapers. Is that your cousin with you, is she the daughter of your uncle Alam in Dhaka?" The woman further asked.

"Yes, my cousin Rokshana, Alam uncle's daughter," Kabil replied.

"But I cannot exactly place you," Kabil asked embarrassingly.

"I am your Hasina aunty. I am from the family who built these plastered brick steps to the pond water. Your father and uncles are my distant brothers. When you go home, tell your mother you met me here. The daughter of brother Alam has grown up," the woman commented, looking at Rokshana. Kabil felt embarrassed for not recognizing Aunty Hasina. She was a close friend of his mother. Possibly his mother had told Hasina that Rokshana was coming to her father's paternal village for the first time in her life. Kabil apologized for not having recognized Aunty Hasina and excused himself and asked her permission to take leave and proceed to meet his mother first.

"Okay, first go and pay respect to your mother. Later, drop by our house when you have some time. We prayed to God for your success in your last exam. God listened to our prayers and you did well. May God bless you more in the future," Hasina added. Both Rokshana and Kabil were touched by what Hasina said and paid respect to her in the traditional Bengali way. Hasina touched their heads with one hand while holding the water pitcher in her midrib with the other hand and said, "May God give you two long life."

After leaving the south end of the village, Kabil entered another open field in the middle of the village. By then the twilight darkness of the early evening had turned into a bright moonlight.

Rokshana felt good walking in the moonlight. She felt like this was her paternal village, and she entered the village for the first time in her life with full recognition of her paternal right. She was wondering how her aunty, Kabil's mother would accept her. She felt determined that from her father's side, she had equal claim and right in her father's traditional family as her aunty Kabil's mother had, and she was not going to allow anybody to deny and deprive her of that right. She was going to claim that her original root was in this family no less than that of Kabil. She felt that her father deeply loved an Urdu-speaking girl of a different culture and tradition, married her, and lived his life shunned by his own older brother, his wife, and their family. Her parents' life together was rooted in a deep love for each other. There was no consideration in this love for their differences in languages, culture, tradition, skin color, or the geography of the places of their birth. She could not understand why her deceased uncle—Kabil's father—could not accept that.

By that time, the two of them crossed the open field, followed the walking pathway, and arrived at the bushy area of the northern section of the village. There was a little darkness in this area even on a moonlit night. At this point Kabil called, "Rokhi!"

"Yes, brother," Rokhi replied.

"It is difficult to see your path in the darkness, Rokhi. Hold my hand," Kabil suggested.

Rokshana promptly held Kabil's hand and said, "So far, brother! I am sweating and I am scared."

"Don't be scared. This is our own village—both yours and mine. Even the ghosts here will recognize me. There might be potholes on the path. Hold my hand and walk carefully," Kabil reassured Rokshana.

"You always tell me that you will someday come to your own village and stay for a while. Will you really do that, Rokhi?" Kabil further asked.

"Of course, I will. Will you not come with me and stay brother?" Rokhi asked.

"Only God knows who will stay where and when. Now I am staying with Uncle, Aunty, and you in Dhaka to further my studies. After that nobody knows for sure who will stay where," Kabil replied solemnly. Suddenly, there was a sound of moving branches and leaves of trees overhead. Rokshana was scared and stopped walking while holding Kabil's hand.

"Don't be scared. It is just squirrel moving around," Kabil reassured Rokshana.

"I understand now. You won't be able to stay in the village for more than two days. How would you manage? You were born in the brightly lit city of Dhaka."

"I sure will be able to stay in my own village. You will see how I will manage," Rokshana countered firmly.

Kabil kept on walking while holding Rokhi's hand and commented, "When you finish your education and become an accomplished lady, Uncle and Aunty will find a princely young man for you to marry. After that you will not even remember this remote village, and you will be embarrassed to introduce this poor, undeveloped village as your own. You will forget all these. Girls forget all about their surroundings after they are married. For you, it will be more normal because you were not born in this village. Nobody will blame you at that time even if you forget us all. That will be normal."

"No, that won't be the case. I will not consent to such marriage, brother," Rokshana replied. She pulled Kabil's hand and stopped walking again.

Kabil laughed aloud and said, "You cannot just say that. You will have to get married one day. My uncle and aunty have plenty of money and other resources. We will find a rich and educated man for you to marry, Rokhi. I do not know at this time who that lucky fellow will be. But I know that he will not care to come to this Montala village for vacation".

"But I know that he will not stop me from coming here for vacation," Rokhi retorted.

"What? Do you already have someone like that? You didn't even bother to tell me that even once all these days?" Kabil wondered aloud.

"I did not because I did not have the occasion," Rokhi replied.

"But I wish very much to know," Kabil said.

"Why so much wish? I am shy," Rokshana said.

"However shy you are—you have to tell me, Rokhi. Who is that young man who will not mind you coming to visit poor people like us? Is it Andaleeb?" Kabil asked in wonderment.

"Oh God! Why are you so jealous of a stupid guy like Andaleeb?" Rokshana quickly responded.

"Then who?" Kabil further inquired.

"Maybe a son of a Syed (dignified) family in this village," Rokshana poured out.

"What do you mean, Rokhi?" Kabil asked.

As soon as Kabil asked that question, he noticed that Rokshana covered her face with two hands and sat on the grassy ground. Kabil slowly sat down next to her but kept a bit of a distance between the two of them. Rokshana did not look up. Kabil then politely put his trembling hand on Rokshana's head.

"I never thought about that, Rokhi," Kabil said softly.

"By God, do not lie. I spoke about my heart's desire like a shameless person. But please do not make fun of me because of that," Rokhi confided.

"I am less shy and less bold than you are, Rokhi. Your courage saved me from a lot of worry and suffering. May God keep you a little less shy in the future for the sake of my deep love for you," Kabil confided back. At that they both laughed aloud.

By the time they reached the open courtyard of Kabil's house, it was already shining in the bright moonlight. On one side of the courtyard, there was a fruit-bearing tree leaning downward with its ample produces. There were two large tin-roofed rooms on the southeast corner. A tin-roofed house stood on the south side. It had cemented verandah with wooden sidings. There were light bamboo curtains on the sidings for privacy. There was a brick boundary wall almost six feet high on all sides of the compound. Tall, straight betel nut trees lined the outside of the wall. The room on the east side perhaps had not been used for a while in the recent past. Kabil's mother lived on the tin-roofed house to the south. There was a dim light in the house. A small flower garden adorned the courtyard on the east side close to the verandah of the darkened unused rooms. On one side of the courtyard, there was a concreted grave without any boundary wall. There was a headstone on the gravesite.

Kabil put down the suitcase that he was carrying on the courtyard and said, "This is our homestead, Rokhi. I heard that Uncle Alam used to live in that room on the east side. Next to it on the left side is my father's grave—that of your arrogant uncle Ahmed Kamal."

"We will look at the house later. But first let us call Aunty," Rokhi said in half Urdu and half-accented Bengali.

"Let me first pay respect to my deceased father by observing a minute of silence at his gravesite, Rokhi. You walk up to the verandah and call your aunty. Say you are Syeda Rokshana Banu-a daughter of this household. 'Can you recognize me,

Aunty?'" Kabil prompted Rokshana. He then walked to his father's gravesite and stood there in silence.

Rokshana picked up the suitcase, walked up to the verandah of the house on the south side, and knocked on the door and called out, "We are here, Aunty. Please open the door."

A woman from inside responded, "Who is there in the verandah?"

"We came from Dhaka, Aunty. I am your niece Rokshana and your son Kabil is also here," Rokshana replied.

Almost immediately, the door opened and there stood an old fair-complexioned woman clad in white saree with prayer beads in her hand. "I am Rokshana, Aunty. Brother Kabil is also here," Rokshana said to the woman. Rokshana immediately bent down to show respect to the old lady who right away embraced her into her arms and cried with joy.

"Oh God! Alam's daughter has grown up."

Rokshana rested her head on the lady's chest and started crying with joy. By that time Kabil also walked up to the verandah and paid respect to his mother in the traditional way.

"Oh God! Will you two keep on crying while you are in each other's arms? Mother, please take Rokhi inside the room," Kabil asked his mother in wonderment. His mother came to be herself at Kabil's urging. She then almost carried Rokshana inside the bedroom and seated her like a child on the traditional family sleeping couch. Rokshana was still intermittently crying. Zakia Banu sat next to her and started caressing her by touching her chin, face, and the long-hair tail and said words of comfort and mock complain, "My poor child! It took you so long to come and see me. The uncle that you all were upset with had long passed away even before you were born. He was crying in his deathbed for his brother whom he had forbidden to return home here. Even a cruel heart could not bear it. I am alive because I am worse than a cruel heart. You all forgive me please," she pleaded. She then started patting Rokhi on her back.

Kabil brought the suitcase inside, opened it, and took out a change of clothes for Rokhi and himself.

"Mother! We are hungry. Please, cook some food for us," he pleaded with his mother.

"Take Rokhi to the bank of the dug water well. Wash your face and hands and freshen up. By the time you come back, I will have dinner ready. I have already cooked all your favorite dishes. But I do not know whether Rokhi will like the same or shall I fry two eggs for her?" Zakia Banu asked.

"No, Aunty. Whatever you already cooked will be enough for me as well. I like rice, fish, and dal. I eat them all the time with my daddy at our home in Dhaka," Rokshana emphatically responded. Kabil was impressed with Rokhi at her attempt to say the things to his mother in almost flawless Bengali. The two of them then picked up towels, soap from the wooden plank, and walked toward the dug water well. Zakia Banu watched them from their back with motherly affection and amazement.

Early the following morning Rokshana woke up with the sound of roosters and cuckoos. She noticed that next to the side of the bed that she shared last night with Zakia Banu, Zakia was sitting on a low prayer couch with prayer beads in her hand. Seeing Rokshana awaken, Zakia smiled a bit and said, "Sleep a little more, my child, if you want. Let me finish my prayer. I will then give you a tour of your paternal house compound. We have a rather big compound. But as there are not many people living in the compound, weeds are growing in some areas. Will you and Kabil stay for a few days?" she asked.

"Yes, Aunty, we will stay for a while," Rokshana replied. She then turned to the other side and closed her eyes trying to fall asleep again.

After early morning prayer, Zakia opened the door and noticed that Kabil was brushing his teeth with a toothbrush. Before going to Dhaka a couple of months earlier, he used to brush his teeth using a neem stick. Zakia also noticed that Kabil had changed quite a bit in the previous two months or so not only physically but also in manners and attitude. She walked a bit closer to him. "Is Rokhi still sleeping?" Kabil asked her.

"Let her sleep a little longer," Zakia replied.

"Mother! You do not know Rokhi. In Dhaka, she sleeps like a donkey. She cannot go to school in time unless someone shakes her out from sleeping. Uncle makes fun about it. Lately, Aunty gave me the responsibility to wake her up. She will not get up before 9:00 a.m.," Kabil reported.

"Oh, so what? Let her sleep for a little longer. She has no school here to go to. She came to her paternal homestead for the first time in her life. Here, you do not have to regulate her activities. I will wake her up in time. Now you rather go to the local morning market and buy some fish, fresh vegetables, a few live chickens, and some fruits. Come inside the house and I will give you money for all these," Zakia told her son.

"Mother, I have money for all these foodstuff," Kabil reported.

"How is that? Where did you get so much money?" Zakia questioned. She further wondered, "Oh, I understand. Perhaps your uncle gave you money for his daughter's expenses as she was coming here for the first time."

"No, Mother. When the news of my good exam result was out, Uncle gave me two thousand rupees to spend as I wish, and Aunty made a suit for me as a present. Uncle did not give me money for Rokhi's expenses here. They know you will feel insulted if he did that. They also know that I would not accept money from them for Rokhi's visit to her paternal village," Kabil elaborated.

Zakia then changed the subject and asked, "How does your aunty look like, Kabil?"

"She looks rather like you, Mother," Kabil replied.

"But I am an old woman, Kabil," Zakia responded.

"Aunty is not old, of course. But she is fair-complexioned like you and tall. She has a smiley face like yours, Mother. And she is a very smart woman, works all day in her fashion and tailoring shop. She manages her own business and earns thousands of rupees. She also stays up late at night overseeing accounts of Uncle's factory and shops. She is a very good woman, Mother," Kabil elaborated.

"Does she like you a lot?" Zakia asked.

"Of course. Why not, Mother? They do not have a son. Besides, they do not have any other close relatives other than us in this country. For nothing, you and Father stopped Uncle from coming to his paternal village just because he had married Aunty Rania. Really, you will not find another human being as good as she is," Kabil said in a subtle tone of complaint.

"Stop. Don't let me hear that complaint again. If you want, go and complain in front of your father's grave," Zakia responded sternly and walked away while wiping tears from her eyes.

ONE WEEKEND MORNING, SEVERAL days after Kabil and Rokshana left for Montala to visit their paternal village, Rania and Alam were eating breakfast together at their Bonogram Lane home in Dhaka. In the middle of eating, Alam asked Rania,

"Did you receive any letter or telegram from Kabil since they went to Montala?"

"Yes, I got a postcard from Rokhi," Rania replied. "They are having a good time there. Rokhi was all praise for her aunty. I am jealous and feel like myself going there to spend a few days with Zakia Bhavi (older sister-in-law)," Rania added in Bengali while pouring tea for her husband Alam. Her Bengali was now perfect and with little or no Urdu accent. She always spoke in Bengali with Alam since their university days together. Yet all her relatives in Dhaka and even most of their domestic help were Urdu-speaking and non-Bengali. Some of them came from Bihar, some from Bhopal, yet some others from Lucknow in India's Uttar Pradesh and from other states. They all spoke either Urdu, Hindi, or Hindi mixed with other Indian state languages. But when it came to literature or even reading newspapers, they always preferred Urdu. Rania's family though, after moving to Dhaka had been transformed into an unusual mixed one. She herself, though a student of English literature at the university, learned to speak, read, and write in Bengali well. Even though most of the employees in her fashionable tailoring shop were non-Bengalis, the majority of the clients were Bengalis. Most of her employees, at one time, supported the idea that Urdu be established/recognized as the working language in the social and political affairs of the then East Pakistan. They could not fathom the depth of Bengalis' love for their language Bengali and their pride in their traditions and cultures. However, the 1952 Bengali language movement and the sacrifices that Bengalis made during that political struggle, convinced these non-Bengali refugees in the then East Pakistan that their inherent support for West Pakistanis to make Urdu as the only state language of all Pakistan was wrong and doomed to fail in the long run. They further realized that their misplaced support for the West Pakistanis in general was the root cause of the general dislike for Urdu-speaking refugees among the local Bengali population. Rania's family from their experience wanted an end to that untenable relationship between the refugees and the local Bengali people. The family wished to integrate into the local Bengali society and culture by establishing a social relationship between the two groups. That was why when Rania met and fell in love with Alam during their student days at the Dhaka University and she wanted to marry Alam, her father Mr. Afsar—a small family businessman—did not object to her wish despite warnings from most of their friends and acquaintances. Afsar was already a widower when he had migrated to East Pakistan from the Indian state of Bhopal with young Rania. He thought Rania being in love with and marrying a local Bengali young man would strengthen his family's roots in East Pakistan. Even though Afsar was heartbroken at the refusal of Alam's family to accept the marriage, he refused to budge from his belief. That was why he willed, before his death, all his businesses and properties to Alam and Rania with an equal share.

The fact that Rania's daughter Rokshana right at that moment was visiting the village of Rania's father-in-law and that none of Rokshana's blood relatives from her father's side was raising any question about it, they all were rather cordially welcoming her and accepting her as one of their own, was making Rania feel extremely happy. She asked Alam:

"You are not saying anything. Wouldn't Zakia Bhavi feel bad, if, instead of Rokhi, I myself would have gone to your village home?"

"Perhaps, after all these years, Bhavi does not hold that grudge anymore, Rania," Alam replied. "She knew very well that I had never done anything else against the wishes of my elder brother— except in the matter of my love for you and consequent marriage with you," Alam further elaborated. He remembered the scene when and where he was leaving the village for good. Zakia and Kabil had come to see him off at the end of the village, and Zakia wanted Alam to understand that she herself had no grudge with Alam. Rather she simply shared the sadness of his elder brother Kamal's soul as his respectful and duty-bound wife and that the decision to break the relationship with Alam was not her own. She just couldn't go against his brother's decision so soon after his death. When Alam got down to the paddy field's narrow mud-path after leaving the village pathway, on his way to the railway station, he turned back to look at Zakia and Kabil one more time and noticed that Zakia and Kabil were still standing under a tree shade on the side of the pathway. Zakia was wiping tears from her eyes with the edge of her saree. Alam walked back to them. He bent down and paid respect to Zakia in the traditional Bengali way by touching her feet and said, "Think it over again, Bhavi. My older brother who cut off relations with me died shortly afterward without having a chance to see my wife and to know anything at all about her family. I know that he had spent just about everything for my education. I want to do my duty and take responsibility in turn for you and my little nephew. But you declined my offer and I cannot force you to accept my offer now. But any time in the future, if you ever think, Kabil could use my help, please do not hesitate to send him to me." With that Alam left them for good.

Ahmed Alam smiled a little on his own. He realized that everything turned a full circle after all these years when his now grown-up nephew Kabil came to Alam's family in Dhaka and took his own daughter Rokshana to their ancestral village home on the basis of their newfound old-blood relationship, and Zakia Bhavi accepted Rokshana wholeheartedly. He felt that somehow the relationship between Kabil and Rokshana was somehow beyond that between two cousins. Rokshana of course carefully managed not to make her parents know until now that her relationship with Kabil was beyond that of two cousins. Alam asked his wife, "Do you think Rokhi likes Kabila a lot?"

"What kind of liking?" Rania asked back.

"I am talking about love between the two beyond that between two ordinary cousins," Alam elaborated.

"You are a fool. Don't you understand anything?" Rania shot back.

"Tell me clearly, Rania. You know about Kabil's parents," Alam asked as if pleading.

"Yes, I know of Kabil's proud, sentimental, rigid parents. Kabil is your brother's son, the brother who refused to allow you to go back to your village because you married me. He did not want to see your face again. Yes, Alam, I know and understand everything," Rania suddenly poured out all the sadness in her heart, dormant for all these years. All these years she spoke to her husband in his mother tongue—Bengali. But that day when her husband revived her dormant emotional wound by referring to Kabil's parents' reaction to his marrying

Rania and their past rigid, inflexible attitude, she lost control of her emotions and started speaking to Alam in her own mother tongue—Urdu. Alam kept silent for a while after his wife's emotional outburst. By that time Rania was able to control her emotions and came to her normal self.

"Your daughter was mesmerized with Kabil on the day that he had arrived in this family. As a mother, I understand everything. I am afraid Zakia Bhavi will also sense this. You know your daughter. She does not know how to hide anything. She will say openly that she loves Kabil and will marry him. Now think what Zakia Bhavi will make of it," Rania explained to Alam.

"What about Kabil? How does he feel?" Alam asked.

"I do not know. But it takes two to tango. You can't clap with one hand only," Rania replied.

"But don't worry. There is nothing to be concerned about. Kabil is a fine young man. He is brilliant in his studies. If they want to marry each other, they will. I think Zakia Bhavi will not object once she gets to know Rokshana," Rania added. At that point, Rania made a move to leave the dining table. Alam indicated with his hand for Rania to sit a bit longer.

"Do you want to say something else?" Rania asked.

"Yes! Of course. What about Andaleeb (Andy), your nephew from your mother's side? He has been eagerly waiting for long for Rokshana to grow up a bit more before proposing to marry her. Do you think about that?" Alam posed the question.

"Yes! I think about that. Andaleeb will be a likable son-in-law. He wants Rokhi with all his heart. He works hard for our business. He is capable of managing your shops, factory, go-downs and all. Your daughter had liked Andaleeb until she saw Kabil. Now she does not care about Andaleeb anymore," Rania replied.

"I do not want to take the side in favor of my nephew, Rania," Alam commented.

"I know that. Why would you do that? We too got married after falling in love with each other. You suffered a lot because of that. All your relatives shunned you for that. You became an outsider in your own country. Now why would you put Kabil in the same situation? Andaleeb is a fine young man. He is in love with your daughter. But if your daughter does not care about Andaleeb, I will not take the side in favor of my nephew either. I know your daughter is now set for Kabil."

"Isn't my daughter your daughter too, Rania?"

"Yes, she was in my womb, but she is yours."

"What do you want me to do now, Rania?"

"You do not have to do anything right now. But we should sound Zakia Bhavi out on this. Otherwise we may have to regret."

Seeing Alam quiet and not saying anything more, Rania got up and walked toward the kitchen. Soon after, Andaleeb walked in with a black briefcase in his hand.

"Come in, my son," Alam welcomed Andaleeb.

"Did you bring the money?" he asked.

"Yes, Uncle," Andaleeb replied.

"How much? Give it to your aunty please," Alam advised.

"Sit down. She went to the kitchen," Alam added.

"I will go and give her the money there. Did you receive any letter from Rokhi?" Andaleeb asked politely.

"Yes, your aunty got a postcard from her," Alam replied.

"Don't worry about Rokhi. I think she is doing well in my village. My sister-in-law Zakia received her with open heart," Alam added. Andaleeb smiled and said, "That's a good news. You will feel relieved of their rejection after many years. Now you take my aunty with you and visit your father's homestead, Uncle," Andaleeb suggested.

"Where will he go to visit, Andaleeb?" Rania asked as she re-entered the room with tea tray in her hand.

"Why? Your father-in-law's village?" Andaleeb replied. Rania didn't answer Andaleeb. She put down the tray on the table and asked, "How much money did you bring in your briefcase, Andaleeb?" she asked.

"Twenty thousand."

"Okay, leave it there. I will count and put them in the locker safe," Rania advised.

"Would you like to have some tea, Andaleeb?"

"No. Thanks, Aunty. I will just take leave of you both now," Andaleeb replied as he walked out. Alam moved the briefcase by the side of the table so he can see Rania. While she was pouring tea into a cup, Alam called out, "Rania."

"Yes."

"I like this nephew of yours very much."

"Do you think I don't know that?"

"I know you are aware of that. The reason I mention that now is because I almost made up my mind that I would give Rokhi in marriage to Andaleeb. He is very capable of managing our business and other properties. And he is a very honest young man. In the future, beyond me, he will take care of you and Rokhi well," Alam elaborated.

"Why are you telling me all these now? I told you of your daughter's love for Kabil. It's my duty to inform you of Rokhi's like and dislike. In our life, Alam, we had love for each other. But for that you had to suffer too. I always felt guilt conscious because my love for you separated you from your near and dear ones. I always think about brother Kamal and worry that one day, my dream about Rokhi's future will be shattered just as I had shattered brother Kamal's dream about your future. I am scared, Alam because your daughter is deeply in love with Kabil. At the same time, my nephew Andaleeb desperately wants to marry your daughter. He loves Rokhi very much. You know that. I wonder what is written in our fate in the future. Andaleeb has been working like your slave looking after your business for the sole reason of winning your and Rokhi's heart with the hope of marrying Rokhi. So far, there was nothing to deter him in his hope until Kabil showed up in our family and completely mesmerized Rokhi. Now Rokhi does not care about Andaleeb at all. Her love for Kabil reminds me of my own mental condition when I had first met you. If Rokhi's mental situation now is anywhere near what my situation was when I first saw you, then only God knows where we as a family are heading to. I am really worried Alam, I do not know what to do." With those words, Rania hugged Alam's neck, put her head below Alam's chin, and started sobbing profusely. Alam started comforting her by rubbing and petting her back.

"Look, Rania! There is nothing for you to worry about much at this stage. You know Rokshana is still very young. She is not yet old enough to make a decision about her future. Like us, she is aware that her own uncle did not allow her father to visit his own village just because her father had married her mother, an Urdu-speaking non-Bengali whose family had fled India for safety and security in 1947 to the eastern part of the newly formed Muslim country of Pakistan. She is upset about my late brother's reaction to our marriage as much as we have been. In the last few months, after Kabil joined our family, he has been able to win over our hearts to a great extent. In the same way, Rokshana also came to convince herself that like Kabil, she is also a child of this country. This is where her father and ancestors are rooted. She did not hesitate to go visit her ancestral village with Kabil to strengthen her newfound roots. Thank God that Kabil's mother and other relatives in our village accepted Rokhi as one of their own. She, after all, has a blood connection with and attraction to Kabil. For all her life so far, she has been hearing that she is an Urdu-speaking Bihari girl and that this is not her motherland and she is a refugee in this country. She had never, before now, been to her paternal village even though she belongs there through her father's blood connection. Once she got Kabil in our family, her belief of belonging to Bengali nation had doubled, and that reinforced her attraction to Kabil. This may not exactly be romantic love between two young people. There is attraction between two young people other than just a romantic one. I do not think you have to be too much worried about the way they interact with each other. Even if it is a matter of romantic attraction between the two, there is nothing wrong about it. Kabil did not come to our family with the hope of sharing our business and other fortunes. You know well, he is the son of two very proud and sensitive parents. Moreover, he is a brilliant student. He will do well in the future once he attends and completes his studies properly and with care. If Rokhi chooses to marry Kabil, I do not think she will make a wrong choice. Like your father used to say that you had made a good choice when you married me. Now, I will not deprive Andaleeb of his rightful claim. He understands our businesses well. But I cannot convince Rokhi to choose Andaleeb over Kabil," Alam concluded.

Rania felt comforted with Alam's words and placed her head against Alam's chest and continued crying.

ON THE DAY THAT Kabil and Rokshana were to return to Dhaka, Zakia Banu woke up early and went to the kitchen to prepare some traditional Bengali cake, known locally as pita. Kabil was still sleeping. But Rokshana woke up earlier than usual even though she had consumed night before a lot of local brand of (binni) rice that has some fermentation characteristics and causes lethargy, drowsiness, and even mild intoxication if consumed in large quantities. She woke up early because she wanted to see and learn how Zakia prepared pita. She told Zakia that she would join her in the kitchen soon, but first she wanted to pour some water on sleeping Kabil's face to wake him up, something that Kabil had threatened her the night before if she did not wake up early in the morning because of her consuming a large portion of binni rice. She did exactly that on her way back from the dug well area after washing her face and brushing her teeth.

"Hey, Rokhi! What is this you are doing?" Kabil asked waking up quickly.

"Have I broken the dream of the son of Syed family about his fairy?"

Rokshana asked as she spread some more water on Kabil's face through his bed room window.

"Rokhi! You pour water all over me."

"It is late. Look, the morning train will leave for Dhaka soon with me and leaving you behind," Rokhi replied.

"Is that so?" Kabil wondered as he grabbed Rokshana's hand through the window.

"Let my hand go soon. Aunty is awake. She would understand what is going on here," Rokshana appealed.

"First tell me what is going on here," Kabil insisted.

"No, I will not tell."

"Then, I will not let go of your hand."

"I am shy. Let me go."

"First, tell me what is going on here that my mother will be suspicious about?

"Shall I tell the truth?"

"Yes, tell me the truth".

"I am blushing"

"No, that is not enough. Tell me the real thing."

"You are madly in love with me—just the same way your uncle—my father was with my mother."

"What about you?"

"I am a daughter of a respectable Bengali Syed family. I have a great degree of shyness and self-esteem."

At that both of them laughed aloud.

Zakia heard everything from the kitchen and understood that something deeper than the normal relationship between two cousins was going on between Kabil and Rokshana. She became worried. *If so, what would happen to Momena,* she wondered. Momena was the daughter of Zakia's deceased brother. She gave words to her father's family that she would like Kabil to marry Momena when the two were of age.

Meanwhile, Kabil released Rokshana's hand and asked, "Shall I open the door? Will you come inside?"

Rokshana said, "Okay, open the door. But remember no touching of me when I am inside."

Kabil jumped out of bed, opened the door, and then went back to bed and covered himself with the bedsheet. Seeing that, Rokshana tiptoed around the bed, smiled naughtily and then ran out of the room and then across the courtyard, entered the kitchen, and took a seat on a stool across from Zakia.

"I just woke up brother Kabil from his deep sleep dreaming about his fairy," Rokshana volunteered.

"Did you pour water on his face?" Zakia asked.

"No, no, he will not wake up from his sleep while dreaming about his fairy princess with a spray of water. I just said a prayer and blew air on his face hoping it will wake him up," Rokshana replied. By that time Kabil came and stood at the kitchen door.

"Mother, do you know what your daughter of affection has done to my bed and came to you to plead for her innocence?" Kabil asked.

"What did she do?" Zakia inquired.

"She made my beddings all wet by pouring water on it," Kabil replied.

"I did not do any such thing, Aunty. It must have been done by his fairy friend." At that Kabil mockingly threatened Rokshana.

Rokshana quickly got up and took shelter behind Zakia.

"Well, Kabil! Leave her alone now. Go and wash yourself. I will serve you some warm pita for breakfast. You may not find this kind of pita in Dhaka," Zakia instructed Kabil.

Kabil returned to the kitchen after wash up, sat on a low stool next to Rokshana, and started eating the pita. Rokshana had already started eating the pita all the while observing how Zakia was making them on the earthen stove.

"Your way of making pita is wonderful, Aunty. I think I now know how to make it myself," Rokshana commented.

"Well then, you make it yourself when you go back to Dhaka and serve them to your parents," Zakia encouraged her with a smile.

"Mother, are you joking? Rokhi will make this kind of pita? She is trying to make us believe that she is a typical Bengali girl and will make Bengali-style pita," Kabil rather jokingly commented. Rokshana suddenly felt offended by Kabil's comment.

"What did you say, brother Kabil? Am I not a Bengali girl? Then whose daughter am I? My own cousin thinks I am a Bihari girl," Rokshana poured out with a deep sense of disappointment. She then covered her face with the palm of her both hands and started crying while Zakia and Kabil stared at each other both not knowing what to say next.

Kabil was sorry and embarrassed and said, "Look, Mother, did I ever say she is not a Bengali child? I was just joking about her cooking skill." Hearing Kabil pleading innocence, Rokshana got up from the stool and proceeded to Zakia's bedroom without paying any attention to anybody and continued crying while lying on the bed. Zakia realized that Rokshana was hurt in her weakest spot in her psychological health. She realized that psychologically Rokshana was desperately looking for her true identity and acceptance in the country by her father's estranged family.

"Why do you say something that hurts Rokhi? Do you not realize after knowing her so long what specifically hurts her? If not, how are you two going to spend life as a couple?" Zakia almost inadvertently poured out her inner sense of the relationship between the two in a way of accusing Kabil of his insensitive comment on the spot. Rokshana heard Zakia's expression, "Spend life as a couple," which immediately caused her to stop crying, and she lay down on the bed in almost total wonderment and pleasant disbelief. Kabil was sorry, ashamed, and embarrassed at his mother's rebuking words and left the room immediately.

Zakia put a stop in her pita making process, went to the dug well site to wash up. She came back to her bedroom, sat on a stool next to the bed, and caressed Rokshana still lying on the bed.

"Rokhi, are you still going to hide your face on the pillow? Are you shy and embarrassed at what I have said? I noticed the two of you interacting with each other. That prompted me to say what I have said about you two spending future life as a married couple. I realized on the first day you arrived here with Kabil that you are in love with Kabil. Now, I am worried about how your parents will take it when they come to know about it. They will think that I may not consent to you two getting married just as Kabil's father did not consent to your father marrying your mother. They may not even come to me to seek my consent. And I will not go to your parent's home because your uncle made me promise on his death bed not to associate with your parents. I thought my attitude had softened a bit over the past years. But you poor children renewed the problem by falling in love with each other. Had I anticipated this earlier, I would not have sent Kabil to your house in Dhaka," Zakia elaborated.

Rokshana got hurt at Zakia's last words. She sat up like a wounded animal and shouted, "Why would you not send brother Kabil to our house, Aunty? Is that because we are Bihari people? Is that because my mother is a foreigner in this country?"

"Did I call you Bihari, Rokshana? So what, if you are a Bihari? Aren't Biharis and other foreigners people like us? Don't they have love and compassion in their heart like we Bengalis do? I do not worry at all about who is Bihari and who is a foreigner. Kabil's father was not upset because your mother is not a Bengali. He was upset with your father—for whom he had invested a lot and he had great hopes—who did not even ask for his consent before marrying your mother. I know your father did not do that because he knew your uncle would be disappointed. He was afraid Kabil's father would not consent to the marriage. Now Kabil is probably going to disappoint your father who may have hopes of marrying you in a richer and better family. But you, poor child, are madly in love with Kabil and are ready to disappoint your father badly. At the same time, Kabil will contribute to his uncle's disappointment despite your parents' hopes and aspiration for you and despite their help and love for him. The hurt which we all hoped would be behind us after all these years would now strike all of us with renewed intensity."

Hearing Zakia's details, Rokshana again covered her head with the pillow and started crying again. With a feeble crying voice, she appealed to Zakia, "Aunty! You give me Kabil Bhaiya. I do not want anything else. I do not care for wealth.

If you don't give Kabil to me, I will not live, Aunty. I will die for him. You forget your anger, Aunty, and come to Dhaka and tell and ask for the consent of my parents on our behalf something that we ourselves cannot ask from them."

All this time, Zakia was caressing Rokshana's back. Suddenly, she thought of some comforting words. She held up Rokshana's chin and said, "Would you promise me one thing, Rokshana? Would you two wait for your marriage until Kabil graduates from the university and until then you refrain from doing anything that will ruin your parents' trust in you two?"

"I promise you that, Aunty. Brother Kabil also will be patient. But if my father insists on marrying me off to my maternal cousin Andaleeb before Kabil graduates, you stop my father doing that. I know you can do that," Rokshana appealed to Zakia.

"I pray to God, Rokshana, so nothing as complicated as that could happen to all of us," Zakia promised. "Now, get ready to go to the railway station on time," Zakia prompted Rokshana.

CHAPTER 3

Life of a Student Activist and a Budding Politician

ONE DAY IN MARCH 1969, a small procession of students from Dhaka University, organized by the Student League was marching toward Gulistan—the center of relatively new DHAKA—while shouting slogans demanding political autonomy for the then East Pakistan. The participants in the procession were quite militant even though they numbered less than two hundred, including no more than four or five girl students. The girls were carrying banners that read, 'Long live Sheikh Mujib." "Accept Six Points Demand," referring to the six-point demands to the central government formulated by the dominant political party Awami League and its leader Sheikh Mujibur Rahman. Kabil and Rokshana were walking side by side at the very front of the procession. They looked tired and both their faces were red in the blazing sun. At one spot, Kabil whispered in Rokshana's ear, "We will slip out once the procession reaches the intersection at Gulistan".

"How?" Rokshana asked, carrying a banner.

"I will enter the big ice cream shop there. You hand over the banner to someone and follow me," Kabil replied. They did just that at the intended spot. A short time later, both were enjoying some milkshake at a nearby restaurant.

"I had to do a lot of maneuvering to hand over the banner to someone else," Rokshana broke the silence. "A lot of people understood that both you and I were slipping out," she continued. "Let them know. I did not open any of my text books as I kept myself busy for the last three months supporting and working for the cause of Six Points Demand," Kabil responded in despair. "I am worried about the results of my last examination. How can I explain the bad result to my uncle and aunty?" Kabil wondered aloud.

"My father does not like at all your deep involvement in student politics, Kabil," Rokshana added. "They see your picture in the newspapers almost every day. They think the Punjabis will not accept/grant the Six Points Demand of Sheikh Mujib. They are worried about Pakistan's survival as one united country if the current turmoil continues," Rokshana elaborated.

"What does Aunty think about it?" Kabil asked.

"Mother is on our side. She says we are not the only students agitating for the causes of Mujib's Six Points Demand. She argues with my dad that most students in the country are in favor of Six Points Demand to stop the exploitation of East Pakistan by West Pakistanis. She believes that students born and raised in this country would obviously protest against the exploitation of their homeland," Rokshana elaborated.

"Okay, if Aunty is on our side, then I don't see reasons for much concern," Kabil observed.

"I am not that sure," Rokshana commented. "Your BA honors examination results will be announced shortly. You did not study very hard before the exam because you were too busy providing leadership to the University Students Union. When the exam result will be announced and you are not happy with the result, then you will blame the student politics and will spend time miserably. I know you well."

"Do you think I will fail the exam?" Kabil asked worriedly.

"No, I do not think you will fail. But I am worried that you may not do as well as you once hoped for and aimed at," Rokshana replied.

"Don't worry much. I studied Bengali literature well and wrote in the exam papers as much as I know," Kabil assured Rokshana.

"Looking at your confidence, I think you might have written the things you did not learn well also," Rokshana teased Kabil, at which both burst into laughter.

Kabil then wondered aloud, saying, "Our future also will depend on my honor's exam result. Remember, Aunty said that she would support our getting married religiously soon after my BA honor's result is out," Rokshana blushed at Kabil's comment. She continued sipping the milkshake to hide her happy but embarrassed facial expression.

"Is that why you neglected your studies so much, worked so hard for Students Union to disappoint my mother?" she asked mockingly.

"You will find out in a couple of days when the result will be out that I also worked just as hard in order to get married to you." Kabil stunned Rokshana.

"May God accept your hard work and may you have a good exam result tomorrow. Let us now go home," Rokshana concluded.

THE FOLLOWING DAY, EARLY in the morning darkness, the police surrounded the house of businessman Ahmed Alam. Two police Jeeps were parked at the front gate. Inside the first one, there were two police officers; in the second one, there were a group of armed policemen. One police officer ordered two of his men to climb over the closed gate and open it from inside. After the gate was opened, the two officers entered the compound, walked up to the verandah, and rang the doorbell. By that time the team of policemen also entered the compound and stood at strategic locations with guns ready in their hands.

Rania opened the door ajar and was taken aback seeing the two police officers with their headgears on.

"What do you want at this hour of the early morning?" she asked.

"Is this the house of Mr. Ahmed Alam?" one officer asked.

"I am Mrs. Alam. Why do you ask for Mr. Alam early at this hour?" Rania asked a little perturbed.

"We are from the police department. We have an arrest warrant against one Mr. Kabil who we believe lives in this house. Please ask Mr. Kabil to come out."

With that, the two officers entered inside the house by pushing the door almost by force even by mildly pushing Rania in doing so. The two officers then seated themselves on the sofa. Rania stood calmly for a few seconds, absorbing their rude behavior and then made a move to go inside. One of the officers then stood up and commanded her, "Wait a minute, madam. Where are you going? We told you that we have a warrant against Mr. Kabil."

"I am going to telephone your boss, the superintendent of police (SP) to find out what kind of warrant has been issued. He is a friend of my husband and perhaps knows more about the warrant than you do," Rania replied. Before she finished, Alam and Rokshana entered the room. Both were uneasy and concerned with being awakened from incomplete sleep. Seeing them, the other officer also stood up out of deference.

One of them said, "You are angry with us, Mrs. Alam. We are sorry to bother you at this hour. We would not come at this time if it was not an urgent warrant." This time their tone was more polite. The information that the SP, their boss was a friend of this family, had an immediate effect on the tone of their voice.

Walking toward the sofa, Alam demanded, "Tell me straight what has happened and what business do you have in my house at this odd hour?"

By this time all of them made themselves seated on the sofa. One of the police officers then said, "Mr. Alam! We have an arrest warrant against Mr. Syed Ahmed Kabil. We know he is now in this house which has been barricaded from all around. He cannot possibly escape. Please ask him to come out. We will treat him well as much as possible if he surrenders himself voluntarily. We ask for your cooperation in this regard. If our boss the SP is your friend, then you can take the matter with him later. We are petty officers. Please don't be angry with us," he then handed over the warrant document to Mr. Alam.

"What is the charge against Kabil?" Alam asked.

"Mr. Kabil's activities as the vice president of DUCSU (Dhaka University Central Students Union) has been endangering the national unity and integrity. A kind of conspiracy to separate East Pakistan from West Pakistan," the police officer replied. At this Alam, Rokshana, and Rania sat quietly for a while. After a while, Rokshana said, "You cannot arrest brother Kabil from this house simply because he is not here at this time. He has not been sleeping in this house for the last several nights—not even eating supper here. Tomorrow his exam result will be announced at the university campus. He will be there for that. If you have the mandate and power, you can go and arrest him from there. You can search the house if you want."

The police officer then suddenly blew the whistle and his men started searching the house frantically. They finished the search with no trace of Kabil in the compound.

THE FOLLOWING DAY RANIA and Alam were eating lunch quietly in the house. Both were in a somber mood. In the middle of their lunch, Andaleeb showed up unexpectedly.

"Did neither of you go to work today?" he asked. Seeing that neither Alam nor Rania cared to answer his question—they rather continued eating silently—he further asked, "What is there to be so worried about? Our Kabil is a well-known student leader. It is not unusual that the government would issue a warrant against him. He is fighting for the rights of his country. He is not a thief. I came with very good news for you two." Andaleeb said this, trying to draw their attention. Both Alam and Rania raised their heads instantly and looked at Andaleeb inquisitively.

"I would have preferred to break the news with Rokhi also present at the same time. Where is she? Is she not eating lunch?" Andaleeb asked.

"Rokhi has been in bed since morning. She didn't even eat breakfast. Go and see if you can persuade her to eat something. But tell us first about your good news," Rania replied.

"Kabil's exam result has been announced. He stood first in his class," Andaleeb declared.

"Praise be to God. Do you know where Kabil is?" both Alam and Rania asked almost simultaneously.

"Yes, I know. He is in a safe place. There is no need for you two to worry about him. I will tell you at the right time. I will now go and give Rokhi the news and then proceed to the shop. No need for you two to be so nervous," Andaleeb said confidently.

Alam felt a bit reassured. He asked while still eating, "How did you find out about Kabil's exam result?"

"Kabil told me himself."

"Did you tell him about the arrest warrant against him?"

"He knew about it before us all. That is the reason he was not here last night. I also told him about the police searching your house last night."

"What did he say to that?

"He is worried about your health, Uncle, knowing that you have a heart problem."

"Tell him that I am okay, and I'm not angry with him."

With that, Alam left the dining table and walked toward his bedroom.

Andaleeb told Rokshana that Kabil was currently at his house and that Kabil did not want Rokshana to try to contact him for the time being. He asked Rokshana to go to the university campus if she could and assure his close friends of his status at a safe place. He also told Andaleeb that police had by that time arrested most other student leaders of Dhaka University Central Students Union (DUCSU). Kabil further cautioned Rokshana that the police might arrest him at any time because the government was aware that the students' agitation would not slow down until the police found and arrested Kabil and that it was through the students' movement that the words of Mujib's Six Points Demand were gaining support among the masses of East Pakistan.

Student groups who were influenced by the ideology of global communism were not yet fully supporting East Pakistan's claim for regional autonomy led and postulated by Mujib's Awami League through its Six Points Demand. The reason for their lack of support was the good bilateral relations between the governments of Pakistan and China. Kabil was one of the senior leaders of that section of Awami League allied Students League whose objective was to attain full autonomy for the then East Pakistan. That was the reason the government was putting pressure on the police to arrest Kabil as soon as possible.

The following day, Rokhsana went to the university campus and met some of Kabil's close friends who could avoid police arrest and told them that Kabil was in a safe hideout. As soon as she got back home, Rania was a little upset and confronted her,

"Where have you been all day without bathing and eating?" she demanded.

"I was at the university campus," Rokhsana replied.

"Did you see Kabil there?"

"No, he is at Andaleeb's house. I shall see him this evening."

"There is a telegram for Kabil from Montala," Rania informed Rokhsana.

"Is there any bad news?"

"Your aunty is very ill."

Rania handed the telegram to Rokhsana. She took a quick look at the message and then put it in her handbag.

"Let me think for a while if I should give this news to Kabil now. The police are on the lookout for Kabil all over the city. Perhaps, it will not be possible for Kabil to go to Montala at this time," Rokhsana said almost to herself.

"I think your aunty's health is not very good. She suffered from typhoid not long ago. Now she again came down with high fever as per the telegram. I am somewhat worried, Rokhi," Rania expressed her concern.

"In the present situation, Kabil will get caught and arrested if he ventured any travel outside of Dhaka. Rather, why not you and Daddy go yourselves? You did not set foot all your life in the village of your father-in-law. You blamed my uncle (Kabil's father) always," Rokshana suggested.

"Not a bad idea, Rokhi. I can go with your father and see your aunty when she is ill. If she did not get better, maybe we can convince her to come to Dhaka with us. Would you also like to accompany us, Rokhi?" Rania asked.

Rokhi kept silent for a few seconds. "How can I go to our village leaving Kabil here in this situation, Mother? He needs me here at this time. I am the only reliable go-between for him and his political allies. Besides . . ." Rokhi stopped halfway.

"Besides what?" Rania inquired.

Rokhi pinned her eyes to the ground silently in the face of her mother's intruding question. Rania came close to Rokhi, put her hand lovingly on her head, and said, "I know, Kabil is a very serious young man. But he is taking a lead role in starting a political storm in this country. Nobody knows where this will lead to. Think, my daughter, if you will be able to ride the storm with him. If not, it is still not too late," Rania told this to Rokhsana as if to express her own inner fear and motherly concern for her only daughter.

Rokhsana kept silent for a while then took Rania's hand in her own. While doing that, she noticed that there was a diamond ring on Rania's little finger. It was not there even a few days ago. Rokhsana remembered that her mother had expressed earlier her desire to complete the religious ceremony of the wedding of Rokshana and Kabil after his BA honor's examination results were announced. Rokhsana guessed that her mother had this diamond ring made for that occasion. But now that Kabil was engaged in raising a political turmoil in the country, her mother realized that and was asking Rokhsana to have a second thought about her love for Kabil and probable marriage to him.

Rokhsana laughed quietly. "Beautiful ring, when did you get it made?" she asked her mother.

"Do you like it? I had it made for Kabil to put it on your finger on the day of the religious ceremony of the wedding between him and you. Do you want to try it on?" Rania asked.

"Now that Kabil has no time to put the ring on my finger, let me try it on myself for a while," Rokhsana commented as she took the ring from her mother's finger and put it on hers.

She smiled at her mother as an expression of her gratitude for the ring.

"I am going out again in the evening. I will be in brother Andaleeb's house. So please don't worry if I am late coming back home. I will try to tactfully tell Kabil about Aunty's health. If I can, then I will also tell him about you and Daddy going to Montala to see Aunty. Now let me go to my room," Rokhsana concluded.

IT WAS SIX IN the early evening. A group of young people was engaged in a heated political discussion with Kabil while sitting on a cotton mat in a closed-door room on the second floor of Andaleeb's house at No. 26 Basu Bazar Lane in Narinda area of Dhaka. One young man complained to Kabil, saying, "Whatever else we can have Sheikh Mujib do, I don't think he will go far enough to demand directly our independence from Pakistan."

"There is nothing to be worried about Sheik Mujib's position on that," Kabil commented.

"Remember, whatever progress we can make toward our total independence from Pakistan with Mujib as our leader will not be possible under the leadership of any other person or group. Sheikh Mujib was one of the leaders who had worked hard for the creation of Pakistan. Despite that, the fact that he is now leading the cause of East Pakistan by raising Six Points Demand for its autonomy is a no mean achievement. His policy of regional autonomy is the right policy for us at this time," Kabil continued.

Before he could finish, the doorbell rang. While someone got busy collecting and hiding posters and other materials from the floor, Kabil got up, walked to the closed door, and asked, "Who is there?"

"It is Andaleeb. Rokhi is with me," the voice from outside the door was heard.

Kabil opened the door ajar and saw Andaleeb and Rokhsana were standing outside. She was wearing a yellow silk salwar kameez with a black scarf on her chest. She used to wear this type of West Pakistani outfit before she got admitted to Dhaka University but changed to wear saree since she started attending the university. She looked stunningly beautiful wearing, after a long while, salwar kameez with colorful pearls on her neck. Kabil's eyes were fixed on her even in the slight darkness of the room.

Rokhsana noticed that and commented, "What a brazen, embarrassing look? Would you at least first let us come inside please?"

Kabil instantly became aware of his awkward look and started laughing aloud in an attempt to lessen the gravity of his rather brazen look at Rokhsana.

"Oh my God! Believe me, Rokhi. I thought brother Andaleeb has brought some Pathan fairy along with him," Kabil murmured.

Seeing some young students inside the room, Andaleeb wanted to lighten the situation and commented, "You people are not the type who would be so mesmerized by looking at a fairy. You all are revolutionary people with your Six Points

Demand. The fairy that I brought with me is not a Pathan. She is a true-blue Bengali fairy. She is very dedicated to the causes of your revolution. She will take care of your needs in my humble house. Now with your permission, I will take leave of you. I will have to attend our spice businesses at this important transaction time."

As soon as Andaleeb left, one of the students said, "Brother Kabil! With your permission, I think we also should leave now. If you want to send some directives to us, you can do so through Rokshana. She will find us in Modhu's Canteen at the campus." With that, the students saluted Kabil and left one by one.

After the students left, Rokhsana took off her sandals, seated herself on the cotton mat on the floor leaning against a pillow.

"Are you facing any inconvenience here in your eating and all that?" she asked.

"No, I am quite comfortable here. If you ever taste the food cooked for Andaleeb by the old lady in the house, you will appreciate what good cooking is," Kabil responded.

"Speak slowly, the lady may hear you. Refer to her as grandmother because she is actually Andaleeb's grandmother. Didn't Andaleeb introduce you to her?" Rokhsana said admonishingly.

"No, maybe he did not have time to do that. I have not told you yet how I ended up taking shelter in this house. That night around 3:00 a.m. I came over and knocked at the door. Andaleeb opened the door. Seeing me standing outside, he smiled and said, 'What's up? Do you need a safe shelter? Go, sleep in the spice storage room. I will hear your story at daybreak.' Since then I casually saw him once or twice to have a conversation. He told me that there was a guardian-type relative in the house who would look after my food and everything. He asked me about my exam results, and I told him that I had stood first and asked him to convey the news to you, Uncle, and Aunty. He did not tell me that this elderly guardian-type old lady is his grandmother," Kabil narrated in detail and felt rather embarrassed.

"Okay, today you introduce yourself to the grandmother and ask for her forgiveness for your previous mistakes. Otherwise, when she finds out our relationship, she would think Rania's son-in-law is an uncultured young man," Rokhi advised.

"Now, I have to give you some bad news," Rokhi continued as she pulled out the telegram from Montala with news of the illness of Kabil's mother and handed it over to Kabil. As he took the telegram, Kabil noticed the shining diamond ring in Rokhi's finger.

"Your diamond ring shines like a cat's eye," Kabil commented.

"Oh! Mother got it made for the upcoming engagement and religious part of our wedding. But as it turned out everything now is uncertain and up in the air," Rokhsana replied. She was distraught and disappointed. By that time, Kabil had a chance to read about his mother's illness in the telegram.

"Looks like my mother's illness is serious. I have to go Montala," he announced.

Rokhsana thought it prudent not to mention anything about Kabil's announcement momentarily. She simply mentioned that her parents were set to leave for Montala the following morning. She also mentioned, "Since the day of the police search of our house, both Mom and Dad stopped attending to the business affairs. Andaleeb is looking after Daddy's business, but mother's tailoring business is suffering. Mother gets upset if I tell her to go to the tailoring shop. She thinks it is pointless to amass more wealth when we both ruined their dreams about our future marriage."

"Sounds like Aunty really felt hurt with the turn of the situation," Kabil observed.

"Yes, she did feel hurt, not so much because of our involvement in student politics, but more so because she could not arrange for our wedding. Moreover, her non-Bengali relatives are constantly advising her to leave this province for West Pakistan, to buy a house there and start a new business there as early as possible, considering the worsening political situation and civilian unrest here. Mother is concerned and worried that things might turn violent and ugly. Her non-Bengali relatives are constantly scaring her of our possible dark future here."

"Does Andaleeb also scare her like that?" Kabil asked.

Rokhsana got startled with Kabil's sudden and unexpected question. Normally, she did not go outside with Andaleeb. But today Kabil himself had asked Andaleeb to bring Rokhsana with him to Kabil's hideout. She couldn't figure out momentarily how to respond to Kabil's question. She just looked at Kabil in wonderment.

Sensing her predicament, Kabil apologetically said, "No, I asked the question because you said Aunty's non-Bengali friends are scaring her of the possible worrying situation in this province."

"But I did not mention Andaleeb's name. You should not have doubt about him," Rokhi replied.

"I am glad to note that suddenly you have a good opinion of him and are increasingly depending on him," Kabil said in a tone of mock jealousy.

"Don't talk rubbish," Rokhsana responded instantly. "Once upon a time, Andaleeb was hoping to marry me. It was quite natural. He is my close relative—my maternal cousin. He is reliable and helps us look after our family business. Do you think it is his fault naturally to want to marry me?"

"No, why should I think that?" Kabil asked with some kind of remorse for his earlier questions.

"Then, why do you look jealous of him? Since I and my parents made the decision that I would marry you, Andaleeb backed off. He now looks at me as his younger cousin sister. There is nothing romantic between us. I told him that. I also told him that I was and am really and truly in love with you and that one day soon I would marry you. I don't want to be without roots in this country by marrying a non-Bengali like my father did. Before, Andaleeb was a little inimical to you. However, since the day I firmly told him of my parents' and my decision, he is now more friendly toward you. He is a good man. Don't unnecessarily make a foe of him. You are involved in dangerous and risky political affairs. God forbid, if anything happens to you, there is nobody else other than Andaleeb who would come to my help," Rokhsana concluded. She then burst into tears of possible despair.

Kabil took her hand in his and started comforting her. He then asked her for advice on going to Montala to see his mother. Rokhsana said, "It is not a good idea for you to leave Dhaka now. The police are on the lookout for you. As soon as you step out, they will arrest and detain you for a year minimum. I am also planning to stay in Dhaka to help take care of you. Otherwise I would have preferred to go to Montala with my parents and spend some time with aunty."

AHMED ALAM AND HIS wife Rania arrived at Montala Railway Station on one sunny afternoon after many years since he had left his nearby paternal village. Alam's marriage to Rania was the main reason why his older brother Ahmed Kamal (Kabil's father) had years ago severed all his family connections with Alam. Alam did not inform anybody in the village in advance of his arrival simply because he had no contact with anybody there. There was nobody present at the railway station to receive him and his wife. His forefathers never had any family relations with any family in their area. His older brother Kamal had married Zakia, a woman from another reputable Syed family from Harashpur which was located another couple of railway stations away from Montala toward Sylhet District town. After Kabil had left their village home to reconnect with his estranged uncle Alam and his family in Dhaka, Zakia brought from Harashpur an orphaned niece of hers by the name of Momena (Momi) to live with her at their Montala home. Kabil had told his uncle Alam and aunt Rania about Momena so that they did not worry about his mother Zakia living alone at Montala. Momena was taught by Zakia how to read and write the vernacular. She used to write to Kabil at Dhaka once in a while, giving him information about his mother's health and other news about their home. Once, in recent months when Zakia was suffering from typhoid, Momi wrote Kabil asking him to come to Montala to visit his mother. Kabil came with Rokshana and stayed for several days. After remission of Zakia's illness, Kabil had gone back to his university studies at Dhaka while Rokshana opted to stay with Zakia and Momena for another two weeks or so. When Rokshana finally had gone back to her parents and Kabil at their home in Dhaka, she spoke highly and fondly of Momi to her parents. She also asked her parents to do what they could to help Momi for her future. She argued that Momi was a blood relation of hers and Kabil's from his mother's side. As Momi was an orphan, Rokshana pleaded with her parents; she had no one else to think about her future other than Kabil and herself as her close blood relatives. Her uncles at Harashpur were in no good financial situation to take care of Momena. Rokshana thought she had been able to convince Kabil and her parents that when Kabil would have finished his university studies and she and Kabil would get married, she would like Kabil's mother Zakia and his maternal cousin Momi to come and live with them in Dhaka.

On that sunny afternoon, as Alam and Rania got off the train at Montala station, Rania noticed that Alam was wiping tears from the corners of his eyes with his pocket-handkerchief. It was an emotional homecoming for him. Rania tried to comfort him by holding his hand. Then a station porter approached them and asked if they needed help with their suitcases.

"We want to go to the Syed family house at Montala," Rania said to the porter.

The porter by then took their suitcases on his head said, "Madam, the station master asked me to take you people to his office first. He's standing there in that verandah. You people arrived a little late. The Syed family matriarch that is Kabil's mother passed away early this morning."

Hearing that from the porter, Alam could not keep himself standing anymore. He sat down on the concrete floor of the station platform. As he had a heart problem from before, he put his hand on his chest and was trying to breathe slowly. Rania looked out toward the station master still standing in his nearby office verandah. Rania signaled him for help with her hand pointing toward Alam sitting there on the concrete platform. The station master Mr. Abdul Hye walked fast toward them.

"You are Kabil's aunty, aren't you?" he asked.

"Yes, and this is my husband Syed Ahmed Alam," Rania said pointing to Alam. He has a heart problem. Could you please help us go to our Syed family household?" Rania appealed to Mr. Hye.

"Don't worry about that, Mrs. Alam. I'll arrange for that right away. I'll also call for two men to help your husband walk home. You can then arrange for Kabil's mother's funeral and burial," the station master reassured Rania. Alam heard the comforting words of the station master to Rania. They inspired and motivated him. He got up himself from the concrete floor where he had been sitting, thanked the station master, and told him that he could manage walking on his own without any help. He and Rania then left the station with the porter carrying their suitcases.

As soon as they entered the Syed family household compound, they first went to the gravesite of Alam's older brother Ahmed Kamal on one side within the boundary wall. Rania noticed that Alam was having difficulty keeping his emotions under control that made him unsteady. She grabbed Alam with her both hands to help him. But Alam got out of her embrace and sat at the foot of Kamal's grave and started crying loudly. He was begging for his dead older brother's forgiveness. Rania sat closely comforting him.

Meanwhile, two middle-aged men came out from the big master bedroom of the house where Zakia's dead body was lying covered with a cotton wrap. They walked to Kamal's gravesite where Alam was still crying with Rania sitting next to him. They helped Alam get up and began comforting him.

They introduced themselves as Kabil's maternal uncles from Harashpur. They took Alam and Rania inside the room where Zakia's body was lying. As soon as Alam saw her covered dead body, he fainted right there. The two men laid him on a couch. Rania noticed a rather confused young girl standing on one side of the room. Rania asked her, "I take it that you are Momena, Kabil's maternal cousin."

"Yes, madam," replied the young girl.

"I'm Kabil's aunty. Hence your aunty as well," Rania added.

"Yes, Aunty! I recognized by looking at you," Momena replied.

Rania had earlier heard about Momena from Rokshana who had spoken very fondly about this orphan cousin of Kabil. She spoke about Momena's physical beauty who she compared with her aunty Zakia's physical features and beauty. Momena used to take good care of aging Zakia for which Kabil was ever grateful to her. Kabil often said that when Momena grew up, he would arrange for her marriage with a good man. Now Rania got a chance to take a close, good look at Momena standing right in front of her. She noticed that Momena was physically well-built, looked a slight bit taller than her own daughter Rokshana. Even though she was not as fair-complexioned as Rokshana was, Momena was bright in her light-brown skin color. Her two eyes were drawn and her eyebrows were like two small flying birds. Rania wondered if Zakia in her younger age was as beautiful as Momena was. Rania never saw Zakia when she was alive. She died with pride and dignity, keeping her promise to her husband in his death bed that she would never ask his younger brother Alam for any help. After her husband's death, she even discouraged Alam to visit her and Kabil at their village home, let alone depending on him for any financial help. Toward the end, she changed her attitude to Alam and his family in Dhaka and permitted Kabil to travel to Dhaka to reconnect with Alam and his family because she no longer could afford to send Kabil for his university education on her meager family income of a widow. When Kabil and Rokshana together had visited Zakia a few months after Kabil's reconnection with his uncle in Dhaka, Zakia had mellowed quite a bit and was influenced and affectionately connected to Rokshana by seeing her teenage romantic attraction to Kabil and Kabil's similar interaction with Rokshana. She then had changed her earlier wish (unknown to Kabil, Rokshana, and her parents) that she would have liked to groom Momena as a possible future wife for her son Kabil.

While Alam was lying on the couch, all these thoughts were crowding Rania's mind. At one point, she called out Momena and said, "Momi, please go and bring a glass of cool water to spray on your uncle's face." It was as if she had noticed for the first time that her husband Alam had fainted and was lying on the couch. One of the two middle-aged men was blowing a handheld fan on Alam's head. The other man was trying to comfort Alam by messaging the bottom of his feet. Hearing Rania talk, one of the two men said, "We are Zakia's younger brothers from Harashpur. We came two days ago upon hearing of Zakia's ill health. We were waiting for the arrival of Kabil and you two from Dhaka. We should not further delay the burial of Zakia's dead body. We have made all arrangements for the funeral and burial. Now, if we get your permission, we can proceed with the burial."

Rania kept silent for a few seconds. She then said, "I'm Alam's wife and Kabil's aunty. I do not think Kabil can make it here in such short notice. Please do not wait for him. Under the circumstance, I request you on behalf of Kabil to proceed with the burial.

Meanwhile, Momena brought a jug of cool water and sprayed it on Alam's face. After a few seconds, Alam opened his eyes. The two middle-aged men helped him get up and sit on the couch. He asked Rania to remove the covering from Zakia's face so that he could have a last look at his older sister-in-law. Rania herself had never seen Zakia's face as the two of them never met each other when Zakia was alive. Rania had heard of Zakia's strong personality and family pride when she was alive. And she used to be scared of Zakia in those days. She, therefore, used to dislike her from a distance. She wrongly thought that Zakia had been responsible for the misunderstanding between her husband Alam and his older brother Kamal in Kamal not accepting Rania as the wife of his younger brother Alam. She thought Zakia had instigated her late husband Kamal to forbid Alam to keep any contact with Kabil and his mother and with their village home. It was only after Kabil had come to Dhaka to live with Alam and his family, and especially after the visit by Kabil and Rokshana together to Montala, that Rania realized that Zakia had no role at all in her husband Kamal's rigid attitude to Alam and his wife.

Yet Zakia never approached Alam and his family for any kind of help from them in raising Kabil until his matriculation examination. Rather she declined politely when Alam had offered to take Kabil and her with him to Dhaka to live with his family soon after her husband's death. She did that out of respect for her late husband and because of her promise to him at his death bed not to accept any help from Alam. Rania realized at that moment that it was her own loss that she did not have a chance to meet such a dignified and proud lady when she was still alive. She was then overwhelmed with emotion and called out to deceased Zakia as her older sister. She started crying loudly while leaning on Zakia's dead body.

Toward the evening, Zakia's dead body was laid to rest beside the grave of her husband within their house compound. Several notable men from theirs and the neighboring villages attended the final funeral prayer in the courtyard of the local mosque. Most of the young people of the villages did not know or remembered Syed Ahmed Alam. But they had heard of Kabil who was a local village young man and was a notable student leader of Dhaka University deeply involved in the country's student movement for the rights of then East Pakistan. Noting that, Alam felt proud of Kabil as his nephew as well as his likely future son-in-law. He felt assured that

Kabil as a rising political figure would one day restore the old reputation of Montala's Syed family in the region.

The only person who felt and looked helpless in that situation was the young girl Momena. She was crying most of the time while remembering her aunty Zakia and calling out Kabil's name. Seeing that, Rania came forward, put her hand on Momena's back, and said, "Don't cry, Momi, you have nothing to worry about your future. I'm also your aunty just like my sister-in-law Zakia was. Your uncle Alam and I will take care of you in Dhaka if your paternal uncles from Harashpur allow us to do that. On the other hand, if you want to continue living in this house, we would make an arrangement for your sustenance, safety, and security in this compound."

EARLIER ON THAT EVENING, Kabil and Andaleeb had run to Dhaka Fulbaria Station as soon as they heard the news of the death of Kabil's mother and boarded the next train going in the direction of Montala. Kabil and Andaleeb arrived at Montala station by train early the following morning. The station master wasn't on duty at that time. Kabil and Andaleeb walked all the way from the station to Kabil's family house. On their walk toward Kabil's village home, he had confided in Andaleeb that he was afraid of being betrayed by his fellow student leaders that might lead to his possible arrest by the police. Andaleeb got the sense that even a student leader as bold as Kabil was scared of internal rivalry among the leaders of various groups of students following different ideologies. At the same time, he noticed a sense of firmness and strength and even anger in Kabil's demeanor in the middle of a great loss at his mother's death.

Having reached their family compound at daybreak, they entered inside and Kabil said, "This is our house, brother Andaleeb," as it was Andaleeb's first visit there. They noticed a fresh grave next to Kabil's father's grave on one side of the front courtyard inside the outer boundary walls. Andaleeb understood that it was where Kabil's mother had been buried earlier the evening before. He held Kabil's hand as he tried to console and comfort him. He said, "Look, brother Kabil, nobody's parents live forever in this world. Look at me. I lost both my father and my mother before I turned even a teenager. I do not know what I would have done if I did not get the love and affection of my aunty Rania and her husband—your uncle Alam. I heard that your parents were very religious and righteous people. With their blessings, you will do alright in your future life. Indeed, as a rising politician, you will be a great leader. Refugees like us depend on your righteous future leadership in this country for our safety, security, and well-being." Having listened to Andaleeb, Kabil walked slowly to the gravesite and stood quietly at the foot of the two graves. Andaleeb was still holding Kabil's arm to keep him balanced. Kabil assured Andaleeb that he'd be okay on his own. Andaleeb looked around the compound. He smelled the fresh air like that in a forest emanating from tall bamboo and betel nut trees all around the compound outside the boundary walls. He could hear the morning chirping of birds from these trees. He liked the house compound and its environment as he did not have the opportunity before to visit one like this in rural areas of this country. He looked up toward the big house and noticed a young girl in her late teens standing in the front verandah. It was Momena. She just woke up from sleep, came out of the big bedroom, and was fixing her saree and hair in the verandah. She was surprised to see Kabil and Andaleeb standing in the front courtyard that early. She was about to shout out Kabil's arrival when he put his hand on his lips indicating to her to keep silent. Kabil then asked her, "Which room are Uncle and Aunty from Dhaka sleeping in?"

"In your room," Momena replied.

"Okay, let them sleep in. Don't wake them up yet," Kabil advised her. "Bring in two rattan stools in the verandah and make some tea for us," he further instructed Momena.

Before she left, Kabil introduced Andaleeb to Momena, "This is brother Andaleeb, Rokshana's maternal cousin. He lives in Dhaka."

He then introduced Momena to Andaleeb.

"Is she the one who used to help your mother here when she was sick?" Andaleeb asked.

"Yes, after I had left for my university studies in Dhaka, my mother brought Momena here from Harashpur. My mother hoped in time I would arrange for her marriage with a good man. Now, I wonder what I can do for her," Kabil replied.

"Why? She is related to you and she is beautiful. Take her to Dhaka with you. Your uncle Alam will arrange for her marriage with a good young man there," Andaleeb suggested.

"If I do that, who's going to take care of this house here?" Kabil asked.

"You can figure that after you will have discussed the matter with your uncle and aunty," Andaleeb replied.

By that time, Momena brought two rattan stools and a tray of tea to the verandah for them. In the meantime, Andaleeb had a chance to take another close look at Momena. Her simple but striking beauty without even any makeup made a deep impression on him.

BACK IN DHAKA, ROKSHANA tossed and turned in her bed until almost two in the early morning without being able to fall asleep. As soon as she closed her eyes, the smiling face of her now-deceased aunty Zakia appeared in her subconscious mind. She could almost smell in her imagination the special flavor of traditional sticky rice that Zakia had cooked for her when she had earlier visited Zakia with Kabil a few months earlier, and Rokshana had enjoyed eating it so much.

After Kabil and Andaleeb had left Dhaka for Montala that afternoon, Rokshana didn't go out of the house. Before leaving for Montala, Andaleeb had repeatedly asked Rokshana not to reveal to anybody the news of Kabil's departure from Dhaka. Rokshana realized that Andaleeb had done that with advice from Kabil. The idea was that nobody including Kabil's friends should know that Kabil was out of Dhaka. But nobody asked Rokshana not to disclose the death of Kabil's mother to his friends. In the evening, Rokshana sent their long-time cook Halim to the Rankin Street house of Kabil's classmate Anjuman with a request for Anju to come and visit her early in that evening. Anjuman (Anju) was also Kabil's fellow activist deeply involved in the student movement at the university. She was also an elected member of Dhaka University Central Students' Union (DUCSU). Rokshana thought it would be alright to inform Anju of Kabil's mother's death, and Anju could then pass the news to Kabil's close friends at the university campus. Rokshana gave a note to Halim and asked him to pass it over to Anju.

Rokshana waited for Anju until about eight in the evening. She then decided to go to bed rather early as Anju didn't show up until then. But sleep evaded her until about two o'clock in the early morning. As she felt drowsy shortly after 2:00 a.m., her brain phased into a long REM dream. In her dream, Rokshana saw herself in an open boat without any sail or rower on it. The boat was moving downstream in a slow-moving current along the edge of a bank of a river. Rokshana dreamt that she was lying down on a wooden plank near a fishing net inside the boat. She could in her dream smell the fish, the algae along the riverbank, and the fresh slow-moving water. She was not familiar with any of the smell as she had grown up in a city all her life. Rokshana could not imagine what wharf or place the boat would stop and who she would meet there. Nevertheless, after a short while, her dreamboat stopped at the edge of a low-lying peninsula covered with wet green grass and bushes. Rokshana further dreamt that she stood with much hesitation in the shallow waters of the low-lying land. The water felt cool and pleasant to her feet and ankles. She looked at the nearby villages on the side of the river bank from where she was standing. As she was standing there with amazement on the land, she dreamt that the sudden wind and the water current floated away her small boat downstream of the river, leaving her stranded where she was. She was scared, at a loss, and couldn't figure out in her dream what to do next. The surrounding was completely unfamiliar to her, and she had no idea at all where she was. She did not know anybody around, neither did she know the names of the villages near the river bank. To make things worse, she was also very hungry and thirsty and didn't have any money on her. In her dream, she felt scared and did not know why she was even there. She realized, in her dream, that Kabil was not there with her because he had gone to his Montala village after hearing the news of his mother's death. Rokshana would like to think of Montala as her own village as well since her father and grandfather were born there. She thought the fact that her father had married a non-Bengali refugee settler girl in Dhaka and involuntarily lost connection with Montala could not deprive Rokshana of her ancestral claim of being a Bengali and of her right to claim Montala as her ancestral village like the ones she was now looking at in her dream along the sides of the riverbanks. She found, in her dream, a stark similarity of Montala with these strange villages. At that moment, Rokshana in her dream thought of herself as much a Bengali girl as any in those villages along the river banks. In her dream, she felt determined to walk through these villages and reach out to someone before sunset and darkness to follow. She got to the nearest bank and took a pathway toward the villages. She felt that the mud path was somewhat warm and comfortable. Night owls and other nocturnal birds were flying low over the paddy fields on both sides of the pathway. Overhead, the flocks of silent bats were flying along the pathway. The night sky was about to be lit by countless stars. And the darkness of the night was about to shut down all human, animal, and bird activities and cover the entire area with oceans of silence and inactivities. In her dream, Rokshana arrived at the nearest village and found that every household door was closed from inside. It appeared that every housewife in every household was preparing to spend the night without any concern after their loved ones had returned home at sunset in the safety and security of closed doors. Rokshana did not know which door to knock on. In the middle of that insecurity and uncertainty in her dream, suddenly the doorbell in her Bonogram Lane home rang. She hurriedly woke up and sat straight on her bed. The just-ended nightmarish dream made her feel exhausted, quiet, and motionless for a few seconds. She never had the experience of waking up after such a worrisome dream. She wondered if Kabil and Andaleeb had reached Montala safely the day before. Meanwhile the doorbell in their house rang again, and she heard someone talking outside.

"It's me Anjuman, Rokhi. Please open the door."

Rokhi heard Anjuman's voice from outside. She ran quickly and opened the door.

"Do you get up from bed so late every morning?" Anjuman asked.

"I'm sorry, I couldn't sleep at all last night. Toward the morning, when I felt drowsy, I had this terrible nightmare which made me exhausted," Rokhi replied.

"I'm sorry that I couldn't come last evening when I got the message from your cook. I had to go out last night because of some urgent situation," Anjuman said with some apology. "You know that none of our leaders can spend the night in the comfort of their own homes these days. I too spent last night away from my parents' home. I was at my sister's house at Ram Krishna Mission Road. In the morning, I came to you as soon as I could without even having any breakfast. Please ask your cook to make some breakfast for both of us. I will listen to your urgent matter when you come back from your morning wash," Anjuman added.

"You come and wait in my room while I go wash up. Meanwhile, I will tell Uncle Halim to bring breakfast here for us," Rokhi replied.

Shortly after, cook Halim entered Rokhi's bedroom with breakfast in a large tray. As they started eating, Rokhi said, "My aunty, Kabil's mother passed away yesterday."

Anjuman was shocked to hear such sad news about her friend Kabil's mother. She was so overwhelmed that she couldn't eat very much. She just sat there with her fingers dipped into the lukewarm water of the finger bowl. She felt that Kabil might have been very saddened with his mother's death at a time when there was a countrywide arrest warrant against him for his political activism. All the while, he was also facing the wrath and the ire of the country's left-leaning political groups and the rivalry of and possible betrayal by his fellow student leadership competitors from his own student organization as well as from other student organizations following different political ideologies. Anjuman was sad for Kabil being in that situation. She was aware that there were rival segments in Kabil's own group—Student League—whose leaders were resentful of Kabil being closely associated with a partial Bihari family through his uncle's marriage to Urdu-speaking Rania. Yet Kabil was the main student representative and spokesperson of Sheikh Mujib for articulating the merits of Awami League's Six Points Demand election manifesto to the public in the country. Besides, Kabil's dedication, hard work, knowledge, and oratory capabilities to explain various aspects of the Six Points Demand to the public had earned him a special and affectionate closeness to Sheikh Mujib. As a close classmate, Anjuman observed Kabil's talents, merits, political and personal interactions with his teachers and other fellow students, and she was very impressed with him. Besides, Kabil was a close friend of Anjuman's fiancé Nisar who was a student of philosophy at the university. She also realized that this was a time of grief and sadness in Rokshana's family. Rokhi had written in her note to Anjuman through Halim the previous afternoon that her parents had gone to Montala. She kept mum for quite sometimes and then said, "I know Kabil has been very fond of and devoted to his mother. He often talked about his mother even in the middle of some heated political debates. He often said his mother always meant his country to him. He used to say that the independence of Bangladesh meant independence of his mother and others like her in the rural areas of this country—independence from poverty and exploitation of all sorts."

"I was going to come and see you even if you hadn't sent the note yesterday. I have news to send to Kabil. We are going to organize a student protest march this afternoon from the university campus and proceed to the Press Club where we will have a public protest meeting. We would like Kabil to lead the march and speak at the meeting. But as I realize now, he must be in a state of grief with his mother's death, isn't he?" Anjuman asked.

"Kabil went to Montala to attend his mother's funeral," Rokhi replied.

"Is that so?" Anjuman was surprised. "None of us students are aware of that. But now that he is outside the city of Dhaka, his chances of being arrested by police is high. What can be done about that?" Anjuman wondered aloud.

"Let that be as it may, sister Anju," Rokshana said. "If Kabil is arrested, he may thereby be diverted from his grief and mourning and escape worry. You know that he has been going through tremendous psychological pressure. He cannot depend on anybody reliably. Nobody is taking seriously any assignment given to them on promoting the Six Points Demand. Everyone has been trying to avoid arrest under any pretext they can find. If everyone loses courage and enthusiasm, then Kabil alone from the Student League has to come to the front," Rokhi intervened.

"Don't say that, Rokhi. If Kabil is arrested, then it will be very difficult for the rest of us to go forward with this movement," Anjuman admonished Rokhi mockingly.

"Please do not tell anybody that Kabil has gone out of Dhaka. If somebody asks you why he is not in his normal hiding place, tell them he has moved to a safer place," Anjuman further suggested. She then got up saying that she had to go to the university campus directly. She looked worried. Anjuman was naturally of brownish complexion, of medium height, a little on the plump side. She was always well-dressed in bright-colored saree with matching sleeveless blouse. She at that moment looked even darker with shades of worry in her face. But she always displayed an aura of courage, intelligence, determination, and firm belief in the cause of the student movement she had been involved with.

Rokshana got up as well and said, "I want to go to the campus with you as well, sister Anju."

"What about your house? Who will look after it?" Anjuman asked.

"Don't worry. Uncle Halim can look after the house while I'm gone for a few hours," Rokhi assured Anju.

"Okay, let's go then," Anjuman agreed.

LATE THAT AFTERNOON, THE students' protest march faced the police barricade as the march reached about one hundred meters west of the landmark High Court gate. The march slowed down its pace. The nature of the slogans being shouted by the march participants was more militant this time. The march organized by the Awami League leaning Students League was then shouting a demand for independence—a step beyond provincial autonomy in Mujib's Six Points Demand. Their slogans were like "Quit Bangla," "Our movement will continue," "Release student leaders from the jail," "Down with Dictator Ayub Khan," etc. Anjuman and Rokshana were walking with the procession up in the front row with one end of the banner in Anjuman's hand. Rokshana was holding Anjuman's other hand.

"Rokhi! Police may open fire. You go in the backside, better even go home," Anjuman suggested.

"No, sister, I'll not retreat," Rokhi replied firmly.

"By God, Rokhi, you at least go to the verandah of the university's Curzon Hall through its back gate," Anjuman pleaded. Soon after, a tear gas shell exploded in front of the procession. Mayhem began. Some students were throwing stones in the direction of the police. A group of policemen then moved forward in force, separated Anjuman from Rokhi's hand, dragged Anjuman by her arm, and moved toward the barricade line.

"Move away from our path. You're Bengali policemen. Aren't you ashamed of yourselves?" Anjuman shouted at the police as she was being dragged along with some other student leaders. Three police officers were embarrassed and speechless being confronted by Anjuman with those words.

One of them spoke on his walkie-talkie, got some instructions from his superior, and shouted out, "You have just one minute. Walk back or . . ."

Suddenly, a flying stone thrown by some student in the back hit the policeman's right hand and dislodged the walkie-talkie from his hand. The other police officer then shouted some orders to other policemen lining up like a human wall beyond the barricade.

Almost instantaneously, a large number of policemen jumped forward and began baton charge. One policeman knocked Anjuman down, pulled her up by her hairs, and dragged her toward the waiting police van behind the police barricade. In the middle of this push and pull, Anjuman's saree came out loose from her body, leaving her only in her blouse and petticoat under her saree around the waist. Other policemen dragged few other student leaders by their shirt collars and loaded them all in the police van. The rest of the students then ran away from the advancing police line. Rokshana managed to be on the nearest sidewalk and was looking at Anjuman in utter shock as the latter was being pulled in her blouse and petticoat. At that point, someone shouted at her, "What are you looking at? Run. Soon police will open fire."

Rokshana turned back and joined the retreating students. She threw away her walking sandals so she could run faster. By then the police already started firing blank shots.

THAT NIGHT, ROKSHANA WENT to bed early, tired and exhausted from the horrifying experiences in the late afternoon with students' protest march and encounter with the policemen, compounded by a sleepless night the day before and a strange REM dream on her imaginary solitary boat trip in rural Bangladesh settings. She fell asleep right away and soon fell into another dream. This time she dreamt that the police officer who had dragged Anjuman from the students' protest march the afternoon before had thrown Anjuman in the back of the police van with help from some of his police colleagues. Another policeman had collected Anjuman's left-behind saree and sandals from the street and threw them at her inside the police van. By then the police had already handcuffed her. Anjuman struggled with her leg and mouth to cover her body as much as she could with that saree.

THE FOLLOWING MORNING, ROKSHANA woke up with the sound of the ringing doorbell as she had done the morning before to let Anjuman into the house. She hurriedly got up and ran to the house's main entrance door. As she opened the door, she found Nisar, Anjuman's fiancé standing there outside. Rokshana stood on one side of the door and said, "Come in, brother Nisar." She understood Nisar had come early this morning to find more about Anjuman's arrest the day before. Nisar walked inside and said, "Today's newspapers reported that eight students had been arrested yesterday afternoon. The scene of the arrest spot published on the front pages of most papers clearly shows your picture as well standing next to Anjuman."

"You probably couldn't sleep last night thinking about Anju," Rokshana commented as she followed behind Nisar into the living room.

"Look, Rokhi, I'm not against your involvement in politics. But the way you people implicate the university and the students' educational matters worries me. Our final year examinations will be held soon. Can you tell me what is going to happen to Anjuman's examination now that she has been arrested?" Nisar asked.

"Don't worry, brother Nisar. Dhaka University will not be allowed to schedule your final examinations until well after all the arrested students are released from jail by the government. You can be sure of that. If you care about sister Anju, bring some of her books and class notes to her in the prison cell. You may not care very much about politics and patriotism, but your fiancée Anjuman cares about them a lot. She is a very courageous lady totally dedicated to the causes of her motherland and to freeing this land from the systemic exploitation by the West Pakistani interest groups. If you had seen the bold way she had approached the police barricade yesterday afternoon, you would have been proud of her, and it would have impressed a budding philosopher like you," Rokshana remarked confidently.

"I'm impressed and that is why I am at your door so early this morning," Nisar replied.

"I understand that by even seeing you here. Otherwise, why a budding philosopher like you would knock on the door of someone like me who has no name or tradition worth noting of," Rokshana remarked to make the gravity of the discussion lighter.

Nisar laughed at Rokshana's remarks. He was earlier very worried about what he had thought of Anjuman's almost volunteering to be arrested by being in the front row of the protest march. He seemed at that time genuinely proud of Anjuman's courage and patriotism. As he was taking a seat on the sofa, he said "Whatever you may say, Rokhi, if Anju cannot sit for the upcoming exams this year, we'll incur losses that will affect us for a long time to come."

"Don't despair, brother Nisar. As I said we will not allow the university authority to schedule exams date until all arrested students are released unconditionally," Rokshana replied with a sense of certainty. She felt proud of her self-confidence. She wanted Nisar to know that she had been more than just romantically linked to an influential student leader like Kabil and that she also was an active participating member of the movement.

"That means you will force the university authority to postpone the examination dates. That would be a wrong thing to do, Rokhi, for a poor country like this. Following this route, you may one day achieve autonomy or even independence. But who is that independence for? Is it for a select group of undisciplined, agitated, uncultured people? That independence will drown in the crying and helplessness of millions of poor, hungry, uneducated farmers' children of this land. You will harm yourselves in this mayhem at the same time deprive the people of Dhaka of their peaceful way of life," Nisar sounded this time like a professional philosopher. For a minute or so, both sat quietly. Then Nisar lit a cigarette and Rokshana asked him, "Do you want some breakfast or just tea?"

"Okay, I'll have some breakfast with you. But, Rokhi, I came to know of Anju's arrest last evening when I went to her parents' house to see her."

"Her parents must have been very sad, weren't they?" Rokhi asked.

"They seemed to be somewhat indifferent to Anju's arrest as if they were not surprised. They accepted it as fait accompli. It looked like Anju had made them somewhat mentally prepared as if it was coming to happen sooner or later. They rather asked me not to worry about Anju's arrest too much. Instead, they had asked me to have dinner with them last night as if nothing significant had happened in the late afternoon," Nisar described the situation with Anju's parents the evening before.

"And you were so surprised with their mental ambivalence about Anju's arrest that you declined the dinner invitation by your future parents-in-law. And you went back to your university dormitory where you missed the dinner time as well," Rokhi asked gingerly.

Nisar could not fully understand how Rokhi was narrating the situation he had faced the evening before. He rather looked blankly at Rokshana's face through the thick lenses of his eyeglasses.

"And you couldn't sleep at all last night in your dormitory bed because you were so worried about your girlfriend Anjuman Ara. This morning you came running to me without having any breakfast at the dormitory to know if the police had mistreated your girlfriend at the time they had arrested her. Correct?" Rokhi asked teasingly.

Nisar was perplexed and kept his eyes fixed on the floor and said, "You guessed it right, Rokhi. Did the police beat up Anju at the time of her arrest?"

"I'm not going to divulge any details about her arrest until you finish your breakfast and then have at least three hours sleep on that sofa, okay, brother Nisar? But first tell me why you love sister Anju so much? Tell me where do you find so much commonality and compatibility in the lifestyles of you two?" Rokshana asked inquisitively.

Nisar was perplexed and not prepared for such heavy questions. He simply said, "I love her so much because of the dis-similarity we have in our lifestyles."

"Yes, you told me the truth. It's not easy to get true, straight forward answers from the philosophers of your kind. As a reward for that, I'll give you some good news. The police did not beat up sister Anju at the time of her arrest. And she told me at the campus yesterday before her arrest that she was madly in love with you. Now relax, let's have some breakfast and then you can sleep in this room as long as you want."

MR. AND MRS. AHMED Alam spent another week or so in his ancestral village after the burial of their sister-in-law Zakia—Kabil's mother. Seeing that Alam's health situation was not getting any better, Kabil mentioned it to Rania, "Aunty, it's perhaps not a good idea for my uncle to spend more time here at the village home considering his health condition. He needs to be closer to his doctors in Dhaka. You take Uncle there. Andaleeb and I will take care of things here, and we will return to Dhaka as soon as we can. Rokhi also must be worried about being by herself in our Dhaka house. I would have preferred you and Uncle left for Dhaka much earlier, but I noticed that our fellow villagers are interested in meeting you and uncle—the real guardians of Montala's Syed family, especially when you two came here after a long time. That's why I thought it would be nice for you and Uncle to spend a little time in the village. But now we have to consider Uncle's deteriorating health condition and take him closer to his doctors in Dhaka as soon as possible."

"But your uncle wants to stay here until he completes the feeding of the village poor people to commemorate the fortieth day after your mother's death. He already gave money to your maternal uncles to buy two cows to be slaughtered for feeding the poor people on that day. On the other hand, what you have noticed about your uncle's health condition is also a matter of concern for all of us. His heart condition is serious. I don't want to take any risk of being here if he needs emergency medical attention. Let me see if I can convince him for us to leave earlier."

"You'll have to convince him, Aunty," Kabil insisted.

"Okay, if he agrees, we'll leave for Dhaka soon. But you at least stay here until your mother's fortieth-day remembrance by feeding poor people. Before we leave, your uncle and I would make some arrangement for Momena to live here in the house. We will ask Majid Meah, your parents' long-time share-crop farmer, to stay with his wife in the compound as well to keep Momena company and to help her in taking care of the house compound. We'll send money from Dhaka on a regular basis for their upkeep."

Kabil didn't know what to say except thanking Rania for her offer of help. Seeing Kabil silent for a while, Rania asked him again, "Do you want to say something else to me, Kabil?"

"Aunty, I can't stay here until the fortieth day after my mother's death. I have some important work to do in Dhaka."

"What important work do you have in Dhaka other than something that might bring the police to our house again with an arrest warrant against you. You are not paying much attention to your studies these days. You weren't even able to come here during the last few surviving days of your own mother. There is a lot of political turmoil going on in Dhaka these days. Students are being arrested daily. When you go back there, you probably have to be in hiding from the police there to avoid possible arrest. Rather than doing that you stay here for a while. Maybe, we'll send Rokhi here as well, and she will bring both your and her books so that you can study here without fear of police raids," Rania said in a tone of motherly command.

Kabil focused his eyes on the ground in front of him for a long while without making any comment. Seeing that, Rania asked again, "Do you think I sound illogical?"

"No, Aunty. You are right. But you know that I have been involved in a very important political and ideological movement in this country. I'm one of the senior student leaders in the country, and I can't stay away from the center of the movement in Dhaka with the excuse of my mother's death."

"I know for sure if I make that kind of decision it will disappoint my co-leaders and followers. It might even make them question my leadership in the movement. Some may even think that the accusations by my competitors for leadership in the movement that I am financially supported by an Urdu-speaking family and that I'm an agent of the largely West Pakistani industrialist families like the Adamjees and the Ishphanis are true. Won't that accusation be too much to tolerate for you, Rokhi, and my uncle?" Kabil asked.

"No, my son. We will not tolerate anybody calling our son a traitor to this province for which he's sacrificing so much of his academic and family life," Rania replied.

Kabil then smiled and said, "I'm not getting any news from Dhaka for the last few days. Soon after you and my uncle leave for Dhaka, I'll find a safe way to return to Dhaka myself and will play a leadership role in our movement to rid the West Pakistani-vested interest groups of trampling the legitimate rights of this province. At this critical situation of our land, we, the university students cannot remain indifferent and silent," Kabil continued.

"I'm scared for you, Kabil. If something happens to you— our only son, your uncle will be very hurt. Then, it will be difficult for me to keep him even alive with his present heart condition. Whatever you do, think of your uncle's mental and physical health in mind. That's all I ask of you," Rania concluded with a tone of appeal in her voice. She then stepped outside of the room into the front courtyard.

Kabil noticed that after spending several days in this village, even a city woman like his aunty Rania had developed a liking for this rural household of her parents-in-law. Rania along with Momena practically rearranged all the furniture inside the house after having them cleaned. She even had the weeds and overgrowths outside in the compound along the boundary walls removed by Majid Meah and had him plant flowers there instead. Every morning after completing her prayer and recitation of Koran on the spot his mother used to do when she was alive, Rania would go out in the compound watering the plants and shrubs just like his mother did. Kabil did not feel at all that his aunty Rania was an Urdu-speaking non-Bengali city woman with a university degree and in charge of running a successful fashion business in Dhaka. He didn't feel least of all that Rania was a refugee settler lady in this province. Kabil felt that his aunty was more like his mother trying to understand, restore, and upkeep the past traditions and reputations of the family of her parents-in-law in this rural area.

THE FOLLOWING MORNING, RANIA having convinced her husband Alam the night before, left their village home for Montala Railway Station on their way to Dhaka. Kabil accompanied them to see them off at the station. His two uncles from Harashpur had left the day before for Akhaura market to buy cows for Kabil's mother's fortieth-day death commemoration. They were likely to return by that evening. At that time, only Momena and Andaleeb were in the house, except for Majid Meah and his wife who had gone to work in the field. Andaleeb wanted to go with Kabil to Montala station, but Kabil told him to stay home and keep Momena company.

Early that morning Andaleeb went to the site of dug water well in the house compound. While Andaleeb was brushing his teeth standing by the well site, Momena called out from the kitchen, "Will you manage to lift water with the bucket from the well? You aren't used to do that in Dhaka. Do you need my help?"

"No, I'm not used to it, but let me try," Andaleeb replied.

"Wait, I'll lift water for you because I don't want you to drop the bucket with the rope down in the well," Momena suggested.

Andaleeb took his sandals off his feet and walked to the concrete slab near and around the dug well and looked down into the well.

"What are you looking at inside the well? Please do not jump down into it. It's a very deep and old well. If you are down there, who's going to pull you up?" Momena asked teasingly.

"If I fall down, would you keep me there in the darkness of the deep old well?"

"Why would you fall? Are you a child?" Momena asked.

"Just think that I jump intentionally into your well. What will you do then?"

"But will I be able to pull up a strong young man like you?"

"Why not? You're also young and very beautiful."

While talking, Andaleeb kept staring at Momena which made her shy and blasé. She promptly covered her head with the edge of her saree and slowly dropped the roped bucket into the well.

"Looking at your youth, I think you'll be able to pull me out of the well," Andaleeb commented.

Momena lifted a bucketful of water and told Andaleeb shyly, "Okay, wash your hands and face while I pour water for you."

As Andaleeb extended his cupped two hands for Momena to pour water into it, Momena had a chance to get a close look at him. She had heard from Rokshana that Andaleeb was an orphan when he had migrated to the then East Pakistan during the 1947 partition of India. He came with his aunty Rania and her father and had been close to their family since then. When he grew up, he had started working with Rokshana's parents in their businesses. Rokhi also told her that Andaleeb was a hardworking man and owned a house in Dhaka.

After washing his hands and face, Andaleeb looked around to see if there was any towel around to wipe his face. Seeing that Momena did a strange thing that she had never done before for anybody else. She pulled out the edge of her saree from her back and extended it to Andaleeb to use it as a towel to wipe the water out from his hands and face.

"Here, use it as a towel. It's clean. I just finished saying my prayer wearing it."

"Wow! You offer me the edge of your saree to wipe my face?" Andaleeb exclaimed with a pleasant surprise. Momena realized Andaleeb was overwhelmed with Momena's offer, and he was looking at her back with admiration and appreciation. She smiled slightly and said, "Okay, leave it. I'll go back to the house and bring a towel for you."

As Momena started to walk away, Andaleeb pulled the edge of her saree and began to wipe his hands and face with it. Momena stood there with her half uncovered back to Andaleeb. She then managed to say, "You're a Bihari Urdu-speaking gentleman. Where did you learn to speak Bengali so well and so fluently?"

"I'm not sure I speak Bengali that well. But I grew up among Bengalis. I learned Bengali from them. Whatever more I will have to learn, I'll try to learn from you."

Momena was surreptitiously looking at Andaleeb. She was awestruck at Andaleeb's well-built physique, his very fair complexion, and his light hair color. Sensing that, Andaleeb noted, "Your aunty Rania and I are originally from Bophal in India. We migrated here because of our misfortune, a result of the communal division of India in 1947. Because most of the refugees here were from Bihar, we are also lumped together with them and are called Biharis. Now, we don't have a country of our own. We consider Pakistan as our newly adopted country. If you ever think that I'm somehow related to you through our common aunty Rania, then think that we are also normal human beings like the Bengalis are."

Momena, a little embarrassed, nervous, and shy, stood there quietly and listened to Andaleeb with her eyes fixed on the ground. Andaleeb broke the silence again, "Don't be shy anymore. You may now wish to make me some breakfast."

At that, Momena walked back to the kitchen.

Kabil was not back home the whole day after seeing Rania and Alam off at the railway station early that morning. Andaleeb and Momena were worried about him. Momena later in the day called their share-crop farmer Majid Meah to the house. Andaleeb told him, "You help Momena taking care of the house for a while and I go to Montala station to look for Kabil."

"Nothing to worry about young Kabil. He has many family friends in this area. Maybe he's visiting some of his friends. I'm sure he'll be back by sunset. You're a guest in this village. You stay home. I would rather go myself and ask the station master about Kabil's whereabouts," Majid replied.

Just then, Momena's two uncles from Harashpur entered the house compound with two cows that they had bought in Akhaura early that morning. They reported that they had earlier in the afternoon met Kabil at Akhaura Railway Junction. According to them, Kabil had gone up to Akhaura to accompany his uncle and aunty on their way back to Dhaka. They also reported that after seeing them off at Akhaura, Kabil would be back home at Montala by the evening train.

KABIL RETURNED HOME BY around ten at night and told Andaleeb that earlier in the day, he had a chance to read the daily newspaper at the office of the station master at Montala; and that according to the newspaper, the police had baton-charged the student protest march in Dhaka the day before and had arrested eight students including his fellow student activist Anjuman. The newspaper also published a spot picture of the scene of Anjuman's arrest. The picture clearly showed Rokshana standing next to Anjuman at the time of the arrest. But Rokshana's name was not on the list of students who had been arrested. Kabil did not share the information with his uncle and aunty lest they became worried. Rather he had decided to accompany them up to Akhaura with the hope that he would be able to telephone Rokshana from there after his uncle and aunty's train had left. He was able to talk to Rokhi from Akhaura. According to Rokhi, there were a lot of searches and arrests going on in Dhaka. Most of the student leaders had been arrested in Dhaka. Andaleeb's house in Basu Bazar Lane, where Kabil had hidden earlier, before he went to Montala, had also been searched by the police looking for Kabil. The police had taken Kabil's all books and other papers from Andaleeb's house. Rokhi was concerned that she herself might be arrested anytime. Kabil said that he had advised Rokhi not to go to the university campus for a while and even go and stay at nearby Anjuman's parents' house if necessary.

"Okay, you advised her that. But what would your uncle and aunty think when they arrive home at Dhaka and find that Rokhi was not there," Andaleeb asked worriedly.

Momena heard Kabil talking to Andaleeb all these things about the situation in Dhaka. She asked as she was going to get dinner for Kabil,

"How about asking sister Rokshana to come and stay here for a while? She will be safe here."

Neither Kabil nor Andaleeb responded to Momena's question. Looking at Andaleeb, Kabil said again, "Brother, Rokshana shouldn't have gone with Anjuman to the students' protest march. In this situation, I don't think I can stay outside Dhaka any longer. I'll walk before dawn tomorrow to Brahman Baria and take a boat carrying jute from there to Narayanganj just outside of Dhaka. I'm afraid that when my uncle and aunty arrive home and they find that Rokhi is not there or if there's more police search in their house, they will be upset, and it will worsen my uncle's heart condition. God forbid, if something happens to uncle worrying about Rokhi and me, I'll not be able to forgive myself. You rather return to Dhaka by morning train tomorrow," Kabil concluded. Andaleeb kept silent because he didn't know what to say.

Momena spread a straw mat on the concrete floor and served dinner on it for Kabil. As he started eating, Kabil said to her, "Please call my maternal uncles here so we can eat dinner together. I also want to talk to them about how they should manage the feeding of the poor on the fortieth day anniversary of my mother's death because I won't be able to stay here until then."

When Momena left to call her uncles, Andaleeb turned to Kabil and said, "Brother Kabil, I want to say something directly to you if you will not mind."

"What is it, brother? Why are you so hesitant in talking to me? Tell me frankly whatever comes to your mind," Kabil asked.

"I like your cousin Momena very much. If I want to marry her, you wouldn't have any objection to it, would you?" Andaleeb asked Kabil directly. "I know you are her real guardian rather than your maternal uncles from Harashpur. That's the reason I ask you directly. If you agree to my proposal, I can promise you that I will never do anything disrespectful to her or anything that will hurt her mentally or physically," Andaleeb further elaborated.

Kabil was a bit surprised at Andaleeb's sudden, unexpected proposal to marry Momena. He looked at Andaleeb for a few seconds. Suddenly, a thought came to his mind. He was thinking that Andaleeb's proposal sounded surreal. A good looking, well-established young man like Andaleeb with a house and good income in Dhaka was proposing to marry Momena—an orphan cousin of Kabil who was born in a remote village and at least partly raised by his late mother. This was obviously good news for Kabil as well as for Momena. After thinking for a few minutes, Kabil collected his thoughts and with a slight show of gravity and seriousness said to Andaleeb, "Brother Andy, you do not know anything about the family circumstances of Momena. She is an orphan and does not own any material possession of any kind. She is very poor, but comes from a reputable traditional family like ours. As such, you will not get any financial benefit by marrying her. She's only marginally educated because of her financially adverse childhood. If you are making the proposal after considering all these circumstances, I'd advise you to think it through again and let me know after a few days."

Andaleeb was pleasantly surprised to know that Kabil was quite serious, diligent, and knowledgeable about such matters as Momena's marriage and his inherited responsibility in the matter. He quickly replied, "Brother Kabil, I have considered all aspects of it and want to marry your cousin. I know she's an orphan, but so am I. She has been living under your mother's patronage as I am still living with continuous support from your uncle Alam and his wife—my aunty Rania. You say Momena is poor, but I'm not exactly a millionaire, neither am I a beggar on the street. I have a shelter in Dhaka where Momena and I can live comfortably. You say Momena is not very much educated. Likewise, I'm not exactly a highly educated scholar, but I'm not totally illiterate either. I had completed my grade-twelve education and joined the business of mine and your common relatives. I have learned the business relatively well. If Momena marries me, she will not starve. If I get your consent to my proposal, I'll put it to our common aunty Rania and uncle Alam who are guardians to all three of us."

Kabil realized that Andaleeb had studied Momena's personality well for the previous few days. He wondered if the two of them by then had developed any degree of intimacy. But he assured himself because he knew that Momena was not that loose type of girl. He thought for a moment and then said, "Okay, brother, a proposal by you to marry Momena is a blessing for Momena and a matter of pride for us. But Momena is a mature woman of age to understand what is good for her. I'll ask her opinion on this matter, and I'll inform you soon of our decision."

Andaleeb smiled a bit and said, "I do not want you to take a long time thinking about this matter. You please ask Momena today of her opinion on this and let me know. Her uncles from Harashpur are also here today. You may consult them as well on this matter. I know that if you wish so, it can happen quickly."

"But, Andy, I don't understand why there's so much hurry in this matter. Momena is my cousin. Hopefully, she'll listen to me and agree to marry you. There's really no need for storming the matter so fast," Kabil commented.

"Storming the matter is as much necessary for you Kabil, as it is for me and Momena," Andaleeb said quietly.

"For me?" Kabil questioned in wonderment.

"Yes, Kabil, for you. I know in the coming few days, it will not be possible for you to avoid political arrest by the government. Once they catch you, they will send you to jail for a long time. Then, Momena will be alone to make the decision about her future here. I know Mr. and Mrs. Alam made an arrangement for Momena's sustenance here and arranged for your parents' share-crop farmer couple to be with her and help take care of this household. But I don't feel it's adequate for Momena," Andaleeb explained his concern for both Kabil and Momena's immediate future.

"You're really in love with Momena, brother Andy. It took me so long to realize that. Okay, I'll ask her and consult her uncles tonight and inform you of their opinion tonight before I leave for Dhaka early tomorrow morning. Once I'm in Dhaka, I'll also ask my uncle Alam and aunty Rania for their opinion as well. We will then arrange for the religious part of your marriage to Momena as soon as we can," Kabil concluded.

KABIL TOOK SEVERAL ROUNDABOUT roads and pathways avoiding the local police and the main rail lines, and after two days of tracking, he arrived by boat one afternoon at Sadarghat area of Dhaka City. From his disheveled look after traveling so many uncommon and unfamiliar roads and pathways, it was obvious that he had gone through a difficult journey. Setting foot in Dhaka, he felt very hungry. He decided to walk a little way past the main road, roundabout, to a restaurant on Johnson Road that he was familiar with. He thought he would have something to eat there. He decided to call Rokhi first from there and depending on the situation at home he would go somewhere like his student friends' dormitory room at the university campus for a badly needed shower and a well-deserved rest. He was not sure what he could do by himself if most of his fellow student leaders of the movement had already been captured by the police. He bought a daily newspaper from a street hawker near the roundabout and noticed on its front page a report that the students had taken out a protest march the evening before. He somewhat comforted himself thinking that the student movement had not been completely silenced by the government. He went inside the restaurant and called home from the phone by the front cash counter.

"Hello, Rokhi, it's me Kabil. Good to know that you are home. How are Uncle and Aunty doing? I trust they had arrived back from Montala safely," Kabil asked Rokhi on the other end of the phone.

"Daddy is in the hospital. He had another stroke of a sort yesterday evening. Mother is with him at the PG Hospital. When did you come back and where are you now?" Rokhi asked Kabil.

"I just arrived back a few minutes ago."

"Would you not come home soon?"

"If Uncle is at the hospital, I will visit him first. What number ward is he in?"

"I went to the hospital this midmorning. Mother had spent last night with him there. You don't need to hurry to visit him. Rather, why don't you come home first, take some rest, and then both of us can go visit Daddy in the afternoon and thus give Mother a chance to take a break herself and get some rest while we stay with Daddy for a while. Mother is worried about Daddy's heart condition and asked that I stay home with you when you arrive back from Montala though she is concerned about your possible arrest by the police."

Kabil was now afraid of his family situation by what Rokshana had just said. He was particularly worried about his uncle Alam's physical health with a heart problem. He didn't know what to say off hand. Suddenly, he blurted out, "Rokhi, I didn't eat since last night. Let me first eat something at the restaurant, and then I'll come home."

"Why do you have to eat at the restaurant? Why not come home straight, take a shower, eat something, and take some rest before we go together to the hospital during the visiting hours to see Daddy? We'll then send Mother home so she can take a break and rest for the night and the two of us can stay with Daddy for the night at his hospital cabin. Moreover, the PG Hospital's private cabin might be a safer place for you to hide from the police lookout. The hospital is near the university campus. I'm not that much worried about myself even though the police might be looking for me as well. I'm hiding because you asked me to stay at places like Anju's. I'm more worried about you, okay? No more discussion. Come home soon, and I'll ask Halim uncle to cook something special for you," Rokshana concluded.

Kabil came out of the restaurant and took a motorized tricycle to their Bonogram Lane home.

Once at home, Kabil shaved and entered the washroom for a long-overdue shower. Just then the telephone rang. Rokshana picked up the receiver and said, "Hello."

"Rokhi, I'm your uncle Doctor Noor, calling from the PG Hospital. Your father's health condition suddenly took a turn for the worse. You better come to the hospital right away," the caller said from the other end.

"Uncle, Kabil just got back from our village home at Montala. He hadn't eaten all day. Will it be too late for him to eat something, and we both will come to the hospital soon after?" Rokhi asked Doctor Noor. It was as if Rokhi had just appealed to the God of misfortune.

"I'm not sure, Rokhi, the heart patients sometimes go through this kind of changing conditions. But we should be ready for the worse. Okay, you feed Kabil and come to the hospital as soon as you can," Doctor Noor advised.

As soon as Rokhi put down the phone receiver, she heard the noise of full-capacity shower from the washroom. She thought Kabil was trying to wash away the grief of his mother's death and the salty taste of long- shed tears by taking a full-blown, satisfying shower. She decided not to disturb him in the middle of his long-deserved shower by giving him right away the news of another potential misfortune. She rather walked to the kitchen and asked cook Halim to send lunch for the two of them to her bedroom. As she walked by the washroom on the way back to her bedroom, she heard the shower was still pouring full speed inside. This time Rokshana decided to rush Kabil and knocked on the shower door inside the washroom. She then said, "Hey, have you gone wild? The food is getting cold. Come out soon."

As she was about to leave after having said that, Kabil came out of the shower with a towel wrapped around his waist with water drops still dripping like crystals on his light-colored hairy chest. Within seconds, Rokhi cast her gaze on the floor in utter surprise and embarrassment. She could sense that Kabil was looking at her body like a hungry hyena with lust and desire in his eyes without saying anything. She hurriedly picked up another towel from the rack nearby and put it on Kabil's shoulder carefully avoiding touch with his body. As she was about to walk out of the washroom, Kabil suddenly pulled her hand and drew her closer to him.

"How about you staying for a second, Rokhi? Stand close to me and let me take a good look at you," Kabil asked.

"What are you doing? Let me go. There are other people in the house. They may see us in this awkward position," Rokhi responded irritatingly. Kabil freed her hand right away and began drying his head and face. Rokshana sensed that Kabil felt embarrassed and sorry for his actions. She stood there momentarily and said, "By any chance, have you been captivated by some supernatural power? You never behaved like this before. You see me all the time. Isn't it still enough? Have I grown some wings like a fairy?"

Kabil feebly answered with his face still covered with the towel, "I'm sorry, Rokhi. Please forgive me. But it's still not enough for me to look at you. I wish I could keep looking at you all the time in the world."

Having said that, Kabil uncovered his face and began drying his back.

"If you wish that much to look at me, why not put that diamond ring on my finger and make it moral and legitimate? Your aunty can hardly wait for you to do that. But thinking about your involvement in politics vis-à-vis your interest in me, she still can't finalize the date for that formal ceremony. If you are too shy about asking my mother for her consent for you to marry me, then give me the permission, and I'll speak to her on your behalf and mine. I'll tell her that I can't wait to marry Syed Ahmed Kabil until he frees this country from the oppression by the West Pakistanis. I'll tell her to urgently arrange for our wedding ceremony so that my father can see you and me getting married before, God forbid, anything serious happens to him. I'll tell her that today while she is with my father near his hospital bed."

In response, Kabil said, "Rokhi, I feel guilty for my irrational and emotional behavior. I have been away from you for quite some time recently, and I missed you badly. That's the reason when I saw you today after such a long time, I felt like holding you tight in my arms and kissing you passionately.

After all, I'm a man of blood and flesh, and I do have passion and desire. Yet I never thought I would behave like this even minutes before I did it. Please forgive me, Rokhi, and help me have the patience to wait for holding you in my arms at the right time. Your honor is greater to me than my life is. I love you very much Rokhi—well beyond I can describe in words."

Rokshana stood there for a few seconds with her eyes focused on the floor. She then said, "Leave your wet clothes there. You might catch a cold. Food is served in my room. Let's eat quickly. We must go and visit my dad in the hospital. His condition is not getting any better."

"What's the matter? Did you get any news from the hospital?" Kabil asked.

Rokshana avoided his question and began walking toward her room. Kabil changed into dry clothes and followed her. Kabil noticed in her room that she had already started eating unlike her normal regular practice of waiting for him to arrive to join her. As soon as Kabil sat down, Rokhi put a plate in front of him and served rice and meat on the plate. As he started eating, Kabil said, "Rokhi, I didn't have time to tell you something important. Cousin Andaleeb likes our Momena very much, and he wants to marry her and marry her soon."

Rokshana was surprised and kept mum for a few seconds. She put down the food she had in her hand back on her plate and asked in amazement, "Has he proposed to marry Momena?"

"Yes, he did. Looks like you are very surprised. Why is that?"

"Is the initiative yours?"

"I know you will say that. But believe me, I didn't take any initiative at all in that matter, and I had no prior knowledge of it. Your cousin Andaleeb suddenly made the proposal to me two days ago before I had left Montala, and he had asked for my approval. How did you think that I would have any idea of Andaleeb wanting to marry a poor orphan girl like Momena?" Kabil counter-questioned.

Now, Rokshana couldn't hide her surprise anymore and while starting to eat again, she asked, "How did that happen? Does Momena know about it?"

"I told Momena about Andaleeb's proposal and asked her opinion. First, she kept silent for a while and didn't respond. I then told her that we wouldn't marry her off to anyone without her prior agreement. Momena then said that she would go along with my choice and agreement. I also asked the opinion of her uncles from Harashpur on this proposal, and they were all happy with it. Now, we need to ask your parents for their approval of it and ask them to arrange a date for the wedding as soon as possible. Andaleeb doesn't want to wait too long. Meanwhile if the police capture and send me to jail before the wedding can be arranged, then you'll have to take the initiative to finalize everything."

Rokshana smiled mildly and sat for a moment with food in her mouth. She then said with a sad look in her face, "When

I can't finalize my own wedding, then I will have to make do with finalizing others'. What else can I do?"

Kabil felt slightly mum seeing the sad look in Rokshana's face.

"Are you blaming me for anything, Rokhi?" He asked.

"Why should I do that? Unlike you, I do believe in fate and destiny. But what I had seen earlier this afternoon of your impatience, please do not advise me to rely on you or trust you anymore. Think, if it were someone else in front of the bathroom or say if it were Momena instead of me, would you not just grab her?" Rokshana asked agitatedly.

Kabil looked down, waited for a while to figure out what to say in response. He then looked up, made eye contact with Rokhi, and said, "Please do not lower me to such level for my momentary lapse of judgment and irrational behavior. I love you too much, Rokhi, to tarnish your respect."

"Keep your love story to yourself. For a long time now, I have moved around hand in hand with you on the roads and streets of Dhaka. For years we lived under the same roof of my parents' house. We spent many, many enjoyable moments together in our village home at Montala. I had never considered myself at risk of my modesty with you until today. Why did you then act like that? Why did I see the fire of lust in your eyes today? Nobody knows better than you do that I am yours. Don't you know what people think of those who do not accept their own rights in front of everybody but rather want to grab through the back door what is rightfully theirs? They are called thief, bad, and immoral . . ."

Rokshana cried out loud before she could complete what she had wanted to say. She got up from her chair and ran out of the room. Kabil sat there for a while. He then washed his hand and grabbed a towel to dry it. He noticed that their cook Halim was standing outside by the door. Kabil realized that the most trustworthy employee of this household must have heard all of Kabil's and Rokshana's arguments inside while he was standing outside by the door.

Halim had come to take away the dishes and the leftover food from inside the room, but hearing their arguments, he did not dare enter the room. Kabil felt embarrassed in the presence of Halim and lowered his gaze. Seeing that, Halim told Kabil, "She went to your room. Go and placate her and help her cool down."

Kabil went to his bedroom and found that Rokshana was lying on his bed with her face buried in the pillow and was still crying. Kabil put his hand on her back and tried to comfort her, but she started crying even more. Kabil was about to say something, but Rokshana's grief and high-pitched, forceful crying kept him silent. Just at that time, Rokshana did something really strange. She lifted her face from the pillow, got up, and grabbed Kabil by her two arms, placed her face on his chest, and said while still crying, "Please forgive me for my bad behavior. I will not be able to live in this world without you. I don't even want to live without you. I could not at that moment and can't even now think straight because of all those thoughts. Please try to understand my predicament."

Kabil realized what was going on in Rokhi's mind and felt remorse for his own behavior of greed and lust. He continued comforting Rokhi by slowly rubbing her back. Just at that moment, Halim entered Kabil's room. He lowered his gaze when he saw Rokshana crying with her both hands around Kabil's neck and her face buried in Kabil's chest.

Halim then quietly said, "Rokhi, you have a telephone call from the hospital."

Hearing that both Kabil and Rokshana regained their composure. Kabil then asked, "No bad news I hope, Uncle Halim?"

"I don't know. They did not want to tell me anything. They asked for a member of the Syed family. It was a nurse from no. 8 Cabin at the PG Hospital, she told me."

Kabil and Rokshana both hurried to the bedroom of Mr. and Mrs. Ahmed Alam where the telephone was. Kabil picked up the receiver and said, "Hello, I'm Kabil, Mr. Alam's nephew."

The nurse from the other end said, "I'm sorry to inform you that Mr. Ahmed Alam breathed his last a little while ago. His wife was present beside his bed at the time of his death. Doctor Noor asked me to relay the message to Mr. Alam's house."

Hearing the news, Rokshana cried out loud calling her father and fell on her parents' bed.

KABIL SPENT THE DAY and the night after his uncle Alam's death in total mental shock and agony. He also had to act like a robot to keep Rania and Rokhi in consciousness. Andaleeb had returned from Montala by the night train and made all arrangements for Mr. Alam's funeral and burial. He consoled Kabil by saying, "Bring yourself together. Do not despair. Help and encourage your aunty Rania and cousin Rokhi to take full control of businesses and properties your uncle had left behind. My aunty Rania loved dearly her husband—your uncle Mr. Alam. I had never witnessed that kind of devoted love between wife and husband be they Bengalis or non-Bengalis. My uncle Mr. Alam was not only a successful businessman, he also owned a lot of landed properties in this city. If properly managed, his family would be one of the rising rich ones in the community, especially among the Bengalis. Now everything depends on you and Rokshana. If you want to live a safe and financially secure life, you will have to leave politics to those infidels and concentrate on helping Rania and Rokhi in managing their sizable businesses and landed properties. Rich and affluent people do not believe in any nation, cast, or creed. They don't care about Bengalis, Biharis, Hindus and Muslims, Indians, and Pakistanis. They pursue wealth and worship money. They don't care about the status of languages in the running of government affairs and businesses. The sound of coins is their language. Your Party's Six Points Demand is not important for them. In reality, business people do not believe in patriotism. Nobody can deny the citizenship of rich people. I'm telling you, Kabil, all these things because you've won the heart of my cousin Rokhi. The worth of her fortune in her inherited properties and businesses is beyond your comprehension. I'm also dreaming about starting a family with your maternal cousin Momena in the near future. I need your help absolutely."

The following day, at the funeral prayer services for Mr. Ahmed Alam in Baitul Mukarram—the city's most famous and central mosque compound—a large number of notable people were in attendance. Most of them were non-Bengali businessmen from Nawabpur, Islampur, Sadarghat, and Waizghat areas of the city. They were all people with whom Mr. Alam had business dealings. Everybody spoke highly of Mr. Alam's honesty, integrity, and pleasant demeanor and personality. After the final prayer, Kabil and Andaleeb slightly uncovered the face of the deceased from the coffin for one last look by friends and relatives. Mr. Alam's face appeared to be peaceful and radiant as if he had no regret in leaving this mortal world.

THE DECEASED WAS LAID to rest at around four o'clock in the afternoon at Azimpur cemetery—the city's noted community graveyard. But Kabil had not been back home from the cemetery. It was now almost nine o'clock in the evening. Rokshana was sitting in the verandah of their silent home and contemplating on repeated calamities that recently befell on her family. The front gate past the courtyard was open that day even though it used to be closed at that time on other days. Looking at the open gate, Rokshana thought maybe one of Kabil's friends or one of her relatives had taken Kabil to their house from the cemetery. Rania, although she had stopped crying by then, was still shaking bodily in grief. Rokshana's eyes were focused on the open gate. At one point, she noticed someone enter through the gate like a shadow in the shallow darkness, walked past the front courtyard, and stood under the porch. Rokshana thought it was Kabil. She asked, "Whose house did you go from the cemetery?"

"I'm not Kabil, Rokhi. I'm Nisar," the response came from the shadow.

"Come, brother Nisar. You were with Kabil when they took Daddy's body from the mosque to the cemetery. Where did Kabil go after the burial? He hasn't come home yet. Come inside, brother," Rokhi invited Nisar.

As Rokhi reached for the light switch, Nisar said, "No need to switch on the light, Rokhi. I will not stay long right now."

"Why is that, brother Nisar?"

"Listen, Rokhi, all your friends and relatives are aware of the situation you are in now. In the middle of all that, I feel sorry that I am here to give you the news of another tragedy that befell on you this evening. Kabil was arrested by police this evening at the gate of the Azimpur cemetery. Kabil and I stayed by your father's gravesite until the evening prayer time when everybody else had left. As we walked out through the gate, we noticed several policemen waiting there in a police Jeep. One officer came down from the Jeep and told Kabil that they had an arrest warrant against him and that Kabil had to go with them to the police station. Kabil could not protest as the police officer almost forced him to get into the Jeep. He told me to relay the message to you."

Nisar felt almost guilty for relaying this sad news to Rokhi at this critical time in her life. He felt like disappearing from Rokhi's presence as soon as he could. He managed to leave the place quietly without Rokshana even taking note of his departure.

NEARLY TWO YEARS AFTER the incarceration of Kabil, the government started in the first half of 1969 releasing from jail some of the political prisoners including low-profile student leaders. However, Kabil was not one of those released student leaders. Meanwhile, faced with the tremendous public and political unrest, the military-turned politician Gen. Ayub Khan relinquished his presidential power and handed the government over to another military strongman, Gen. Yahya Khan who immediately declared martial law in the country. Ayub Khan then disappeared from the political scene of Pakistan. The political situation in the then East Pakistan was at that time boiling over Mujib's Awami League Party's Six Points Demand for decentralization of federal government powers leading to provincial autonomy.

There were student protest meetings and processions from the university campus marching through the city streets demanding the release of Kabil from the jail. The daily newspapers published Sheikh Mujib's statements, urging the government to release Kabil from the jail immediately. The newspaper reports also carried Kabil's pictures describing him as the most effective student leader in articulating Awami League's Six Points Demand and voicing arguments against the government's notorious Agartala conspiracy and sedition case against Sheikh Mujib.

ONE MORNING AT THE breakfast table, Rokshana drew Rania's attention to a news item in an English language newspaper on a speech by Sheikh Mujib. She said, "Look, Mom, Sheikh Mujib criticized the government for Kabil's continued imprisonment and demanded his immediate release. It's possible that Kabil will be released by the end of this week."

Drawing the newspaper closer to her eyes, Rania looked at Rokshana and commented, "That's good news indeed. But I wonder if it would bring anything good for you."

Rania's voice was mixed with worry and uncertainties. Rokshana realized her mother's inner thinking and made a move to leave the table without finishing her breakfast. At that point, Rania commented, "Finish your breakfast before you go, Rokhi. I didn't say anything bad for you to leave the table before finishing your breakfast.

Rokshana turned back and said, "I'm not leaving because you said something bad, Mom. I didn't feel hurt by what you've said thus far. I know that you always have my well-being in your heart and say the right things for me. After Kabil was arrested, you asked me to stop my involvement in student politics and pay more attention to my studies and our family businesses. My late father had left behind a sizable amount of money, car, house, properties, and successful businesses in this city. Like you, I don't want to see that my father's hard-earned assets mismanaged and spoiled. I'm also the daughter of a businessman like you are. I stopped even going to the university following your advice. I understand that I have nothing to gain by being involved in politics. I had been involved in politics for someone who was very uncertain about our future together. Because of that, I'm now trying to learn from you and cousin Andaleeb to well-manage and maintain our family's economic prosperity. I may not be as good as you are in business acumen, but I'm trying my best to learn from you."

"I know you may someday in the future blame me for not pursuing your higher education. I had told you to devote more time to your studies keeping yourself detached from student politics. I was feeling helpless in managing our businesses after your father's death and Kabil's incarceration. I was afraid that the police might arrest you as well. I told you to stay away from student politics but not to give up your university education. Moreover, my decision should not always dictate your future. I know Kabil has been in touch with you by correspondence from the jail. To say that you quit your studies and joined full-time on our businesses without his consent is beyond my comprehension. I tend to think that it's just a way of complaining against me and my nephew Andaleeb."

Rokshana did not comment on Rania's remarks and was about to walk away toward her bedroom. Just then, the doorbell rang and she stood there. Halim opened the door and Anjuman walked in. She went straight to the dining table.

"I came to give you good news, Aunty. But first, please ask Uncle Halim to bring me a cup of tea," Anjuman said as she sat down on a chair next to Rania.

Rokshana also sat eagerly next to her mother to listen to Anjuman's good news.

Rania took a quick glance at the front page of the daily English newspaper then put it down and asked Anjuman, "What good news did you bring, Anju? Is it the release from jail of your friend Kabil?"

"You guessed it right, Aunty. How did you do that?"

"I guessed by looking at your facial expressions."

"Aunty, when Kabil is released from jail this time, you please arrange Rokhi's wedding to Kabil as soon as you can," Anjuman suggested.

"Anju, you talk like I'm responsible for delaying their wedding."

"No, Aunty, I didn't mean that. I know you had bought an expensive diamond ring for Rokhi for their wedding more than two years back. It was our political setback that came in the way of their wedding. Because of that, my uncle

Alam could not see the wedding of his own daughter and his nephew Kabil before his death. Our involvement in politics is to blame for all that. That is the reason I'm suggesting that we should proceed with their wedding as soon as possible after Kabil's release."

"Okay, Anju, then tell us a bit more about Kabil's impending release. When can we expect him back at home?"

"Possibly this afternoon or tomorrow evening," Anjuman replied.

"Isn't any of you going to the jail gate to receive him?" Rania asked further.

"Student leaders will be there if they get the exact information and timing. But the government may anytime now release him unannounced to avoid the crowd in front of the jail gate. If I get the exact time of his release, I'll be there with my fiancé Nisar. Nisar can hardly wait to have a good look at his friend Kabil—now a student leader famous throughout the country."

As Anjuman finished, Rokshana got up and said, "Let's go to my room. Halim will bring tea for us there."

As both got up, Rania asked Anjuman again, "Where did you get the news that Kabil will be released today or tomorrow?"

"Nisar came to know about it yesterday at the university campus. Student leaders probably got the news earlier. Moreover, the government will hesitate to keep Kabil in detention further after Sheikh Mujib's strong demand for

Kabil's release which was published in all newspapers today," Anjuman sounded somewhat certain about Kabil's impending release from the jail.

Rania asked again, "Anju, if people are kept in government custody for a long time, does that change their way of thinking and looking at the world and their perspective about themselves?"

"Why do you ask that question, Aunty?"

"Because of the way you had changed after spending some time in jail yourself. Before you went to jail, you were a shy girl. You used to behave in front of people as if you wanted to hide your face. But after your jail time, you got used to delivering passionate speeches at all sorts of public gatherings and protest meetings. You look more self-confident. Jail time had changed you a lot, Anju."

Anjuman burst into laughter and sat down on her chair again and said,

"I understand your concern, Aunty, and I know exactly what is going on in the back of your mind. You are worried that Kabil might have changed after spending long two years in jail. The entire country is protesting in public meetings and marches demanding Kabil's release from the jail. There are large posters on house boundaries and other walls throughout the country with pictures of nationalist leader Kabil on them urging the government to release him. That kind of fame and publicity might make you worried whether after release from jail, Kabil would maintain his close relationship with Rokhi and you or not. Let me assure you, Aunty, that after his release from jail, Kabil will not do anything that might make his closest relatives—you and Rokhi—in the city of Dhaka uneasy and uncertain of his family ties with you two.

"Rather, when he finds out that Rokhi, his dear and closest companion for the last decade or so, has abandoned her university education while he had been in jail, and she had been working hard to succeed in her father's businesses, he will be very disappointed. He will think that life goes on, and the world does not wait for anybody. You're afraid of Kabil's success in politics, lest it might take him away from you and Rokhi. You are worried that Kabil, sheltered and supported for the last decade or so by you and your family but now famous, adored, and popular among masses throughout the country will change his attitude, respect, liking, love, and closeness with your family. I can assure you, Aunty, Kabil is not that kind of a young man. He will not change his attitude, and he will not do anything that might hurt yours and Rokhi's feelings."

As soon as Anju finished her mini-speech, Rokhi took her hand and both walked toward her bedroom.

THAT HOT AFTERNOON, AT around three o'clock, Kabil in his T-shirt was reading an English novel while sitting on a wooden stool on the verandah in front of his third-floor room at cell no. 27 in Dhaka Central Jail. The Bengali newspaper of the day which he had finished reading earlier was lying on the concrete floor next to his feet. The statement by Sheikh Mujib demanding Kabil's immediate release had been published in the Bengali newspaper on its front page. There were now only a few prominent political prisoners including Kabil remaining in government custody at Dhaka Central Jail in addition to some fifty or so hardcore Marxist politicians detained earlier by the government. Kabil could not understand why the new military government led by Gen. Yahya Khan was so reluctant to release him. After lunch at the prison canteen that day, most detainees were taking their usual midday nap. Kabil habitually used to spend these quiet moments for studying his regular university course books or other materials of his interest. He was by nature not used to daytime snooze. Neither did he ever spend time while he was in jail by playing cards like most other political prisoners did. Kabil would rather spend time doing some gardening in the small plot of land in front of his cell building. The walkways around his cell building were laid with red bricks with sides marked with white-painted brick corners. Beyond that, there were small gardens with chrysanthemum and other colorful flowers. Kabil could never have imagined from outside the jail that the inside environment could have been so well organized, well maintained, and attractive looking. Seeing this inside environment, nobody could imagine that this could be a place where human souls were subjected to punishment beyond limits. Here, a few prisoners get rehabilitated to normal, societal life unlike those in prisons in advanced and developed western countries. Most here only get punishment year after year for crimes they might or might not have had committed.

Some were hanged for murders; some other get life sentences. Some get reduced punishment for grave offenses because of loopholes in the law while some others suffer heavily for petty thefts or other minor crimes. In all cases, human spirits shrunk once inside the boundary walls of these prisons. Although it was said that the political prisoners like Kabil were entitled to special treatment, Kabil being confined here for over two years without judicial trial knew or felt no differences, not at least in its psychological aspects. Kabil lived the last two years of his prison life without any real companionship to speak of. Even though every month his widowed aunty Rania and his fiancée Rokhi, sometimes along with Andaleeb, would visit him at the gate of the jail compound, and they would bring for him his favorite food in a tiffin carrier, Kabil himself never encouraged them to make those visits. Every month, he would tell Rania, "Aunty, I'm not here in that bad conditions. Eating here is somewhat good for one to maintain health. There's no need for you and Rokhi to take the trouble of getting permission from the authorities to visit me every month. I would rather request you to take care of your health and help Rokhi understand and take control of my uncle's hard-earned properties and businesses. I don't want her to turn out like me. Politics is not good for someone in her position. I wasted my life by getting involved in politics and thus incarcerated. But there's no going back for me now. If you think that it is up to you to restore and uphold the past reputation of Montala's Syed family, then you will have to help groom Rokhi for that.

I will not be of much help to you all in that regard. My parents died with pains of broken hopes, aspirations, and dreams. I do not want you to face and suffer the same kind of pains."

Listening to Kabil, Rania one time broke down in tears while hugging Kabil. Kabil himself could not stop weeping. But Rokshana turned her face the other way trying to stop the tears in her eyes. Despite all that, Rokshana came every month to visit Kabil at the jail gate with a tiffin carrier full of Kabil's favorite cooked food. Kabil never saw her shaken with emotional weakness.

THAT DAY WHILE BUSY reading his English novel, Kabil noticed that the chief of Dhaka Central Jail accompanied by his deputy jailor and a few sepoys were walking toward his cell building. He assumed that they were coming to see and talk to him as they usually never came to this building at this unusual time, and there was no other major political prisoner left behind in this building. He quickly went inside his room, put on a shirt, came out again, and sat back on his stool in the verandah. By that time, the chief jailor and his associates were behind the wall on the ground floor. Kabil wondered what news the chief jailor might be bringing for him. Was it going to be the news of his imminent release or of a possible transfer to another jail in some remote corner of the country? The chief jailor and his entourage climbed up to the third-floor verandah of Kabil's cell building and started walking toward Kabil. Kabil sensed their arrival but pretended not to have noticed them. He focused his eyes on the novel in his hand. When the visitors reached in front of his room and gave usual salutations of respect, Kabil looked up and said, "What happened? You're all here at this time? Are you going to send me somewhere else outside of Dhaka?"

"Oh, no no, Mr. Kabil. We bring you good news. The Home Affairs Ministry has issued your release order. We just received the order a few minutes ago. We'll release you this evening and send you home in our Jeep. Please be ready with your books and other belongings. Just before sunset, a sentry will come here and escort you to my office at the front gate. After the release formalities in my office, a Jeep from our special branch will drive you to your Bonogram Lane house," the jailor gave Kabil the planned details.

"That means you will not allow any welcome reception by my friends and supporters at the front gate. And there will be no press reporters present at the time of my release."

"You guessed it right, Mr. Kabil. The government doesn't want any undue publicity and unnecessary gathering of crowds and thereby create confusion and commotion. We can do nothing about it. It's the order from the ministry," the jailor commented and left with his entourage. After they had left, Kabil sat there quietly for a few minutes reflecting on how life would be like in the outside world after two years of his confinement in the jail compound. He heard from Rokshana that during his time in jail, Momena had convinced everybody to postpone her marriage to Andaleeb even though Rokshana had gone to Montala to convince Momena not to delay her wedding. Momena refused to agree, saying that with Kabil in jail, she couldn't and wouldn't go through her wedding. Andaleeb was considerate enough to respect Momena's decision in that regard and agreed to wait until Kabil's release from jail so that Kabil could, as Momena's legal guardian, give Momena's hand in marriage to Andaleeb.

Kabil was sure that he would find everybody in the family in the same condition as he had left them two years ago, except for Rokshana even though she had come once every month for the last two years to visit him at the jail gate with a tiffin carrier full of his favorite cooked food. Kabil was emotional during her routine visits, but despite his repeated attempts to engage Rokhi in meaningful conversation, she resisted his attempts simply by responding to his questions in monosyllables. Kabil would ask her, "How are you, Rokhi?"

Rokhi would keep silent for a long time and then would respond, "Okay."

Once Kabil asked her, "Why did you stop going to your university classes?"

"Because your friends look at me with greed and lust in their eyes," Rokhi replied. "Moreover, I wrote my BA final exams. Being simply a graduate would be good enough for me," she added.

"What am I going to do with too much higher education? My father was a successful businessman, and he left behind a lot of wealth for me. I'm learning to manage my parents' business well so that the heap of wealth doesn't fall. You do not have to worry about me that much," Rokhi continued.

This was Rokshana's once only a full-time statement while she was visiting Kabil at the jail gate. Other than this Rokshana never spoke a complete sentence except by responding with yes or no to Kabil's all sorts of inquiries. Kabil was wondering if she was unhappy with Kabil himself more for his own arrest and incarceration than with the fact of his arrest altogether. It could have been quite possible that she was unhappy with Kabil himself. Everybody who had known them well knew that Rokshana had wholeheartedly hoped that Kabil would agree with her mother Rania to have completed at least the religious part of their wedding despite the seriousness of the political turmoil in the country. Rokshana had remembered that her mother had bought the expensive diamond ring with great hopes that Kabil would put that ring on Rokshana's finger at that religious ceremony. Rania of course at a later stage backed down a little bit after seeing Kabil's hesitation to her proposal, especially after seeing the government's arrest warrant for Kabil. In the end, Rokshana forced herself to put that ring on her finger only to avoid social embarrassment. Kabil was not sure why all those past things were crowding his brain at that moment of his impending release from the jail. His aimless sight was fixed on the light post outside. He noticed that at the crying sound of a lonely crow on the lamp post, another crow joined in trying to cheer up the lonely bird, and the two birds started rubbing each other's body and thus playing joyfully. For some reason, this day of

Kabil's release from the jail after two long years seemed like any other day to him. He did not feel any excitement about his impending release and freedom. He folded the novel he was reading late that afternoon, placed it on his knees, and started to think what he should do after being released from the jail. He thought he would definitely have to, at least partially, shoulder the leadership of the student movement. He had learned from Rokhi that wall posters with his pictures were pasted all over the city, indeed all over the country demanding his release from the jail. Most politically aware men, women, and young people all over the country would recognize his name as a rising political star who was dedicated to fighting for the legitimate rights of the then East Pakistan. Syed Ahmed Kabil was now an undeniable personality of the autonomy-demand movement of the province. But only Kabil knew how relatively easy it was for him to reach that stage in his political career. He had only spent two years in jail as a political prisoner. There were scores of other student leaders who had spent a lot many more years behind the bars for their lifelong political struggle. Kabil remembered that it was mainly because he had been able to earn the trust and confidence of their leader Sheikh Mujib for his (Kabil's) dedication and in his capabilities in articulating the rationale of the demands of their Awami League Party.

Kabil wondered in what situation he would find himself both at home and at his students and party organizations once he was out from jail after two long years. Rokshana, of course without reservation, had told him that she would have nothing more to do with student politics. She had said,

"Whatever else I can do, I would not be able to extricate East Pakistan from the continued exploitation by the West Pakistani-vested interest groups. Once I was motivated by you and took part in student meetings and protest marches. But on the day I had seen the police pull sister Anjuman by her hairs from a protest march, I realized that politics was not my cup of tea. My father was a successful and wealthy businessman, and he had left behind a good fortune for me. I grew up in a wealthy and financially comfortable family. I have no capacity to take in police brutality, insults, beatings, and other sufferings. Moreover, after my father's death, I realized that we do not have capable and reliable people to take care of my father's assets and businesses. It's not possible for Andaleeb to look after everything by himself. My father once hoped that you would help me and Andaleeb in taking care of his properties and businesses. But he realized before his death that his hopes were not to be materialized as you are deeply involved in the country's politics. After your imprisonment, I took over the management not because I don't trust Andaleeb, but simply because it is my business and my responsibility to run it effectively to the best of my ability."

Rokshana told Kabil all these at the jail gate during one of her monthly visits to him in the later part of his incarceration. Somehow, lately she had learned to speak directly and without emotions. Maybe she had changed lately by having to deal with real-world business people. Kabil couldn't fully understand but somehow felt how much Rokhi had changed when he had heard that Rokhi had moved from the university classes and campus activities to the business districts of Nawabpur and Sadarghat. It would have been probably unlikely if Rokhi didn't have the genes of the professional and traditional business community through her non-Bengali mother Rania who had been herself a highly educated and seasoned businesswoman. Kabil lately noticed some sense of authoritative attitude in Rokhi's demeanor and interactions, and he realized that Rokhi was a personality different from what she had been two years ago.

Kabil, after completing the release formalities at the front gate office of the chief jailor, came out and found things different from what he had been given to anticipate earlier by the chief jailor. There were a lot of young men and women outside the gate shouting, "Long live Ahmed Kabil," "Our movement will continue," etcetera. Most of the student leaders of his organization 'Student League' were present there waiting for him to come out through the gate. They had flower garlands in their hands to put around his neck as a way of welcome and greetings. Anjuman was the first one to put the garland around Kabil's neck. She then said, "Let's all go to the Shahid Minar (the 1952 Language Movement Martyrs Monument). We want to hear a speech by you there."

Kabil smiled and quietly asked her, "Nobody from our house got the news?"

"The student leaders came to know of your release only a short time ago. I didn't have time since then to phone

Rokhi. Please forgive me for that. But I had informed them earlier today that you might be released either today or tomorrow. Now let's go to the Shahid Minar," Anjuman hurried in leading Kabil forward followed by the people who had gathered together there earlier. At the front line of a medium-sized procession, garlanded Kabil's face looked somewhat faded. His eyes were looking at a small portion of the blue sky in between high-rise buildings on both sides of the road. A crowd of vultures was flying low, navigating skillfully in between the buildings looking for their sources of food and intimidating some sporadic flying crows who made frightened noises. Kabil breathed a sigh of relief and felt the smell of freedom after two long years of confinement. The procession kept moving slowly toward the national Shahid Minar.

AROUND EIGHT THAT EVENING, Rokshana received a phone call. After that she came to the dining room and found her mother there. She said to her, "Your nephew has been released from the jail early this evening. Rania was a bit puzzled at the subdued way Rokshana abruptly broke this very happy news. She was confused by Rokhi's reference to Kabil as "your nephew" rather than her usual "brother Kabil". Yet she couldn't conceal her excitement, emotions, and happiness, but at first couldn't say anything for a few moments. Meanwhile Halim put dinner plates on the table for both Rania and Rokhi. But Rania told him, "I'm not going to eat now."

Rokshana looked up at her mother's face. By that time Halim put some paratha on Rokhi's plate.

Rania asked again, "Is Kabil coming home soon?"

"I don't know. Brother Nisar just telephoned me from Sheikh Mujib's house and told me that brother Kabil had been released early this evening. He went to Shahid Minar first accompanied by his friends and supporters. From there, the student procession took him to Sheikh Mujib's residence in Dhanmondi. He's there now. Anju and Nisar had gone earlier to the jail gate to receive him upon his release. They couldn't have called to tell us of his release ahead of time."

"How's Kabil doing health-wise? Did you ask Nisar when Kabil might be coming home?"

"It wasn't possible for me to discuss with Nisar all those things over the phone. Now that he's out of the jail, he'll come home sometime. Moreover, why should I ask Nisar about Kabil's health condition? I know he's physically alright," Rokshana replied.

"I don't understand that you speak so coolly and nonchalantly about Kabil's release from jail after long two years. You managed to sit down for dinner before our son's arrival home after all those times. Wouldn't it be nice if we wait a bit so that we can have dinner with him at home after such a long time?"

Rokshana kept silent for a while without answering her mother. Then she stood up to leave the dining table and said, "Okay, we'll eat together when brother Kabil gets home. I'm not feeling well. Let me go to my bed and lie down for a while. When brother Kabil gets home, please wake me up."

As she was about to leave, Rania asked worriedly, "What happened? You said you weren't feeling well. I hope you aren't coming down with fever or something."

"Probably not. I spent the whole day in our factory. There, the workers are always talking in groups. There's murmur about General Yahya's proposed forthcoming general election. If Sheikh Mujib's Party campaigns with his Six Points Demand, no other Party is likely to win any parliamentary seat from East Pakistan at the National Assembly. The Bihari workers at our factory think that if Awami League under Sheikh Mujib's leadership wins majority seats at the National Assembly, the local Bengalis will make it difficult for the non-Bengali refugees to live in East Pakistan. The workers in our factory are congregating by spreading this unlikely fear. I found the workers at the factory stopped working and were congregating to discuss their future because of this baseless rumor. They were worried about their lives and livelihood in the future.

"They were busy discussing in groups what the future will hold for them in that situation. They were scared that if Mujib wins the election, there might even be a mass killing of refugee settlers in East Pakistan. When I tried to dispel their fears and concerns, someone sarcastically remarked, 'She's a Bengali even though her mother is a refugee settler. She will not understand the concerns of the refugees.' Cousin Andaleeb was also there with me. I didn't feel good and came home early. Now I don't feel well physically either."

"Didn't Andaleeb say anything to the workers?" Rania asked, worried about the laborers' unrest at their factory.

"Yes, he did. He mildly scolded them for believing and spreading unfounded rumors and asked them to get back to work. He then told me that it was my father who had employed these poor, helpless refugee women in our factory to help them make a living. There is not a single Bengali woman working in our factory. If Father had employed at least some Bengali women here, then the feelings of other non-Bengali workers wouldn't be so much anti-Bengali. But my father couldn't foresee that the country would come to this turbulent political situation. If this level of fear and concern among the workers persists, then it would be difficult to keep the factory functioning."

Having said all that Rokshana went to her room.

KABIL CAME HOME AROUND nine o'clock that evening. Anjuman and Nisar also came with him. Kabil paid respect to his aunty Rania in the traditional way. Rania in turn gave him an affectionate hug and blessed him by giving a kiss on his forehead. She asked him to go, take a shower, and then say a prayer to thank God for his release. Kabil thought as if he was hearing after a long time the voice of his deceased mother advising him to do so. Rokshana was standing nearby on one side observing with admiration the reunion of a nephew with his aunty who didn't happen to have a son of her own. She noticed teardrops on the eyes of both. She decided to leave them alone there and said before leaving the scene, "There's hot water in the bathroom. I will put fresh towels etcetera for you there. I'm going to take Nisar and Anju to my room."

Kabil for the first time focused on Rokshana. She was wearing a standard eleven feet long, legendary Tangail brand traditional saree with lots of intricate works on it and wrapped around her body as most fashionable Bengali city women did. She was also wearing a matching sleeveless blouse underneath, showing a generous part of her midrib. Kabil immediately felt attracted to her fair complexion and inviting outfit.

As soon as Rokhi left with Nisar and Anjuman, Kabil babbled out, "Our Rokhi has become quite healthy in the last two years and you, Aunty, have become thinner. What happened? I hope you are not suffering from any kind of illness."

"No no, nothing wrong has happened to me. I'm pleased to hear that Rokhi looks more attractive to you. I have been always praying to God for the health and well-being of you both. Thank God you also look healthy. They must have fed you well in jail."

Kabil burst into laughter at Rania's remark about his health and said, "This fatness will not last long, Aunty. This is the result of being inactive in the jail cell year after year even though they fed us only rice, lentils, and green leaves. This is false fat. Going to university back and forth and eating at legendary Modhu's canteen at the campus for a week or so will bring me back to shape. Then you'll see your nephew Kabil has not changed at all in two years of incarceration as the guest of the martial law government."

That made Rania also laugh aloud. Kabil then went to take a shower as per Rania's advice. Later that evening Kabil came to the dining table and sat next to Rokshana. Nisar and Anjuman sat on the opposite side facing them. Rania sat at the end of the table and tasted Kabil's favorite dish freshly cooked by Halim. She then served a generous portion of the same item of food on Kabil's plate. Others took their respective choices on their plates. While everyone was enjoying dinner, Anjuman wanted to engage Kabil on recent political developments in the country. She said, "I went with you from the Shahid Minar to Sheikh Mujib's house, but I couldn't talk to you anything about our plans for the near future vis-à-vis current political situation in the country. I noticed that Sheikh Mujib called you aside while we were in his house and talked to you privately for quite some time. Would you mind sharing with us at least some of what he talked to you about, especially if anything about the future directions of our movement?"

Kabil replied with a deep sense of seriousness, "The leader told me that in the time leading up to the forthcoming election, he would undertake campaign and speaking tours to as many outlying cities and towns of this province as possible and that he would like me to accompany him in those tours as his student representative. He wants to start those tour programs within a week or so, and he would like me to start planning for those from tomorrow. He apologized for having to ask me to engage in political activities so soon after my release from jail. But he said we couldn't afford to lose time before this crucial nationwide election called by Gen. Yahya Khan. He also said that he needed me by his side as his chief student spokesman to elaborate the economic, social, and political aspects of Awami League's Six Points Demand election manifesto to the public."

Nisar raised his eyebrows and asked, "And you conceded to his proposal with great pleasure, right?"

"What can I do? He is the boss, he's the leader, and he gets his way with his followers. Moreover, the main issue in the forthcoming election will be his Six Points Demand from the government, and we, the student arm of his party Awami League, i.e., the Student League had assumed the responsibility of explaining these demands to the public. I'm his chief student representative to do this. Therefore, I can't back away from my duty when he asks me to do just that."

Just then, Andaleeb walked in from outside and said, "Sorry, I'm late. There were many customers in our shop in the evening. I came after attending to them and balancing the cash."

He then left his briefcase on the floor next to Rokshana and said, "Today's income of forty thousand rupees is in here."

Kabil looked up and noticed that there had been a change in the way the businesses and the family affairs were being managed as Andaleeb gave the daily business income to Rokshana rather than to Rania as he used to do before Kabil went to jail.

Kabil then said to Andaleeb, "Come, brother, take a seat and join us for dinner. I've something to tell you afterward. I got a letter from Momi a few days ago when I was in jail. She's doing okay."

Andaleeb felt a bit awkward. He took a chair and sat next to Kabil. He then said, "We haven't seen Momi for a long time. Now that you're out of the jail, let's all go together for a few days to visit Momi at Montala and to celebrate your release."

Both Rania and Rokhi discreetly smiled at Andaleeb's suggestion. But Kabil said with a voice of seriousness, "No, brother, I'll have no time at all now to go to Montala—not even for a day. Rather I would suggest that Rokhi go to Montala alone and bring Momi here. Momi wants to come to Dhaka anyway. Besides, then Aunty can act for both sides and decide on a date for your wedding to Momi. I do not want to delay your wedding any longer. What's your opinion on that, Aunty?" he asked Rania.

Rania replied, "Now that you're back home, we really do not need to rush things. Let Rokhi stay home. Rather, I go to Montala for a few days. After Momi and I come back here, I would like to settle both the weddings—yours and

Andaleeb's around the same time. Now, everything depends on you, Kabil."

As soon as Rania finished, Rokshana got up from her chair and said,

"I'm finished with my dinner. If you all excuse me, I want to go to my room."

Everybody noticed surprisingly Rokhi's sudden departure from the dining room. Anjuman laughed loudly to make the environment a bit lighter. She then addressed Rania, "You're right, Aunty. When it comes to marriage, if you have to take into account everybody's opinion, convenience, and otherwise, timing, then we all will be middle-aged by the time we get married. Rather, you decide on a date for all concerned, and others will adjust and comply with that. We all then would start the celebrations."

Rania smiled a bit and said, "Are you indicating that I should call for your wedding to Nisar as well? If you do, I'll not shy away from my assignment and will work on it with pleasure. What do you say, Nisar?"

This remark by Rania made everyone laugh aloud, and the environment in the room became lighter even though the shade of hesitation did not disappear from Kabil's face. He couldn't fully understand the motive behind Rokshana's leaving the dining table so abruptly. Kabil knew Rokhi's patience had run out much earlier like a straw floating away in a heavy, fast-moving current of water. By that time Kabil thought Rokshana had come to the conclusion that she would not have a peaceful, rich family life with a common political man. Kabil had noticed that when he was talking about touring various parts of the province with his leader campaigning for the election, Rokshana turned her face the other way as if she was absorbed in other thoughts. He thought he should come to a clear understanding with Rokshana on this soon. If Rokshana waited for months, years, or even a life dreaming about a kind of quiet, peaceful, and affluent, apolitical future with Kabil, he would not be able to provide that to her. In that case, it would be intolerable for both sooner or later. He realized that he himself was responsible for creating that situation for both himself and for Rokhi. He thought about explaining the situation to Rokhi that very night. He thought about telling Rokhi that he did not have the time, qualifications, or the competence at that stage in his life to accept the social and family obligation of marriage even though he loved Rokhi and without her in his life, he would not care very much to live. But he did not have the courage and the strength to ask his aunty Rania to postpone his marriage to Rokshana as Rania had planned for. He would rather ask Rokhi to convince her mother that Rokhi herself needed some more time to think things through.

Kabil hoped that Rokshana could convince her mother that it was not Kabil, it was rather Rokshana herself who did not want Kabil at the time to abandon his political responsibilities for the sake of their marriage and thus disappoint his leader and other political associates. He thought that once Rokshana could get her mother to their side on this issue, then everything else would be in order. Kabil was confident that Rokhi would agree to undertake the responsibility of convincing her mother to that effect once he would have made the suggestion to her. However, he was somewhat skeptical that Rokhi would agree to convince her mother because she herself was no longer sure of her future with Kabil anymore. He was skeptical because he thought Rokshana might be mentally prepared to release Kabil from all his love for and promise to her. *Otherwise,* he thought, *why would Rokhi leave the dinner table with such dismay and trifling manner when everybody was engaged in discussing the timing of their wedding?*

After dinner, when Nisar, Anjuman, and Andaleeb had left, Kabil got up and sat on a sofa in the living room. By that time, Rania went to her bedroom. The lights in the room were dim. A lot of thoughts were going through Kabil's tired brain. Suddenly, he felt that a somewhat indistinct shadow entered the living room and sat on the sofa at a distance. Kabil was scared and quite subconsciously shouted, "Who is there? Who is there?"

"Don't shout. I'm Rokhi," came the reply.

"Oh! You came after so long. Everybody left a while ago. I thought you were not feeling well and went to bed in your room."

"I left the dining table early because I wasn't feeling well physically. I lay down on the bed until now but could not fall asleep. I thought after everyone left, I would come to your room and talk. But I noticed you were sitting here quietly with all the lights off. What happened? Is that what you have been used to doing in jail?"

"Not really, Rokhi. While I was sitting here, I was trying to bring my uncle—your father's face in my imagination—that polite, affectionate face. But I couldn't do that, Rokhi. Instead, I saw in my imagination an unhappy, sad face of his—one that I had never seen when he was alive. I don't know why I imagined such a look in his face while I am quite awake."

"That's nothing. It's a reflection of your thought. Maybe, you were thinking that Daddy, if he were alive now, would have been very angry with all your political involvement. That's what probably came to your mind as a reflection of imagination. Let's go to your room because if we talk here, perhaps Mother will hear us from her bedroom. I will not turn the lights on. Here, you hold my hand."

Rokhi herself extended her hand and took Kabil's hand in hers, and they walked toward Kabil's bedroom. Once, they were outside the living room, Kabil suddenly stopped on the hallway, took Rokhi's two warm hands, pressed them against his chest, and said, "Believe me, Rokhi, I love you very much. My political involvement, fame, and influence are all for you. I just need some time because I do not want to keep you worrying about me day and night. If I do not get this much consideration for my love from you, then who else can I beg it from?"

Rokshana was a bit stunned at this kind of reaction from Kabil. But she didn't move her hands from Kabil's chest. She quietly and softly said, "Whatever you can't say in front of our family and friends, you can say that to me when we're alone in this dark night if you feel comfortable to do so. But why swear anymore by the words of love etcetera? I do not have the capacity like you have to keep so much love hidden in my heart. I can live my entire life without being touched by love. Whenever you are ready, just tell my mother, and she will arrange for everything. I will also stay fixed like all other furniture in this house until that time. Please do not worry, I'll not move."

"Are you saying these because you know that I have no answers to this kind of loving accusations of yours?"

"No, there's nothing like a loving accusation in here. You love me, you will not be able to live without me, your involvement in politics is all for me, yet would I not be able to hold a lifetime or my prime time of youth waiting for you? Okay, I'm willing to do that. You will not have to back away from anything for me. But I can't take the burden of convincing your aunty of this. Even though she is my mother, she thinks I am to be blamed for my failure because I had told her even in my late teen years that I'm in love with you. Now, please release my hands and let's both go to our respective bedrooms and go to sleep."

TWO DAYS AFTER KABIL'S release from jail, Rania and Andaleeb arrived at Montala Railway Station one early morning. The station was quiet. Rania found it uninviting because the previous station master had been transferred from here to Akhaura Junction. Unlike during her previous visits at this station with her now-deceased husband, nobody approached her this time, invited her for a cup of tea at the station master's office, neither did anybody come forward offering to carry their luggage for them. The previous station master was a good friend of her late husband's reputed Syed family of the nearby village of Montala, and his wife was a good friend of Rania's now-deceased sister-in-law Syeda Zakia Banu, i.e., Kabil's late mother. Rania heard that the current station master was a non-Bengali. Despite that, neither she nor Andaleeb felt like going to his office to introduce themselves and to say hello to him.

Both Rania and Andaleeb waited for a while on the concrete station floor hoping that some porter would come to carry their luggage. They noticed other incoming passengers going on their respective ways to their respective final destinations outside the station. Rania remembered that this was the place where her late husband Ahmed Alam had abruptly sat down during her first trip here when he heard the news of the demise of his sister-in-law Zakia Banu. That specific scene came back flashing in Rania's memory and saddened her.

After a short while, Andaleeb said to Rania, "Let's go, Aunty. I can carry both our suitcases. We don't need a porter."

"Okay, let's go then, my son. I was a bit nostalgic remembering my last visit here with my husband."

Just as they were about to start walking, a porter came along, took the suitcases from Andaleeb's hand, and started walking alongside them.

IN THE EVENING AFTER seeing off Andaleeb and her mother on their way to Montala, Rokshana came and sat inside Kabil's bedroom on his bed. Kabil joined her and sat on a chair next to his study table. Nobody said a word for a long while. They both knew why Rania went to Montala with Andaleeb. They knew that she would come back to Dhaka after a couple of days with Momena. And that after their return, Rania would like to arrange for completing the religious ceremony of the wedding between Andaleeb and Momena and that between Rokshana and Kabil. Rania had made it clear to all four of them that she would not like to wait for their wedding much longer. Rania had also planned to invite Momena's uncles at Harashpur to come to Dhaka to attend the wedding once the date would have been fixed.

Now, sitting in his bedroom in their house in Dhaka, Kabil could not think of any way to delay Rania's initiative this time for his marriage to Rokshana. At the same time, he also could not think of saying anything that might hurt Rokshana's pride and self-respect. All the while, he wanted the wedding between Andaleeb and Momena to go ahead as per Rania's wish and timing. After a while, he looked up at Rokshana and asked, "What are you thinking about?"

"I'm thinking how surprised and confused Momi would be seeing mother and Andaleeb all of a sudden. I'm sure she would not know what course of actions she should take relative to her proposed marriage to Andaleeb."

"She would first question and complain why I did not go with them after my release from the jail. But I'm sure she would be happy to see Andaleeb after almost two long years."

"Oh! You think your cousin Momi hasn't seen Andaleeb for two years when you were in jail? The fact is that Andaleeb used to visit Momi at Montala every month with the excuse of taking her sustenance allowances and other supplies. He didn't dare disclose that to my mother, but he used to tell me before going to visit her. Momena is a very good girl. You'll see that Andaleeb will be happy when they are married."

Kabil just sat there looking on the floor with his brain crowded with all sorts of thoughts. Seeing him in that confused situation Rokshana asked, "What happened? What are you thinking about now? You didn't respond to any of my comments and questions. Momena is coming with my mother and Andaleeb in a couple of days. After a long time, the festivities of a wedding will take place in our house. You can at least feel good about that and look cheerful. Instead, why do you look so sad and serious? I told you your cousin Momi is a very lucky girl. She is also very beautiful. The empty house of my cousin Andaleeb will lighten up and be filled with joy by Momi's presence there. You should feel happy for them."

"Do you think I'm not happy for them? I'm as happy for them as you are, Rokhi. You praise Momi's physical beauty.

Let me then tell you an old story about her. This had happened long before I came to Dhaka to meet your father—my uncle. My mother once took me to my maternal grandparents' house in Harashpur. I was only about seven or eight years old, and Momi was even younger. When one of my maternal aunties brought Momi to meet us, my mother put her hand on Momi's head and affectionately said, 'Oh, little Momi! One day in the future, I'll take you to live with me in Montala. I'll train you well so that when you grow up, I'll arrange your marriage with my son, Kabil. You two will match well with each other. I will talk to your uncles—my brothers about it soon.'"

"Is that so?" Rokhi said with a look of jealous surprise in her eyes.

Kabil laughed and said, "This was my mother's sudden thought. As a young boy, I felt shy and embarrassed. My aunties all laughed aloud at my shyness and commented, 'Our future son-in-law is feeling shy.'

Later, when I came to Dhaka to live with you all and you and I visited my mother in Montala, she noticed the interactions between you and me. She changed her earlier intentions. Nevertheless, after we had come back to Dhaka, my mother brought Momi to live with her at our home. But she then made me promise that I should find a suitable groom for Momi when she grew up. Now, if Andaleeb marries Momi, I'll feel as if I would have kept my promise to my mother."

"Does Momi know and still remember that your mother once chose her for you to marry?"

"When Momi had heard for the first time, my mother's hopes and aspirations for her and me, she was still a little girl in her frocks. I don't think she remembers that after so many years."

"Girls never forget that kind of incident. Why only girls? It seems that even boys don't forget these events. If they do, you would not meticulously remember the whole thing suddenly after such a long time. Maybe, you have some regret about the turn of events in your life after you came to Dhaka. Momi might have grown up in a village, but it's a fact that she's a more beautiful and full-sized woman than I am. She catches the eyes of any man. She's even more beautiful now than she was before. When you'll see her in a few days, your eyes will be dazzled, and maybe, you'll regret that your mother had changed her earlier intentions about you two."

Kabil could feel the subtle poke in Rokshana's expressions. He laughed aloud and said, "What's the point in my regretting my mother's change of her earlier intention? I can't even fulfill and materialize my mother's latest choice for my marriage. Momi somehow can depend on somebody in the person of Andaleeb and is going to be rewarded for falling in love with him. On the contrary, I have nothing to offer except my words of love and promise to reward the one who loves me with all her heart. Nobody among my friends is perhaps as unlucky as I am."

"Why are you saying that?"

"Because nobody understands me."

"I told you that I'll wait as long as it takes for me to understand you."

"That sounds like a very angry pronouncement of a promise. Don't I know that you will wait for me? The real matter is if you think that I am taking advantage of your helplessness, then I should not keep you in this situation any longer. It's okay with me whatever Aunty wants to do about us when she comes back from Montala. Don't you worry about it anymore for nothing. Now, I have to go to Anjuman's house for something. Nisar will also likely be there. I'll be late coming back home." With that, Kabil got up and left the house.

Rokshana did not say anything in response. She just sat there, keeping her eyes focused on the slowly blooming evening flowers outside near the window. A beam of light from inside the room traveled outside through the window on the bunch of blooming flowers. Rokshana was deeply absorbed in her thoughts about Momena, Kabil, Andaleeb, and herself. She thought how time played out the relationship between Momena and Kabil in their childhood, between her and Andaleeb before Kabil came to Dhaka to live with her family, and between her and Kabil since then and now between Momena and Andaleeb who became drawn to Momena because Rokshana herself had rejected Andaleeb since Kabil's arrival at the scene. Thinking about all these, especially about how to save face for Kabil and yet convince her mother to give both Kabil and herself some more time to think through about their future together, Rokshana fell asleep on the bed in Kabil's room.

Kabil returned home well after 10:00 p.m. and found Rokshana sleeping in his bed. To wake her up, Kabil slowly drew his face near Rokshana's ear and whispered, "What happened? You fell asleep here. Will you not eat supper?"

Hearing Kabil's voice, Rokshana woke up hurriedly, sat on the bed, and asked, "What time is it?"

"Well, after ten."

"When did you come back?"

"Right now. I was chilling with Nisar and Anju. I have made up my mind, Rokhi."

"What did you decide?"

"I don't want to make Aunty and you unhappy anymore. You and I will also get married at the same time as Momena and Andaleeb do. I will have to accept this situation if I want to spare Aunty any further worry. Besides, there is a limit in your patience as well. How much longer would you have to wait? We should make good use of your favorite diamond ring that your mother had bought long ago for you to wear at our wedding."

Hearing that, Rokshana slowly got down from the bed while fixing the edge of the saree on her shoulder. She then asked, "Is that the advice of your friend Anjuman?"

"Not only Anju. Nisar also concurred with that for peace and family stability. I should now respond positively to

Aunty's initiative. Besides, many of my political coworkers are married. If they have no problem, why should I?"

"Well, that's right. Like a good boy, you found a solution to the mathematical simplification problem."

Kabil couldn't understand Rokshana's comments. Was she shy or simply upset with what he had just described to her.

Rokshana fixed her saree properly and said, "Look, cousin Kabil! Whatever else you do, please do not insult me for nothing. Whatever obligation you feel here is between you and your aunty—my mother. You want to do this because you think I am responsible for your aunty's impatience. I know that you do not at this moment agree at all with this initiative of your aunty for our marriage. I also know that you do not have political and mental stability at this time to go along with your aunty's initiative. Under these circumstances, you decided to go along with my mother's initiative simply for our family stability. I do not want you to go through this unwillingly or half-heartedly simply because you feel an obligation to your aunty's mental peace and happiness. For your information, I have thought about a way out of this for both of us for the time being. Let's go and we'll discuss this further at the dinner table."

She then walked out of the room while putting her saree over her head.

RANIA SOON AFTER ARRIVAL at Montala for the second time in her life, established a good rapport with a number of respectable ladies in the village. She told them that she was going to revive the old respect and reputation of her late husband's famed family in the locality. She also told them that she had been planning to arrange the marriage between Kabil and Rokshana and that between Andaleeb and Momena in the near future in Dhaka. She also expressed concern about Kabil's safety and security because of his deep involvement in national politics which was well-known in the whole country including Montala areas. Every family she talked to was happy to know of her intentions of strengthening the old respectable Syed family by way of these marital arrangements.

One day, Rania invited Momena to join her for late afternoon prayer. After the prayer, she said to Momena, "Look, Momi! You like Andaleeb, don't you? I would like to take you to Dhaka with me and arrange for your wedding with Andaleeb there later this week. I am confident this marriage will be good for both of you. If I get your clear consent on this marriage, I'll send for your uncles in Harashpur for their consent as well. If they also agree, I'll invite them to come to Dhaka to attend the formal ceremony there. Is that okay with you?"

This proposal by Rania was not something new to Momena. There had been talks about this marriage in Rania's family even before Kabil was arrested by the government for his political involvement and sent to jail. But when the formal proposal came directly from Rania who was Andaleeb's aunty and local guardian, Momena's young mind was filled with subtle happiness and normal shyness. She looked down and started picking on the prayer mat with her finger—a normal sign of shyness and silent consent. Observing that, Rania picked up the subject again. "You may have one question about this proposal, and that is that Andaleeb is a non-Bengali refugee settler in this country. The depth of his family relationship in East Pakistan is not that well established. Look, Momi! I'm also a refugee in this country and didn't have much roots here. You see, now you all are my roots in this land. This house in Montala is my father-in-law's, and therefore my own house now."

Seeing no visible sign of objection from Momena, Rania continued, "I would have liked to arrange for the wedding between you and Andaleeb and that between Kabil and Rokshana on the same date. But Kabil has just been released from jail. Right at this moment, he would probably need some time to sort things out for himself before his wedding to Rokshana. However, I do not wish to delay the wedding between you and Andaleeb for Kabil's uncertainties. Now, you tell me candidly, if you have any reservation of your own in marrying Andaleeb."

After a few moments' silence, Momena said, "What can I say, Aunty, over your and cousin Kabil's choice of a husband for me? I'm an orphan. Cousin Kabil and you are my guardians. My aunty Zakia, before her death, left the responsibility with cousin Kabil for arranging my marriage. If Kabil and you choose Andaleeb as my future husband, I would have no objection to it."

With that she left the room.

A LITTLE LATER, SHE came back with tea for Rania. After serving Rania with her tea, Momena took Andaleeb's tea to his room. She left the tea on the table and made a move to leave the room. At that point, Andaleeb said, "Look, Momi, I'd like to have a few words with you. If it is okay with you, please stay for a few minutes." Seeing his eagerness, Momena didn't make any objection and sat on the bed next to his chair. Andaleeb opened the conversation, "I love you, Momi. Whether you love me or not is up to you. Aunty Rania, who is the guardian of both you and me, would like to arrange for our marriage soon if you do not have any objection to it."

"Aunty Rania just told me of her decision a few minutes earlier."

"Why do you talk like that, Momi? Do you have any doubt about my love for you?" Andaleeb asked with a sense of worry in his voice.

"Rokhi once told me that you used to love her very much and wanted to marry her. But . . ." Momena replied.

"But what, Momi? Please tell me clearly."

"But Rokhi changed her mind about you after she had met cousin Kabil."

"That's true, Momi. But where is my fault in that? I wanted to love one, but she liked someone else other than me. I made way for her and helped her. This is proof of my great respect and consideration for her. Nobody can blame me for that. It wasn't my fault."

"No, definitely not your fault. I'm only talking about your love. You tell me that you love me. Once you also loved Rokhi enough to have wanted to marry her. People need to accept their luck or fate rather than relying on their love alone. You could not do anything once Rokshana decided not to love you. You accepted that. Surely, you're a good man. People's hearts never remain empty, and because of that, I got a place in your heart. I'm grateful to you for that. My happiness will not be hampered because you once used to love Rokhi. Our marriage would be the greatest thing in life for you and me."

"But," Momi continued, "if I do not tell you something now, I'll feel guilty myself after we get married. Just as I'm willing to marry you, having known about your past love life, I feel that you also must know, before we're married, something about my past unfulfilled dreams about my future bridegroom."

Andaleeb was impressed with the way, Momena expressed things clearly and candidly. He said, "Okay, if you want to say something on your own about your past, I'm willing to listen and you can say whatever you want without fear of anything."

Momena kept silent for a while. She felt Andaleeb's eagerness was merely his curiosity. She understood that any man would be upset and unhappy with what she had intended to disclose. Yet Andaleeb had confessed about his past love for Rokhi and that love might have included some of his hopes and aspirations for sharing, after his intended marriage with Rokhi, the considerable wealth that Rania and her husband Alam were likely to leave behind. In the same way, Momena also should confess that once she was brought to Montala's Syed family by her late aunty Zakia Banu with the promise and hope that she would marry Kabil—the only scion of that family. Kabil also was not completely unaware of that promise, hope, and aspirations of not only his mother but also of Momena herself. Momena wondered if any man could completely forget the past family promise and hopes because of changed circumstances in his life. Momena knew that Kabil had not completely forgotten that either. That was the reason Kabil told everybody about his responsibility to find a suitable groom for Momena.

After a few minutes, Momena said, "My aunty Zakia had brought me to this family in order to groom me as her son Kabil's future bride. I stepped into this family thinking that I would one day marry Kabil. I loved Kabil with my heart and was dreaming all my life that one day we'll have a family together. However, when Kabil met Rokshana, fell in love with her, got access to her family's considerable wealth, he could not keep an orphan, village girl like me in his dream or in his heart. Also, when my aunty Zakia saw her son Kabil coming with Rokhi to visit this village before I was brought here, her dream about me and Kabil together was shattered.

She nevertheless brought me here, raised, and trained me to her liking, and before she died, she made Kabil promise that he would find a suitable husband for me. To me, love is not everything in life. Rather, if two people can meet each other's needs and wants then they can complement each other and can find in each other something more than just love, hopes, and aspirations. That is the reason I agreed early this evening to Aunty Rania's proposal to marry you."

AFTER SPENDING SEVERAL DAYS at Montala, Rania returned to Dhaka along with Momena and Andaleeb. Back at their Bonogram Lane home, she found that Kabil had gone on a political tour to Mymensingh, another district town north of Dhaka along with Sheikh Mujib. He had told Rokhi that he would be back in Dhaka the following day. But two days after, when he was not yet back, Rokhi telephoned Anjuman's house and came to know that Mujib had fallen sick after their first public meeting at Mymensingh and returned to Dhaka. He had delegated other Party and student leaders including Kabil the responsibility to address the subsequent public, political mass meetings at Bhairav Bazar and Brahmanbaria. Kabil could not have returned to Dhaka as he had hoped for because of this changed situation.

Rania was unhappy when she heard on arrival home that Kabil had gone out of Dhaka. She said to Rokshana, "You shouldn't have let Kabil go out of Dhaka so soon after his release from jail."

"What can I do if someone is not happy staying home? Besides, if he has important work outside, why should I stop him from leaving Dhaka? But he told me that he would be back after only one day."

"Kabil should have stayed home for a few days until after I come back from Montala. Doesn't he know why I had gone there?" Rania said with a sense of worry in her voice.

"Of course, he knows. There isn't going to be any impediment in your arrangement for the wedding between Momena and Andaleeb. You might as well go ahead with your plans."

Rania felt a sense of setback at what Rokshana had just said.

"It seems to me that you have come to some sort of agreement with Kabil about your own marriage at the same time. I thought I had told you before I went to Montala that I would like to arrange for the religious ceremonies of both marriages together. Do you two want to keep me waiting longer with uncertainty and lack of my mental peace?"

Having asked that question, Rania sat down on a chair, keeping her handbag on the dining table. Andaleeb followed Rania on another chair, but Momi, not knowing what to do just stood there by the door. Rokshana then called her out, "Come, Momi! You have a change of clothes in my room."

As they were about to leave, Rania asked, "Before you go, answer my question, Rokhi. Does Kabil want to delay the wedding of you two longer yet?"

"No, Mother. He's willing to conform to your wish. But I need a little more time to think through the matter."

"What are you saying, you unlucky, poor child?"

"No, Mother. Don't just rebuke me for nothing. The young man Kabil whom you have been waiting for over a decade now to marry me off with, the man Kabil I used to know and love was my cousin brother. Today's Kabil is not that man anymore. I need to check out today's Kabil who is a famed leader of this country. Please do not hurry anything mother. Have patience. I can wait for a while longer. Come, Momi."

Andaleeb looked at his aunty Rania and said in a manner of comforting her, "There's no rush on my part either, Aunty. If you wish to have both the wedding together at a time, then maybe Momi and I also must wait for a while. I'm sure Momi will not object to our waiting once she understands everything."

"I'm not willing to wait for even a week, Andaleeb. I will not postpone your wedding for Kabil or Rokshana. Did you hear what my daughter just said? She can't make up her mind after being madly in love with Kabil for so many years. Yet you, me, all our relatives here, and all my employees know that your uncle Alam and I had to change our plans because my daughter declined you—my nephew as her possible future husband and opted for her paternal cousin Kabil. Now after so many years, my same daughter says that she needs more time to understand Kabil more before marrying him. Now, you tell me what I can say and do," Rania poured out with a sense of much frustration in her voice.

"Aunty! You do not worry about Momena and me. We're willing to wait for a while even though we are also willing to respect your wish as you like. But you don't need to make an elaborate arrangement and extravagant celebration during my wedding with Momena. We'll celebrate the two occasions together on a grand scale when Rokhi and Kabil feel comfortable to marry each other. I understand how much Rokhi loves Kabil. When she says she needs some more time to think things through, let's give her that extra time. After all, it's a lifelong commitment," Andaleeb said in a considered manner. With that, he politely took leave of Rania and left for his own house in Narinda area of Dhaka.

ONE EVENING, AROUND EIGHT o'clock, Anjuman and her fiancé Nisar came out of Anjuman's parents' house on Rankin Street. They talked while walking on the sidewalk. Anjuman said, "I'm giving you company tonight only up to a short distance. You can go by yourself from thereon. I can't go up to the medical college roundabout to see you off as I normally do on other days. I'm scared to walk back alone all this distance after seeing you off there. I'm afraid, one of these days, the secret police in plain clothes might pick me up without any arrest warrant."

"So, you're also afraid to walk alone. But you used to say all these days before that the local hooligans recognized you as a high-ranking political student leader and were afraid of you," Nisar teased Anjuman.

"The hooligans are not only afraid of me they also salute me and move away from my path. But I'm talking about plain-clothes policemen. Besides, considering what you have told me inside our house a while ago about possible suppression of Awami League's student affiliate, I have to be careful about my movement for a while."

They reached the end of Rankin Street as they talked. There they stopped near the corner of the so-called Poetry Place under a well-blossomed, large Krishnachura flower tree. It was dark under the tree this time of the night, and there were very few pedestrians going by this place. Nisar picked up Anjuman's two warm hands in his own and said, "This morning, I heard at Modhu's canteen in the university campus from the leaders of your counterpart students' union that the head office of Pakistan Special Intelligence Service had issued strict orders to stop East Pakistan's student movement agitating in favor of Mujib's Six Points Demand. The Home Ministry of the East Pakistan provincial government is soon going to implement that order. Soon there will be a large-scale arrest of student leaders. It's likely that Kabil will be arrested again soon. I'm scared that you yourself might not escape arrest again. Your name, your speeches at students' gatherings along with your picture are published every day in the newspapers. I worry and am afraid for you, Anju."

"If you're so worried, tell me what I should do."

"I'm an apolitical man, Anju. You will not like what I want to say. Besides, you have gone far in your political involvement. I can't ask you to leave the political activities against your will and concentrate more on your studies."

Anjuman felt as if Nisar's words dropped water on her forehead like water drops from the flowers of the Krishnachura tree.

"Why can't you? You love me yet you're hesitant to pressure me to do anything."

"I fear because my suggestions may not be to your liking," Nisar replied.

"The real thing is that you never once forcefully told me that you loved me and therefore would like me to leave politics behind and start a family with you. With that kind of pressure from you, Nisar, I probably would have left politics long ago. I don't think that anybody could give me anything more important than your love. You're such a lovable and mild-mannered person. You tolerated all my wild manners. It's also true that I love you more because you're so opposite of my wild nature. You tell me what you want me to do, and I will not do anything contrary to your wish," Anjuman said breathlessly.

"I don't want to pull you out from your political activities right away. Nobody should do that with the excuses of love. Neither can it be done because this is such a thing as one's love for one's motherland," Nisar replied.

"Is there such a thing as love for the country in the books of a budding modern philosopher like you? If there is, it's good. The thing with me is that I'm a politician with a history of imprisonment for political reasons. My future is uncertain. Yet I want to make you happy as much as I can. If you ask me to marry you tomorrow, I'm willing to do so. In that case, you'll have to have the courage to formally ask my parents for their consent. They're waiting for your proposal. I'm not putting pressure on you to do that. But if that will give you some comfort physically and mentally, then I'll go along with your wish. I will not shy away from it with the excuses for my political activities. Moreover, you will not have to carry the financial burden of having a wife until you complete your studies."

Anjuman made a liberal and irresistible proposal mixed with love and emotion to her long-time fiancé. They were both standing in the dark shade of the large Krishnachura tree.

"I feel the urge right now to hug and embrace you in my arms and kiss you madly on your lips, Anju."

Anjuman didn't respond to Nisar's wish. She rather slowly walked on her own closer to Nisar, embraced him with both her arms, and kissed him on his cheek and lips. She then rested her head on his chest and began sobbing out of joy. Nisar drew her even closer and then said, "I don't merely love you, Anju. I have a seat of great respect for you in my heart where your shadow has been established like that of a queen. You are a courageous woman. This country needs a woman like you at this critical time. I do not want to ruin your established reputation in the country for the sake of my love for you. Rather, I'll follow the suggestion you just made and go to your parents directly and beg them for your hand in marriage to me. If they agree, then we'll get married as per their plan."

Hearing what Nisar had just said, Anjuman extracted herself from his embrace and said, "Let me then walk with you for a while to see you off."

"Up to the medical college?" Nisar asked teasingly.

"No, all the way to the gate of your student dormitory," Anjuman replied. At that, both of them laughed aloud.

IN THE EVENING OF Momena's arrival at Rokshana's house in Dhaka, Rokshana after supper invited Momena to her bedroom for some chatting. It was raining outside—one of the last rains of the fading monsoon. The weather was warm and overcast even the day before. But this evening with rain, it suddenly felt like early fall. The sound and sight of the falling rains could be felt inside the room through the windows. Momena sat on the bed looking out to half wet betel nut trees outside near the window. She was wondering where she came to be and where she might end up with here in this strange, new, unfamiliar city. She knew nothing about this big metropolis as she had spent most of her young life in the rural areas of the villages of Harashpur and Montala. She was aware that people of this household were her close relatives, yet socially she felt like a stranger here. The one closest relative of hers in this household was Kabil with whom she once dreamt of a life together. Yet she had not seen him once since her arrival here. She knew that he had been deeply involved in his political responsibilities. She considered him very much as her real family guardian even as a cousin. She also knew that he had in his heart a genuine interest in her future well-being. But Rokshana had recently been able to move Momena away from Kabil's mind perhaps by the wealth and position of her parents. Momena thought she should never again expect to reclaim this lost romantic idol of hers. She got used to the reality and had agreed to marry Andaleeb as a second choice for a future husband.

Yet Momena got the impression so far that Kabil was somewhat indifferent about his relationship with Rokshana because of the way Rokshana talked to her mother about Kabil since Momena's arrival at her house. Momena felt a sense of low tide in Rokshana's eagerness toward Kabil and about her possible marriage to him in the future. She was not quite clear about Rokshana's feelings about Andaleeb and Momena's hoped-for marriage soon. Momena understood that although Kabil was said to have really and truly loved Rokshana, yet her parents' wealth and even her love didn't mean very much to him when it came to his political fame throughout the country and his love and passion for his country. Momena figured that Kabil's life would not be a failure even if Rokshana did not marry him. His life would be rewarded with his hoped-for political fame and power. In those circumstances, perhaps the relationship and even sexual attraction to Rokshana would probably not play too big a role.

The worst thing was that this change in Kabil's attitude was somehow clearly exposed to Rokshana which made her life almost unbearable as of then. Moreover, just in front of Rokshana's eyes, the wedding of the girl who Kabil's mother had dreamt of as Kabil's future wife was to be held within the following few days with Andaleeb who had once dearly loved Rokshana and whom Rokshana's parents also once wanted her to marry. And this was all happening according to then changed wish and initiative of her own mother. And her mother was doing this because Rokshana had rejected Andaleeb once she had met Kabil and fell in love with him. This whole thing was all too confusing, complicated, and made life miserable for Rokshana. Momena fully understood the mental burden and sadness this situation had been imposed on Rokshana's mind. She turned her eyes from the scenery outside of falling rain and focused her attention on Rokshana. Rokshana by that time had changed her Urdu-culture day outfit of salwar kameez and was wearing a loose-fitting, soft silk nightdress. She looked beautiful in that silk dress. Her tall body was flawless in proportion to her body parts. Momena felt a bit of a letdown with Rokshana's inviting, youthful and luscious body appeal. Right at that moment, Rokshana asked Momena,

"Momi, do you want to change your daytime outfit of saree with something more comfortable for sleeping?"

"Do you think we sleep in silk nighty as you do?" Momena replied.

"If you want to wear silk nighty, there's another one of mine, washed and pressed in the closet. You can wear that and go to sleep," Rokshana said.

"No need for silk nighty. I feel comfortable sleeping in my saree. You look beautiful though in that nighty, sister! You're so pretty."

"Don't cast your evil eyes on me, you jealous girl. I'm turning the lights off right now. Oh my God, this girl came to swallow my cousin Andaleeb and now she casts her evil eyes of jealousy on me as well," Rokshana said teasingly.

She then turned the light off, pulled Momi next to her inside the comforter and they tickled each other for a while. At one point, Rokshana started the conversation again.

"Did you ever look at your body and appearance in the mirror or in the dug water well at our Montala village house compound?"

Momena was startled a bit and asked, "Why, sister?"

"Tell me first, if you ever did?"

"Yes, I often see myself in the mirror or at the well water deep down. So, what's in it? Why do you ask?"

"You're very beautiful, Momi. I'm nothing compared to your physical beauty. You got the look of my aunty—Kabil's mother. I've never seen such beautiful eyes as yours. I might be a bit taller than you are. But your body form is incomparable. My cousin Andaleeb fell in love with you for nothing, you think?"

"You are exaggerating a little, sister Rokhi," Momi commented shyly.

"Not really. You were born with all the stolen beauty of my aunty Zakia. It's for that she once wanted her son Kabil to marry you."

Momena was quite surprised and speechless hearing what Rokshana had just disclosed. She hid her face under the blanket. Seeing her quiet, Rokhi asked again, "Hey, Momi! Why are you so quiet suddenly?"

"How did you come to know all these, sister? Why are you telling me all those old things? You know they're all irrelevant now."

"Who says they're irrelevant? They're relevant if you think they are.

"I'm afraid, sister Rokhi. I'm a simple village girl. I am not that much educated like you are. The one you mentioned—Kabil—wants to marry you, not me anymore, if he ever did at all. He's highly educated and famous for his political activities throughout the country. I've heard and seen that you also love him dearly. Besides, I'm not qualified for him. Now, one good man—your cousin Andaleeb has fallen in love with me, maybe out of his kindness. He wants to marry me and our wedding is supposed to take place shortly in this very house of yours. If you raise all those earlier things now, maybe they'll mean trouble for me. What will you gain out of that? I'm not an obstacle in your way, sister."

Rokshana laughed aloud and said, "Just think that I'm interested in marrying a man whom you once dreamt of marrying from your childhood years. And you are about to marry a man who once loved me dearly and wanted wholeheartedly to marry me. Then, don't you think we need to have some sort of understanding between you and me?"

"What understanding, sister? I'm a girl who has been defeated in the matter of love. My aunty Zakia taught me not to pursue the so-called golden deer—the impossible or unlikely—at best. She had told me that you loved Kabil very much. She cried over the fact that she could not keep her earlier promise to me and my guardians at Harashpur village. She also made me promise that I should never be jealous of your fortune and curse Kabil. She taught me to accept the reality in life under different circumstances. I parted with my childhood dream of life with your Kabil though it had hurt my young heart a great deal at that time. Now, after so many years, I came to this place with the hope of marrying your cousin Andaleeb. Please do not confuse my little brain by raising all those things of the past. I love your cousin and I think he loves me as well."

"Okay, Momi! How do you know that Andaleeb once loved and wanted to marry me?"

"I know because Andaleeb told me himself."

"Don't you doubt Andaleeb? If I give him some signal today, he may leave you in midstream and come back to my feet to beg for my hand in marriage."

"I don't think that you'll be able to do that at this stage. Andaleeb promised me in the name of God, and I trust him."

"You want to try it out?" Rokhi asked with a challenge in her tone.

"No, sister. I'm not in a position to win in any kind of challenge with you. I beg of you. Please do not try to prove anything related to my luck right now. You got one of the most politically famous men in the country. Why are you jealous of a poor girl like me? I'm soon to be married to Andaleeb, and I'm grateful to you and your mother for that. What would you gain by putting me in trouble? I beg your forgiveness if I have been disrespectful to you in any way. But please do not ruin my hopes and aspirations this time as well."

Rokshana laughed aloud again and said, "Listen, Momi, I just tested you a bit. I thought you might still have some hopes and longing for Kabil. Even if you have, you are not to blame for that. Now I see that the non–Bengali Andaleeb has completely won your heart. I've no conflict with you. I'd rather be sure and certain by helping you marry Andaleeb. Now, go and sleep with no worry in your little head. Don't have a nightmare out of fear of what I had said."

ROKSHANA WAS USUALLY THE first one in this household to wake up early in the morning. She got the habit from her father who used to do his morning walk holding tiny Rokshana in his arms until at least the hawker delivered the daily morning newspapers. Rokshana would then play in the front-yard garden chasing the early flocks of butterflies when her father would sit in the verandah reading the newspapers. She kept the habit of walking in the early morning at their garden even after her father's death.

This morning as usual, Rokshana woke up early and noticed that Momena was fast asleep. Usually, the village girls wake up early in the morning. Momi possibly couldn't sleep well last night because of the nature of things they had discussed before going to sleep. Rokshana felt pity for Momena. She didn't want to wake Momi up. She thought Momi might be extraordinarily beautiful, but intellectually she was a fool. She was really scared of Rokshana's probing last night about her relationship with Kabil earlier and then with Andaleeb. Rokshana thought, if Momena were smart, she could have scared Rokshana herself instead. Last night, Momena was trembling in fear when she came to know that Rokshana had been aware of Kabil's mother's dream of Kabil's future marriage with her. She repeatedly told Rokshana that those were things of the past and were irrelevant in the current changed circumstances. Yet everybody knew that Kabil consistently felt an obligation for Momena. *Was it only Kabil's sense of duty because of his earlier promise to his mother, or there was something more to it?* Rokshana wondered. She was trying to find more about it last night from Momena. But Momi did not volunteer any secrets in that regard. She was totally devoted to Andaleeb from her heart. Rokshana thought it was because Momena had no other choice.

Rokshana loved Kabil from the bottom of her heart. Her clear and open announcement to that effect since long in this household swayed her parents as well as the others, including Andaleeb. Rokshana's father Ahmed Alam had hoped that as Rokshana's once- thought- of future husband, Andaleeb would one day take care of his properties and businesses. Kabil's mother, on the other hand, had the dream that Kabil one day would marry her niece Momena who would help restore her family's past fame and reputation in their locality which had taken a hit when Alam had married an Urdu-speaking refugee settler's daughter Rania, leading to his elder brother Kamal severing all family relations with Alam. Both Alam and Zakia had their own respective, intended choice of spouses for their respective child in line with their respective interests and positions. But on the day that Rokshana saw Kabil walking into her family and introducing himself to his long-estranged uncle and his family, she thought he was her closest relative in this country other than her father. She took his appearance as a way of connecting her roots in this country beyond her father and establish herself as a Bengali by birth and kinship. She wanted Kabil in her life forever. All other issues and considerations were insignificant to her lifelong burning desire to prove herself as a Bengali in this land. Her parents' wish and Kabil's mother's disappointed silence could not stand in the way of Rokshana's youthful joy with Kabil. Kabil's early reciprocation of her young sentiments reinforced her love and devotion to him. She thought neither her parents nor Kabil's mother perhaps wanted to object to the way she and Kabil were interacting as two young love birds. Otherwise, Kabil's mother could have said that her earlier promise and dream of bringing her niece Momena to her house and groom her as Kabil's future wife was to her more important than Kabil's love affair with the daughter of her estranged brother-in-law Alam. Or perhaps Zakia was afraid that if she did not accept Kabil's love for Rokshana, she would probably lose Kabil from her life, just the same way her husband Kamal had lost his younger brother Alam from his life when the latter married Rania.

Rokshana was walking barefoot on the dew-covered, well-mowed grass of their front lawn inside their house compound. She was still wearing her silk nighty. She felt a bit cooler in the light breeze of the pre-winter morning. She was also concerned that someone from the upper floors of their neighboring houses might be watching her in her nighty. After a while, she walked up to the verandah and put on a wrapping shawl around her body. As soon as she had put back her sandals, the bell at the front gate rang. She thought it was the usual newspaper hawker. But then she heard Kabil calling out their cook Halim from the other side of the gate. Rokshana hurried to the gate and opened it from inside. She noticed Kabil was standing there right in front of her.

"What's the matter? Where's Uncle Halim? Why are you here early this morning in your nighty in this cool weather?" Kabil asked.

"I woke up just a few minutes ago and was taking a walk in the lawn."

Kabil came inside and closed the gate behind him and said, "I couldn't sleep well last night and have a headache now. Can you ask Uncle Halim to make some tea for me, please?"

"No need to wake up Uncle Halim at this early hour. I'd go myself and make tea for you. You go to your room and rest. I'd be there soon with your tea."

As Rokshana was about to leave for the kitchen, the bell at the front gate rang again. This time Kabil went and opened the gate when the hawker gave him two newspapers one in English and one in Bengali, Kabil handed the Bengali newspaper to Rokshana and the two of them sat down on two rattan round stools (Mora) in the verandah to read the newspapers.

"I see that the *Daily Observer* has published my speech of last evening in full," Kabil remarked.

"Look! the Bengali *Daily Ittefaq* also published the speech with your picture as well," Rokshana added. She then handed the *Ittefaq* to Kabil and walked toward the kitchen to make tea for them.

Right at that time, Momena appeared at the scene, and seeing Kabil sitting there, she bent down and paid respect to Kabil in the traditional way of touching his feet lightly with her hand.

"How are you, brother Kabil?" she asked respectfully.

"Oh, Momi! When did Aunty Rania and you come from Montala?" Kabil asked with a pleasant surprise.

"Yesterday," Momi replied.

"How have you been, Momi? How do you like Dhaka from what you have seen of it in one day?"

"Dhaka looks very unfamiliar, especially when you were not home yesterday."

"Momi, I can't stay home always these days. But brother Andaleeb is here and I'm sure he will take good care of you."

"He's there, of course. But for some reason, I don't feel scared when I see you around. That's perhaps because I know you from my childhood."

Kabil laughed and said, "Poor girl! Brother Andaleeb loves you a lot. You love him as well. There's nothing for you to be afraid of. We, rather Aunty Rania is going to arrange for your marriage with Andaleeb soon. You have spent your life so far in rural villages. From now on, you will be living in Dhaka in your future husband's own house. I should be rather jealous looking at your face."

As he was talking, he noticed, as if with wonderment, the extraordinary beauty and perfect, proportionate figure of Momena who had just woken up from bed and was still in her untidy saree. She looked stunningly beautiful and lustrous. Her hair almost touched her buttocks below her waistline. She looked physically very fit. He had already been familiar with her beautiful eyes which were like two large butterflies competing with each other for their restlessness. At the same time, her eyes were indicators of simplicity and inquisitiveness.

Kabil couldn't, as neither any other man could, resist admiring such beauty.

"You look very beautiful, Momi! I didn't realize before that you're so beautiful. Perhaps you became more beautiful because you are so happy to be married to Andaleeb soon."

"Maybe so. But what would you have done if you had realized it earlier?"

Kabil was startled at the nature of Momena's sudden, unexpected question. He couldn't figure out momentarily what to say in response. In the middle of his nervousness, he blurted out, "Then I would have arranged your marriage with a real-life prince."

"No prince ever falls in love with a poor but beautiful village girl, brother Kabil. Those are just fairy-tale stories told by grandmothers to the little village girls."

With that she hurriedly left Kabil's presence in the verandah and ran toward Rokshana's bedroom. Rokshana, while carrying tea cup on a tray to Kabil in the verandah, noticed Momena leaving in a hurry with tears running down her cheeks. She was a bit surprised and asked Kabil, "What is the matter? Why did she leave in such a hurry?"

Instantly, Kabil decided to divert the subject of his conversation with Momi and replied to Rokshana's question by saying, "Oh, nothing! I raised the question of her wedding, she blushed and ran away."

Rokshana understood that Kabil was trying to hide the real reason for Momi's hurried exit. She wondered if Momi had told Kabil what the two of them had talked about the night before. She felt sad and regretted that she had probed Momi the night before about her feelings for Kabil. If Momena had told Kabil about those things, how would Kabil take it? She handed the cup of tea to Kabil and asked, "How about fixing the date of the wedding between Momi and Andaleeb this coming Friday? Mother will be able to arrange everything by then. We'll also help her."

"Whatever Aunty decides is okay with me."

"Mother wanted to settle our wedding also on the same day. I thought about your uncertainties and difficulties with your political activities, took all faults on myself, and was able to save you from trouble with her for the time-being."

"But, Rokhi! I didn't ask you to take all faults on yourself and pour cold water on Aunty's wish? I just told you that my future was uncertain voluntarily or involuntarily. I thought I shouldn't drag you in my uncertain future simply because we fell in love with each other. If I do drag you in, then you'll blame me and question my love day in day out in the future. You may or may not know that I could be arrested again even tonight. Sheikh Mujib called as soon as I returned to Dhaka and asked me to be ready for possible arrest. You tell me now should I entangle you in any kind of formalized relationship in these uncertain times in my life?"

"If that is so, then why are you blaming me again? I have already convinced my mother to postpone any formal arrangement between you and me."

"Yes, you convinced her alright. But I didn't ask you to tell her an unacceptable lie for me and thus break her heart by postponing our wedding. I said I would agree with aunty's proposal and wish."

"You agree, but I don't. This is exactly what I told my mother. I told her that I needed more time to think things over thoroughly."

"You probably can't realize how deeply hurt she must have felt by what you had told her. Why did you have to tell her lies like that? Why didn't you tell her that you are asking her to postpone our wedding because of my political uncertainty and other difficulties? That would have at least kept the hopes in her heart. But instead, what you have told her would make her think that her own daughter was not sure about her marrying Kabil," Kabil said that very angrily and got up from the rattan stool he was sitting on.

Rokshana kept her head down for a few minutes and then said while biting her nail, "You may be angry with me. But what I told my mom wasn't all lies. I, myself, at this stage am not mentally prepared for marriage. Why should I blame your politics only? All these days, we did not take into consideration the matter of businesses that my late father had left behind. Actually, our assets and businesses are worth more than I had thought. They're also not well looked after. I'm determined to streamline them. Even though Andaleeb is there, it is not possible to look after everything by him alone. Moreover, I'm the owner of my father's properties and other businesses. I need to gain skill, experience, and control over how they're managed. There was a time when I used to think that you and I will do the management together. But you'll agree that it will not be possible on your part to do that, at least not for now. In these circumstances, what I told my mother came out from my heart. I didn't lie to her on your behalf for your political difficulties."

Kabil was stunned at what Rokshana had just said and tried to look at Rokshana's face, but she turned her face down in such a way that he couldn't see it. He couldn't exactly figure out Rokshana's facial reactions in raising suddenly all those feelings and concerns of hers. He rather foolishly said, "But you didn't tell me all those things ever before. I used to think that I had for so long deprived Aunty of the joy of seeing us two married and seeing me put that expensive diamond ring that she had bought for the occasion on your finger. Now, I see you yourself aren't a hundred percent sure of us getting married at all."

"Tell me why you're blaming me again. Did I tell you that I am not willing to marry you or that I had changed my mind? You should know that I might also need some time to think the whole matter over, just as you need some time yourself. Because of that, should you have any doubt about my love for you? I don't need that much punishment, cousin Kabil."

Having said all that, Rokshana raised her head and noticed that Kabil had already left the verandah. She took the empty teacup in her hand and walked inside the house.

EARLY THAT EVENING, ANDALEEB came to the house and asked Rania, "Aunty, may I take Momena out for her to see my house? If you permit, I'll also like to take her to the market and then maybe go to see a movie."

Kabil, Rokshana, and Momi were all present there when Andy asked Rania the question. Rania smiled a bit and said, "Why not? Nothing wrong in just going out and about for a while! Momi didn't have a chance to go out and see the city since she had come to our house. What do you say, Kabil?"

"You don't need my permission for that, Momi. If it's okay with Aunty, you go ahead and I'll have no objection to it. Go get dressed and enjoy the sights and sounds of the big city."

Rokshana looked at shy and blushing Momena and said, "Come, Momi! I'll help you put your makeup etcetera. When you come back from the market, just don't forget to bring some paan (digestive natural leaf traditionally taken after dinner) with sweet betel nut for me."

Shy and blushing, Momi got up from the evening tea session and headed for Rokhi's and now their shared bedroom. Rokshana and Andy followed her closely.

Inside the bedroom, Rokhi asked, "Shall I dress her in saree or salwar kameez, cousin Andy?"

"As you like, Rokhi. What shall I say?"

"Your soon-to-be-bride. Whatever you prefer, I'll dress her in that today."

"First, let the wedding take place, then ask me about my liking. Today, let Momi decide whatever she wants to wear. What do you say, Momi?"

"I'll wear saree, sister Rokhi. And tell your cousin to go outside the bedroom while I get dressed."

Andy felt embarrassed and said, "That's right. I shouldn't be here while Momi gets dressed. Okay, I'm going to wait in the sitting room."

RANIA AND KABIL WERE still in the evening session of sipping tea. They were quietly discussing the preparations for Andy and Momena's forthcoming wedding. Rania said, "Even though Momi's uncles left everything about her wedding to me, you, Kabil, are the real guardian of Momi. As such, you tell us what my nephew Andaleeb will need to give Momi in the way of her wedding ornaments and other jewelry. You'll also have to consider the matter of Andy's affordability."

"Aunty! You needn't ask me anything on that matter. Whatever you decide in that regard, Momi, her parental uncles, and I will accept that without any question. Momi is lucky to have your patronage. Because of you, she will hopefully have a good husband and a happy family. If my mother were alive today, she would have prayed to God for your well-being. My mother didn't get what she had wanted for Momi. I admit it's perhaps because of me, my mother's wish did not come true. You're arranging for the marriage of her orphan niece with your own nephew. We should all be happy and thankful to you for that."

Before Kabil could finish, Rokhi and Momi entered the sitting room in front of Rania and Kabil. Kabil was suddenly thrilled to look at Momi—all dressed up with good makeup. He said without even thinking, "Wow! Momi looks like a princess."

Rania was also quite impressed with the physical beauty of the soon-to-be bride of her orphaned nephew Andaleeb.

Rokhi turned to Kabil and said, "Momi got the physical beauty of my late aunty Syeda Zakia Banu."

Hearing that Kabil lowered his gaze on the floor.

Andy then suggested to Momi, "Let's go, Momi! It's getting late."

Andy hired a man-pulled rickshaw. He and Momi sat on it next to each other. Once the rickshaw started moving, he said to Momi, "I want to show you my house first. Then from there, we'll go to the market in Sadarghat and Islampur, buy somethings for you and then maybe go to Mukul Cinema Hall to see a movie. Afterward, we'll have dinner at a restaurant in Gulistan area. I'll then take you back to Aunty's house at Bonogram Lane. By that time, you'll have seen almost one-third of Dhaka City."

Andaleeb then directed the rickshaw puller to take them to his house in Narinda area of Dhaka. Andy pulled the hood of the rickshaw overhead. Seeing the slight uneasiness of Momi, he tried to keep a little distance from her body. As intelligent as Momi was, she realized Andy's efforts to keep a physical distance between them. She said, "I don't have any contagious disease. You need not have to sit so far away from me."

Andy felt at ease and came closer to her and said, "I don't see today a human being in Dhaka more fortunate than I am."

"Is that so? Can't you see anybody around near you?" she asked rather teasingly.

Andy quickly corrected his earlier comment and said, "No, there's another one who seems to be just as happy and lucky as I am, and that one is sitting right next to me."

"Why do you refer to me as a lucky one? You know that there's hardly any girl as unlucky as I am in this world."

"Don't you say that, Momi! Tell me truly, are you enjoying this evening with me?"

Momi kept silent. Seeing that, Andy said again, "If you do not respond, I'll ask the rickshaw puller to turn back to Aunty's house."

"If I tell you the truth, you'll be angry with me," Momi said hesitantly.

"Even so, I want to hear from your mouth what is going on in your mind."

"I'm afraid."

"Are you afraid of me?"

"Cousin! I've never set foot outside the house with a strange man, not even with my own male relatives. I never went out like this. Not even cousin Kabil ever took me alone anywhere outside the house. You know that women from our family are not allowed to go out alone with a man. If my Zakia aunty, who raised and taught me the rules and manners of life for women in our family were alive today, I wouldn't probably dare go out like this with you."

In response, Andy said, "I understand your situation, Momi. I'm aware of the conservative reputation and high tradition of your family. Kabil told me everything about your family. Don't worry, I'm your well-wisher just like Kabil who is your most trustworthy relative and your real guardian."

"You aren't just my well-wisher. You are going to be more close relative to me than that. You're going to be my husband soon. I just told you of my fear and my conscience. Please do not fault me for that. I do not have, right now, a closer man than you to whom I can express my feelings without any fear and reservation."

"If you think that way, then there's nothing for you to be afraid of. I'll not do anything before our marriage that will bring dishonor to you. But I'll like to remind you that your aunty Zakia Banu did not disapprove of the way that Kabil and Rokshana had been interacting with each other," Andy said that in the way of slight teasing, hoping that it might lessen Momi's regret, if there was any, in coming out with him.

Momi quickly replied, as if in defense of her late aunty, Zakia's high moral standard, "Yes, my aunty didn't object to Kabil and Rokshana's free and liberal interactions, but she definitely did not like it. She once told me with great regret that the day she had seen Kabil and Rokhi coming in each other's arms to her house at Montala village, she had realized that she could not exert family's moral standards of boys not mixing freely with girls on Kabil and Rokshana. She was afraid that if she tried to do so, she might have lost Kabil from her life the same way that her husband had lost his brother Ahmed Alam when the latter had married Aunty Rania. She didn't want to go through the pains of losing in life her only son Kabil because of his love for Rokhi."

Andy realized that his raising the subject of Kabil and Rokshana's love and free mixing was not appropriate at that time on his part. But he was surprised knowing some new facts about Zakia not having unconditionally and wholeheartedly approved, but for a genuine concern, the relationship between Kabil and Rokhi. He came to know that Zakia's dream was to groom Momi as a future wife of Kabil. Andy remembered that it was Rokhi, who after having met Kabil for the first time in her life in their house in Dhaka, wanted him in her life to prove her Bengali roots. Subsequently, Rokhi had rejected Andaleeb's expressed interest in marrying Rokhi when she grew up. She had ignored the plans and hopes of her father Alam to marry her off to Andaleeb who he had thought would be capable of managing his properties and businesses beyond him as Rokhi's future husband. Rokhi also dashed the hopes of Kabil's mother Zakia to have her niece Momi as Kabil's future wife. However, earlier today, he had noticed something different in Rokhi's attitude. Her eagerness to prove her Bengali heritage had been replaced by her keenness to become a successful businesswoman, learning and controlling her father's left-behind properties and businesses.

By that time, their rickshaw arrived at Narinda area and stopped in front of Andaleeb's house at Basu Bazar Lane. Andy's house was a bungalow, except there was a small room on the roof. It was an old house with cement plastered on outside walls recently. Momi realized that Andy had kept the house in good shape. As she climbed down from the rickshaw, she asked, "Is there no other guardian in the house other than you?

"For some years now, I had brought in here my maternal grandmother from Bhopal in India. She now desperately wants to go back. She doesn't have anyone there to look after her. But she wants to be buried there next to her husband's grave. So far, I have persuaded her to stay with me here with the hope that pretty soon she would be able to see her granddaughter-in-law here. Tonight, she'll be happy to see you here."

"Does she do the cooking for you?"

"Oh! No, I have a female domestic help who does the cooking and cleaning for us. Her name is Jubi. She's an orphan, refugee here from Patna in India."

Once inside the house, Andaleeb introduced Jubi to Momena. Jubi greeted Momi and then took her to another room. Andy also followed them. Inside that room, an elegant-looking, very fair-complexioned elderly lady was sitting on an ornamental postal bed made with milk-white bed sheets and colorful pillows with handiwork done on the pillow covers. She had a thick, full head of gray hair hanging loosely behind her back. She was wearing typical Bihari-style salwar kameez unlike pure-white saree traditionally worn by Bengali widows. The lady turned her eyes toward the door and asked in Urdu, "Who's there?" as she pulled the scarf over her head.

Andy stepped forward and said, "Grandma, Momi has come to meet you—Momi, Kabil's sister."

The elderly lady took out her eyeglasses from its case and put them on. She then clearly saw Momi's face—all done with full makeup. Momi paid respect to the old lady in the traditional South Asian way, stood politely in front of her, and said, "Grandma, I came to pay respect to you. Please pray to God for me."

"Wow! What a pleasant surprise! My competitor for my grandson's love has finally come," the lady replied. She then jumped out of bed and hugged Momi with loud laughter. She held Momi against her own body with love and affection for a while. She then released Momi from her embrace, took Momi's chin on her hand, and said, "Wow! Very beautiful future wife of my grandson. Hey, Andy! Where did you get such a beautiful girl in this land with lots of water?"

"Grandma! Don't be too profuse about her physical beauty and let that go into her head. After our wedding, you would hardly wait to go back to India to sing ghazal (Urdu classical song) at the gravesite of my grandfather. And then, I'll have to put up with her pride of beauty here all by myself. Who will then help me to manage her temper?"

Hearing Andy's complaint, the old lady laughed aloud and said, "Young man! Don't you have confidence in your masculinity? Be courageous, boy."

At that everybody including Jubi laughed aloud.

AT AROUND 8:00 P.M., Kabil was in his bedroom. He was turning the pages of a recently published book written by Reginald Debrer—a noted Latin American revolutionary. At one point, their cook Halim appeared at the door and said, "Someone is on the phone for you."

Kabil closed the book and walked to Rania's room where the telephone used to be kept since Rania's husband Ahmed Alam had been alive. Kabil picked up the receiver and said, "Hello!"

A voice on the other end responded, "I'm calling from Road No. 32 at Dhanmondi (Sheikh Mujib's private residence). The leader wants to talk to you."

By that time Mujib picked up the telephone himself on the other end and said, "Kabil?"

"Yes, leader, it's Kabil here. Is there any instruction for me, leader?" he asked.

"Did you finish your supper, Kabil?"

"No, leader, not yet."

"Then come over to my house. You will have supper with me here. I need to discuss something confidential with you. Be careful on your way. Try to avoid your student friends as you enter our house. Come upstairs straight. I have instructed my people downstairs to allow you unhindered to come to me directly."

"Yes, leader. I understood. I'll leave our home at Bonogram Lane right away."

As Kabil put down the receiver, Rania asked, "Who was on the other end of the phone, Kabil?"

"Our leader Sheikh Mujib."

"Are you going to the dinner table? If so, wait a few minutes. Rokhi went to Anjuman's house after she had seen Andy and Momi off to the market in the evening. She'll probably be back soon."

I know, Aunty. Rokhi had told me before she left. I'm not going to eat supper at home tonight, Aunty. Sheikh Mujib had just asked me to have supper with him tonight at his house. He wants to discuss something important and confidential with me alone. It could be that he wants to know the concerns and positions of the student leaders regarding some political decisions." Kabil then headed for the door. Rania at that point signaled Kabil to wait for a moment.

"Yes, Aunty. Do you want to tell me something?"

"Come here and sit next to me for a moment."

Kabil sat on the side of the bed next to Rania.

"Since you came out of jail, I didn't have a chance to take a closer look at you. You're the one who didn't allow me to do that. You have been so busy with your political activities. I had no idea where you have been eating, sleeping, or what you have been doing day and night. When you were younger and came to live with us in this house, you used to spend a lot of time with your books. Your uncle, my husband Alam, and I used to peek at your room quietly, and we used to feel so proud of you seeing you busy studying your books. Your late father had cut off all family connections with his brother Alam because he had married me—a refugee-settler girl from India. I used to think that I would do all I could so that you could get a proper education, perhaps go back to your ancestral home, and restore the old reputation of your grandfather's family. I used to think that by helping you get a good education, I would earn your parents' forgiveness for causing their heartache by marrying your uncle—the last hope for the restoration of their family's old reputation. Now both your parents and your uncle are no longer with us in this world. But at least your mother and your uncle came to know before their death that you are a talented student, well on your way to complete your university education. I'm also happy to notice that you're in love with my only daughter Rokhi and that one day you two will get married, have a family, and take care of our properties and businesses. The broken family ties between your parents and your uncle will be restored."

Having recounted all those old memories, Rania's voice almost got choked. Kabil quietly took his aunty Rania's hand in his own in a way of comforting her.

"I understand your disappointment, Aunty. I wouldn't like to see your hopes and aspirations unfulfilled. But if you had a son like me, you would give him the chance to become an influential university student leader like I am. Then, he would also like to see the remedy of all the discriminations and exploitation of this province by the vested interest groups of West Pakistan."

"I understand that and feel proud of your reputation throughout the country as a top-ranking university student leader. I also fully support the causes of your collective struggle. But I'm worried about your safety and security. You're our only son. Sheikh Mujib is a great leader of Pakistan. Politics is for great people like him. Nobody would dare harm them. Temporary imprisonment only makes them more popular among the masses. But worrying about your own safety, security, and future make me spend sleepless nights."

Kabil tried to lighten the situation with a slight smile and said, "You don't have to worry about anything, Aunty. I'll not do anything that will cause mental stress on you and Rokhi. So long as I'm a student leader, how can I stay away from the students' struggle against the oppression of East Pakistan?"

"Then, why do all the young people around here talk about you alone? They say you are the leader of the movement against Pakistan. Do you all want to break up Pakistan which was created after such oppression of Muslims in the subcontinent with so much struggle and sacrifice by great leaders including Sheikh Mujib."

"Aunty, I know the people who tell you all the bad things about me. They're your non-Bengali friends and relatives. In reality, their exploitation and oppression of the majority of the people of Pakistan—the Bengalis—are the real reasons for any possible future breakup of Pakistan," Kabil said that with a great deal of emotions. He then got up to leave.

"Are you going out now?" Rania asked.
"I shall come back soon after eating supper with the leader."

"Sheikh Mujib likes you so much. Tell him on my behalf that he is the leader of all of us. Our appeal is for him not to do anything that will end up breaking the solidarity of Pakistan. If that happens, where shall we all refugee settlers go?"

Kabil never noticed this sense of insecurity in Rania's expressions. To cheer her up, he said, "You worry too much for nothing, Aunty." With that, he left the house.

NISAR, ANJU, AND ROKHI were chatting and laughing while the three of them were standing on the sidewalk outside the front boundary wall of Anju's parents' house under the shade of two overhanging branches of a large Kamini flower tree from inside their house compound. Nisar and Anju came out of the house to see off Rokhi who spent some time in the afternoon in their house. Anju started the conversation, "Rokhi! Tell Kabil that I was about to faint by the kind of courage his budding philosopher friend Nisar had shown today. Nisar told my parents today that he would like to beg them for their daughter's hand in marriage. He told them without any hesitation that he loved me and that he would not be able to live without me in his life. He promised them that he wouldn't stand in the way of my involvement in the political activities of the country and that I could do whatever I want in politics after our marriage. He also promised them that he would never cause any hurt or sadness to me for even a moment and that he would love me so long as he will have lived. It's a pity, Rokhi, if I had known that he would make a proposal in those words to his future parents-in-law, I'd have gone outside before that."

"Oh! I get it, you coached Nisar on how to present the proposal to your parents, and now after he has done it, you pretend to be embarrassed by his words. But I'm very pleased that Nisar proposed directly to your parents and convinced them and obtained their consent for you two to be married. Really Nisar! Anju may think that you are a philosopher-type man, but you're the most broad-minded and courageous man among our circle of friends. The sense and knowledge in real life that you have shown today is living proof of that, and it's wonderful. Nobody else in our girlfriends' group was lucky enough so far to have met a man like you. And congratulations to both of you. May you have a happy and long conjugal life together."

Both Nisar and Anju could sense the inner pain that Rokhi felt in her heart as she expressed those words. To make Rokhi feel easy, Anju suggested, "Okay, Rokhi, let's leave the praise for the budding philosopher for now. Let me go inside and see how my parents are celebrating the courage of their soon-to-be son-in-law. Nisar will walk you himself this evening to your house."

With that Anju walked inside their compound while Nisar and Rokhi headed for her house.

THAT EVENING, KABIL HAD supper with Sheikh Mujib and his close family at No. 32 Dhanmondi Road. After supper, Mujib called Kabil to his study to give him some instructions on Kabil's political assignment for the following few days. Mujib began by saying, "Listen, Kabil, you're my chief student spokesman to explain to the public the political, economic, and social aspects of our Party's Six Points Demand from the government. Nobody else, not even your other senior student leaders can better present and elaborate on the implications of our demand to the public as well as you can, especially to our large non-Bengali refugee-settler communities. I've, therefore, decided that you'll provide leadership to the large student and public protest march that has been called by our Party for tomorrow afternoon from the Shahid Minar. From there, the procession will march through different city roads and culminate at a large public meeting at Paltan Maidan in Gulistan area of the city. You'll address the meeting, explaining our Six Points Demand election manifesto to the public. I've discussed the matter with other senior student leaders, and they all agreed with my decision."

Kabil was a little embarrassed at this sudden expression of confidence in him by Sheikh Mujib, bypassing other senior student and political party leaders. He smiled a bit and looked up to Mujib for a few seconds. Mujib, at that point, asked him, "Do you want to say something to me, Kabil?"

Kabil suddenly remembered what his aunty Rania had told him to ask Mujib, shortly before Kabil left home earlier in the evening. He said to Mujib, "Yes, leader! Before I left home early this evening, my aunty Rania Alam had asked me to convey to you a message from her. She asked me to tell you on her behalf that you are the most popular leader of the majority of the people of East Pakistan—both Bengalis and non-Bengalis, including the refugee-immigrant settlers. Her request to you was that you do everything in your capacity to safeguard the political unity and integrity of Pakistan for which you yourself worked hard and contributed so much in your early political life. She was concerned about the safety and security of refugee-settler communities including her own if Pakistan is politically broken up into two countries. In that case, she's worried that she will have no other country to call her own. Her non-Bengali friends are telling her that the Six Points Demand that her nephew (Kabil) has been fighting for would break up Pakistan."

Mujib felt a bit flattered by what Kabil had just told him. He said, "I once met your uncle late Syed Ahmed Alam. I was told that he was an honest, successful Bengali businessman. I also heard that he had married a refuge-settler girl. Tell your aunty that I would do my best to safeguard the unity and integrity of Pakistan."

Then, a rather somber look fell on his face. He wondered why the Bihari wife of a wealthy, noted Bengali businessman like late Ahmed Alam still considered herself as a refugee immigrant in East Pakistan and did not consider this as her own country. *If that's the case then,* he thought, *his Party would have to do a better job of explaining the political and economic aspects of their Six Points Demand to the public, especially to this minority group. Otherwise, they wouldn't,* he thought, *support the Awami League and would refrain from voting for the Party.* He then said further to Kabil, "Tell your aunty that if, God forbid, Pakistan ever breaks up politically, it will not be because of actions by the Bengalis, rather by the stupid, arrogant, and unjust actions of West Pakistani political leaders, military generals, and other vested interest groups." He then shook hands with Kabil and saw him off.

Kabil came out from Mujib's house feeling rather relieved and empowered for his newly assigned duties by his leader for the following day. It was past ten o'clock at night. The flow of pedestrians had been reduced on the sidewalk. There were only a few sporadic vehicles plying on the road. Kabil looked around on the main road for an empty three-wheeled, motorized scooter to take him home. For a long time, Kabil couldn't find an empty scooter. He then started walking toward the rather busy New Market area where he thought he would find an empty scooter in front of the Balaka Cinema Hall. It was a moonlit night with a clear blue sky. It was as if the city was bathing in clear moonlight and he himself was swimming in its easy waves. He walked past a children's playground and was thinking about how he would play the lead role in the large student public protest march the following day called by his Party. He was dreaming about Sheikh Mujib himself introducing Kabil as one of the lead speakers at the planned public meeting at the Paltan Maidan the following day after the protest march through the streets of Dhaka.

In the middle of all these thoughts and excitement, Kabil didn't even realize when he had left the sidewalk and started walking on the relatively empty road. He was rather enjoying the walk while thinking about the exciting things to come in his political career the following day. A short distance past the playground, Kabil became aware of his surroundings and sensed that a scooter with loud muffler noise came out from a side lane and suddenly stopped in front of him, blocking his way forward. Before he realized what was happening, two middle-aged men came out from the scooter—one on each side—and stood there with Kabil standing in between them. Kabil was surprised and asked,

"Gentlemen, what's in your mind?"

"Not much, Mr. Kabil. We saw that you're going home walking alone at this hour after your meeting with Sheikh Mujib and thought that we'd give you a ride home in our scooter. You wouldn't get any other transport at this hour of the night. Come onboard our scooter. We're also going to nearby where you live," one of the two men concluded as the other man came around and stood very close to Kabil. Kabil instantly realized that these men were from the Government Intelligence Bureau. To keep them distracted and make them feel easy, he smiled a bit and said, "I see you are very kind gentlemen! But if you want to take me in your scooter, you got to have at least a warrant paper. Do you have one?"

The two men laughed loudly and Kabil pretended to join them. The other plain-clothed policeman stepped in front of Kabil and said with a slight smile, "No, Mr. Kabil. We don't have an arrest warrant. We do not want to arrest you either. We just want to have a private conversation with you at our branch office for an hour or so and then we'll let you go free. If you agree, we'll even give you a ride to your Bonogram Lane home in our office Jeep. Now, would you come to our scooter please?"

Having said that, the man got hold of Kabil's right arm and was about to pull him to their waiting scooter. Kabil momentarily looked at him and suddenly cast a hard blow with all his force right on the man's eyes. The man instantly fell on the road. The other man, before figuring out what had happened received a strong kick on his groin from the metal-tipped shoes that Kabil was wearing. He sat down on the road instantly as well with a moan and his hands on his groin. Kabil momentarily ran toward a side lane and disappeared. With severe pain in his eyes, the first man that Kabil hit with his blow, by that time took out a pistol from his pant pocket and aimed at the side lane. But he didn't have the energy to focus and pull the trigger. His hand slowly gave in and the pistol dropped on the road. As the moon went behind the waves of clouds, the lane became slightly darker. A night owl flew away from a lamp post with strange sounds as if it was giving witness to an unfortunate (or fortunate for Kabil) event on that lonely night.

LATE THAT EVENING, BOTH Rokhi and Momi were lying in bed side by side. They were talking about Momi's experience with Andaleeb early that evening in exploring the sights and sounds of the city. None of them could fall asleep--- each for their own reason. Rokhi was worried because Kabil had not returned home until then after his supper at Mujib's house. On top of that, her mother Rania was not feeling well early that evening and went to bed earlier than her usual time. Momena could not fall asleep because of her newfound deep feelings for Andaleeb. What a simple easy-going man God had provided for her to marry soon. She could hardly believe it, yet that was going to take place soon. She spent the whole evening trying to understand Andaleeb better. She could not remember the names of the roads and places that she had been to earlier that evening because all along she was thinking about Andy and how he had been always paying attention to her, making sure of her comforts, needs, and preferences. He was, as if, born as a butterfly glued to Momi's roselike face. Who could imagine that this man once begged for the attention and love of another woman—Rokhi—now lying in bed next to her, only to be rejected by Rokhi. The other evening, Rokhi took pride in her rejection of Andy's love for her and threatened Momi that she could at any time, even now, take Andy away from Momi. This evening, Momi felt more confident and was determined to tell Rokhi if she bothered Momi again about Andy, that with all her city girl's education, family wealth, and personal sophistication, she will not be able to snatch her beloved Andy from Momi's life. Rokhi might try to do that if she wanted to. Momi then turned toward Rokhi in their shared bed and said, "Hey, sister Rokhi! Who're you thinking about as you chew paan and sweet betel nut and lying on bed sleepless?"

"Poor jealous, Momi, you bring bad luck to others. If I tell you, you'll snatch him away from me," Rokhi replied.

"Oh! You think only you can play the game of snatching and counter snatching. Nobody else knows how to play that game. Is that what you think, Rokhi?"

Momi posed that question in such a way, it instantly reminded Rokhi the incident of that early morning when Momi left Kabil's presence in their verandah with tears in her eyes and ran past Rokhi as she was carrying tea tray for Kabil. Rokhi had asked Kabil what the matter was with Momi and why she had run away in a hurry with tears in her eyes. Kabil had surreptitiously told Rokhi what she thought was a white lie to hide the truth from Rokhi.

"Oh, Momi! It looks like you also by now have mastered how to play that game."

"If I say, I'm not playing any game. Rather, I found my old playing marble that I had lost earlier. It was within my touch to grab. But I couldn't see it. Tell me who isn't happy when a lost thing is found, sister Rokhi?"

Rokhi was stunned at what Momi had just said. She wondered if this village girl was not totally possessed this evening by some sort of evil spirit. She couldn't lie down any longer. She threw away the covering sheet she was under and sat up straight on the bed.

"What happened, Momi? Tell me frankly what you and Kabil were talking about that morning in the verandah before you left hurriedly with tears rolling down your cheeks? Get up and sit, you poor kid. I'll understand everything if I see your face."

Momi was made to sit up with an angry jolt by Rokhi. She instantly cooled down seeing the rough and fearless smile on Momi's face. She was momentarily lost for words. Only the reflections on the bedside mirror of the two extremely beautiful, luscious young women dressed in thin nightdress with competitive, mysterious looks in their faces persisted for a long while. Rokhi realized that the power of jealousy and competition was somehow in the full grasp of this young village girl. She also realized that if she bothered her too much now, it might be counterproductive and something undesirable might happen. She silently regretted having threatened Momi the other night.

"Listen, Momi, I never thought of you as my competitor. I'm sorry that I had treated you badly several nights ago. I did that because I wanted to find out if you still have some sadness in your heart for having lost Kabil to me. Trust me, sister, I do not have jealousy or competition for you and Andaleeb. I'm making all the arrangements myself for your marriage soon.

Now, sister, you tell me honestly what did Kabil say to you that morning in our verandah and what made you run by me with tears in your eyes. Please do not hide anything from me. Here, come and touch my heart and feel how badly my heart is throbbing to know what is going on, if anything, between you and Kabil."

Rokhi then pulled Momi's hand and placed it on her chest.

Just at that moment, the telephone rang on Rokhi's bedside night table. Rokhi picked up the receiver. It was Andy on the other end. He said, "Hello, Rokhi! Kabil is going to spend tonight with me here at my house. I'm calling so you and Aunty do not worry about him."

"Why is he going to stay with you, cousin Andy? Please tell me a little more about his situation."

"Kabil got the responsibility of leading the student public protest march tomorrow. Sheikh Mujib personally picked Kabil for this leadership role by passing over other senior student leaders. If Kabil sleeps tonight at your house, the police may arrest him to stop him from carrying out this important job tomorrow. That's the reason Kabil decided to spend the night at my house. Don't worry about him and there's no need for you to be in tension."

"There won't be any harm to him, I hope, will there be?"

"Look, Kabil is now Sheikh Mujib's most favored associate, and one of his top student spokespersons. Nobody would dare harm him. And listen, where's Kabil's dear sister now? Is she snoring heavily in her beauty sleep?"

"Are you talking about Momi?"

"Other than that, who's dearer to Kabil? All this evening, she could barely talk about anybody else. She could hardly concentrate on choosing the merchandise that I bought for her."

"Is that so?"

"Yes, Rokhi. I'll tell you all when I meet you face-to-face. You won't understand how difficult it is to go shopping with such a simple and beautiful girl."

"Aren't you happy, cousin, to be married soon to such a girl?"

"I'm grateful to God. I never dreamt that God would sanction such a golden girl as a wife for me."

Rokhi couldn't think of what to say in response. She held the telephone receiver silently and was softly swinging in her mental wave caused by Andy's restlessness for Momi.

THE FOLLOWING NIGHT, AT around 9:00 p.m., Andy came to Rokhi's house. He had a grave look in his face. He went straight to Rania's bedroom and closed the door behind him. Rokhi and Momi had just come to the dining table when they saw Andy walking into Rania's room. They looked at each other's eyes with the fear of something grave and serious. Rokhi pushed the empty dinner plate aside and said to Momi,

"Seems like Andaleeb has some bad news for us. You eat whatever you want. Otherwise, when you hear the sad news, you'll end up with an empty stomach all night."

"Don't scare me for nothing. Kabil had a public protest meeting this afternoon. He's not back home yet."

Rokhi didn't bother to respond to Momi. She just sat there looking toward the closed door of her mother's bedroom. Shortly afterward, the doorbell of the living room rang. Rokhi got up to open the door. Before she reached the door, their cook Halim already opened it, and Nisar ran in with the speed of a storm. He stood in front of Rokhi and asked, "Didn't you get the news?"

"Waiting to get it," Rokhi replied, pointing to her mother's closed bedroom door.

"Kabil has been arrested again."

"Before the public meeting?"

"No, in the middle of the meeting. As Kabil started his speech, the police barged in with baton charge to break up the meeting. Tear gas canisters started to fall on the speakers' stage as well. At that point, when Mujib asked the public to counter the baton charge, the mayhem started. With great efforts, we're able to escort Mujib to his car waiting nearby. It looked like Kabil was one of the targets of the police baton charge."

"Was he beaten badly?" Rokhi asked.

"When he was being escorted to the police car, he was holding his hands pressed on his head. There was blood on his clothes."

A COMPLEX, FOUR-SIDED LOVE STORY AND A CIVIL WAR

With Nisar's explanations, Rokhi stopped asking further questions and started walking quietly toward her bedroom. By that time, Andaleeb and Rania came out of her room and joined Nisar and Momi in the dining room. Rania pleaded with Nisar to go to Rokhi's room to bring her back to the dining table to see if he could convince her to eat something. Nisar went and came back with Rokhi shortly after, and they all sat around the dining table.

After a while, Andaleeb made an appeal to Rania, "Aunty! If you permit me, I can take Momi to my house tonight. Rokhi perhaps will feel better if she's left alone without any hindrance."

Hearing Andaleeb's suggestion, Momi intervened before Rania could reply to Andy.

"Please do not say unreasonable things at the wrong time. I don't want to go anywhere tonight leaving my sister Rokhi alone here. If you want, you can take me back to Montala tomorrow morning or the day after for a few days."

Rania couldn't figure out any reason for Momi's forceful reaction. She responded as she started walking back to her bedroom, "Since what I had wished and hoped for in the next few days is not going to happen any time soon, there's no reason for me to hold you back in Dhaka. You may as well go back to Montala until things get sorted out around here. Nobody knows when Kabil might be let out from the jail. When he does, someone will go to Montala to bring you back here."

At that point, Rokhi said, "Let me also go with Momi to Montala for a few days. We want to leave tomorrow. If I go with Momi, cousin Andy will not have to go, and he can help you look after all our businesses."

Everybody around the dining table was surprised at Rokhi's proposal. But nobody said anything. Only Rania stopped on the way to her bedroom, turned back, and said, "Nisar said that our son Kabil had been beaten up by the police who had taken him away in a police van. If he's seriously hurt, he may be sent to the hospital outside the jail for treatment. In this situation, it's not a good idea for Rokhi to go out of Dhaka. Even Momi can wait for a few days to assess Kabil's situation before she goes to our village home at Montala."

Rania meant as if that was her order to the two girls. She then went straight to her bedroom.

At around eleven that night, Rokhi moved the blanket covering her body in bed, pushed Momi, and asked, "Are you sleeping?"

"No."

"Why were you suddenly so angry with Andaleeb?"

"You tell me first why your cousin Andy doesn't have any discretion."

"Actually, Andy was concerned about my mental distress following the news of Kabil's injury and arrest. He wanted to take you to his house so that I have some space and time to be alone myself. He knows me from my childhood. He knows that I like to be alone when I'm under tension. I get angry when someone asks me the reason for my tension. Concerned about me, he wanted to take you to his house so I can be alone for a while. But you, poor little girl, got suddenly mad at him for his innocent suggestion."

"I did it to teach your cousin a lesson, sister Rokhi."

"But you never asked me how I felt about Kabil's injury and arrest by the police."

"You just said that you get angry if somebody asks you those kinds of questions."

"Oh yes, but you came to know of that because I just told you how I feel being questioned for my tensions. Before knowing that, you could have simply wanted to know how I had been feeling after hearing the sad news about Kabil."

"What do I have to know? I've seen everything with my own eyes. You have a lot of patience, sister Rokhi. You can wait for everything."

"You can't wait?"

"No, not at all."

"Because of Kabil's arrest, your planned wedding with Andy will likely be postponed for a few months. But rest assured, it's going to happen sooner rather than later."

"You speak like a fortune-teller. Can you foretell about our future?"

"I don't know about my own future, let alone other's. But I know yours, sister. Andy will not keep you hanging much longer because of Kabil's arrest, not even because of my mother's inconvenience. Andy is in love with you, sister. You haven't seen men in love. But I've seen a man in love in Andy."

"Andy once was in love with you, Rokhi. How did he look like at that time? Now that he's in love with me, did he change?"

Rokhi decided not to respond to Momi's question. She couldn't yet understand the reason for Momi to be suddenly so angry with Andy earlier in the evening. Neither did Momi ever disclose the reason why she had left Kabil's presence in the verandah that morning with tears rolling down her cheeks. Did she still wish that Kabil should have more respect and consideration for his mother's intention of having Momi as Kabil's future wife? Did she believe and was she trying to give hints to Rokhi that a man's liking and love for any woman were not permanent and were not worth waiting for a lifetime? In the game of love, whoever won whomsoever was a matter of fate, just as there was no rule and morality in the war.

Seeing Rokhi quiet for a while, Momi asked her again, "Hey, sister Rokhi, are you angry with me? I'm not feeling well. Please forgive me if I did something wrong to you."

"I'll never forgive you unless you answer my one question. Do you still deep in your heart wish to marry Kabil as you once hoped for when Aunty Zakia had chosen and promised you that one day she would welcome you to her home as Kabil's wife? Think for a moment that you have an opportunity to choose either Kabil or Andy and both are willing and available to you for marriage. Who would you choose in that situation?"

Momi at first couldn't figure out the reasons for Rokhi's sudden behavior like this. She thought Rokhi might have some ulterior motives behind asking her such strange questions at this critical time in both their lives. She turned to Rokhi with an angry look in her face and a perceived threat from Rokhi. She took Rokhi's probing as a challenge and asked her a counter-question, "Do you really want me to tell you the truth?"

"Yes, Momi, please tell me the truth without any fear or reservation."

"If you give me the choice, I'll choose that untrustworthy Kabil who I thought all my life would be my future husband as per the dream of his deceased mother—my beloved aunty. Why should I not choose Kabil? Why do men like me? I may not have as much education or wealth as you have. But what I have in my body is enough for any young man to have a desire for me. I have told you the truth, and now you can go to sleep. It's rather late." Momi then turned to the other side of the bed and tried to fall asleep.

RANIA WOKE UP EARLY the following morning. After finishing her early morning prayer, she sat down on a low rattan stool in front of the kitchen where Halim was making some paratha and cooking goat brain that everybody in the house liked to eat with paratha. Halim suggested to Rania, "You didn't eat supper last night. Shall I serve you paratha with some goat brain? Rokhi and Momi can eat breakfast when they wake up."

"Okay, I'm hungry. I couldn't sleep at all last night worrying about what is happening to my son Kabil in police custody."

"Don't worry. He's involved in politics. Politicians either become ministers when their time comes or spend time in jail. Either of these two may happen to Kabil anytime."

Halim has been a cook for Rania's father for a very long time since their days in India. He was always treated like a family member by everyone including her father and husband when they were alive. Halim served paratha and goat brain to Rania. As she started to eat, Halim said again,

"Kabil is a smart, intelligent young man. Politics will not be able to consume him. You do not have to worry about Rokhi's marriage with him. Maybe, you'll have to delay their marriage for a while. But God willing, it will happen."

"May your words come true, brother Halim. Just think, there's nobody else in this country except Kabil whom you, Rokhi, Andy, and I can call our own close relative."

Right at that moment, Rokhi, all dressed-up with full makeup and everything appeared at the scene. Rania looked up at her daughter and asked, "Where are you going so early? Won't you have breakfast before going?"

"I'm going to cousin Andy's house. I'll have breakfast there. Then I'll go with him to our Nawabpur shop. I'm going in my car."

"You're going to open the shop there? Shouldn't you first inquire about what happened to Kabil last evening, where the police took him to?"

"Oh yes, just a few minutes ago, some student leader called me from Sheikh Mujib's house. He told me that police had taken Kabil to Central Jail in Dhaka last night and admitted him to the hospital facilities inside the jail. Kabil's injuries are not that serious. Mujib had instructed the student leader to call to assure you and me not to worry about Kabil's safety. So there you are. I'm on my way."

As Rokhi was about to leave while putting the edges of the scarf on her head, Rania called from her back, "Listen, Rokhi!"

"Do you want to tell me something, Mother?"

"Isn't Momi awake yet?"

"I didn't wake her up. She argued and quarreled with me a lot until late last night. I thought I let her catch up on her sleep."

"What do you two quarrel about so much all the time? Her fate is troublesome as it is. On top of that, you hassle with her instead of consoling her?"

"You only see Momi's bad fate. Do you think the rest of us are floating in the clouds of joy?"

"I didn't mean that. I know you also don't have peace of mind these days. We can only ask for God's blessing at this time. What else can anyone do?"

"Would you like what I want you to do?"

"Let me hear your advice in these days of crisis."

"Okay, I'll give you my suggestion. You go ahead, as per your earlier plan, and arrange for Momi's wedding with

Andaleeb without waiting for Kabil's release from jail. Why should Momi and Andy wait and suffer from Kabil's political activities and their consequences? If you do not, you may not be able to arrange for their wedding either, let alone mine with Kabil. Just think about it."

As Rokhi headed out, Rania called her back again, "Listen, Rokhi, what if Momi and Andaleeb do not agree to go through their wedding while Kabil is in jail?"

"That they may not agree is your guesswork only. You didn't ask for their opinion on this yet. After the news of Kabil's arrest last evening, everybody was sad. Why did you in that situation think about sending Momi back to Montala? Why should your nephew, my cousin Andy, have to give up his own plan and pleasure for the activities of your politician nephew Kabil? Is that because Andy is employed in your family business and therefore should pay for your inconveniences and abide by your decisions?"

"No, I didn't think about all that. I thought it might not be appropriate to arrange for a wedding ceremony for Momi when her real and legal guardian is in jail. Andy may agree, but Momi may be wondering who would give her away in marriage while Kabil is in jail. Moreover, when Kabil comes out from jail and finds that during his absence, we set aside the matter of his real guardianship of Momi and gave her away in marriage to Andaleeb, Kabil may feel hurt inside even though he may not say anything openly."

"Mother! I know that Kabil will be happy with whosoever you arrange Momi's marriage with. Besides, you know full well that Kabil has full consent in Momi marrying Andaleeb. You have just lost your judgment because of my own bad fate. You leave my fate to me. You just tell Momi today that you'd like to arrange for her wedding with Andy within a week. I'm going to Andy's house now. There, I'll try to convince Andy myself for their wedding. I'm sure Andy will go along with it. If Momi is willing, then there's no reason for Andy to wait. Since Kabil is in jail, maybe we should downsize the celebration."

Having said that, Rokhi left the house.

After Rokhi had left, Rania sat there quietly for a while. Seeing that, Halim brought her another cup of tea. Halim then sat squatting on the floor at a modest distance from Rania and said, "Rokhi ma'am sahib said the right thing. Once you made the decision for the wedding of Andy and Momi, and both of them as well as Kabil had expressed their consent earlier to this wedding, then there is no reason for delaying the matter because of Kabil's arrest."

"So you also agree with Rokhi's suggestion. But I still have to get clear consent from Momi about the timing. Let me go and wake her up."

THE NIGHT BEFORE, AFTER a lot of argument with Rokhi and the resulting tension, Momi turned away in bed from Rokhi, covered herself with the comforter, and tried to fall asleep. But she had not been able to do that until well past midnight. This morning, she didn't have the courage to face the consequences of saying such true but reckless words about her feelings for Kabil directly to Rokhi's face. She was panting underneath the comforter. She couldn't understand why Rokhi liked to pick up arguments with her for nothing often before going to sleep. Why was Rokhi always doubting and probing Momi? Rokhi knew that Momi had forgotten her past feelings for Kabil and now loved Andaleeb wholeheartedly. Yet Rokhi's doubt about Momi's childhood hopes and longing for Kabil hadn't been lessened. Momi told Rokhi that her aunty Zakia had wished and promised her and that she grew up from her childhood dreaming of Kabil as her future husband. But after Kabil left their village home, came to Dhaka, reunited with his estranged uncle Alam, and started living with his family in an affluent environment and in close proximity to Alam's beautiful young daughter Rokhi and fell in love with her, he forgot about his mother's earlier dream and promise of marrying Momi. He thus broke the dreams of both his own mother and that of Momi. Momi therefore now considered Kabil a totally untrustworthy man. Rokhi knew that her mother Rania had brought Momi to their house in Dhaka with the objective of arranging her wedding with Andaleeb. Yes, Momi would have liked to marry Kabil—the man of her lifelong dream who had been snatched away from her by Rokhi with her parents' wealth and affluent lifestyle.

Momi did not tell a word of lie when she had told Rokhi about her feelings for Kabil after the persistent probing by Rokhi. Love was not a stone that would not melt with kindness, hopes, and aspirations. Didn't Rokhi have a past or a memory of Andaleeb's earlier love for her? When a heart wished to get someone but did not get that someone, nobody could wash away that longing of heart with soap and water. Yes, the reflection of Kabil's face in Momi's heart had not faded away, would never do. That did not mean the other needs of her youth had become forbidden for her. Now Momi loved Andy with all her heart and that was what counted to her. She was now swinging like a large leaf of a tall palm tree with the winds of Andy's desire. She was madly waiting for Andy's expected touch. Thinking about all these, Momi could not sleep well last night. Toward the end, she dozed off and didn't even sense when Rokhi had left their shared bedroom. Now that it was early in the morning, the sun's rays came in through the window; she felt comfortable and relaxed. Soon she phased into an REM sleep and a strange dream about Kabil. She dreamt that she was lying on the broad chest of a strong young man on their honeymoon night. She thought in her dream that it was Kabil's chest. She dreamt that no other man's chest could be so warm and comfortable. She felt as if she was spending her honeymoon night in the comfort of Kabil's warmth and the security of his presence. In her dream, she felt that suddenly Kabil woke up, pushed her away from his chest and shouted, "Hey, Momi, how did you come here in this outfit? Why are you wearing Rokhi's wedding saree?

How did you enter our honeymoon suite? You are supposed to be with Andy in your own honeymoon suite."

In her dream, Momi replied to Kabil, "Why should I be with Andy on my honeymoon night? Your mother—my aunty dressed me up in this saree to spend my honeymoon night with you. I'll stay with you."

Hearing Momi's response, Kabil in Momi's dream shouted again, "Be careful, Momi. I forbid you, Momi. Never again say those words. I'll kick you off my bed right now, Momi, if you don't leave me alone."

At that stage of Momi's bittersweet REM dream, Rania came to her bedroom and woke her up. Momi hurriedly sat up on the bed and asked while rubbing her eyes, "What time is it, Aunty!"

"It's about nine o'clock."

"Has sister Rokhi gone out already?"

"Rokhi has gone to Andaleeb's house to pick him up to go to our Nawabpur business. You get up, wash your face, and come to my room. I would like to talk to you about something important."

Momi got down from the bed and went to the washroom. There with toothbrush in her hand, she stood apprehensively and wondered,

Is it possible that Rokhi, before going out earlier this morning, told Aunty Rania about their silly argument last night and that Momi still deep down in her heart apparently wanted Kabil as her future husband and that her marriage to Andy, on the contrary, would be

kind of imposed on her so that she could not lay any claim on Kabil as per his mother's dream and promise earlier to Momi? Rokhi might have even asked her mother to send me back to Montala village to keep me away from Kabil.

Having finished washing up, Momi told cook Halim to send some breakfast for her to Rania's bedroom. She then walked in there to see Rania with some apprehension and trepidations in her heart about what she might be faced with in both short and long terms. Seeing her come in, Rania affectionately called her name and said, "Come in, Momi, and sit close to me."

Momi was a bit apprehensive and sat on Rania's bed, keeping a respectable yet modest distance from her, not knowing yet what to expect soon.

"You are definitely feeling sad for Kabil. You can see when Kabil is not present in this house. Everybody is worried about his safety and security, and nobody feels at ease and comfortable. You also know Rokhi's mental condition when Kabil is away from our house. In this situation, you must have thought that no festivities on your wedding with Andaleeb could be possible or appropriate in this house. Perhaps for that reason, yesterday you got upset with Andaleeb and expressed your wish to go back to Montala for a while. Like you, I also had the same line of thinking." Rania took a pause as if she couldn't figure out how to tell Momi about her now changed plan for arranging her wedding within a week or so.

"Aunty, you were right yesterday evening. There's no reason for me to stay here now. Moreover, I don't feel like staying here either. If you permit me, I'd rather go back to Montala. You may wish to arrange for bringing me here for a few days later during the wedding celebrations of sister Rokhi."

Rania smiled and said, "I know you're a bit disappointed, Momi. Now you tell me, my little girl, who are you disappointed with? If it is with me, let me tell you again, I had brought you to this house with the hope that I would arrange for your marriage with my nephew Andaleeb this week. But if your disappointment is with Kabil, then I'll tell you that Kabil's genuine wish was to see you married with Andaleeb this week with much festivities and in his presence. Your aunty Zakia had left with Kabil a pair of gold bracelets—her own wedding bracelets—for you to wear on your wedding day. Kabil gave the bracelets to me and asked me to put them on your hand on your wedding day as a symbol of his mother's love for you. Think about the fact that Kabil's mother did not ask for giving her own wedding bracelets on the hands of the wife of her own son. Kabil did not make any sentimental claim on those bracelets on behalf of his future wife either. Now, you tell me, is it right for you to be disappointed with me or with Kabil under the present circumstances?"

Rania, with these words, politely and affectionately tried to lighten the mood for both Momi and herself.

Momi remembered that her aunty Zakia always used to wearing those bracelets, and she used to say that she would put them on Kabil's wife's hands on his wedding day. Suddenly in her imagination, Momi saw those bracelets in her late aunty

Zakia's hands. Her vision became somewhat hazy with tears without her realizing it.

"I'm not disappointed with anybody, Aunty, for anything. Nobody in this house anticipated that Kabil would be arrested again. Now things being as they are, and Kabil being away in jail, how can I think about any wedding celebration in this house? Rather, until Kabil's release from jail, I may—"

"I want to discuss that with you, Momi. I would like to complete the religious aspect of your wedding with Andaleeb this week as both Kabil and I had planned earlier. Maybe, we'll skip the social celebration part until our son Kabil comes back from jail. What's your opinion on that?"

Rania made this changed proposal, interrupting Momi in the middle of her earlier comments. Momi now thought that Rokhi must have, for sure, told Rania about their argument the night before. Otherwise, why was Aunty so eager early this morning to arrange for her wedding with Andy, even in the absence of Kabil, changing her thoughts of yesterday evening?

Even yesterday, she didn't indicate anything like this. Rather she had agreed yesterday as per Momi's wish for Momi to go back to Montala for a while. *Does Aunty think like Rokhi does, that any claim on Kabil by Momi may bring danger to Rokhi's relationship with Kabil?*

Does that mean that Kabil may now think that Momi is just as worthy as Rokhi is for his attention and possible future marriage? She further thought that Kabil might even have given Rokhi at some times hints about his weakness for Momi. Maybe that was the reason why Rokhi brought that issue time and again to ascertain if she (Momi) still had any hope and longing to marry Kabil.

All these complicated thoughts suddenly made Momi get quite stressed mentally. Yet on her facial expression, she maintained her polite and rural simplicity and responded to Rania's new sudden proposal for arranging her wedding to Andaleeb within the coming week.

"Aunty! I'll not be able to repay you ever for your all kindness and attention to me. But please do not tell me about my wedding at this critical time. I want to go and stay in our village home until cousin Kabil comes out from jail. You please explain my wish to your nephew Andaleeb. I'm confident that he will understand. He might also not think about our wedding in the absence of Kabil. You and Rokhi have done a lot for me. Please give me a little more time, I beg you."

Rania was moved by Momi's appeal and said, "Okay, Momi. If you do not agree, then this wedding will not take place at this time. Alright, Andy will take you back to Montala tomorrow. I see good reason in your argument as well. Okay now, finish your breakfast and go, do some packing for you to go to Montala tomorrow for a while."

AFTER THE ABSOLUTE MAJORITY victory by Sheikh Mujib's Awami League Party in the first-ever democratic federal parliamentary election in Pakistan, there was widespread jubilation in the hearts and minds of

Pakistan's majority population of Bengalis in the then East Pakistan. At the same time, there was a somewhat depressed excitement in the city of Dhaka. The reason for depressed excitement was that the Bengali nationalist leader Mujib had started the election campaign with his Six Points economic and political demands and was able to make it clear to the ruling West Pakistan-controlled martial law government that the Six Points Demand was the only election issue as far as East Pakistan was concerned. Syed Ahmed Kabil was one of the top-ranking student leaders and Sheikh Mujib's top student spokesman to explain the ins and outs of the Six Points Demand to the public. The student leaders, including Kabil, had forsaken their studies, daily food, and sleep, traveling all over East Pakistan as Mujib's emissary to explain the message of the Six Points Demand to the rural masses. Their objective was to win as many parliamentary seats as possible in East Pakistan that would give their Awami League Party an absolute majority in the Pakistani National Assembly. Kabil had recently been released from jail for the second time in his political life. But he had resumed his political campaign throughout the country soon after his release.

On the day of his release from jail this time, he was bedecked with flower garlands and was surrounded by students and the general public and well-wishers who were escorting him on the main road in front of the jail gate. On the way, Kabil noticed that at a distance near the start of a lane, Rokhi was standing while leaning against her new Austin car. Seeing that, Kabil avoided the crowd and walked directly to Rokhi. She embraced him heartily and invited him to get into the car.

"Would you go first to your leader's house at No. 32 Dhanmondi Road?" Rokhi asked as she started the car.

"No, I want to go to our house first to pay respect to my aunty Rania. How is she doing health-wise and mentally?"

"Mother isn't doing very well lately."

"How are you doing?"

"I have no health issue. I'm keeping well."

For a while Kabil kept quiet simply because he couldn't figure out what to say. Once he thought of asking Rokhi about Momena and Andaleeb. But on second thought, he decided not to for time- being. Rokhi didn't look at Kabil even once as she was concentrating on her driving.

Meanwhile Kabil had an opportunity to have a good look at Rokhi from the corner of his eyes. She looked a little heavier than she had been before. Earlier, Rokhi used to wear gold bangles on both hands. Now she only had a watch with a gold band on her left hand. Kabil also noticed that the diamond ring which aunty Rania had bought for Rokhi's wedding to Kabil was not in her ring finger anymore. It was a favorite of Rokhi's to wear before Kabil had gone to jail. Now she had a thick silver mood-ring with an emerald stone on her ring finger. Kabil knew that this kind of mood- ring was generally popular at that time among non-Bengali young girls. She didn't have any gold ornament on her ears either. This made Kabil think that Rokhi consciously gave up on the ongoing practices of wearing jewelry by young Bengali girls of her age. Otherwise, Kabil would have noticed at least the thin gold chain around her neck. Suddenly, Kabil almost inadvertently remarked, "You seem to have gained a little weight lately."

"Is that so? Maybe, because I had no worry about food and shelter since I was born. Women my age look healthy when they are happy and have nothing to worry about."

"Rokhi! I wish at least today you wouldn't talk like that. You know prison is a place with a lot of difficulties for the inmates. I was happy that I saw you soon after I stepped out of the prison gate. Yet I noticed for all these times, you never once had a good look at me."

At that Rokhi turned her eyes to him. She saw for a moment the sadness in Kabil's eyes but quickly turned her eyes back on the road, concentrating on her driving. But she managed to say, "You can see that I'm driving and you also know that I'm not a very experienced driver. Even then, I could sense that you were looking at me very closely noting any and all changes in my features. I enjoy that with a bundle of happiness, brother Kabil. My hands, indeed my entire body shakes with joy when I sense that you are looking at me with desire in your eyes. I do not know how you would like me in your eyes after you spent a long time in prison. But I have to tell you that it was not possible for me to remain as a little girl Rokhi as I used to be in your eyes after such a long time. I had to work hard day and night looking after my family business. You do not have to worry about the future because maybe one day you will become a government minister in this country.

But I have no other means of survival if I can't learn how to manage my father and grandfather's business."

Kabil remained silent for a while. Then he said, "So you think I'm involved in politics because I want to be a government minister someday?"

"Everybody thinks that way and says that too."

"I do not want to argue with you not at least today."

"Okay, if you do not want to argue, then please forgive me for my indulgences and promise me that you will enter the house with a happy look in your face so that mother will think that her son Kabil and daughter Rokhi are happy around her like they used to be before."

Hearing this Kabil understood that his aunty Rania's illness was because of his and Rokhi's uncertain wedding plans and indeed their uncertain future together. He couldn't respond to Rokhi's appeal to him then because he himself was not sure what lay ahead in his own future. He decided to change the subject and said, "I don't understand why Momi in the end refused to stay in Dhaka with you and Aunty. Andy had told me during one of his visits to me at the jail gate that Momi had been staying with her uncles at Harashpur village. I also do not understand why Momi decided to postpone her wedding to Andaleeb as per aunty's wish just because I was in jail."

"You know better than I do, cousin Kabil, why Momi decided to postpone her wedding to Andy. But I can somewhat guess why she didn't want to stay at our Montala village home."

"Tell me why. Let me hear your guess."

"Momi is not my mother's maidservant. She is Kabil's cousin sister. Once, Kabil's mother promised Momi that when both Momi and Kabil grew up, she would like them to marry each other. Momi remembers that and so do you. Momi feels that even though circumstances have changed because of your love for me and vice versa, she herself as of now did not hear from your mouth directly that her marriage to you is not likely anymore because of the present changed circumstances. She didn't dare refuse my mother's proposal for Momi to marry cousin Andaleeb because at that time she didn't have any other real guardian and protector other than you. That is why she didn't want to go through her wedding until you came out from jail and personally give her hand in marriage to Andy. Momi does like Andy as well. But he's a non-Bengali refugee in this country. Momi is self-conscious that she is a very beautiful, well-endowed girl even though she grew up in a village and has very little education and no worldly possessions to speak of. Momi became aware of her physical beauty and attraction since she had come and spent some time with us in Dhaka. It's not unusual for a young girl to belatedly gain enhanced self-respect and pride when she is extremely beautiful. Possibly because of that self-estimation and pride, she decided to stay with her poor uncles at Harashpur rather than stay at our village home in Montala as its caretaker even though it was more comfortable for her financially with my mother and Andy's generous help. I do not blame her for doing that."

Kabil listened to Rokhi with stunned silence, looked at her intensely for a while, and then suddenly asked, "So are you the one who made Momi insane by giving her all those ideas?"

"Do you think I would accept defeat by a poor, helpless, uneducated village girl like Momi and beg you from her claim on you and tell her that she is like our maidservant and that she shouldn't dare lay claim on my first and much-loved, intended future husband? No, brother Kabil, I couldn't do that whatever lies ahead in my fate in the future. I couldn't be that cruel. You do not know how much Momi loves you, cousin Kabil."

She then pulled out a handkerchief from inside her blouse and wiped her eyes with it. Shortly after, she drove the car inside their house compound.

IN THE MIDDLE OF post-election somewhat-subdued joy and excitement in Dhaka, another family on Rankin Street was getting ready for a celebration of a wedding ceremony. That was in the house of Anjuman's parents and the wedding was of Anjuman with her long-time beau Nisar—the budding philosopher and Kabil's close classmate at the university. The wedding date was fixed exactly ten days after the election results were announced. Most of the invited guests to the celebration at the large gated front courtyard of Anju's parents' house were young university student leaders of different groups affiliated with different political parties in the country. Guests were seated around numbers of decorated tables placed on large-sized carpets on top of the well-cut, green grass of the lawn with a beautiful large shamiana (canopy) overhead. On almost every table, the topic of discussion among the guests were the results of the recent national election and the possible political directions to which the country might be heading to following the election results. Everybody was concerned and worried about the process the country's prevailing military government leader General Yahya might opt for in transferring governmental power to Sheikh Mujib, leader of the political party Awami League which won the overall majority number of parliamentary seats in the upcoming National Assembly. People were concerned whether General Yahya, surrounded by powerful West Pakistan-based military, economic, industrial, and corporate interest groups would ever accept Awami League leader Sheikh Mujib as the legitimate, elected, future prime minister of the whole of Pakistan. General Yahya also had to deal with the lobbying and incitement of Mr. Z. A. Bhutto, leader of the Peoples Party which had won most seats in West Pakistan, against transferring governmental power to Sheikh Mujib's Awami League Party.

People were skeptical that the leader of the Peoples Party with the majority number of National Assembly seats from West Pakistan but still fewer than the total number of seats won by the Awami League would ever accept Sheikh Mujib as the prime minister of the whole Pakistan, especially with Mujib's Six Points Demand as his main election promise to the people of the then East Pakistan. They were aware that Bhutto was already lobbying with the country's military government and urging General Yahya not to transfer the power to Awami League Party. He was even threatening of possible widespread public protest in West Pakistan should General Yahya decide to do so.

Here at Anjuman's wedding celebration, the mood among the top-ranking student leaders was somewhat somber because of this mixture of hopes and apprehension and the possible bloody confrontation between East and West Pakistan. Kabil was standing by the front gate of the courtyard receiving and directing the incoming guests to their respective seats. Next to him, the prominent male and female student leaders were standing greeting the guests. They all liked Anjuman not only as a prominent student leader, but also as a very friendly, popular, and congenial person. Whatever her political ideology and party affiliation was, she was well-known and well-liked by both teachers and the student leaders of all political leanings for her courage and amiable personality. Kabil was standing there looking anxiously toward the direction and the time when his friend Nisar—Anjuman's soon-to-be husband—was supposed to be arriving. He was curious how Nisar would look like in his traditional groom's formal costume. Suddenly, a little girl in a bridesmaid's costume approached Kabil and said, "You are asked to come inside the house where the bride is getting dressed."

Kabil turned to the girl and exclaimed, "Who is calling me inside at this hour? Let's go and see."

"Come with me to the room where the bride's friends including sister Rokshana are dressing sister Anju."

"What! Is it appropriate for me to go there at this time? I am supposed to greet the groom's party who will arrive any time now."

"I don't know. Sister Anju herself asked me to take you there urgently."

Kabil understood that it might be something important and urgent. Otherwise, Anju would not have sent for him at that hour. He followed the little girl inside the house and up the stairs to the second floor. He noticed Anju's mother standing at the top of the stairs. Seeing Kabil, she said, "Come, Kabil, my son. Listen to my daughter Anju's arrogant talk here. She says she will not spend her honeymoon night at our house. We had earlier agreed with Nisar's mother that the couple after their wedding would stay with us in our house until both of them finish their university education and find their own place of residence." Having said all that, Anju's mother looked at Kabil with a sense of desperation in her face. Kabil replied, "Aunty! I understand your concern about their future. We'll find a solution to your concern later. But please tell me what your immediate problem is."

Before Kabil could complete his question the soon-to-be-married Anju, clad in her deep-brown Benarasi silk wedding saree appeared on the scene and stood in front of Kabil. Rokshana hurried behind her and commented, "Look, sister Anju ignored my advice, pushed aside the makeup kits, and ran here in front of you."

Kabil instantly made the decision to make the situation lighter and said with a laughter, "Anju! You look more beautiful than the queen of Mainamati ever was. But what was so urgent that you had to leave your dressing room?"

"No, brother Kabil! If I and Nisar stay here tonight after the wedding, our neighbors would think of Nisar as my kept husband. Please ask your friend Nisar to arrange for a place where we can spend at least a couple of days soon after the wedding formalities. After that we can come back to this house for a while until we both finish our studies. Nisar has many friends in the city. Let our neighbors think and see that I would have left my parents' house after my wedding."

Hearing that both Rokshana and Kabil burst into laughter. Rokshana turned to Kabil and said, "Sister Anju has a valid point. After saying, 'I do,' the newlywed lady doesn't have to spend her honeymoon night in her own old bedroom. That will not be fair to sister Anju."

Kabil assumed a grave composure, turned to Anju's mother, and said,

"Listen, Aunty! We'll have to consider Anju's point of view as well. Nisar is a simple young man. He's my close friend. I'm sure if I propose something to him, he will agree. He came by boat this morning from his rural village home with a few close relatives and friends, did some shopping for Anju and himself, got himself ready at his dormitory room, and will soon be here for the ceremony. Since Anju doesn't think it is appropriate and prestigious for her ego to spend the honeymoon night in her own bedroom, then we would consider another arrangement for them."

He then turned to Rokhi and whispered something in her ears as if to consult her privately and turned to Anju's mother again, "Listen, Aunty! If you permit, Rokhi and I would not mind taking Nisar and Anju to our house after the ceremony tonight. They can spend a couple of nights together with us and then come back to your house here."

Anju's mother felt a sigh of relief at Kabil's proposal. Seeing that Anju also showed her agreement by her silence. Anju's mother then replied, "What could be a better solution than that? You, Kabil, are a really good friend to both Nisar and Anju. I'm grateful to you and I don't know how I can return your favor."

"You don't have to do anything, Aunty. Now, if you can please manage things here with Anju's other friends and let Rokhi go to our house to tell her mother all about this matter and prepare the bed in my room for Nisar and Anju with clean sheets and everything. Aunty Rania loves Anju and she will be happy to welcome them to our house. What do you think, Rokhi?" Kabil asked as if to get Rokhi's approval.

Rokshana looked up for a moment toward Kabil's eyes then lowered her gaze. She then asked Anju, "Come, sister! Let me finish your makeup and dressing. Then I'll go home soon."

She then almost pushed Anjuman toward her dressing room—ignoring even a glance toward Kabil. Kabil wondered if he did the right thing, sending Rokhi home early and leaving all the festivities at Anju's house. He realized it might have been a bit insensitive of him to Rokshana, but by then both Rokhi and Anju left the scene.

HAVING GIVEN UP HIS own bedroom to Anju and Nisar for their honeymoon that night earlier, Kabil returned home late from the wedding venue at Anju's parents' house. He decided not to bother anybody at that hour and quietly went to sleep on the sofa in their living room. He woke up early the following morning as it was not very comfortable to sleep on the sofa. He slowly walked into the small study cum office room of Rokhi's deceased father Ahmed Alam and started composing a letter. Shortly after, Rokshana woke up and learned from cook Halim that Kabil had been up and was in the study room. Rokhi slowly entered the study herself. Kabil by that time completed writing the letter and was putting it inside an envelope.

"Are you sending an important letter to an important person in your life at this early hour?" Rokhi asked Kabil rather pointedly with a subtle, hidden surprise in her voice.

"I'm writing to my uncle in Harashpur, requesting him to send Momena back to our village house at Montala. I'm planning to go to Montala next week to bring Momi here," Kabil replied.

"Perhaps, Momi will not like to come and stay at Montala by herself at this time. On the other hand, she also may because you are asking her to do so. But know one thing. Momi has changed quite a bit during all these times that you were in jail. You may find Momi next week as a girl with a different mind-set with firm conviction and determination of her own."

"Is that so?" Kabil asked with a sense of surprise in his voice. "Then I will have to find out how far you have smartened up our village girl Momi during all these times when I was in jail."

"I didn't do very much except I encouraged her not to be afraid of me or my mother and to express openly the hidden wish or desire implanted deep down in her mind by my pious aunty late Syeda Zakia Banu. She did exactly that. She said her paternal aunty—your mother had wished to raise and prepare her to be fit as a wife for her son Kabil. She thinks she is now good enough to be Kabil's wife."

Kabil looked at Rokshana with the full gaze of his eyes and said, "Do you enjoy the warmth in this wintery morning by setting a fire inside me, Rokhi?"

Rokshana decided not to respond to Kabil's question and said casually, "Let me go now and awaken my mother. The honeymooners will probably be ready for breakfast."

As she stood up to leave, Kabil asked again, "You're ignoring my question, Rokhi. Do you think by hurting my feelings, you'll solve all our family problems? I'm involved deeply in politics. Is that my unforgivable fault?"

"I'm not raising the issue of your involvement in politics. I'm talking about your mother's early promise to Momi. You were aware of her promise, and to date, you never denied that, did you?" Rokhi shot back.

"My mother knew well that I loved and will continue to love you. You do also want me. Having realized our feelings for each other, my mother silently and expressly approved of our relationship. Your parents knew and hoped that someday we will marry each other. Only you brought Momi into this as a punishment to me for my involvement in politics. Now I'm doubtful about your choice. Have you really changed your mind, Rokhi?"

Rokshana couldn't take anymore. She slapped Kabil on his cheek with the full force of her hand and then placed herself against Kabil's chest and started crying. "I can't take it anymore. You strangulate me to death and thereby relieve me of this pain. Why did I have to come to know that someone else once had wanted you? I'll kill your cousin, that stupid Momi. I don't want her to come to this city anymore. That monster would silently want you even if and when she will be married to Andaleeb. Indeed, I don't even want Andaleeb to marry her. You arrange for her to marry someone else in the village, and I'll pay for all her jewelry and other expenses. I don't want to see her face anymore."

Shortly after this, Rania called out for Kabil and Rokhi to come to the dining table for breakfast. Nisar and Anju by that time had already been seated themselves—one on each side of Rania. Cook Halim began serving them all kinds of sumptuous food he had cooked for this special occasion. While everybody was in a good mood enjoying the food, the telephone rang in Rokshana's room. Halim went to answer the phone and came back shortly. He turned to Kabil and said, "It is for you. Shall I bring the receiver here?"

"Whoever it is, please ask to call back a little later unless it is very urgent," Kabil told Halim.

"He said it was urgent and that Mr. Tajuddin wanted to talk to you," Halim replied.

Kabil instantly stood up and said, "Okay, I'll answer the phone."

Soon after Rokshana, Anju, and Nisar also finished eating. Rokshana invited them to her bedroom to chat the lazy morning away. As the three of them entered Rokshana's bedroom, they found Kabil talking on the phone with a gloomy look on his face.

"I am leaving home right away and tell Mr. Tazuddin and other leaders that I'll be there soon to take part in the discussion. Tell them that we, the student leadership, will not organize any procession or meeting and will not speak out publicly contrary to the advice of the party leadership." He then put down the receiver. He turned his eyes toward Anju with a deeply anxious look and said, "Bhutto is conspiring trouble. He says that his Peoples Party won majority parliamentary seats in West Pakistan. Hence, Sheikh Mujib, according to Bhutto, cannot claim the overall majority in the parliament because Awami League's overall majority is based on almost all the seats in East Pakistan. According to him, there is no clear-cut solution to this scenario in the country's constitution which was earlier abrogated by the military administration. After Bhutto's claim, General Yahya telephoned Sheikh Mujib and told him that Yahya would arrive in Dhaka this evening to have a direct, face-to-face talk with Mujib."

Nisar looked at Kabil with no words in his mouth. But Anju came out, forcefully saying, "If the pigs can't find a solution, we'll dictate one to them."

Kabil then left the house, saying that he would be in a closed-door meeting with the party leadership and would probably not be home until late at night. He also said that Rokhi would be able to take care of Anju and Nisar for the rest of the day.

SEVERAL DAYS LATER, THE political situation in the then East Pakistan transformed into severe apprehension and political unrest. General Yahya had come to Dhaka with his entourage and held several rounds of discussions with Sheikh Mujib and his associates. He also held political consultations with other minor political party leaders. He, however, went back to Islamabad without having achieved any significant progress on the crucial issue of transferring governmental powers to the party which had gained overall majority National Assembly seats in the recently held national election. This lack of progress gave rise to a lack of hope among the public for a peaceful transfer of power to Sheikh Mujib's Awami League Party. That resulted in more worries, fear, and depressing concerns for the political future of the country. The people of East Pakistan clearly understood that the predominantly Punjabi military establishment based mostly in West Pakistan and its ally rich and vested interest groups controlling most of Pakistan's economic, industrial, and large commercial establishments had no intention of giving up their privileges by transferring governmental power to Sheikh Mujib's Awami League Party. Bhutto himself was fueling conspiracy with his political clout in West Pakistan. Bhutto publicly raised the claim that since his Peoples Party had gained majority seats in West Pakistan, the Awami League Party was not entitled to form the government with Sheikh Mujib as the prime minister of the united Pakistan. Since then the image of united Pakistan started to crumble down in the eyes of Bengalis in East Pakistan. At the same time, the West Pakistani-vested interest groups and their lackeys—the Urdu-speaking non-Bengali refugee settlers in East Pakistan started openly criticizing Sheikh Mujib and his Awami League Party as the agents of India bent on breaking up Pakistan into two countries and accused Sheikh Mujib of sedition referring to allegation known as Agartala conspiracy case by the earlier government led by military strong man Gen. Ayub Khan. The partisan media in both wings of Pakistan controlled largely by West Pakistan-based capitalist groups began accusing Sheikh Mujib as the agent of mostly

Hindu India and for protecting the Hindu minority group in East Pakistan by diluting the social and religious culture of the majority Muslim population in East Pakistan. This partisan propaganda blitz expectedly and rightfully motivated the Bengali youth organizations to turn against the Urdu-speaking refugee settlers in East Pakistan. In response, the better organized erstwhile refugee settlers along with their local fundamentalist Muslim collaborators organized as Shanti Bahini, Rajakars, Al-Badr, etc., placed their wrath on volatile, poor, and less-organized Bengali workers in mills, factories, and other industrial and commercial establishments owned and operated by West Pakistan-based vested interest groups. Every day, there were reports of communal riots and killing even though both communities were believers in Islam. At the same time, the minority Hindu population of East Pakistan was the special target by these fundamentalist groups of people. The law and order situation and the political, economic, and socio-religious situations were rapidly growing out of hand of the soon-to-be outgoing military administration. Dhaka had turned almost into a ghost town except for frequent militant student group's protests and demonstrations. Meanwhile the employees of the local and provincial administrations claimed to abide by the instructions from Sheikh Mujib and his Awami League Party leaders.

A fearful and anxious environment prevailed in Kabil and Rokshana's ethnically mixed household. It was impossible for Rokshana and Andaleeb to keep their businesses running especially after sunset. Their mostly non-Bengali refugee women workers didn't dare come to work in their factories and spice-grinding machine shops.

Likewise, in the refugee-settler dominated areas of Mirpur and Mohammadpur, the local Bengali laborers didn't feel safe to go to work. The atmosphere of mutual trust and amicable social greetings between the two communities that had existed for years evaporated overnight. It felt as if a cloud of distrust and hatred was prevailing all over Dhaka City that might rain down in bloodletting and indiscriminate killing.

One early morning, Rokshana received a telephone call from her maternal cousin Andaleeb.

"How are you doing, cousin Andy? Aren't you going to attend to our shops today?" she asked.

"I'm not feeling well this morning, Rokhi. Besides, the situation in my home area of Narinda doesn't look very good. Last night, someone threatened me over the phone and said, 'You damn Bihari refugee! Leave your house and escape if you care for your life.' He also called me all kinds of bad names."

"Are you afraid just because of that?"

"No. I'm not afraid. I know some extortionist young kids in the neighborhood are threating the immigrant community to extract money from them. But the political situation in the country doesn't look that good. It appears that—"

"What do you think of the current political situation?"

"No. Nothing serious, Rokhi."

"Brother Andy! Please do not hide your fears from me. Tell me frankly of your true specific security concerns."

"Okay. If you insist. I think General Yahya will not transfer governmental power to Sheikh Mujib. And in that situation, no immigrant settlers like you and me in this country are totally safe, my cousin."

Rokshana understood Andaleeb's security concerns but didn't know what to say to alleviate his fears. She just kept quiet for a few seconds and then said, "Okay. If you aren't feeling well, then do not go to the shop for a few days. I'll attend to the shop myself in your place. Maybe, you'd rather go to our Montala village home to visit Momi there for a few days. It will be okay if you want to leave as early as tomorrow."

Andy was moved by the sympathetic words of Rokshana.

After a few moments of silence, he asked, "Will Kabil approve of my going there by myself at this time?"

"Where will you find Kabil to ask for his approval? You think he comes home on time on a regular basis?"

"Why? Is he not home now?" Andy asked sounding genuinely concerned about Kabil's whereabouts in these increasingly precarious political and security situation in Dhaka.

"No. Cousin Kabil has been spending these last three or four nights at the university students' dormitory. He called me once in between and asked me to tell my mother not to worry about his physical safety. He also told me that Momi's uncle in Harashpur had sent Momi to our village home at Montala. He asked me to pass on the message to you, cousin. If Momi is staying at our house in Montala, we need to send her money for her upkeep. I think you better look after Momi's welfare now as you had done earlier."

Having heard that from Rokhi, Andy felt a sigh of relief. He said, "In that case, I'll leave for Montala tomorrow morning. I'll come to get permission and approval of Aunty Rania tonight."

SHORTLY AFTER, KABIL STORMED into the house. He looked tired and dishevelled. He took a quick shower and went to bed in his room. Toward the evening, Andy came to the house to ask for Rania's approval for him to go Montala the following morning to visit Momi there. Rokhi was not home. She had gone to attend to Rania's fashionable tailoring shop and lady's fashion garment shop beside Dhaka's then only five-star Intercontinental Hotel. Rania had been managing this reputable and profitable business since its founding many years ago when her husband Alam was still alive. Lately, however, she had not been physically and mentally well enough to look after this rather challenging business. In her place, Rokhi had been trying to manage the business with the help of some newly recruited employees.

Andy was greeted by the cook who told him that Kabil had earlier in the day come back home and was in his bedroom. Andy walked toward Kabil's room and knocked on the closed door. Kabil responded from behind the door, "Come in please! The door is not locked."

Andy entered the room and sat on a chair next to Kabil's study table.

"Rokhi told me that you had been spending the past several nights at the university campus." Andy started the conversation.

"Yes, I have been," Kabil nodded.

"I know the political situation has not been good these past several days. But I don't understand the underlying root cause of tension between the two communities of Bengalis and the Biharis. The Biharis have been settled in this province for over twenty years now. I'm scared this tense situation might escalate into a widespread communal riot any time."

"It is not impossible, brother Andy. We have to be ready for all eventualities resulting from the continuous misleading propaganda by leaders of both the communities."

"What is the stand taken by you student leaders in this situation? I noticed a sense of hatred in some of their statements against the immigrant settlers' communities. I don't think General Yahya will transfer the governmental power to Sheikh Mujib soon, if at all. I don't understand why he will not do that. After all, Sheikh Mujib is the leader of Awami League which received numerically majority of seats in the National Parliament in the last general election. Mujib is therefore now entitled to be the legitimate prime minister of the whole of Pakistan. He had earlier fought for the creation of Pakistan when he was even a student in those earlier days. I hope Yahya will not be misguided by the nefarious advice of the eccentric and power-hungry Bhutto and invite Mujib to form the central government in Islamabad."

Kabil smiled at Andaleeb's simplistic ideas and belief and said, "May you be right, brother."

"By the way, Kabil," Andaleeb changed the subject, "Rokhi and Aunty Rania want me to go and visit Momi for a few days at your village home in Montala. I hope you have no objection to me doing that."

"No, brother Andy! I'll be even grateful if you will do that since I myself cannot do that at this critical time. You really love Momi, brother. She is one lucky girl, and I'm happy for her—my little cousin and my mother's all-time favourite," Kabil responded.

ANDALEEB ARRIVED AT THE Montala railway station toward the evening of the following day. He was carrying a suitcase and a handbag. He brought a few sarees and blouses for Momi in his suitcase. The handbag was full of cosmetics and other essentials for Momi. He passed the railway station and was on his way to Kabil's home following the village path. As he walked, he was overwhelmed by a sense of shyness and apprehension. This was his first visit alone to see Momi. He was apprehensive of how Momi and her neighbours would take his visit to Momi all by himself. He knew Momi had always kept a share-crop farmer and his wife in Kabil's house compound for her own safety and security. Amidst all these thoughts, Andaleeb arrived at the gate of the Syed family compound and knocked on the closed gate. Shortly after, Momena appeared and opened the gate.

"Oh! It is you!" she exclaimed.

"Yes. It's me. Aunty Rania and brother Kabil have sent me to inquire about your well-being," Andy replied.

The following morning, Momi briefed Andaleeb at the breakfast table about the Bengali-Bihari tension at nearby Montala railway station. Andy told her that the situation is even worse in Dhaka. He noted that a murderous situation could trigger anytime between the two communities all over East Pakistan.

That evening after dinner, Andaleeb returned to the bedroom assigned to him by Momi the night before. He noticed there were significant changes in the way the room was arranged compared from the night before. The beddings and pillows were nicely rearranged. The mosquito net was properly tucked in under the mattress. A glass of water with a cover was placed on the bedside table. There were a few burning Indian incense sticks emanating pleasant fragrance in the room. Andaleeb realized that Momi herself, instead of her young domestic help, had prepared everything in the room. He sat down on a chair next to a table, took a sip of water from the glass, and looked outside through the window. In the wide open sky full of millions of stars, the full moon was visible like a large golden plate. Occasional bats and night owls were flying by the window in the sea of moonlight. The night was filled with unpolluted air emanating a kind of rural fragrance of freshness. There were mild sounds of moving long, straight banana leaves from the garden nearby inside the compound. Outside the boundary wall, rows of straight beetle nut trees were standing tall as if to guard the compound against any possible intruders. From far away bamboo gardens, flocks of fire flies were moving around fast, emanating harmless, romantic flames of fire.

Andaleeb realized he would not be able to fall asleep this night. Various thoughts and anxieties would keep him awake, tossing and turning in bed as if to punish him for his honesty and love for Momi and for his unfortunate situations in various stages of his life since his childhood. Yet, he loves dearly the natural beauty of this lush green, mostly unspoiled virgin countryside of Bangladesh. He had spent most of his young life in Dhaka, ever since he had migrated to the then East Pakistan after having fled the Indian State of Bhopal during 1947 communal riots in India when he had lost both his parents. He came to Dhaka with the family of his aunt Aunty Rania and her widowed father and ever since living and working with the family.

He had liked Rokshana, daughter of Rania and her Bengali husband Ahmed Alam, both of whom also showed their liking for Andaleeb. He had hoped that one day when Roksahana grew up, he would like to marry her; his uncle Alam also seemed to have liked the idea. However, when Kabil showed up in Dhaka and reconnected with his paternal uncle Alam and his family, Rokshana seemed to have been mesmerized by Kabil and has been deeply in love with him. Kabil also reciprocated Rokshana's love.

Having thus been rejected by Rokshana, Andaleeb slowly fell in love with Momena, Kabil's erstwhile simple and rural maternal cousin who like Andaleeb had lost her parents at an early age. Momena was raised by her paternal aunty Zakia, Kabil's mother, instilling in Momena from her early age that Zakia would like to welcome Momena as Kabil's wife when both of them grew up. In the middle of all these mixed feeling in the comfort of pleasing surroundings, Andaleeb soon fell asleep while sitting on the chair.

A short while later, seeing Andaleeb's door open and Andaleeb asleep on the chair, Momena felt kind of drawn and akin to him. She put her hand-carried lantern outside the door and entered the room. She dimmed the inside hurricane on the table. Only the burning Indian incense was making circles in the air, emanating a romantic fragrance.

Andaleeb was fast asleep on the chair. Momena first thought of leaving him alone as he was. But then she thought that he might get a backache or stiff neck if he slept long in a sitting position on the chair.

She hesitantly brought her mouth close to Andaleeb's ear and whispered, "Brother Andy! You fell asleep on the chair. Please wake up, close your doors from inside, and go to sleep in the comfort of your bed."

Andaleeb woke up instantly and found Momi standing next to his chair.

"Oh, Momi! Please sit down and put the hurricane light a bit up. I fell asleep thinking about the political situation in the country and our consequent future—you, me, Kabil, Rokshana, and Aunty Rania with her house and good, profitable business in Dhaka."

"It's rather late and you're also sleepy. Besides, you are planning to go back to Dhaka tomorrow morning. You better go to bed soon and I should leave you alone now."

"It's okay if you want to go. I at least fulfilled part of what I had intended to do on this visit. I assure you, Momi, that your regular support money will continue to reach you."

"Yes! Kabil had assured me and my uncle at Harashpur about that in his letter when he had asked them to send me here."

"Then—" Andaleeb suppressed what he wanted to say.

"Then what? If you want to tell me something else, brother Andy, please do not hesitate," Momena said with some eagerness in her voice. She had figured out that Andy had really come to Montala to see and talk to her.

"You see, Momi, you know how much I'm in love with you. Our planned wedding had to be postponed because of difficulties with Kabil's political activities resulting in him going to jail and the problems in Aunty Rania's household. I can't blame Kabil because politics is his passion in life. His own safety, security, and well-being were at stake. Therefore, he didn't have much time to think about our wedding. But my feeling is that if you were serious about us getting married, then our wedding did not really need to be postponed."

He then got up from his chair and sat on the bed. Suddenly, Momi didn't feel like leaving the room. She sat herself down on the chair which Andaleeb had just got up from.

"You're right," Momena said. "It's because of my indecisiveness that our wedding had to be postponed."

Andaleeb was a bit taken aback by Momena's honest and straight confession.

"No. I'm not blaming you either. I recognize you may have some reservations because I'm not ethnically of Bengali origin."

"Yes. That's there, of course. But you know that there is another matter that I myself had never brought to your attention. You might have of course heard from Rokhi who wants to deprive me of what I had all along thought was mine. Therefore, she is interested in you and me getting married as soon as possible, so that I'm out of her way in her claim to what I always thought was mine since my childhood. My wedding with you is her guarantee in that respect."

"I know that, Momi! Please do not torment me by reviving all those past things. You are vainly going through tormenting yourself as well by holding on to the past and thinking about Kabil all the time. I know very well Kabil loves Rokhi and that he doesn't love you. But Rokshana is still doubtful whether you have been able to take Kabil out of your life once and for all. She thinks you still love Kabil, and she feels guilty that she turned Kabil away from you."

"I see, you know everything."

"Yes, Momi. I also know that if Kabil is today willing to marry you, you will not even consider me as your future potential husband. But I'm in love with you, Momi, and I will not be able to live without you beside me. I'm sure you will not kill yourself if Kabil refuses to marry you. You will marry someone else. Why could it not be me even if I am not your first love?"

"Brother Andy! Rokhi is not as certain as you are that Kabil will not marry me."

"Rokhi is for nothing jealous of your physical beauty and attractiveness."

"But Kabil is a man. He's old enough to be attracted by a woman's beauty and physical attributes."

"Yes. He's old enough. But I don't know what Kabil himself had told you lately. But he doesn't have time to look at any other woman other than Rokshana at this critical time in his political life. Even if he has, his life is not as emotional and common as ours. You don't know where you are heading to, running after this mirage in your life. On the other hand, Rokhi had turned you insane by showing her inner, imaginary shadow of jealousy," Andaleeb expressed a slight, bitter smile on his face.

Momena sat there quietly for a while. A lot of mixed thoughts crowded her head. She then said, "What then, do you advise me to do, brother Andy?"

"I didn't come here to advise you to do anything, Momi! I came to inform you once again of my love, devotion, and consideration for you. The future of the country is bleak.

There are reports of bloody riots between the Bengalis and the Bihari communities in various parts of the country. The immigrant settlers here are apprehensive whether Pakistan as an united country will survive. Most Bengalis hate Urdu-speaking people as if Urdu is a forbidden language. I pray for you, Momi, my love. May God take care of you. I'm leaving for Dhaka tomorrow morning. I don't know when I'll have another chance to come and see you. But, remember, I—a Bihari refugee settler—love you from the core of my heart. If you ever feel any real, genuine love for me in your heart, then just send me the news, and I'll come to you from wherever I may be."

Andaleeb then put his head down on the bed and lay there looking up at the ceiling. He was tired, disappointed, and afraid of what might be in store for him in the near future. Seeing him in that distraught condition, Momena got up and stood close to his bed and said, "Please forgive me, cousin Andy! If I'm tormenting you. But I beg you to decide for me who I should choose as my life partner."

She broke into tears and bent herself down on the head side of Andaleeb's bed. Andaleeb sat up on the bed and pulled Momi unhesitantly in an embrace and asked, "Do you want me to tell you who, between Kabil and me, you should choose as your future husband?"

"Yes, I want you tell me exactly that as an objective, unselfish well-wisher of mine. Because, I, like most women, cannot decide whom of the two strong, able men will be a better match when not one of them is within possible reach as my future husband. I need an outsider's advice to make that decision for me. I count on you to make that objective choice for me, please."

With that, Momena, with tears still running down her cheeks, placed herself firmly against Andaleeb's chest.

BACK IN DHAKA THAT day, at Rania's Bonogram Lane house, Kabil spent all day sleeping off the previous days' exhaustion. Rokshana came twice to peak through his window and turned back seeing him sound asleep. She wasn't feeling well herself on this day. Andaleeb was not back from Montala yet. There were reports in the daily newspapers of sporadic communal riots in various parts of East Pakistan. But nothing was of major concern. As such, they didn't cast significant doom and gloom in the daily lives of the citizens of Dhaka. There were no significant outbreak of dislike and hatred for the Urdu-speaking Bihari refugee settlers' community among the common, low-income majority local Bengali working class. However, there was an undercurrent of discontent, mistrust, and ill-feelings toward the Biharis among the educated middle- and upper-class people like students, teachers, professors, professionals, and Bengali business people, fueled mostly by the partisan propaganda by media, politicians, and other religious fundamentalists and vested-interest groups. Low-ranking Bengali government and private sector employees were trying to paralyze the functioning of the government and private organizations and incite hatred between the two communities.

Seeing Kabil sound asleep in his room late into the day, Rokshana ate some light lunch, returned to her own bedroom, and lay down on her bed trying to go through the daily newspaper. But she could neither concentrate on the paper nor fall asleep for an afternoon nap. She was restless and was eagerly waiting for a chance to spend some time alone talking intimately with Kabil. She so badly wanted to be in close intimate company with Kabil and spend some quality time with him—alone, just the two of them. But Kabil seemed to have been trying to avoid that lately with one excuse or another. Rokshana set aside the newspaper, got up, and sat on her bed and covered her chest with her usual scarf. She then stood up and on an impulse ran toward Kabil's bedroom. Kabil was awake but still lying on his bed quietly with a thin bed sheet covering his body. He was looking out aimlessly through the open window. He didn't see Rokshana quietly entering his room from his back side. Rokshana slowly sat on the side of Kabil's bed and even more quietly lay down on the back side of Kabil, sharing that side of his pillow. There was a pin drop silence for a while and Kabil couldn't hear or feel anything. He kept his aimless gaze out through the window on the opposite side of the bed. Rokshana could not tolerate the deafening silence any longer.

"Who are you thinking about so deeply?" Rokshana quietly asked. Kabil suddenly got startled by a question like that from the side of his pillow. He instantly got up and sat on the bed.

"Oh! It's you! When did you come in?" he asked.

"I came and went back several times. You can sleep like a donkey."

"You could have woken me up."

"If I did that, you would find an excuse to leave the house on some urgent political business. Rather than that, I contented myself looking at you when you were asleep," Rokshana replied with a slight bitterness in her tone. Kabil looked at Rokshana silently for a long few minutes—not only at her face but with an inspecting eye on her entire body, as if he was truly inspecting some undiscovered sensual parts of her person. In the end, when his eyes reached a birthmark like a blood spot right at the middle of her chest, they were filled with a mild smile of self-contentment.

"Do you think I avoid being with you with fake and false excuses?" Kabil asked.

"Why *think*? I know that for sure. Tell me, aren't you avoiding being with me day and night?"

"Your impression of me is wrong, Rokhi! I do not possess any power of avoiding you. Rather, whenever and wherever I may be, I'm always anxious and restless to have an opportunity to have a look at you. You're full of doubt about my feelings and longing for you because I do not know how to explain to you my pains of being away from you. Neither do I know how to make myself trustworthy for you. I live an active life because I feel surrounded and secure by your unlimited love and devotion. You're the source of my daily stamina. Yet I don't know of any way to remove your doubts about me and about our future together. I have no doubt about your feelings for me. Nor am I afraid of anything or worried about our future together. Now, you tell me how I can lessen or remove your uncertainty about our future life together."

Kabil said these things with a tone of seriousness in his voice. Yet he finished them with a smile and happiness in his appearance. He looked over again on symbols of youth and attractions of Rokhi's young, beautiful body with joy and enchantment. Rokshana also felt happy that her beloved fiancé had been enjoying the beauty and attractions of her youthful body with joy and enchantment. Yet she felt her congenital shyness, embarrassment, and cultural inhibition of a conservative Muslim young lady. She instantly sat up on the bed and covered her brassier with her scarf.

"Please do not look at my body like that. I feel embarrassed," she murmured.

"I feel embarrassed too. But when I'm alone with you, I can't control my eyes."

"If you find me irresistibly attractive, then, why not ask my mother for my hand and make our relationship moral and formal as a married couple?"

"Aunty Rania isn't opposed to our marriage, she will rather welcome it and be happy with it. It's me who's holding it off. When I am responsible myself, I have to suffer the punishment alone."

"If you prefer to punish yourself, what else can I say? Then, I'd rather go and bring a cup of tea for you."

Rokshana then got up from bed. Her eyes were about to shed showers of tears. She turned aside and tried to wipe her eyes. Suddenly, Kabil put his hands on her shoulders and said,

"I'm sorry, Rokhi! I made a grave mistake. Please forgive me. I shouldn't have said that only I was suffering for my indecision. I know I'm causing a lot of psychological pains to you as well. But I'm hopeful our days of uncertainties will be over soon. I'm confident that there will be a compromised solution to the present political turmoil in the country. The day Sheikh Mujib is sworn in as the prime minister of Pakistan, I'll ask Aunty Rania to formally announce the date of our wedding. The diamond ring that your mother had bought for your wedding will for sure start emanating radiance."

Rokshana couldn't hold herself back any longer. She embraced Kabil with both her hands and started crying like a young teenage girl.

WITHIN A FEW DAYS, a sense of disappointment and despair gripped most middle-class Bengali residents in Dhaka. The city had been filled with all kinds of rumours, political excitement, and uncertainties. Everyone in the city had been waiting for so many days with the hope that good, sound common sense would prevail among the leaders of West Pakistan, including the military leaders, and that General Yahya Khan would in the end ask Sheikh Mujib to form a democratic government in Islamabad after years of military dominated rule in the country. Even Yahya himself had been in Dhaka to carry on political negotiations with Sheikh Mujib to that effect vis-à-vis Mujib's Six-Points election manifesto. He had arrived without any press coverage, but rather in complete state-controlled secrecy. Perhaps, Yahya had now realized the practical implications and political realities in East Pakistan as far as Mujib's Six Points Demand were concerned of which he had been ambivalent and rather somewhat indifferent as of that time. Perhaps he wanted to ascertain for himself in direct face-to-face negotiations with Mujib number of issues—like if Mujib and his Awami League Party were to form the central government in Islamabad and his government concentrated on implementing the party's election manifesto of Six Points Demand, how would Sheikh Mujib address the concerns of Pakistan's military and most West Pakistani political, industrial and business communities about the country's unity and integrity? As the president of the prevailing military government, General Yahya was well aware of the sentiments and the demands of the young people and the student communities in East Pakistan. Some political party leaders and student groups went even as far as raising the demand of independent, sovereign state of Bangladesh. As such, they were closely watched by the powerful Pakistani armed forces. The students movement was not simply aimed at political, economic, and cultural autonomy. They were also aware of the fact that East Pakistan had been deprived of their share of representation in Pakistani armed forces. Indeed, the military government for decades encouraged and facilitated a colonial type of administration, exploiting the economic and natural resources of East Pakistan for the benefits of West Pakistan. The common religious traditions and practices among the majority population of both wings of Pakistan failed to establish in the past twenty-five years, a strong common bond between them as was hoped for in 1947 during the partition of the subcontinent. This was mainly because of the way the national power centers in West Pakistan had treated the interest of the people of East Pakistan.

The tragedies involving the police shooting of students who had died in the 1952 Language Movement when the central government tried to impose Urdu as the only state language of Pakistan, ignoring Bengali—the language of majority of the population of Pakistan — were revived in people's memory and bore a stark similarity to the attitude of the prevailing power structure in West Pakistan. All these thoughts of past tragedies and injustices to the people of East Pakistan and their strong resistance to these were crowding General Yahya's head as he lay down on a reclining chair in the verandah of the presidential palace in Dhaka late that afternoon. The half-full whisky glass on a low side table was emitting yellow intoxicating bubbles. The General was trying to figure out how to solve the prevailing political dilemma of widespread discontent and anger among the people of East

Pakistan that was threatening the very integrity of united Pakistan.

Is military crackdown an option? he asked himself. *That would be declaring war against a section of the people of his own country,* he said to himself. He picked up the whisky glass and wanted to see the intoxicating bubbles through the side of the crystal glass. He then swallowed the contents of the glass in one quick gulp. Soon, he fell into a deep state of intoxication and slumber and began to snore heavily well into the early evening.

THE DIALOGUE BETWEEN GENERAL Yahya aided by his military and civilian advisors and Sheikh Mujib and his team was scheduled to begin the following morning. The city of Dhaka was again flooded with long processions of people from all ranks and walks of society to show solidarity with their elected leader, Sheikh Mujib—the legitimate future prime minister and the only man who could, given the chance, preserve the unity and integrity of Pakistan. This time some people were raising the slogans of straight independence from the tyrannies of West Pakistan with a view to strengthen Mujib's negotiation stand. The student procession, which began from the university campus through Lalbagh, Chowk Bazar, Islampur, and Sadarghat areas, was now proceeding through Nawabpur toward Gulistan. The procession was being led by student leaders like A. S. M. Abdur Raab, Sheikh Fazlul Hoque (Moni), Abdul Quddus (Makhan), and Shah Jahan Siraj. Kabil was leading the slogans in the front row of the procession.

As the procession approached the front of Rokshana's shop in Nawabpur, Kabil took a quick look and noticed that Rokshana, dressed in her typical Bihari salwar kameez, was standing in front of the closed door of her shop. Andaleeb was standing next to her with a chain of keys in his hand. Most of the shops owned by non-Bengalis in this area were locked down and the shop owners were waiting for the procession to pass by so that they can reopen the shops again once the procession had passed by their area. They were all awestruck by the size and length of the procession. An image of despair and fear was visible on their faces. Most Bengali shop owners were of course clapping and cheering the procession as it passed by their closed shops.

Seeing Rokshana stand there, Kabil passed on his hand-held microphone to his friend next to him in the procession and said,

"I'm thirsty. Let me go and get a glass of water. You keep on leading the procession with the slogans."

The young man took the microphone eagerly and shouted with the full force of his throat, "Heroic Bengali people! Take arms in your hand! Make Bangladesh free and independent!" The crowd in the procession repeated the slogan and moved on.

Kabil stepped aside from the main stream of the procession and began walking in the opposite direction. A short distance back, he met Rokshana and Andaleeb standing in the verandah of their shop and said, "Let's go somewhere and have some cold drinks."

Both Andaleeb and Rokshana were surprised at seeing Kabil break away from the procession and coming there to meet them. Andaleeb smiled and said, "What happened, why did you break away from the procession? What would your fellow leaders think of you, leaving like that?"

"Let them think whatever they want. I'm thirsty and hungry. I want to take Rokhi to some place where we can have something to eat and drink," Kabil replied.

"Okay then. You two go. I'll re-open the shop when the procession is out of our sight," Andaleeb commented.

Rokshana then suggested to Kabil, "Let's go by our car. We can go straight by Narinda round about. That way, we will not face the procession anymore. Otherwise, your friends would think their leader Kabil had abandoned the procession for the company of his Bihari whore girl."

"If you think that way, then you need not accompany me, Rokhi. My friends know you well. I never heard so far anybody making any disrespectful comments like that about you. Rather, you sometimes make comments critical of my friends and political associates. Once, you yourself were involved in student political movements. I do not say that you can't criticize anybody you want. But it is not fitting for you to be critical of the political demands of the students' movement. Remember, you're also a Bengali by birth. Your father was a Bengali."

"But my mother is not a Bengali. Her father was not a Bengali either. I do not accept that I will not have a place to live in this land because of part of my heritage."

"Who's telling you to accept that argument?"

"Why? Only a few minutes ago, you and your friends at the front of the procession shouted some slogans which clearly demonstrated just that."

Andaleeb was shocked at this sudden argument between Rokshana and Kabil. He couldn't understand why the two of them suddenly got into this unpleasant, untimely argument.

He said innocently, "Oh, Rokhi! Why are you starting all these arguments at a time and place like this? Do you want all these people around you make fun of you two? You guys don't have any patience."

Neither Kabil nor Rokshana answered Andaleeb's question. Kabil took a quick look at the crowds in the verandah of neighboring shops. They were leaning forward trying to overhear the argument between a Bengali young man and a Bihari-looking young girl.

Most of them were non-Bengali shop owners. Some of them knew of Kabil and Rokshana and of their relationship. Everybody was discreetly and looking sideways at Kabil's face reddened with embarrassment. He couldn't look up anymore. He instantly started walking out on the sidewalk. Before, Andaleeb could come and stop him, Kabil started running toward the direction of the procession. Both Andaleeb and Rokshana, out of their desperation, walked back to their shop—both in deep shock and sadness, not knowing what to do next.

ROKSHANA RETURNED HOME THAT afternoon and learned from their cook Halim that her mother had gone to visit a friend of hers in the refugee settlers-dominated Mohammadpur area. Halim had tried to convince Rania not to leave home because of her ill health. But she wouldn't listen to him.

Halim also told Rokshana,

"Your mother heard some disturbing, floating news and left home in a hurry."

"What disturbing news?" Rokshana asked with concern in her voice.

"The news that there was a large-scale riot among the laborers at the Adamjee Jute Mills (largest jute mill in the country owned and operated by West Pakistan-based industrialist Adamjee Business Groups). Apparently, the Bihari labourers stabbed a Bengali officer there. In the end, the local villagers came out and set fire to the Bihari laborers' colony in the slum area. The Bihari families fled the area in groups and headed for Mohammadpur area. Your mother wanted to know more about it from her friend Ayesha."

After hearing the name of Ayesha, Rokshana breathed a sigh of relief and said,

"If mother went to visit Aunty Ayesha, then she will be okay. Aunty Ayesha will bring her back in her car before it is too late. You please make a cup of tea for me."

A COMPLEX, FOUR-SIDED LOVE STORY AND A CIVIL WAR

"Why do you want to drink tea at this odd time? I have finished cooking. You go and take a shower and I'll put lunch on the table," Halim said in a subtle tone of affectionate order.

"I wanted to wait a bit for Kabil before I eat lunch. I had a big argument with him earlier this morning. I told him some wrong things and he just walked away. I don't know where to find him so that I can apologize for my indiscretion. What can I do Chaca (Uncle)?"

"Oh! Is that the matter? Kabil came home around noon— shortly after your mother had left home. He went straight to the washroom. He hasn't come out yet."

Rokshana instantly felt happy and relieved knowing that Kabil was already home. She lowered her eyes and walked slowly toward her bedroom. Shortly after, Kabil came out of the washroom with a large heavy towel wrapped around his waist.

"Uncle Halim! Please put lunch on the table. I'm really hungry. I'll go get dressed and come out soon," Kabil said as he walked toward his bedroom.

"Okay. I'll put lunch on the table for both you and Rokhi. She is also back in her room."

Soon after, both Rokhi and Kabil entered the dining room almost at the same time from the opposite ends and took their seats. Rokshana broke the silence trying to make the situation lighter.

"You came home early. Doesn't the situation in town look that good?"

"I hear there are sporadic riots between the Biharis and the Bengalis here and there in the city. I will have to leave for the university campus soon. Looks like, I'll not be able to come back home for a few days. I wanted to tell Aunty myself not to worry about me. But I hear she had gone to her friend in Mohammadpur."

Kabil said all these without even looking at Rokshana once. He served himself some lunch and pushed the serving plate to Rokshana.

"Please forgive me, cousin Kabil, for my behavior at the shop earlier today. It was wrong of me to have been engaged with you in an argument in front of all those people," Rokhi said apologetically.

Kabil did not respond to her apologies and continued eating quietly. Seeing no reactions from Kabil, Rokshana realized Kabil was still upset with what happened between them earlier in the morning. She on her own said again.

"I'm sorry for my misbehavior this morning. I ask for your forgiveness."

Even after that, Kabil didn't look up at Rokshana. Rokshana then stopped eating and started watching Kabil eat his lunch with his face looking down. She said again,

"Don't leave without seeing Mother. She went to visit Aunty Ayesha who will bring her back early in the evening."

At that, Kabil raised his face and said,

"I don't think I can wait until evening. The students have asked me to deliver a speech at a gathering at four in the afternoon. You tell Aunty on my behalf that I will spend a few days at the university campus. No student leader is expected to return home until the political negotiations between Sheikh Mujib and General Yahya is over. I'll inform you later the room number in the students' dormitory where you can reach me at night."

"What am I going to do then during these few days? The situation in town is tense. I don't feel safe to go and attend to our shop in Nawabpur (the older part of Dhaka)."

"Don't go. The political situation and the social environment are critical. Everybody should pay attention to the situation. Aunty shouldn't have gone to the non-Bengali dominated area of the city today. There are riots between the two communities all over East Pakistan."

Rokshana understood that Kabil was genuinely concerned about her mother.

"Don't blame me for Mother leaving home in this situation. She had left before I came home. If I were home, I wouldn't let her go. Mother was worried about the ongoing riots between the two communities. Aunty Ayesha's husband works with the pro-Pakistan daily, the *Morning News*. Perhaps, Mother wanted to get some ideas about General Yahya's intentions during the high-level negotiations. She wouldn't listen to my concern about her ill health. Perhaps she would listen to you."

Rokshana picked up some rice and by-then cold fish curry from her plate and put it in her mouth. Outside, it started raining heavily soon afterward. Kabil didn't say anything further. He got up and walked toward his bedroom. Rokshana just sat in the dining chair for a few more minutes but couldn't eat anything. In the end, she looked blankly toward Kabil's bedroom for a while and then walked slowly toward it. Inside, Kabil put on his long raincoat and looked in the mirror for a minute. As he heard Rokshana's footsteps, he turned back and said,

"I'm leaving now. If there is something urgent, you call Anju's house. Anju and Nisar will pass the message to me."

"Why should I call Anju? I can go to the university campus myself and find your whereabouts."

"It will not be wise and safe for you to go there alone. Moreover, I do not want you to leave home at this critical time and go anywhere. Cousin Andaleeb will have to manage all our businesses by himself until the political situation becomes quiet and normal. This is my order. It's up to you to obey it or not. I came home to inform Aunty of my decision."

"Then why not wait for a while until your aunty is back home? If you go a little later, will it hurt your heroism?"

"I said I'll have to deliver a speech at a student gathering at 4:00 p.m. I have been asked and I want to do that. Moreover, Sheikh Mujib gave me instructions to motivate and guide students to do something to diffuse the tension between the Bihari and the Bengali communities. He asked for me to say something to that effect in this afternoon's student gathering. I can't just sit home because of the rain. The students are planning a large protest march tomorrow as well."

Rokshana listened to Kabil quietly and carefully. She looked up at Kabil for a few seconds with an aimless expression and said,

"Okay then, go if you have to, but it's not late yet. If you want, I can ask our cook to make a cup of tea for you before you go."

Kabil didn't respond but sat down on a chair with his raincoat still on as a sign of his agreement to Rokhi's suggestion. Rokshana ran to the kitchen to ask Halim to make tea. She quickly came back and sat on Kabil's bed.

"Before you go, please forgive me for this morning's incident in front of our shop in old Dhaka," she said again.

What she said did not affect Kabil's thought process at all. He looked up at Rokshana, and for a while they fixed their look on each other's eyes.

"I tried to look at things from your perspective," Kabil began to speak. "You said the correct things this morning in front of our shop. There is nothing in it for you to apologize. And I have no reason to be upset with you because of that."

"What?" Rokshana asked quite surprised.

"What I mean to say is that by talking about Aunty Rania's sentiment and feelings, you expressed the doubt and pains of the entire non-Bengali refugee settler community. I don't know if you had noticed this morning, the non-Bengali business community members of old Dhaka who were present there at the time were surprised and very pleased at your courage and outspokenness. I saw the expression of their sentiments in their eyes. That is also the view of you, Aunty, and cousin Andy, which you articulated very well. The effect of political victory of the Bengalis on the economic gain and loss of the immigrant settlers' community is a matter of great concern for most of the top-ranking Awami League leaders. Naturally, you are worried about this not only as a business woman, but also as a part of that community. After all, your mother—my aunty Rania—is a successful, established, non-Bengali business lady even though you are a real Bengali from your father's side. The present political situation will perhaps push the Bengalis toward something more consequential and vengeful than what they had wanted with their original Six Points Demand. Under these circumstances, you all are going through some psychological turmoil because of what might happen to you and all the non-Bengali settlers here. Their hopes and aspirations of finding brotherly cohesion in this province on the basis of common Islamic religion, misused as they were, are at stake now. You are carrying all these pressures on you because of your love for me. I fully understand that."

Rokshana felt much relieved at Kabil's long explanation. She tried to feel at ease with a mild smile.

"I didn't deeply think about all those implications, when I wrongly and impulsively engaged myself into an argument with you this morning, as I often do with you. I realized later that I shouldn't have done that, at least not in a public place like that in front of others. I cried a lot afterward because of my indiscretion. Please forgive me before you go," Rokhi said in sincere repentance.

"Don't worry. I fully understand your sentiment of the moment. You did nothing wrong. You were upset with quite natural human anger. You are not a Bihari nor a Bengali only.

You are a decent, beautiful, normal human being. I am not upset with you at all, Rokhi."

Rokshana put her head down and began to bite her finger nails. By then, the rain outside subsided a bit and Kabil walked out in his raincoat without even an umbrella.

AROUND EIGHT IN THE evening, Andaleeb came to Rokshana's house. Her mother Rania was perched on the bed with a sad and gloomy look on her face. Rokshana was sitting on a rattan stool on the floor near her mother's bed. She was leafing through an English daily newspaper. Andaleeb began by giving them an update on what was going on in the old city area of Dhaka during the rest of the day.

"The non-Bengali refugee settlers all over the old city are spending days with great fear and apprehension. The small business holders and traders are more worried about their safety and security. The Bengali hooligans of the area are threatening them for their lives. Already, the low-income refugee settlers and the daily laborers are vacating their makeshift, roadside shops, and their shelters in adjoining slum areas and are moving toward Mirpur and Mohammadpur areas, where large numbers of refugee immigrants are settled," he said.

Andaleeb himself was threatened over the phone as he had been several times before. Andaleeb continued,

"Even though, I'm not too much worried about my own safety, my old grandmother is really scared. She desperately wants to go back to her late husband's old village in Bhopal, India, which she had fled from almost two decades ago."

Hearing all these, Rania commented,

"It will perhaps be better to send your grandmother back there to her nephews and nieces who are still there. The situation in this country doesn't look very good. My gut feeling is that General Yahya's intention is not very encouraging. If Mujib does not play according to Bhutto's tune, he will urge and Yahya will opt for military crackdown on the students and general protesting public. This is the impression I got from my talk with Ayesha and her husband in Mohammadpur earlier today. Ayesha's nephew Captain Khaleq works with the Baluch Regiment of Pakistan army. He had been transferred along with several other members of his Regiment to Dhaka earlier this month. He had advised Ayesha and their other relatives in Dhaka to move to Islamabad. He said that General Yahya had come to Dhaka this time to silence Sheikh Mujib once and for all."

Both Andaleeb and Rokshana were terrified at Rania's remarks. Nobody could gather courage to respond to Rania's comments. Rania herself took a deep breath of despair and continued.

"Only God knows what is in store for us in the near future. Ayesha told me something today which she had never dared before. She said that the Bengalis were infidels at heart and that they really wanted to be reunited with their Bengali Hindu brethren across the border in the Indian State of West

Bengal. She also told me that I had made a great mistake by having married a Bengali man."

"And you accepted that silently, Mother, and did not respond to her comments?" Rokshana asked obliquely.

"What can I say to that under the present situation after so many years of my happy marriage with your father in this country?"

"There was a time when you used to oppose forcefully any adverse comments by your relatives against marrying my Bengali father. Now, perhaps, you have lost that fire of your love for my father. Otherwise, you would have taught your Urdu-speaking friend Ayesha a fitting lesson for making all those nasty comments about my father and his fellow Bengalis."

Rokshana was upset with her mother this time and quickly walked out of the room.

Both Andaleeb and Rania were dumbfounded at Rokshana's sudden emotional outburst. They stared at each other with utter disbelief. Andaleeb felt a kind of sympathy in his heart for Rokhi. He realized that Rokshana was going through a difficult mental phase in her life. On one side, there were her non-Bengali mother and her Urdu-speaking refugee settler friends and relatives who were in danger of losing their houses, properties, and other worldly possessions; and were even at the risk of losing their lives for the second time within the span of a little over two decades. On the other side, there was her beloved fiancé and Bengali cousin

Kabil whose life's mission was to fight for the rights and rightful place of his fellow Bengalis preferably within the framework of one united Pakistan. Andaleeb understood that Rokshana—his beautiful, young cousin whom he himself once loved dearly—was standing at a difficult crossroad in her life. Besides, he reminded himself that he too was truly in love with Momena—a beautiful, traditional Bengali girl.

ON MARCH 20, 1971, both Andaleeb and Rokhi put Andaleeb's aging grandmother on an Indian Air Lines flight to Delhi. Afterward, they drove to their fashion-tailoring shop in Sakura behind the Intercontinental Hotel. Rokhi invited Andaleeb in for a cup of tea before his departure to attend their shop in the old city of Dhaka. Inside the shop, Andaleeb sat on a sofa. Rokshana asked their new tailor master Mr. Abdullah to arrange for two cups of tea for her and Andaleeb. Andaleeb started the conversation as he took a sip from his tea cup.

"Rokhi! If you can, please try to find the whereabouts of Kabil. He shouldn't have gone to stay at the university campus in this dangerous situation. The dialogue between General Yahya Khan and the Awami League leadership has created some discontent among some student groups affiliated with other local political parties. These groups have become more militant and violent even to Kabil's Student League affiliated with the Awami League. There is an atmosphere of despair in the city. I know the nature and intent of the speech that Kabil was likely to have delivered this afternoon in front of the students group. But that will not pacify the more militant students. Rather, it will make them hostile to Kabil himself. He should have stayed home at this critical time. Moreover, Yahya—the drunkard General that he is—will not give in to the demands of the violent and hostile student groups, nor would he spare the unarmed young students. He would, if necessary, hit them hard with full military force. Consequently, I'm afraid, the situation may turn into a murderous confrontation between the Bengalis and the pro-Pakistan, non-Bengali refugee settlers' communities. You should not allow Aunty Rania to go to the immigrant settlement areas alone anymore."

"Does she ever listen to me? She is always worried about what might happen to us—you, me, and especially Kabil," Rokshana interjected.

"I'm also worried about Kabil," Andaleeb added.

"What can I do worrying too much about Kabil? Is he going to quit politics if I ask him to?"

"But Rokhi! If Pakistan is split into two separate countries, what do you think will happen to us immigrant refugees? Where shall we go?"

"Why should you go anywhere? You will stay here. You all, including my maternal grandfather left everything in India once before in your lives and came here because of political division of the subcontinent in 1947. Now, this is your country. There is no other country for you and my mother other than this place. Why should the innocent refugee immigrant minority community pay such a heavy price of being uprooted time and again because of political disputes among the leaders of any country?" Rokhi asked.

There was a kind of childlike solution in Rokhi's assertion to the recurring, widespread human tragedies in many countries throughout the world. Even though, there was a glimmer of truth in her childlike question. Andaleeb set the empty tea cup aside and said,

"You're very correct, Rokhi! But the prevailing situation indicates that the non-Bengali community leaders here think that God has sent an angel in the form of General Yahya to ensure the unity and integrity of Pakistan by teaching the rebellious Bengalis a lesson, once and for all. These leaders refuse to accept that Mujib's Six Points Demand are right and legitimate. Every non-Bengali immigrant businessman thinks that if Mujib becomes prime minister of Pakistan and implements his election manifesto of Six Points Demand, his party hooligans would either kill or drive away all the non-Bengali immigrant settlers. This is the message that is being delivered by their leaders everywhere among the settlers' communities. If the general Bengali public understood these vicious propagandas in Urdu, no non-Bengali family's business establishments would be safe and secure by now. Considering that, I would think that Bengali young people are by far sober and patient."

Having said his piece, Andaleeb left Rokshana and the tailoring shop.

TOWARD THE EVENING, ANJUMAN suddenly dropped by Rokshana's house. She was rather in a hurry and asked:

"Isn't brother Kabil back home yet?"

"Why? He's at the university campus. He wasn't supposed to be home so early," Rokshana replied.

"There was a violent chaos at the campus because of the speech that Kabil had delivered there late this afternoon. Some students labelled him as a traitor and stooge for the Biharis. A few of them got into fistfights with each other as a result of that."

"What? We haven't heard anything like that, Sister Anju!"

"Yes. That was the case. Kabil, during his speech, had called for a unified stand by both the Bengalis and the Bihari settlers in opposing General Yahya's conspiracy against the legitimate rights of East Pakistan under the disguise of military's on-going negotiations with the Awami League leaders. He said that this was the wish and instructions of Sheikh Mujib, who wanted a unified front against the conspiracies by West Pakistani industry and business elites and the upper military echelons. Kabil's statement caused turmoil and commotions among some student participants in the gathering. Nisar was also present at the gathering. Nisar said that Kabil's friends whisked him away safely from the crowd and out of the campus. Nisar came back home and asked me to inquire if Kabil had returned home."

"No. He hasn't come back. Then, where else could he have gone?"

"There is no reason for you to panic about it. Nisar had seen Kabil being escorted safely out of the meeting site by his close associates. Maybe he has gone to Sheikh Mujib's house. Let's go and check," Anju continued while she began walking to the telephone set in Rokshana's bedroom. As the two of them entered Rokhi's bedroom, the telephone rang.

"Hello!" Rokshana answered.

"It's me, Kabil. I'm calling from our leader's house at Dhanmondi. Did you hear about the incident in our meeting at the campus this afternoon?"

"Yes. I just got the news from sister Anju."

"Don't worry. It was not that serious and I'm safe and well. I'll brief our leader about it and will soon come home after the briefing. Please do not tell Aunty about it. It will simply cause her more pain and she will be more worried about me."

With that Kabil put the phone down. Rokhi turned to Anju and said, "Kabil says he is at his leader Mujib's house and will come home soon. He asked me to tell you that he planned to visit your house with me when he will have returned home later this evening."

MARCH 21, 1971. THERE was a report circulating in Dhaka that Mr. Z. A. Bhutto, leader of the Peoples Party which won majority parliamentary seats from West Pakistan but overall fewer parliamentary seats than Mujib's Awami League Party, had come to Dhaka to take part in a tripartite dialogue with Mujib and General Yahya. Kabil expressed to Rokhi, Anju, and Nisar at a dinner at Anju's house that evening an optimistic view of the report. He said at the dinner table,

"If Mr. Bhutto is in Dhaka today, it might be a good thing. Maybe, the three of them would find a compromise formula so that General Yahya can hand over the power to a civilian government headed by Sheikh Mujib."

Nisar did not share the views expressed by Kabil. He remarked,

"No way, Kabil. Yahya will never ever transfer governmental power to a civilian government headed by Sheikh Mujib. Both you and your other party leaders are running behind a mirage. There is no 'lake' of peace and hope ahead of that mirage—only a river of flowing human blood."

The news of Mr. Bhutto's arrival in Dhaka was received with mixed reactions by the general Bengali public. Some thought that a compromise solution would be found this time around. Perhaps, General Yahya had asked Mr. Bhutto to come to Dhaka to see if he could come to a mutual agreement with Sheikh Mujib. Others thought that Yahya had asked Mr. Bhutto to come to Dhaka as a pretext to buy some time for his military generals to prepare for a military crackdown. Yahya might be using Bhutto's presence as a camouflage for his ulterior motives with the pretence of tripartite political negotiations. Because whatever Mr. Bhutto had been saying in public meetings and news conferences in West Pakistan since the election results were announced, did not reflect his intention to accept the election verdicts of majority of the people in the whole of Pakistan. Rather, Mr. Bhutto gave the impression to the students and the intelligentsia of East Pakistan that he was the leader of the elected majority party in West Pakistan, regardless of whether or not it was united with East Pakistan as a single united country of Pakistan. These groups of people thought that General Yahya representing the Pakistan's armed forces based mostly in West Pakistan would be compelled by his military associates to support Mr. Bhutto's stand in order to safeguard their own position among the people of West Pakistan, who overwhelmingly had voted for Mr. Bhutto's party.

Meanwhile, the youth and student movements all over East Pakistan somewhat forcefully and unofficially designated Sheikh Mujib as their elected prime minister and trusted him with the day-to-day administration of the government businesses. The administrative machinery all over the province was taking day-to-day orders and instructions from his Awami League Party leaders. The prevailing general environment was such as if East Pakistan would never again take orders from a central government based in West Pakistan and headed by someone other than Sheikh Mujib. They maintained that Sheikh Mujib should unequivocally tell General Yahya and Mr. Bhutto that his Awami League Party had won majority of the seats in the National Parliament and as such, he as the Awami League Party leader was the unequivocal prime minister of the whole of Pakistan. If Mr. Bhutto and Mr. Yahya cannot accept that fact and act accordingly, then East Pakistan would go alone and declare itself as a separate, independent, sovereign state.

MARCH 23, 1971. AT around seven o'clock in the morning, Rokshana drove Kabil to Dhanmondi main road in front of the lane leading to Mujib's private residence at No. 32. Kabil asked her to stop the car at this place and drop him there—a short distance from No. 32.

"I can walk to No. 32 from here," Kabil said.

"I can drive all the way and drop you right in front of his residence," Rokshana replied.

"No need for that. Moreover, look at the line of cars trying to get there to see the leader. Once you go in, it will be difficult and time consuming for you to turn back."

With that Kabil got out of the car.

"Shall I wait here for you? Or shall I go back home? I have nothing urgent to do at home. I don't feel like going to attend the shop either this morning," Rokshana asked.

"Then wait for me in the car. The leader has promised to see me at around seven thirty. He is usually on time and keeps his appointment schedule. If you can wait, I'll go back home with you soon after my brief discussion with him," Kabil responded before he walked away. Rokshana parked the car in a close by secured place.

Kabil returned from No. 32 much earlier than both of them had anticipated. He had a rather sad look on his face.

Rokshana got out of the car and met Kabil in front of the lane with a worried and inquisitive look on her face.

"What happened? You're back early?" Rokshana asked.

"Why did you get down? Let's go inside the car and I'll tell you everything there."

Kabil took Rokshana's hand in his and guided her back to the car. He sounded rather disappointed.

"Did you get a chance to see him?" Rokshana asked as she started the car and drove out.

"Yes, I did see him briefly."

"Then? Why do you look so disappointed? Tell me a little of what you talked about."

"There's nothing much to tell, Rokhi. He didn't say much either. But I got the feeling today that there is hardly any other person in the whole of Pakistan as simple and straight talking as Sheikh Mujib. He's even willing to compromise on our Six Points Demand and accept Bhutto's claims of majority parliamentary seats in West Pakistan. He thinks his softened stand on our Six Points Demand will impress both General Yahya and Mr. Bhutto with the goodwill of the Bengalis. This, in turn, will motivate General Yahya to issue a Presidential order inviting Awami League to form a civilian government in Islamabad with its leader as the Prime Minister. This way, he will be able to maintain the unity and integrity of Pakistan and yet will be able to slowly implement our Six Points Demand of regional autonomy for East Pakistan in the long run. He's hoping a lot of positive developments in today's planned negotiation with both Bhutto and General

Yahya. Yet the student leaders and the Bengali intelligentsia feel that today's dialogue is simply a ploy by both Bhutto and the military leadership under Yahya to buy time for them before they unleash something horrible that might lead to the division of the state of Pakistan."

"Your last words are mere reflections of a small militant group of students predicting a future for the worst. If your leader thinks that a compromise solution is possible through negotiations, then why are you student leaders so impatient?" Rokshana asked with rather a vexed tone in her voice.

"We're impatient because we know our leader. The West Pakistani leadership didn't reciprocate so far in the negotiation at all to whatever our leaders had indicated to accept a compromise formula on our Six Points Demand. Sheikh Mujib made all those concessions for preserving the territorial integrity and political unity of Pakistan which has always been a priority in his mind. The student leaders are afraid that the military leaders are harboring an ulterior motive and that Mr. Bhutto knows well about the nefarious plan and that is the reason why Bhutto has taken a rather uncompromising stand in the negotiation process. Only the Bengali leaders are ill-informed of the military's plans and preparations. They foolishly think that matters can still be resolved amicably through dialogue and negotiations involving compromise on both sides. We, the students, aren't so optimistic of that compromise any longer."

"Why don't you tell your leader directly about your concerns?" Rokshana asked innocently.

"He knows our views and our collective feelings. But we haven't asked him yet for his reactions to our doubts about the intentions of the West Pakistani political and military leaders. Today, I told him directly that we do not think Bhutto is interested in any political compromise, and the military is not capable of imposing a political solution on Bhutto's Peoples Party because of the widespread support the party enjoys in West Pakistan. Bhutto surely doesn't want to see Mujib as the prime minister because Bhutto thinks he is the leader of West Pakistan and doesn't want to play the role of an opposition leader. I asked him to give us instructions in time, so that if Yahya embarks on a military crackdown, we do not find ourselves totally unprepared and take heavy losses in our resistance. I told him that the responsibility lies squarely on his shoulders."

"What you said is pressuring him to declare war openly. What was his response?"

"He put his hand on my back and asked me to go home, and I left right away."

MARCH 24, 1971. EARLY in the morning, Andaleeb arrived at Rokshana's house and rang the bell outside the closed gate. Kabil came out and opened the gate. He was surprised to see Andaleeb standing outside.

"What happened, brother Andy? You're here so early in the morning."

"It seems like it is impossible for me and my domestic help Jubi to stay at our home in Narinda any longer. The local young thugs threw stones at our roof, doors, and windows all night long yesterday. Some even threatened from behind trees outside that they would set my house on fire unless we vacate the house on time. I woke up early this morning and decided that I should bring the situation to your attention and seek your advice. All non-Bengali families living in the area have already left and moved to Mirpur and Mohammadpur area where there are large concentrations of non-Bengali settlers. I'm not that much afraid, but nobody can predict misfortune," Andaleeb narrated as he walked inside the gate. Kabil looked at Andaleeb's face as they stepped up on the verandah. He found Andaleeb—normally a courageous man—visibly worried and afraid. There was widespread fear and apprehension among the non-Bengali immigrant settlers all over the city. Have they somehow got the hint that General Yahya would soon call off the negotiation process and unleash a thunderous rain of military crackdown on unarmed Bengali citizens? *Are they anticipating revenge on themselves by local majority Bengali populace?* Kabil wondered silently. He sat on a chair in the verandah and directed Andaleeb to sit on another one.

"No, brother! I'll make sure you will stay safely in your own house in Narinda. Now, let's go, have some breakfast," Kabil said with a glare of confidence on his face.

"Maybe, I and my domestic help Jubi can come here and spend a few days in this house, since the miscreants in this area are aware of you and sister Anjuman's status in the Awami League Party. Hence, hopefully, they will not dare take any action against refugee settlers like me and Aunty Rania," Andaleeb asked with a terrified look in his eyes.

"Why? You shouldn't vacate your own house. Neither should all the other refugee settlers. If you all do that, the local miscreants will find an excuse and will carry out widespread looting. If the situation were not this tense all over East Pakistan, I would have suggested that you go and spend some time with Momi in our village home at Montala. However, my thinking is that the non-Bengali settlers should demonstrate the strength of their moral character and show solidarity with the Bengalis in their legitimate grievances against perpetual injustices for decades now. They shouldn't leave the unarmed majority of Bengali civilians of Dhaka to face any possible military crackdown by Yahya's army and leave for some safe areas for themselves. If they do, the Bengalis will think that they all are with their enemies of Yahya's military forces and supporters of rich industrialists and capitalists of West Pakistan," Kabil said with some skepticism in his tone. Andaleeb was visibly scared at Kabil's narratives and asked,

"Is the Bhutto-Yahya alliance then going for military actions against the Bengali civilians?" he asked nervously.

"Personally, I don't think that they will. But I spent last night at the university campus and just came home shortly before you arrived. All student leaders are almost unanimous in their opinion that Bhutto had come here to encourage and incite military crackdown on public and the students."

"Why do you then think differently?"

"The only reason I have is that Sheikh Mujib told me that he didn't think General Yahya would be that foolish to give in to Bhutto's pressure and, thus, risk breaking up Pakistan by taking widespread military action against unarmed Bengalis. Mujib told me that he didn't get so far any indication to that effect from General Yahya in their on-going dialogue. Mujib is a seasoned politician, and has been involved in politics all his life starting from his student days in united India in the 1940s when he had fought hard supporting the cause of creating a separate sovereign state of Pakistan in the Muslim majority areas of India.

If General Yahya had any nefarious motive to do anything involving military force that will surely lead to the breakup of Pakistan, Mujib would have sensed it during their negotiations. In that case, Mujib would do everything he could to persuade General Yahya not to do any such thing. Since Mujib thinks that the negotiation is on the right track, then, I have no doubt that a compromise solution would be found to solve the present political impasse," Kabil explained confidently.

"I feel hopeful with your words, Kabil."

"Like I said, there is no immediate danger for any of you to be worried about. Let's have some breakfast now and then you can go home with confidence. I'll drop by your house as soon as I can to handle the miscreants who are threatening you in your own house. I'll tell our local party leaders to ensure your personal safety and security."

Kabil then asked their cook Halim to serve breakfast for Andaleeb and himself. Andaleeb felt reassured with Kabil's words of encouragement and left for his house after the breakfast.

EARLY THAT EVENING, KABIL was dressed smartly ready to go out. Rokshana came to his room and asked,

"Are you going to the university campus?"

"No. I was thinking about going to Anjuman's house to spend some time with her and her husband, Nisar. Do you want to come and join us?"

"Better, why don't we go and visit Andaleeb in his house at Narinda area? He seemed to have been visibly scared this morning with the situation in his neighborhood. He will feel reassured if we pay him a visit there at this scary time for him."

"Good idea. On our way back, we can drop by the Ittefaq office and find out more about the latest progress in the dialogue between General Yahay and Sheikh Mujib. I know many journalists in that office whom I haven't visited for a long time now."

"Okay. You wait for me for a few minutes in the verandah. I'll get ready and join you there."

Soon after, they decided to take a man-paddled tricycle rickshaw to Narinda area instead of taking their car because the lanes in Narinda area were rather narrow and congested in the evening time. Rokshana was wearing a silk saree with matching short-sleeve blouse showing her fair-skinned arms and mid-rib. Kabil was wearing a typical Bengali style well-pressed, white dress pajama, a long brown Punjabi, and a matching no-sleeve Mujib-style vest. The two of them sitting close to each other on the rather narrow passenger cabin of the rickshaw looked very much like a typical happy Bengali couple out for some quality time in town in the early evening. Rokshana felt happy that Kabil, after a long while, agreed to spend some time with her alone instead of his regular visits alone to the university campus in the recent past.

It took them about twenty-five minutes to reach the Narinda area. They got down from the rickshaw in front of Andaleeb's house on Basubazar Lane. Kabil noticed a group of three mischievous-looking young boys sitting on the low front boundary wall of Andaleeb's house. They were chatting among themselves with visibly evil looks in their eyes. They were somewhat nervous upon seeing Kabil and Rokshana there and hurriedly got down from the wall. Kabil hurriedly paid the rickshaw puller and then, without letting Rokshana sense anything, walked toward the boys. He grabbed the shirt collar of one of the boys who looked like the leader of the group and asked,

"Who threw stones at the doors and windows of this my brother's house last night?"

Seeing Kabil's sudden and unexpected move, the young boys felt numb and dumb momentarily and looked at Kabil with blank, fearful eyes. Rokshana didn't know how to react herself. Kabil held on to the boy's shirt collar, forcefully shook him up and shouted again.

"You thugs! Tell me who threw stones last night at my brother's house? Who threatened him to vacate his house? Tell me his name, otherwise, I'll break your neck."

"Why are you holding me?" the boy finally answered. "I don't know anything about it. You ask your non-Bengali brother if he has seen me or not."

The boy was visibly shaken and scared. Seeing the look on his face, the other two boys ran away from the scene. Meanwhile, a few passersby stood nearby. They don't know Kabil in this area. But noticing the way he was dressed, they realized that he was one of the student leaders and was somebody important.

Realizing the commotion outside his house's boundary wall, Andaleeb opened the gate and came out himself. He was awestruck seeing Kabil still holding the young boy by his shirt collar with rage in Kabil's eyes, as if, he was about to beat the young boy. Rokshana quickly ran to Kabil, freed the young boy from Kabil's grip, and told the boy,

"Go and escape! Never again come to hang out around this house."

As the young boy started to walk away, Kabil shouted to him.

"If I ever hear again that somebody threw stone at this house, then remember, whosoever's son you might be, I'll pick you up from your father's house, and cut your ears off. You think you hooligans can go unpunished for your sectarian crimes."

Suddenly, the crowd started walking away from the scene. Andaleeb came forward and said,

"Let's go inside."

All three of them then walked across the front courtyard and stepped up on the verandah.

"Let's go inside the house. Come to my bedroom and we'll chat there. I have some important news to share with you," Andaleeb suggested.

They entered Andaleeb's bedroom. He motioned to Kabil and Rokshana to sit on the bed while he himself sat on a round rattan stool nearby.

"Tell me if you would like to eat something with your afternoon tea now, and I'll ask Jubi to bring some food along with your tea," Andaleeb asked them.

"No. No need for any food right now. Just tell her to bring some tea for now," Kabil replied.

Shortly after, Jubi brought some tea for all three of them inside the room. Andaleeb took a sip from his cup and said,

"I heard from some source close to the immigrant settlers' community that some of Bhutto's close associates who had come to Dhaka with him for discussion with Sheikh Mujib are leaving for West Pakistan later this evening."

"What does that mean?" Kabil asked with keen inquisitiveness. "Does that mean the negotiation broke down?"

"I don't know about the status of the negotiations. All daily newspapers reported today that the negotiation was continuing.

There were some indications in the daily Observer that some progress in the negotiation has been made. In that situation, why would they leave Dhaka before the final outcome of the negotiation has been achieved? There is no way for common people like me to predict the status of the negotiation. Maybe, we'll get some information in tomorrow's newspapers," Andaleeb said to calm Kabil down

Kabil put down the tea cup on the tray and said:

"I thought I was going to spend the evening and have dinner with you here Cousin Andy. But at this moment I feel I need to see our leader Sheikh Mujib right away. The Awami League Party leaders would probably be home before ten p.m. from their evening discussion with General Yahya and his team. I would like to know the outcome of their discussion as soon as I can. Rokhi and I would therefore like to leave now, brother."

"If you have to go, then you must go. But before you leave, I'd like to request you something, brother Kabil. Whatever march or procession, etc., that you take part in these critical days, please do not stay overnight at the university students' dormitory. You rather come back home and stay at night with Aunty Rania and my cousin Rokhi. Aunty has been really sad and demoralized lately. She can't fall asleep worrying about you if you are not home at night. You know that yourself. She cannot explain everything to you for various reasons. But you must think about her situation."

"I'll return home at night unless I am held up for something important and urgent. I promise you, brother."

"Okay then. You do whatever you have to do," Andaleeb commented as he stood up.

As he escorted Rokhi and Kabil to the street in front of his house, Andaleeb said to Rokhi,

"It is not possible any longer for me to stay at home and do no business, more so considering our businesses' poor performance of late. I need to go and tend to our businesses from tomorrow onward. The spice-grinding machine shop is near closing down condition. Our workers are secretly and fearfully coming to work from Mirpur/Mohammedpur areas. There are many absentees as well. Maybe we need to hire some new people to fill the vacancies as well."

"I will go to the factory from tomorrow onward brother Andy," Rokhi replied.

"I'm not saying that you will have to come."

"Don't worry. Whatever happens to the political situation, we are business people. We can't sit idle by locking up our businesses. From tomorrow onward, I'll spend part of my days in all three of our business locations. We'll have to earn money to survive."

Andaleeb felt encouraged and motivated by Rokhi's determination. He remembered that her father Syed Ahmed Alam was a shrewd businessman and used to talk like that. Rokhi has got some business acumen from both her father and mother's side.

"I'm finding it difficult to keep all spice-grinding machines running with many absentee workers," Andy further commented.

"If they don't come to work, what can we do? We'll have to hire new workers—Bengali or Bihari—and train them to do the job," Rokhsana concluded as she got into the cycle rickshaw with Kabil sitting next to her. As the rickshaw kept rolling, Kabil suddenly became aware and worried about the deteriorating condition of their family businesses. He did not have time lately to pay much attention to the running of the family businesses. Rokhsana has been supervising all the family businesses by herself as her mother was not of late in good health to do so. Yet she does not seem to be much worried about their future prospect in business. Seeing the worried look in Kabil's face she broke the silence.

"Don't you worry too much about our family business. I can handle that myself."

Kabil couldn't and didn't say anything for a while. He just kept staring at Rokhsana in the corner of his eyes. Her all too familiar fair-complexioned appearance suddenly looked more beautiful and inviting to Kabil at that moment. He found a kind of emanating radiance in her appearance that helps a man feel self-reliant and bold. A man with exceptional congenital luck deserves the love and affection of such a woman. Kabil felt good with his own luck and divine fortune. He silently kept on looking at Rokhsana sitting very close next to him inside the rickshaw cabin. Rokhsana felt slightly embarrassed and uneasy by Kabil's oblique stare. She said,

"Why are you looking at me like a hungry hyena?"

"You, Rokhi, are really a wonderful, strange girl," Kabil could not resist pouring out.

"I'm really nothing wonderful or strange. You find me strange because of your own unstable and uncertain situation. I thought you were going to say how beautiful and attractive you find me at this moment. Once in a while you say that whenever you find the opportunity. But today you said something different."

"You are somewhat different, Rokhi."

"If I'm not different, then who will look after the business that my father—your uncle—left behind? My father hoped that you yourself would take care of his sizable business beyond him. But you and I know that you would never have time for that because of your involvement in safeguarding the rights of our people in this province of Pakistan. But we'll have to depend on these businesses for our family's economic survival. You find me strange because you always look at me as your dependent future wife. Would you find me strange if you looked at me as your helpless cousin sister?"

"You'll look wonderful and beautiful to me from whatever angle I look at you, Rokhi! Because I love you from the core of my heart, from all directions."

Rokshana felt a little shy and embarrassed by Kabil's genuine self-confession. Out of her usual habit, she covered her head and said in a way of changing the subject,

"We are in front of the Ittefaq office. Go inside if you want. I would wait for you outside the front gate."

"Why do you want to wait outside the gate? Why not come inside the building with me? I'd go and see the news editor Shiraj Bhai, get a piece of information, and come back right away. I want to know whether the news we just heard about most West Pakistani leaders leaving Dhaka this evening in the middle of their serious political discussion with Awami League is correct or not."

"You go alone. I'd spend the time reading the *Ittefaq* pasted on the outside boundary wall of the building. You finish your talk as soon as you can and come down quickly. If I go with you, a lot of people there will rather keep staring at me. You know how uncomfortable that makes me feel."

"All right! I'll come down shortly."

As soon as Kabil walked upstairs inside the Ittefaq office and Rokshana moved on the sidewalk outside the boundary wall to read the day's copy of the paper pasted on the wall a short distance from the front gate, two young men walked out from inside through the gate. They noticed Rokshana as they walked by on the sidewalk. They looked like university students. As Rokshana tried to concentrate on the newspaper on the wall, she overheard one of the young men tell the other,

"That is our student leader Kabil's Bihari whore."

"What is she doing here reading the *Ittefaq*?" responded the other.

"She is definitely waiting for someone. Shall we knock her out?" asked the first one.

"Leave it for now. No need to invite pedestrians to gather around her. When time is ripe, we'll get the whore on another occasion."

Rokhsana's two ears became unusually hot overhearing the conversation between the two guys. Her heart started pounding hard. She felt as if the boundary wall of the Ittefaq office by the sidewalk fell down on her head. She could hardly see anything. Suddenly, the news headlines on the paper pasted on the wall appeared to be a hodge-podge to her eyes. She walked a little farther by the wall, leaned on it with her back, and tried to steady herself by looking at the road in front. The fast-moving traffic and the pedestrians on the road appeared as hazy smoke in her eyes. She felt like crumbling down on the sidewalk if she did not lean back on the wall. She could not remember how long she had been leaning on the wall. Suddenly, she felt the touch of Kabil's hands on her back. As she grabbed him with both hands she said,

"I'm feeling dizzy. Please hold me firmly for a minute or so."

"What's the matter? What happened all of a sudden?" Kabil asked.

"I'm not feeling well. Please call a rickshaw and help me get on the seat."

As a rickshaw pulled over by the roadside, Kabil lifted Rokshana with his both hands and got her seated inside the canopy. He then sat himself by her side. Rokhsana grabbed him with both her hands, put her head against his chest, and fainted. Kabil looked around. Nobody was paying attention to anyone. The flow of vehicles and pedestrians kept moving as usual. As the rickshaw came to their house on Bonogram Lane, Rokshana came out of her fainting. Kabil helped her get down.

"I can walk home inside," Rokshana said.

"Maybe not. Let me help you climb the stairs up to the verandah."

"No need. If Mother sees us, she would think something serious happened to me, and she would be worried."

"Your condition seems serious to me. You didn't tell me anything. What happened for you to suddenly faint?" Kabil asked.

"I'll tell you later. Now I can go on my own. No need to call my mother. I'll go to your room."

Kabil paid the rickshaw puller his fares for the ride. When he got to his bedroom, he noticed Rokshana was lying flat on her back on his bed and was staring at the ceiling. Rokshana signalled him toward her and said, "Come this way and put your hand on my head."

Kabil silently went near Rokshana and put his hand on her forehead.

"What happened to you suddenly?" he asked.

"As soon as you went inside the Ittefaq office building, two students came outside the gate on the sidewalk. It appeared they knew both of us. When they saw me standing and reading the paper on the wall, they made some nasty comments about me as they passed by. I couldn't hold myself with rage and sadness. If you didn't come back as soon as you did, I probably would fall down on the sidewalk."

"What did they say?"

"They said that I was Kabil's Bihari whore and that one day in the future, they will knock me down, etc."

Kabil kept silent for a few seconds and then said, "Why would you faint like that because of those ruffians' irresponsible words?"

"I don't know what happened to me."

"You should have gone forward, hold one of them by his shirt collar. Generally, they are cowards. If you challenged them, you would have realized that they have very weak spine with no moral strength."

"I would have slapped them with my sandal if you were with me."

"You slap them from now onward even if I'm not with you. They are eunuchs without any ideals. They can only terrorize and insult women—nothing else. If you challenge them, they will not hesitate to lie down on your feet."

Rokshana suddenly got up, embraced Kabil with both hands, and put her head against his chest. Kabil put his hand on her back and said,

"You lie down on the bed and get some rest. I will have to go to the Leader's house for a while."

"What did you learn from the Ittefaq office?"

"I didn't get a chance to tell you, Rokhi, considering your condition. The news in general is not good. Some West Pakistani leaders are leaving Dhaka tonight. The local media is skeptical even though our leaders are telling them that the negotiations are still going on. *Ittefaq* news editor told me that General Yahya was meeting separately with his military advisers. That means he is planning for repressive military actions."

Hearing that, Rokshana embraced Kabil more closely and said,

"What are you then going to the Leader's house for?"

"It is my duty, Rokhi, to see him at this crucial time. He is very affectionate to me and trusts me a lot. He tells me about things that he would not share with his other political associates. I'll not feel good being away from him at this time."

Kabil then gently and carefully put Rokhsana on the bed and left home.

KABIL CAME BACK HOME from Mujib's house at around eleven that evening. As he entered the house compound, he found Rokhi near the gate. He was surprised to see her there and asked,

"What's the matter? Where's Uncle Halim?"

"I was awake, so I came to open the gate for you."

"Why are you awake so late?"

"I was talking to mother after dinner. Nobody went to bed knowing that you would be back soon with some news."

"Is that so? Actually, an unlikely fear has taken its grip in our household. The one who can lessen this fear, is really making it worse."

"Are you referring to me?"

Kabil didn't respond to Rokhi's question. He walked straight to the dining area and stood beside Rania who was sitting on a chair behind the table. He told her,

"Aunty! You aren't supposed to stay up so late. Why do you wait up for me? Now let's get up and I'll take you to your bedroom." With that he took Rania's arm in his hand.

"I heard that you had gone to see Sheikh Mujib, and I thought we would get the latest news from you."

"Aunty! You aren't feeling well. You should not be tensed anticipating any bad news. If you continue doing that, you'll put yourself in danger one of these days."

"What danger are you talking about? The worst could be that I'd die and be with your uncle Alam. In that case, you and Rokhi will be spared and will not have to put up with me," Rania said with a kind of motherly complain. Rokshana was standing quietly at the corner holding the dining table.

"Why would you die? Why are you unhappy? There will be political ups and downs in this country. You need not be worried and scared about it," Kabil put emphatically.

"Everybody is scared and running away from this locality like the time when we fled from India fearing for our lives. And you say there is nothing to be afraid of?"

Rania replied with a sense of irritation and tension in her voice. Kabil had no response to Rania's comments. Yet he said as if to divert Rania's attention,

"No. You have nothing to be afraid of."

339

"Why don't I have anything to be afraid of? Simply because I had married a Bengali man a long time back?"

"Yes! You don't have anything to be afraid of because you are my aunty."

"But I'm not a Bengali, my son."

Kabil was taken aback at the tone of Rania's voice as if Rania's last words shot Kabil's heart from the front and went out through his back. Yet Rania was right. She was not a Bengali. She had doubts in her mind about her safety and security like many other refugee settlers, perhaps even for their lives. Kabil took Rania in his arms in an embrace and said,

"So what if you aren't a Bengali? You are still my aunty and your son—this Kabil—is a true-blue Bengali."

"Yes, you're a Bengali and my own daughter, Rokhi is a Bengali, but I'm a Bihari. I'm a refugee settler in this land. I have no country of my own. I have no compatriot. The local people think I'm their enemy. They want to kick me out of this land."

Rania freed herself from Kabil's embrace and walked quickly toward her bedroom. Both Kabil and Rokhi were dumbfounded at Rania's quick disappearance from the scene.

Kabil had his late dinner. While he was eating, Rokshana just sat quietly by the dining table with her head down. She felt the silence of the night piercing into her heart because of the way Rania had just disappeared earlier into her bedroom. She didn't say a word while Kabil was eating. She didn't bother to ask Kabil about his meeting in the evening earlier with Sheikh Mujib. She just sat there by the table while Kabil was eating. Only cook Halim said, as he was serving food to Kabil,

"There was a letter for you in the mail box. I picked it up and left it in your room."

Kabil looked at Rokshana for a split second when she said,

"It's from Momi from Montala. I saw the envelope and it's on your bed."

"You could have opened and read it. She might have written something about her needs and difficulties in these trying times."

"It came only today. You can go and read it." With that she got up and went to her bedroom. A short time later, Kabil, after finishing his dinner, also retired to his bedroom.

As Rokshana lay down in her bed, she couldn't fall asleep. Tossing and turning, she became overly curious about what Momi might have written in her letter to Kabil. Momi usually does not know very much about the current political tension engulfing Dhaka and what is going on in the lives of Rokhi, Rania, and Kabil. Momi doesn't know what terrible mental and circumstantial conditions this family in Dhaka was going through. She wondered what Momi might have written Kabil about. If it was about her financial or other difficulties, she usually wrote either to Rania or to Andaleeb. She never before wrote directly to Kabil—not that Rokshana knew about at least. Rokshana was now feeling somewhat uneasy about the whole matter of Momi's unusual letter to Kabil. What did Momi write to Kabil about? Does Momi still have hopes and her childhood claim for Kabil through his mother's previous promise to her? Or is she worried about everybody in this family during the current political turmoil in the country? If Momi is worried about Andaleeb's safety and security because of the prevailing Bengali-Bihari tension in the country, should she not have written to Andaleeb himself? Rokshana knew that Momi had written letters to Andaleeb before from time to time. Momi was not educated enough and didn't think much about politics in the country. If she did, then it would be all right to write to Kabil about the current political situations. And it wouldn't bother Rokshana and would not cause her to have difficulty in falling asleep over her letter to Kabil.

Rokshana got up and sat on her bed. Then suddenly and impulsively she walked toward Kabil's bedroom and peaked through his normally open window. She noticed that Kabil was fast asleep and snoring vigorously. In the dim light of the room, she saw that Momi's now opened letter was lying on the window side table. Rokshana quietly picked up the letter through the window. She came back to her own bedroom and read the letter.

Momi wrote:

Dear Cousin Brother Kabil:

"I'm writing to you today to inquire about the well-being of all of you. I heard that the political situation in Dhaka is not that good. Apparently, sporadic riots between the Bengalis and the Biharis are going on in Dhaka. I'm worried about all of you being in this situation. Please write me back as soon as you can with details of how you, Rokhi sister, Rania Aunty, and cousin Andaleeb are doing. There are some communal troubles near the railway station close to our home in Montala. Some people from our village carried out widespread lootings in the households of Bihari railway porters, pointsmen, and even the Bihari Station Master. Consequently, most Bihari families in and around Railway Station have fled to Akhaura Railway Junction, fearing for their lives. Some students from our Montala village came to our compound and warned me saying that they knew about a Bihari man who came from Dhaka to this household on a regular basis in the past and that I were to be married to that man. They threatened me saying further that if that happens, they would set our house on fire. I'm terrified, brother Kabil. For God's sake, please do not send cousin Andaleeb to Montala at least for a while.

I feel sad and embarrassed to write cousin Andaleeb directly about all these. Hence, I write to you about my concern.

Other than that, I'm doing all right here.

Yours affectionately,
Momi

After reading Momi's letter, Rokshana was dumbfounded. She felt relieved but kept staring through her window into the quietness of the moonlit night.

CHAPTER 4

Despairs of Two Student Activists

EARLY DAWN OF 27TH March, 1971. Kabil was at the tail end of his long REM dream in his escape boat on the Titas River rowed upstrem manually by a single man on its way to the Indian border town of Agartala. The only other passenger on the boat was Anjuman---Kabil's long time fellow student activist and wife of Kabil's close friend Nisar who had been killed by the the Pakistani army on the night of 25th March. Anjuman woke up a while ago and was listening to a portable hand held radio which Kabil had carried with him. Anjuman was trying to tune in to various frequencies to get news from Dhaka. At one point, she tuned into a certain unknown wave band where she heard news of quite an unexpected but hopeful announcement. She excitedly rushed back to the inside of the canopy of the boat and shook Kabil up and said:

"Wake up brother Kabil. Listen, I just heard on the radio a very reassuring announcement"

"What announcement? Whose announcement?" Kabil asked as he sat up on the mat still rubbing his eyes.

"It sounded like some Bengali Major of the East Bengal Regiment of Pakistan Army had just announced his defection from the Army. He supported the cause of Bangladesh

Liberation Struggle and made from a clandestine radio, on behalf of Sheik Mujibur Rahman an announcement proclaiming Bangladesh as a sovereign State fully independent of Pakistan. He identified himself as Major Ziaur Rahman."

"Thank God Anju. Sounds like our struggle has not totally stopped on the night of 25th March. The armed struggle for total independence has just started. Jai Bangla Anju, Jai Bangla (victory for Bangladesh)" Kabil announced excitedly with determination in his voice. Anjuman hugged Kabil with emotion and excitement. She said loudly:

"I want to take revenge from the Pakistan Army for shooting death of my husband, brother Kabil. I want to take part in whatever way I can in this armed struggle for our total independence. I will learn how to use rifles, machine guns and fight the beastly invaders until they are forced to leave our country".

Soon their boat reached a point near Akhaura Railway Junction. Kabil paid the rowman to his satisfaction and got off the boat helping Anju by holding her hand. They walked across the rail line and started walking toward the Indian border town of Agartala. They crossed the border and were cordially received by the Indian border police. Kabil introduced Anju and himself as student leaders and they were taken to the city where they were given political asylum. Soon they met up with other Mukti Bahini fighters from Bangladesh under the sector command of Major Jalil- a senior officer of the East Bengal Regiment who had also defected and was busy setting up his command in that sector. Kabil was given the command of a Platoon with seven other escapees from various rural areas of Bangladesh. None of them had any previous military training. But each one of them was willing to undergo rigorous training and to lay down their lives fighting the Pakistani army. Anjuman was designated as Kabil's assistant looking after the logistics for the Unit. Thus began the armed guerrilla type struggle by two prominent Dhaka University student leaders from across the Indian border along with many other such Bengali youth groups. The struggle was to last for nearly nine months. During these nine months, things moved fast in Dhaka which were devastating personally for Kabil.

MID DECEMBER, 1971. THE civil war in the then East Pakistan was almost over. The combined Bangladesh Liberation Forces (Mukti Bahini) and its coalition partner Indian Military had defeated the Pakistani occupying forces and liberated from its brutal control most areas of Bangladesh outside of the capital Dhaka. The coalition forces had surrounded Dhaka. General Niazi, the commander of the Pakistani forces in the then East Pakistan had agreed to surrender with his over one hundred thousand soldiers. The struggle of some seventy-five million (at that time) Bengali people lasting nearly twenty-five years for self-determination and liberation from the colonial grip of Pakistani exploiters and brutal military forces was coming to an end. The new nation of Bangladesh with a red-glowing eastern sun in the lush green background of its countryside on its new national flag was about to be born.

One very early morning, Kabil and Anjuman, two of many prominent, high-ranking student leaders of Dhaka University, who played direct military roles from across the Indian border in defeating the Pakistani military forces arrived back at Demra—just outside of Dhaka. They had fought for nearly nine months with other groups of the Mukti Bahini—mostly carrying out cross-border attacks from India on the Pakistani forces inside Bangladesh territories. After the rural areas of the country outside of Dhaka had been freed from the occupation of Pakistani forces, most of the units of Mukti Bahini had crossed over to Bangladesh.

Both Kabil and Anjuman had played earlier prominent roles in the student movement against the Pakistani dictatorship up until the latter's brutal military crackdown, mass murder, and the arrest and detention in West Pakistan military prison of their leader Sheikh Mujibur Rahman on March 25–26 of that year.

On this early morning of mid–December 1971, the group commanded by Kabil and assisted by Anjuman, along with their fellow group fighters, made their way to Demra. They started walking toward Dhaka while shooting in the air from their rifles and SLRs. The countryside was covered with dews of cool December morning. Even though they could identify each other from close proximity in this heavily fogged environment, Kabil and Anjuman could barely see each other's face. Each of them was carrying the arms on their shoulders. The arms felt heavier as they kept on walking long distances.

"How much farther is Dhaka, Brother Kabil?" an exhausted Anjuman asked.

"We will have to walk still quite a distance, Anju," Kabil responded as he lighted a cigarette.

"This rifle really seems heavier now," Anjuman commented.

"Give it to me. I'll carry both yours and mine for the rest of the way."

Kabil then took Anjuman's rifle and hung it on his other shoulder.

The other boys and girls of the unit under Kabil's command were also walking alongside, a few steps behind them. There were altogether nine of them, including Kabil and Anjuman. Each had their own weapons plus some spares for the group. The other seven were all from outside of Dhaka. They came from different rural districts of Bangladesh. They didn't know very much about the country's politics before the Pakistani military crackdown on March 25–26, 1971. They had heard Sheikh Mujib's name on the radio and television, but never saw him in person. This and other similar groups of seventeen to twenty-five years old boys and girls had started crossing borders to India to join the Mukti Bahini after they had witnessed the indiscriminate killings of innocent civilians, rape and murder of young, helpless girls and women, and setting systematic fires on rural peoples' houses by the Punjabi men of Pakistani armed forces. They became the backbone of the true dedicated Mukti Bahini. They did not need any motivation by others because they had witnessed the dishonor of their mothers and sisters, setting on fire of their houses, forceful occupations of their lands and properties by the Pakistani forces and their local collaborators. These motivated them to join the Mukti Bahini in large numbers to take revenge from the invaders. They couldn't care less about Pakistan being politically broken into two countries. Their main grievance was about the dishonor of the women and their concern was their livelihood damaged by the Pakistani looters and by their collaborators. They were not moved by the illusion of common religion anymore. They felt that this liberation of their country that day came as a result of their wholesale sacrifice and acceptance of possible martyrdom.

The following day, December 16, was the scheduled date for the official formal surrender by the Pakistani General Niazi and his forces. The seven young fighters under Kabil's command in previous nine months in the border towns of India, came at one stage flocking around Kabil and Anjuman on this day. Kabil turned to them and said,

"Are you all eager to enter Dhaka in victory?"

"Sir, tomorrow, General Niazi and his soldiers will formally surrender to the combined command of Mukti Bahini and our ally Indian military. We want to see that before we go and see our families in our respective districts."

The only things that Kabil could think about at this stage of his life were the faces of his beloved Rokshana and his venerable aunty Rania. He told the group,

"It's still another hour before the break of dawn. We'll march toward Dhaka after the ritual call for the Muslim morning prayer. When we reach Dhaka, my command will come to an end. After the surrender by Pakistani forces, you turn in your weapons to the higher command of the Mukti Bahini and then you can go back to your respective villages."

"Okay, sir," the group members replied.

Kabil then suggested, "Let's then spend the hour and have some tea before we set off."

He directed the group toward a roadside tea stall where the vendor had just started his earthen fire stove.

There, Kabil told the group,

"After we arrive at Dhaka, I'll not be able to lead or accompany you all anymore. I'll first have to look for my family, my fiancée, and my aunty and our house. I'm not sure if everything is all right with them there."

With that Kabil formally disbanded the unit, said "Goodbye," thanked them for their support and sacrifices, and wished them well in their future endeavors.

Anjuman then held Kabil's hand and said,

"Let's go home, brother Kabil, after we reach Dhaka."

Kabil looked up and saw a mix of smile and sadness in her face and he liked it. It was, as if, the morning rays that were about to come out from the eastern horizon flashed on Anju's face, hairs, her woolen shawl, and her body. Kabil was a bit startled when Anju said, "Let's go home." For him, going home was to go and see Roksahana, his aunty Rania, and their longtime house cook Halim. He hoped everybody was alive and well. He also wished that Rokshana's house on Bonogram Lane was in the same condition as when he had left nearly nine months ago. While thinking all that, Kabil felt energized. To cheer Anjuman up he said, "Long live Bangladesh. Let's go home, Anju."

He then took Anjuman's hand in his and started walking rather spiritedly.

ON A COMFORTABLE SUNNY WINTER MORNING IN MID- December of 1971, Kabil and Anjuman arrived back at Rankin Street in Dhaka after having been away to neighboring India for almost nine months. They didn't see a car or a rickshaw from Jatrabari area to the intersection of Tikatuli area of Dhaka. When they reached the intersection, they noticed the remnants of the now-destroyed office of the Awami League supporter, the daily *Ittefaq*. There, they found a rickshaw coming from the direction of Ram Krishna Mission. Kabil signalled the rickshaw puller with his hand, and the peddler stopped by the sidewalk. Kabil and Anjuman got into the tricycle. The puller first objected saying he didn't want to go to their area. He had agreed to that when he noticed that both Kabil and Anju were carrying guns. But when Kabil explained that they just wanted to be dropped off at Rankin Street, the peddler didn't object any further. They got down from the cycle rickshaw when it reached the front of Anjuman's parents' house on Rankin Street. They were shocked to notice a rather large-sized padlock hanging from the gate. They looked around and felt that the neighborhood people were watching them through their open windows. Surprised and shocked, Anjuman said,

"Perhaps, there's nobody in our house."

Kabil took a quick look around and said,

"Maybe, your parents weren't staying in Dhaka for these past few months. Perhaps, they all went to your village home in the rural area."

Right at that moment, an old man from a close-by small shop appeared before them. He apparently recognized Anjuman and told her,

"Your parents left your house three or four months after the trouble had started. They left the keys with me. Shall I open the gate for you?"

"Do you know where they might have gone?" Anjuman asked.

"People from your in-law's village came and took your parents to their village home. Your husband's mother and uncle came to Dhaka when they heard the news of your husband's death. Soon after, the local people advised your parents to leave the house and move to the rural areas. They were afraid of possible repercussion by the military and or the local Bihari people because of your past political involvement against the Pakistanis. Before leaving, your parents told me to keep watch on your house. I've been doing that ever since with the help of my sons. By God's grace, there was no looting or damage to your house."

The old shopkeeper then handed the keys for the house to Anjuman.

Anjuman turned to Kabil and said, "If my parents have gone to the village of my parents-in law, then they're hopefully well in the middle of grief, mourning, and sadness. Perhaps they'll be coming back soon. Now what shall I do alone in an empty house? Rather, let's go to Rokhi's house at Bonogram Lane and see how they are doing."

"I was going to tell you the exact same thing. God knows what's in store there for us. I'm scared, Anju."

Anjuman did not respond to Kabil's comments. Instead, she turned to the old shopkeeper and said, "Uncle, I'm taking our house keys with me. But you please keep a watch on the house for a few more days as you have been doing so far until I come back. Was there much looting in this area?"

The old man was touched by Anju's addressing him as "uncle." He became somewhat emotional and said,

"Oh my God! It wasn't just a lot of looting. You'll never imagine what had happened to this Dhaka city of ours in the last few months. The hooligans—both Bengalis and Biharis—broke into all vacant houses and got away with whatever valuables they could find. They even terrorized with arms a few home occupants who couldn't leave their houses for some reasons. They looted the contents of their occupied houses as well. The hooligans tortured the house occupants who dared resist them. You'll understand everything in time. I and my young sons somehow managed to safeguard your parents' house with the help of some strong, influential men in this locality."

"I understand everything from your description, Uncle. But now I have to go to Bonogram Lane area where some relatives of ours used to live in their house there. We want to find out what conditions they are in now and how they managed."

The old man was a bit taken aback when he heard Anjuman mentioning about Bonogram Lane and said,

"You talk about Bonogram Lane? God helps! There's hardly any house left in that area which had not been looted. The looting, torture, rape, and killing were much worse in that Lane compared to those in this Rankin Street area. The Biharis from Mirpur and Mohammadpur areas escorted truckloads of soldiers and looted and or destroyed every household in that Lane. There used to be more Bihari people living in that Lane. Most of them had fled their households for fear of their lives before the military crackdown on the night of March 25. After that day, they all came back with truckloads of Pakistani soldiers and repossessed their houses that they had abandoned earlier. At the same time, they looted the few houses in that Lane where a few Bengalis used to live. Rumors were that the soldiers also raped the Bengali women and tortured the menfolks. There was a kind of a man-made disaster in that locality. After March 25, your father visited that area occasionally to inquire about some of your friends or relatives who used to live in that Lane. Indeed, on March 26, there was supposedly a death in their family that your father visited. The deceased was an elderly woman. Your father came and requested my young sons to help with the burial. Soon after that, your father once lamented that it was impossible for that family to stay in that house."

From the way, the old man described the whole situation, both Anju and Kabil suddenly became distressed and worried about some uncertain and possible sad news awaiting them at Bonogram Lane. They looked at each other for a split moment and hurriedly started walking toward Bonogram Lane without saying anything to the old man or to each other.

They stopped in front of the gate of Rania's house and were shocked to note that both door planks of the gate were missing. They could see the verandah on top of the stairs to the house inside the compound. The doors of the house behind the verandah were also open. That indicated that someone had removed and taken away the door planks and the frames as well. Kabil ran to the stairs and cried out calling, "Aunty!"

Anjuman followed behind him. It looked like there was nobody present inside the house. A sound of quietness like that of fireflies was coming out from inside the house even in the broad daylight. Anju, by that time, was holding one of Kabil's arms.

Kabil composed himself and took in his hand the Chinese rifle that he was carrying on his shoulder, as if he was trying to keep himself alert in case he faced any unseen adversary. Anjuman let go of Kabil's arm and ran inside the house. Kabil cautiously and quietly followed her step by step. The sitting room was completely empty. There were no traces of any furniture inside the room. Sofa, antiques, expensive oil paintings and other wall hangings, and even the carpet on the floor were gone. Kabil stood for a second on the dusty floor of the room enclosured by walls that had no plasters or other coverings. The room looked strange and almost unfamiliar to Kabil. He couldn't imagine this was the sitting room of his prosperous uncle and aunty where he had spent more than a decade before he left Dhaka only nine months or so ago. Kabil momentarily made himself psychologically prepared to learn about other possible heartbreaking things. He put the rifle back on his shoulder. On his way from the sitting room to their former dining area, he almost bumped into Anju who was returning after having seen all the bedrooms of the house. She was running almost breathless like a frightened little girl.

"There's nobody living in this house, Brother Kabil," she announced sadly.

"There's nobody, what do you mean, Anju?"

"No, brother, there's nobody. Hopefully, they are all safe someplace else, by the grace of God. Perhaps they left this area and went somewhere else safer than this place. Maybe, they went to your village home at Montala to stay with Momi there. For God's sake, Kabil, please do not lose hope and patience. You heard earlier that Bonogram Lane was one of the worst affected. In that case—"

Kabil stopped her mid-sentence and said, "Let's visit all the rooms again please . . ."

Kabil made the request so sadly, as if to mean that Anju didn't find anybody because she didn't look thoroughly.

"I looked at all the bedrooms in one go, Kabil. There's nobody here. But if you want, I'll go with you again."

A COMPLEX, FOUR-SIDED LOVE STORY AND A CIVIL WAR

Anju held Kabil's arm again and felt that his arm as well as his whole body was shaking like that of a frightened child. After they visited the former dining area, now without any chairs or table, Kabil let go of Anju's hand and ran straight to the kitchen which Anju had neglected to check earlier. Anju now followed Kabil without saying a word. They suddenly stopped motionless as they entered the kitchen. There, they found someone sound asleep and snoring on the floor with knees folded and covered with an old, torn blanket. Kabil wasn't sure who it was because the whole body, including the head and the face, was covered. He nevertheless knelt and put his hand on the lying body which was trembling. Kabil called out quietly,

"Uncle Halim!"

Hearing his name, the lying man moved his blanket away from his head and face and sat up. His head was full of long gray hair and his beard was gray, long, and unkempt. He looked as if he was a homeless insane man one would find in the streets. He looked at Kabil and Anju for a few seconds, as if he couldn't believe what he was seeing, and then managed to say,

"So you finally came back?"

Kabil momentarily put his hands around the man and began crying out loud,

"What happened to you, Uncle? Where's my aunty and where's my Rokhi?"

Cook Halim then hugged Kabil with both his hands and began crying with wailing sounds. Anju sat down on the dusty floor next to Kabil and Halim and began patting their backs. Halim then in his wailing rhythm began telling Kabil,

"You're a very unlucky man, Kabil. Nobody stayed waiting for your return. I couldn't hold anybody back for you."

"Why, Uncle, who could you not hold back for me? What happened to my Rokhi? Tell me please. Don't delay, and tell me everything openly. Is my Rokhi okay?"

"Rokshana and Andaleeb fled to Pakistan, Kabil."

"Pakistan?" Kabil echoed not believing what he had just heard.

"Yes, it was not safe for them to stay in this country any longer. The hooligans attacked this house just an hour after they had left. They thought some Biharis had been living here. They tied me up and looted everything. I could manage at the last minute only Rokhi's last letter for you and some other documents she had left for you. I used them as my pillow to safeguard them. And I was waiting for your return."

"Where is my aunty?"

"Your aunty, of course, could not go anywhere leaving you behind in this country. She loved you very much like her son she never had. That's probably the reason she couldn't leave this country."

"Where is she then?"

"She's in this compound. We laid her down on one side of the courtyard. You probably did not see her grave on the right side by the boundary wall as you came through the gate. She died the night you left this house almost nine months ago. She died of a heart attack."

As Halim continued his wailing narratives, Kabil sat on the floor without saying anything and kept staring at Anjuman.

Anjuman at that point asked cook Halim,

"Uncle, will you please show us the letter Rokhi left behind for Kabil?"

Halim picked up the letter and other documents Rokhi had left behind with him from underneath his pillow. He handed them over to Anju and said,

"Here they are. She had written the letter the night before she left this house. She handed them over to me and then went to her mother's grave site and cried there for long time. A military jeep was waiting outside for her and Andaleeb. A non-Bengali friend of your aunty, who used to tell her to move to Mirpur area and then to Pakistan, had arranged for the military jeep to safely escort Rokhi and Andaleeb out of this house. It was good of her to do that. Otherwise, our Rokhi's honor could have been at stake. She went to Pakistan with her maternal cousin Andaleeb. May God make her safe and happy."

"Stop, Uncle! Don't say anymore," Kabil said rather loudly. "Anju, please give me Rokhi's letter," he continued.

"Let me read it for you, Brother Kabil."

"Okay then, go ahead and read."

Anju then began reading aloud Rokhi's letter.

"Dear Cousin Kabil:

You'll not get many things back when you will have returned to Dhaka. You will not have your former country of Pakistan. You will not find your beloved Aunty Rania- my late mother. You will not find your close friend Nisar. And you will have to bear the pain of not finding me—your one-time dearest love and fiancée who had reciprocated your love from deep down in her heart. After a lot of thought, I've decided to leave with Andaleeb. I do not know how much, if at all, I had loved Andaleeb. However, faced with a choice of life and a fear of possible dishonor, even death, I hung on to Andaleeb and learned anew to love him.

I hoped and thought that when you would have returned to Dhaka after winning the liberation war, there will be compensation for you for the things you had lost in the gruelling process. Because you'll get a new country for which you had sacrificed so much and fought gallantly. But I also thought about what would be there for a Bihari refugee settler like Andaleeb in this country—neither a country nor a woman he had once loved so dearly. Andaleeb had come to this country with my grandfather and my mother from India during its 1947 partition as a mere child. He had worked hard as an employee of my parents' businesses and built a life for himself including a modest house. But now he has to leave involuntarily and almost broke financially for Pakistan, leaving behind his house and this city of his youth, simply because he's not a Bengali by birth.

A COMPLEX, FOUR-SIDED LOVE STORY AND A CIVIL WAR

At this time, even if I could probably save myself because my father was a Bengali by birth, (but my mother was not), I could not possibly save Andaleeb from certain misery and likely murder. I therefore, held on to his hands because he was quietly leaving for fear of his life with the pain of losing everything he had ever worked for, including Momi whom he had genuinely wanted to marry after I had earlier rejected his love for me. He is also a cousin of mine just as you are one. I can't let him go alone, financially almost broke, and destined for an uncertain future in a strange country. I know that Andaleeb is an experienced, hard-working man who worked for my parents and helped them build up their sizeable assets and businesses in this country. I'm leaving behind for you the documents and records of all our cash, businesses, and land properties in this country. Hopefully, you'll have no difficulties in taking possession of all these assets of ours. Moreover, nobody will dare deprive you of your rightful claims on these because you were a freedom fighter for this country.

Don't be angry with Andaleeb. Don't speak ill of him and call him an infidel or a traitor. For he had wanted to stay back in Dhaka taking the risk on his life, so he could offer my hand in marriage to you. But I encouraged him to leave this mindless, cruel, indiscriminate massacre in this country, taking me with him to a country where at least our lives would be safe. You know how badly Andaleeb had once wanted me as his wife.

We managed to take with us only a small portion of our cash and other liquid assets. We plan to start a family either in Karachi or in Islamabad all over again with a lot of hard work. Andaleeb is an intelligent man and he understands business well as he came from a business community. I also inherited some business acumen from both my parents. I'm hopeful that we'll make it good in life. Don't worry about us. I left behind with our cook Halim, the diamond ring for you, which my mother had bought for the occasion of my wedding with you which she had hoped for so much in her life.

Andaleeb tells me that he'd be very happy if you would marry Momena, your other cousin, whom he loved madly since I had turned down his first love for me. I did that because I was deeply in love with you ever since I had met you first in our house when I was only a teenager. I discussed all these with Andaleeb. He cried a lot for Momena and wanted to go clandestinely to Montala just to see her one last time before we leave for Karachi. But I persuaded him against doing that because of my concern for his safety on the way. If you can forgive me and Andaleeb, then I would suggest that you start a family with Momi. I knew that Momi was once madly in love with you just as Andaleeb had once loved me deeply. Now that I'm going to learn anew to love Andaleeb with all my heart, why should you be so miserly in loving Momi in the future?

My mother has been buried in the compound of our house at Bonogram Lane. I probably will not be able to come back again to pay a visit and respect to my deceased mother at her grave site. If you choose this house as your future residence, then I'll have mental peace and happiness even by hearing that news, maybe after a very long time. The house needs some overdue repair works. You may, in the future, have some natural hatred toward Biharis based on ethnicity because they had always sided during the bloody civil war with the oppressive West Pakistanis as they spoke the same language Urdu. You might also rightfully have some grievances against the West Pakistanis for the unjust and unequal way they had treated the Bengali people of the then East Pakistan. You might have legitimate reasons for hatred against the Pakistanis for their military's brutal suppression of the Bengali people's rightful struggle for political autonomy and proportionate sharing of the national wealth. These oppressive actions ultimately broke Pakistan into two separate sovereign countries. If you ever reminisce in the future on the pains of this bloody separation of a country and want some mental respite from it for a few minutes, you may wish to remember and think of our mutual, unlimited love for each other. You may also wish to remember that one of your Bengali cousins by the name of Roksahana will be living in Pakistan. It might be of some mental comfort for you and rapprochement toward your erstwhile countrymen.

I tried to write this letter in Bengali as succinct and organized as possible even though I had to write it under tremendous mental pressure amidst fear for our lives. Our longtime cook Halim refused to leave this house and go to Pakistan with us. Please take care of him as much as you can. It was just as well perhaps for me not seeing sister Anjuman in her present situation as a young widow. She's the widow of Nisar who was your close university friend. I do not have the audacity to remind you of your moral responsibility to her. Please tell her that I seek her forgiveness for any of my past irreverence to her. And I seek your blessing for my future. I wish you well and happiness in life. Long live Bangladesh.

Yours affectionately,

Rokhi

November 12, 1971

After Anju had finished reading Rokhi's letter, Cook Halim got up, went to a corner of the kitchen, picked up a small packet of papers and handed that to Kabil. He then said,

"Here, take the diamond ring. Your aunty Rania had it made for Rokhi as your future wife, but as it turned out, perhaps for Momi as your possible future wife. Just think that by a twist of fate events over which none of you had any control, your paternal cousin Rokhi got to pretend as if the ring was made for her and played with it for a while. Just think that way, my son, and be patient."

Kabil took the packet and opened it. The ring radiated bright shiny rays. As Kabil took a look at the ring, he began wailing in sadness like a child. Halim then put his arms around Kabil as if he was the son Halim never had in his life.

Upon seeing Kabil wailing like that, Anjuman realized that there had been some serious, longtime, pent-up emotions inside Kabil, and they were now erupting inside him. She decided instantly that she had to be strong herself at this critical time in Kabil's life and manage that reaction inside Kabil. Otherwise, he wouldn't be able to concentrate on any after-war political activities and duties. He would not go anywhere and nobody would come looking for him. She slowly put her hand on Halim's back who turned toward her. Anjuman then said to Halim,

"Uncle, how do you manage alone in this ransacked house? I noticed you do not have any proper bedding, pots, and pans and other essential things."

"No, Anju, there's nothing left. The local hooligans looted everything from this house."

"How do you feed yourself?"

"I go to a nearby roadside restaurant owned by an acquaintance of Kabil. He feeds me for free and asks that when Kabil would be back from the cross-border war, I should put in a good word for him to Kabil."

Halim attempted to chuckle in the midst of his immense sadness.

"Now, you get ready, we'll go to our Rankin Street house which somehow got spared in all this chaos. One of our neighbours safeguarded it while my parents had earlier left and gone to my in-law's village home to escape the massacre by the Pakistani soldiers in early April this year. You come with us there and cook some food for us. We both are very hungry."

By that time Kabil stopped wailing. He stood up and said,

"Yes, Uncle, let's all go to Anju's house. But before we leave, I want to pay respect to my deceased beloved aunty by visiting her grave site. Tomorrow morning, I plan to go with you to our village home in Montala."

At that point, Anjuman intervened,

"I too want to see Momi after such a long time. Will you not take me with you two, Brother Kabil? I'll not feel safe alone in our house either."

"Yes, Anju, you can also come with us, if you so wish."

By that time Kabil put the diamond ring on the middle finger of his left hand.

DECEMBER 16, 1971. THIS WAS the day scheduled for the formal official surrender of Pakistani forces in the then East Pakistan by their commander, General Niazi, to the combined Indian military and the Mukti Bahini of Bangladesh Liberation Forces commander, General Jagjeet Singh Arora. The city of Dhaka was in a frenzy to celebrate its victory. There were a series of victory marches by hundreds of thousands of spontaneous Bengali citizens. There were sporadic blank shootings of guns in the air. Some people even indulged in taking control, in the name of Mukti Bahini, houses, shops, cars and other properties previously owned by known non-Bengalis who had earlier abandoned these for fear of their lives and, so, fled the country. Indeed, the members of Indian military and the genuine Mukti Bahini forces were busy safeguarding the security of defeated Pakistani soldiers, officers, and the members of the trapped non–Bengali families.

Kabil, Anju, and Halim spent the previous night at Anjuman's parents' house and returned in the morning to Rokshana's Bonogram Lane house. On arrival there, Halim tried to tidy up the place; he put new locks on former bedrooms of Rania, Rokshana, and Kabil. These bedrooms were all earlier stripped of their expensive furniture by the local hooligans, leaving open only the doors intact. Kabil didn't bother going to the formal surrender ceremony of the Pakistani forces. Nobody had asked him either. Anjuman once tried to tell him,

"Brother Kabil, let's go and move around the city once. Let's go at least to our university campus. Maybe, we'll meet some of our old friends or even some of your fellow student leaders. You'll then establish your old contacts with them."

Kabil silently looked at Anjuman's face for a while and said, "I don't want to go anywhere, Anju. If you wish so, you can go, look around, and then come back. I do look forward to seeing the place where Nisar had been shot dead. I thought, I'd go there with you sometimes to at least identify the location of Nisar's martyrdom for our country. But if we go there now, we'd be late in leaving for our village home in Montala. You, of course, know that it's important for me to go to Montala as soon as possible. Perhaps, Momi there had been watching over our village house, while looking forward and waiting for Andaleeb. And if for some other reason, she might have gone to her uncles at Harashpur, then also it's my responsibility to inquire about her situation. Perhaps, Momi doesn't know that my aunty Rania had died and that Rokhi and Andaleeb had left for Pakistan. This news would be a great shock for Momi. If I myself can't console Momi about these shocking events in her life, you and Uncle Halim can be of help to me. Moreover—"

"Then, why did we come here this morning? We could have left for the railway station from our house," Anjuman replied.

"We came so the people around here realize that I've come back from India and that this was never a house occupied by non-Bengalis alone. At least three true-blue Bengalis—my uncle Alam, his own daughter Rokhi, and I myself once lived here before it was ransacked by local hooligans. I do not believe that somebody from Mirpur or Mohammadpur areas came here to loot and vandalize our house," Kabil replied.

"Let's then head for the railway station. We'll wait at the station and board the first train going to Akhaura Railway Junction and then go to Montala from there," Anju suggested.

"You're right, Anju! We'll go and wait at Dhaka Fulbaria Station. But where shall we leave these firearms behind here?"

"Why should we leave the firearms behind? We'll carry them with us. Do you think it is safe for us to move around unarmed anywhere in the country at this critical, uncertain time? Do you not remember that we had taken oaths not to disarm ourselves until the safe return of our leader Sheikh Mujib to Dhaka?"

A COMPLEX, FOUR-SIDED LOVE STORY AND A CIVIL WAR

"Yes, I remember Anju. But—"

"What's 'but' then?"

"What if someone challenges us for carrying guns after the official surrender by the Pakistani military?"

"Okay with the surrender, if someone challenges just to harass us, I'll open fire at them in self-defence. We were freedom fighters. We don't want to be harassed or insulted. We sacrificed everything for the liberation of this country. We have nothing left except these weapons on our shoulders."

At that point, Halim suggested, "Maybe, I stay back in this house. You two go and bring Momi here."

"No, Uncle, you come with us. Momi will feel much better if you are with us and talk to her," Anju replied.

"Okay then, let's leave for the station soon," Halim responded.

THE SUN SET ON the evening of December 16 in the rural areas of the new nation of Bangladesh in a scenario quite different from the one in the city of Dhaka. In the previous nine months, the villages and towns near the areas bordering India had seen an unparalleled scale of looting, rape, mass killing, and destruction by the Pakistani military and their local collaborators in response to sporadic hit-and-run armed guerrilla-type attack by Mukti Bahini fighters from across the Indian borders. The unarmed innocent people on Bangladesh side of the border had suffered from the atrocities committed by the Pakistani forces looking for Mukti Bahini fighters presumably sheltered by the local Bengali families. This had been done with the help of their local collaborators organized in the name of Shanti Bahini (Peace Forces), Al-Badar and Rajakars, etc. Members of these groups helped the Pakistani military in identifying families whose young sons and daughters had joined the Mukti Bahini and had crossed over to India. They then punished the remaining innocent members of those families. Additionally, they had set fires on vacant houses in rural areas whose occupants had left the houses in anticipation of coming Pakistani forces to their areas and took shelters in nearby bushes for fear of their lives. Some of these families were also victims of nightly armed excursions by members of the Mukti Bahini looking either for possible Pakistani collaborators or simply looking for food and shelter for rest for themselves. They also punished and or killed the suspected collaborators in public and burnt their houses. After having lived in this nightmarish environment for nearly nine months, the innocent, simple local people breathed a sigh of relief on this victory day of December 16. They welcomed their first carefree peaceful evening without any fear of disturbance by any of these two opposing forces. Most of them sat after evening prayer on their doorsteps or in their verandah with radios in their hands, eager to listen to the news of the day broadcast by the open and free Bangladesh Radio and Television Services.

That evening, Momena's uncle, Mr. Hashem from Harashpur, who had been visiting her at Kabil's village home in Montala, was sitting near the door of the house with a small radio in his hand waiting for the day's news from Dhaka. Momena had called for him to accompany her on an intended trip to Dhaka to inquire about Andaleeb, her aunty Rania, and Rokshana. She had not received any news about either of them for a long time, and she was worried about their well-being. Momena had spent the last nine months in dreadful fear and agony with all kinds of rumours about the situation in Dhaka as did most of the villagers in towns and villages near the Indian borders.

This evening, Momena came to the door and sat on a low wooden stool (*piri*) near her uncle Hashem. Mr. Hashem was sitting on a prayer mat with prayer beads in his right hand.

Mr. Hashem asked Momena, "Have you finished cooking supper, my child?"

"It's likely done, Uncle. This evening, our share-crop farmer Majid's wife has been doing that. I've been busy packing my suitcase for our forthcoming trip to Dhaka. I might have to stay there for a while this time," Momena replied.

"Yes, you may have to. My hunch is that this time, soon after you arrive at Dhaka, your aunty-Alam's wife Rania would probably make all arrangements for your wedding with Andaleeb. They probably could not come to this area in the last few months because of the riots between the Biharis and the Bengalis followed by the war between the Punjabis and the Mukti Bahini. My nephew Kabil is a supporter of Sheikh Mujib's Awami League Party. He must have crossed over to India and joined the freedom fighters. God knows, if he has come back to Dhaka yet, now that the country is liberated from the grip of Punjabi soldiers. Moreover, you told me that you had earlier written a letter to Kabil asking him not to send Andaleeb to Montala because of tensions between the local Bengalis and the Bihari railway workers in this area because his life, as a Bihari himself, could have been in danger in this vastly Bengali-dominated area. It was good that they took your advice and did not come to this area," Mr. Hashem commented.

"Even so, Uncle, someone could have inquired about me during this long, terrible war in the country," Momena said in a tone of grievance.

"How could they? Especially, if Kabil had not been in Dhaka or even in Bangladesh? And it was wise for Andaleeb not to have left Dhaka during this time when Biharis had been at risk for their lives in rural areas."

"What about my aunty Rania? How could she forget about me for such a long time? I have a fear, Uncle, that this time when I go to Dhaka, I might have some surprising and shocking news waiting for me there."

"Don't worry, my child. By God's grace, you'll find everybody safe and sound. The war is over today. Perhaps, someone might come from Dhaka in a day or two to visit you. But you insist on going to Dhaka yourself tomorrow morning and asked me to come here to accompany you. I have left urgent work in my cropping farm to accompany you there. Otherwise, you'd think that I didn't stand by your side in times of your need."

"I'm really scared, Uncle. That's the reason I had sent message for you to come here urgently to accompany me to Dhaka. I'm scared for Andaleeb because he's a non-Bengali refugee settler in this country. He was an orphan like I am. I'm worried that some misfortune might befall him. My heart trembles and aches for him as I hear that many Bihari people were killed in various railway stations where they worked."

Momena disclosed her deep feelings for Andaleeb to her uncle ignoring the normal traditional hesitation of young unmarried girls to share such feelings with their elders.

"No, my child. You did the right thing in calling for me to come here. Now, it's our duty to inquire about all our relatives in Dhaka as we are all safe here, especially when most communal riots and fighting took place over there in Dhaka."

As her uncle had continued the conversation, both heard footsteps outside the closed gate of their house compound. Someone knocked on the gate and called out Momena's name. It was the voice of a woman. Momena ran and opened the gate. There, she found herself standing face to face with Kabil, Anjuman, and Halim. Rifles were hanging on the shoulders of both Kabil and Anjuman.

"You all managed to think about me after such a long time? How are my aunty Rania and sister Rokhi doing, Uncle Halim?" Momena asked with genuine pleasant surprise in her voice. She took a quick glance at all three of them and then fixed her focus on Halim. Even though she couldn't clearly see their faces in the early evening darkness, her inner instinct of anxiety made their facial sadness all clear to her. Nobody could find words to respond to Momena's questions. Kabil was also speechless, even though he almost didn't recognize right away Momena's full-bodied appearance and the changes in her demeanor. Her tall body was standing there holding one open plank of the gate. For a moment, everybody was silent like the evening darkness of rural Bangladesh.

In that tense, uneasy moment, Anjuman first stepped inside the gate, hugged Momena, and asked,

"How are you, Momi? The people you were asking about are all okay. Let's first go inside the house and we all want to hear about you."

"Come in, please. My Hashem uncle is here. He has been sitting inside the door with the radio in his hand trying to get some news from Dhaka. He and I had planned to leave for Dhaka tomorrow morning to inquire about you all. You could have brought cousin Andaleeb with you as well. He wasn't in any danger, Sister Anju. Was he?"

Kabil was a bit surprised hearing that Momena this time asked directly about her beloved man Andaleeb with whom she was about to be married before Kabil was sent to prison for his political activities for the second time by the Pakistani authorities. Momena just couldn't hide the murmur inside her chest thinking about Andaleeb's well-being. Her worry over Andaleeb's well-being now took over the natural shyness and modesty of this village girl from a traditional conservative Bangladeshi family. Kabil was silently watching Momena intensely. Hearing Momena's words of worriness about Andaleeb, he lowered his gaze to the ground.

Halim, in his simple mind, couldn't figure out what to do with himself at this difficult moment for all of them. He suddenly stepped inside the gate and blurred out weeping,

"How can I now console the members of this family now? The dreams of all you people have been shattered and broken, Momena, my child. Your aunty Rania had died. Your cousin Rokhi left for Pakistan with her other cousin Andaleeb. Anjuman's husband Nisar had been killed by the Pakistani military. I'm an old man. I didn't come here to console you by hiding the facts or with false hopes. I came to tell you the truth. Why are you waiting for so long with false, unrealistic hopes in your mind? Go inside the house, lie on your bed, cry your chest out, and make your heart as comfortable as you can."

Everybody suddenly became stone-still with Halim's wailing and plain, honest, simplistic disclosure of fateful events of the past nine months affecting every member of this family. None of them had any real control over these events. It's the cost paid by this one family, like many others in the country, because of this cruel civil war. The civil war broke the natural, reasonable, and attainable dreams of extended family members, especially those of its four young men and women.

Once, they all came inside the house, nobody said anything to anybody before dinner time. After dinner, Kabil said to Anjuman, "You and Momi can sleep in my mother's bedroom. Uncle Hashem, Uncle Halim, and I will all sleep in the front sitting room. I'll have to disclose everything to uncle Hashem."

In the middle of the night, Anjuman told Momena all about the sad things that had happened in Dhaka affecting the members of Rania's family. Momena listened silently and breathlessly to Rokshana's last letter written to Kabil as Anjuman had read it to her.

After reading the letter to Momena, Anju asked, "Momi, say something. What do you want to do yourself now? We've all accepted our fate. Now, you'll have to accept your fate as well."

Momena didn't respond to Anjuman's question. She left enough sleeping space between Anjuman and her in Zakia's rather large bed, turned her back to Anjuman and covered herself from head to toe pretending to fall asleep. Anjuman realized that there was no point at that time to aggravate the sorrow of this unfortunate girl by asking her more questions. She decided to leave her alone until the next day in the hope that Momena might feel lighter, at ease, and would be willing to share her feelings by that time. Anjuman had thought that Momena would put an end to all her sorrow and sadness as an orphan by accepting Kabil as her future husband. After all, she said to herself, Momena had been preparing herself during her childhood and early youth as a possible future wife of Kabil as her aunty Kabil's mother had wished for. What a wonder!

Fate had now prepared a possible honeymoon for Momena and Kabil as his mother had hoped for both.

Anjuman sighed a long, deep breath.

SHORTLY BEFORE SUNRISE THE following morning, Kabil woke up by the call to morning prayer from the local mosque. He sat up on his bed, heard the sound of roped bucket with which Momena was drawing water from the dug water well in their house compound. He walked over to the well site without thinking very much about it. Momena was performing ablution for her morning prayer.

Seeing Kabil there, she asked, "Why did you wake up so early? Didn't you sleep well last night?"

"No, I didn't sleep well. I heard sound of your drawing water from the well and came out here. I have something to talk to you, Momi," Kabil replied.

"Let me first finish performing my prayer. Then we can talk in the kitchen."

"Okay, you go and finish your prayer. I'll brush my teeth and then come there. I want to talk to you alone before others wake up."

"Okay, you do that," Momena replied.

The tone of her response was mixed with some sadness and indifference. She then walked out of the well site back toward their kitchen. Kabil could not figure out exactly what was going on in Momena's mind. He wondered if Momi had learned last night from Anju the contents of Rokhi's last letter to him. Kabil, shortly afterward, walked to the kitchen. Momi had just finished her prayer. Kabil sat on a low rattan stool (*mora*) next to Momena who was still sitting on her prayer mat. Kabil thought that Momena after saying her prayer, would sit on a low wooden stool, *piri*, next to him, shy and reserved as she used to do in earlier days. He was a bit confused seeing that Momena this time did not leave the prayer mat on a small slightly raised wooden platform. She had her eyes focused on the intricate shapes woven at the head of the prayer mat. Kabil was surprised because he had never seen such indifference in Momi's demeanor. He remembered seeing in his early years his mother performing prayers on this same platform. Suddenly, the face of his deceased mother appeared in his subconscious mind. He lamented silently that if his mother were alive that day, she probably would have been happy seeing that Kabil was now back from all his early life adventures and was about to propose to Momena to marry him as his mother had always wanted and wished for. And that, together with Momena by his side as his wife, the two of them would restore the past reputation of his father's family in the locality. It also came to his mind that the sizeable landed properties and businesses left by his uncle Ahmed Alam and now abandoned by his daughter Rokshana would also help in that regard. He imagined that it would have made his mother very happy to see all her hopes and aspirations fulfilled. On second thought, Kabil also wondered if his mother would have been sad noting that her erstwhile estranged brother-in law Alam and his wife Rania had died before all her hopes would have come true and their daughter Rokhi- Kabil's erstwhile beloved fiancée- had to leave Bangladesh with her maternal cousin Andaleeb for reasons over which none of them had any control whatsoever. He thought his mother would probably have been very sad because of his own defeat in his love life.

Kabil snapped out of his deep thought, as if by hearing his deceased mother's cry in his imagination.

He then called out, "Momi, have you finished your prayer?"

"Yes. I'm ready to listen to whatever you have to tell me."

"You can at least look at me, Momi."

"I can hear and pay attention to you, cousin."

Momi's voice was steady, firm, and intense. As if she had turned into a stone with all the shocking news she had heard the previous night from Anjuman.

"Did you come to know from Anju last night about the letter that Rokhi had written to me before she left for Pakistan with Andaleeb?"

"Yes, cousin. I came to know the contents of Rokhi's letter to you."

"I have no objection anymore to what Rokhi had suggested in her letter about you and me for our future, Momi. Even my mother had wanted to see us in this position. Now, it seems like God has brought us together in this situation," Kabil said with emotion in his voice.

Seeing Momena still silent, Kabil continued, "Anju and I came here to take you to Dhaka, Momi. I'm glad that uncle Hashem is also here. I discussed with him last night our situation and our future together as a married couple. He seemed to be pleased with it. We intend to call our other relatives from Harashpur to come here shortly and we can complete the religious part of our marriage right in this house which would have made my mother happy. After that we'll move to Dhaka. All the assets and businesses of Uncle Alam and Aunty Rania are unprotected now in Dhaka. We'll have to take care of those. After that, sometime in the future, we'll fix a date, invite all our friends and relatives and celebrate the social aspects of our wedding ceremony."

Kabil said all those in almost one breath. Momena continued her silence and kept her gaze down on the intricate shapes on the prayer mat and was biting her nail. Seeing Momena quiet, Kabil was a bit surprised and said again,

"You aren't saying anything, Momi. Do you have something to say? I know your heart has been broken by Andaleeb's departure like mine by Rokhi's. What can we do? This is our fate. Let's accept our fate and start a family together. You yourself once wished me in your life as your husband. Didn't you?"

"Yes, cousin. I did wish for that for a long time. But then I was a fool. I didn't understand very much of anything. Now I do not wish for that any longer because Andaleeb had shown me what real, selfless love was."

Momena pulled down her head cover a bit, turned her neck toward Kabil and responded in those words.

A heartless, breathless ray of smile flushed on Kabil's face and then quickly disappeared.

"I can understand your sentiment, Momi," Kabil said in desperation.

"No, cousin, I'm not being sentimental, and I don't have a grievance of any kind against you. I didn't even know anything about love and devotion until I met Andaleeb. I did not know what love between a man and a woman was supposed to be. Your mother had brought me to your house when I was very young because I was an orphan. She had raised me as her own child. She was my mother even though she had not carried me in her womb. I do not remember anything about my biological mother who had died soon after I was born. Your mother—my aunty was my real mother for all I knew. She had hoped to restore this family's reputation in this locality by arranging my marriage to you when we both grew up. But you didn't look at me from that point of view. You fell in love with your paternal cousin Rokhi who was a city girl with university education and whose parents were wealthy business people in Dhaka. You had a long, loving relationship with Rokhi and many memories of her. You and I did not have that kind of relationship and memories of us together. You came yesterday to seek my hand in marriage because you were unable to get Rokhi in your life and because she had asked you to do so. But you know that I wasn't waiting for you either in recent years since I had met and fell in love with Andaleeb. Recently, I had been waiting for him to come and take me in his loving arms. He had earlier saved me from yours and Rokhi's indifference and, even, occasional insult. You don't know how much love and fond memories of us together we have between Andaleeb and me. I remember feeling his loving touch and the smell of his manliness everywhere in this compound and in Dhaka when I was there with him. I do not feel that way about you, my cousin. Please forgive me for that."

She then covered her face with both hands and started weeping.

"Listen, Momi! Andaleeb was helpless and had to flee this country with Rokhi for fear of their lives. They had perhaps no other choice to save their lives and Rokhi's respect and modesty. You know that I had never thought about my life without Rokhi with me. But what can we do under these precarious circumstances in this country and in our lives? Our fate was definitely not in our favor in what we both had wished for ourselves in this life."

"I do not want to accept that kind of fate in my life, cousin. I do not want Rokhi to win the battle of love in life because of a twist in our fates. She had left holding Andaleeb's hand voluntarily or compelled to do so by the turn of circumstances. She first broke my heart once when she stole you from me and then she ran away with Andaleeb who was like a piece of my heart. Then she had the audacity to write to you asking you to do me a favor by marrying me as an act of kindness to me on your part as well as hers. I do not know how much Rokhi had loved you, but she knew very well that I had loved Andaleeb very much. I can't forgive Rokhi for breaking my heart first by stealing you from me and then again by stealing Andaleeb.

I definitely do not want to marry you as your second choice for a wife. If I have to start a family with someone, considering the rest of my life, I do not want to do that with Rokhi's love doll Kabil. My uncles and other guardians will hopefully be able to arrange my marriage with some farmer young man of this country, and I will learn to love him. I'll spend the rest of my life with him in good times as well as in bad. Yet I do not want to accept Rokhi's favor and her 'leftover' by marrying someone abandoned by her. She may possibly know a long time from now that I wasn't a beggar in the matter of love in life. I would rather be a 'thorn in memory' in her life with Andaleeb."

With that Momena suddenly stood up from the prayer couch and made a move to leave the scene. Kabil stood up from his rattan stool and cleared the way for Momena.

THE FOLLOWING DAY AT around three o'clock in the early morning, Kabil, Anju, and Halim were at the Akhaura Railway Junction, waiting for the arrival of the Mail Train from the southern port city of Chittagong on its way to Dhaka. Both Kabil and Anjuman had their rifles hanging from their respective shoulders. The passersby looked at them with some sense of fear, but nobody dared come near them. Kabil and Anjuman sat side by side on a long railway station bench in a quiet area with dimly illuminated light from the nearby lamp post.

Kabil then asked Halim, "Uncle, you please go and have a cup of tea in the local tea stall. When you finish, please bring two cups of tea for us as well."

As Halim left, Anjuman put down her rifle on the ground next to her and somewhat intentionally came closer to Kabil's body. She lowered her gaze and called out in a whisper, "Kabil."

"Do you want to say something to me, Anju?" Kabil asked.

"Yes, I was thinking that the diamond ring on your middle finger is very consequential. It's an expensive piece of jewellery worked by a professional expert. It's shining brightly in the dark. I feel sad that there is no woman in your life to wear that ring."

"Are you making fun of my misfortune, Anju?" Kabil asked.

"No, Kabil, trust me. I don't dare make fun of your misfortune. I had spent the last nine months with you while we were both fighting the Pakistani military to liberate Bangladesh from the oppressors. I've never seen in my life another man like you who is so sacrificing, so dedicated to the cause of our country, yet so unfortunate in your own personal affairs. Why did it have to be like that, Kabil?"

"I don't know, Anju. Maybe I had someone's curse on my life. It could be my mother or my aunty Rania. I spoiled the dreams and hopes of both. You're right, Anju. There is no one more unfortunate than I am in this world."

Anjuman then came closer to Kabil, their two bodies now touching each other. At that point, Kabil said,

"Anju, at this very moment, I feel like throwing this unlucky diamond ring into the bush and save myself from the piercing pains of a lot of memories."

"After all that, do you want to throw this expensive ring into the bush?"

"What am I going to do with this ring now, anyway?"

"If I tell you that there is still a woman who is willing to share her life with you, will you put that ring on her ring finger?"

"Anju, please tell me frankly what you have in your mind."

"Shall I tell you more directly?"

Kabil was surprised and looked at Anjuman with somewhat blank eyes.

Anjuman's face was not clearly visible in the shade of darkness. But her wind-swept hair bunch touched Kabil's face.

Anjuman then said,

"Why don't you put that ring on my finger, Kabil? There's nobody else left."

"You—," Kabil could not finish his sentence.

"Yes, me, Kabil. I was never a woman of your choice. But you need me now more than anything else in your life. We may not be in love with each other right now. But we need each other for mutual support and for reminding each other of our duties and responsibilities in life toward our families and to our newborn country. I may not be of your liking, but your close friend Nisar once liked me for sure. Please put that ring on my finger."

"DO NOT DELAY ANY longer, Kabil, my son. Put that ring on Anju's finger," an almost commanding ghostly voice came from their back. It was that of Kabil's longtime cook, well-wisher, and revered Uncle Halim.

"Hold these tea cups. I brought some tea for you two," Halim continued. Kabil took the tray with tea cups from Halim's hand and put that on the other side of the bench they were sitting on. As Kabil then slowly and obligingly put the diamond ring on Anju's left-hand ring finger, Halim, from their back quietly took Anju's scarf from her head and covered both Kabil and Anjuman with that scarf.

INDEX

A

Akhaura Railway Junction, 24–25, 27, 135, 342, 344, 367, 382

Alam, Ahmed, 25, 28–31, 34, 36–39, 42–44, 47–48, 50–51, 66–76, 87–91, 101, 103–8, 127, 134, 140, 150–52, 211, 253

All India Muslim League, xiii

Andaleeb (Andy, Rokhi's cousin), xii, 13–19, 21–23, 47–48, 60, 71–74, 76, 90–91, 96–97, 99–101, 109–12, 115, 127, 131–40, 147, 151–52, 162, 164–65, 168, 173, 176–78, 180, 182–85, 187–89, 191–99, 204–5, 208–11, 214–17, 219–26, 228, 238–47, 249, 251–59, 261, 263–64, 273, 277, 279–90, 298–300, 308–13, 321–25, 327–31, 340–41, 357–61, 366–67, 370–74, 378–82

Anjuman (Anju, Rokhi's friend), 10–13, 16, 24–25, 113, 116–26, 135–36, 142, 157–60, 169–71, 173–75, 178, 180, 189, 199–203, 231–33, 265, 267–71, 274–75, 305, 314–16, 346–47, 349–56, 358, 363–68, 372–73, 375–76, 378, 382–85

approval, 147, 279–80

Awami League, xiv, 2–3, 14, 20–21, 92, 117, 120, 154–55, 167, 172, 176, 200, 235, 259–60, 266–67, 275–77, 281, 295, 307, 311, 314–15, 317, 319, 322, 329, 333, 350, 370

Ayesha (Rokhi's aunt), 301, 303–4, 309–10

B

Bangladesh, vii, xiii, xv–xvi, xviii, 1–2, 19, 118, 284, 295, 343–47, 371, 378

Bangladesh Liberation War, vii, xi

barricade, 120–21, 123

Bengali-Bihari tension, 283, 341

Bengalis, xiv, xx, 2, 11, 14, 19, 22–23, 32, 34, 41–46, 48, 54–55, 66–67, 70, 82, 114, 133–34, 151, 173, 211, 213, 231, 234–35, 260, 276, 281, 289, 298–300, 303, 306–7, 309–10, 312–14, 316, 319, 323, 331, 339, 342, 345, 352, 359–60, 362, 370

Bhutto, Z. A., 2–3, 14, 266–67, 274–76, 282, 309, 315–17, 319–21, 323–24, 328

Biharis, 8, 22–23, 54, 82, 134, 151, 281, 290, 303, 305, 307, 314, 331, 339, 342, 352–53, 357, 362, 370–72

Bonogram Lane, 8, 17, 27–28, 31–33, 66, 115, 143, 164, 196, 221, 228, 237, 335, 350, 352–55, 361

burial, 15, 17–18, 104, 107, 127, 151, 153, 353

C

chief jailor, 163, 169

civil war, iii, xi–xii, xiv–xv, xviii–xix, 1, 3, 5, 7, 9, 11, 13, 15, 17, 19, 21, 23, 25, 29, 31, 33, 35, 37, 39, 41, 43, 45, 47, 49, 51, 53, 55, 57, 59, 61, 63, 65, 67, 69, 71, 73, 75, 77, 79, 81, 83, 85, 87, 89, 91, 93, 95, 97, 99, 101, 103, 105, 107, 109, 111, 113, 115, 117, 119, 121, 123, 125, 127, 129, 131, 133, 135, 137, 139, 141, 143, 145, 147, 149, 151, 153, 155, 157, 159, 161, 163, 165, 167, 169, 171, 173, 175, 177, 179, 181, 183, 185, 187, 345, 361–63, 373–75

communal riots, 22, 277, 281, 284

D

Dhaka, vii, xii–xv, xviii–xix, 2–5, 8, 11–14, 19–22, 24–32, 35–36, 38, 45, 52, 54–56, 58, 62–64, 66–68, 70, 76–77, 79–81, 83–84, 91, 93, 95–96, 101–3, 106–9, 111–14, 118–19, 123, 125, 127–31, 133, 135–38, 140–41, 148, 160–61, 163–64, 177, 184, 186–88, 191, 196–97, 199, 203, 214, 216, 221–22, 224, 236, 244–45, 250, 253, 260, 263–65, 275, 277–80, 283–84, 286, 289–90, 294–97, 304, 306, 308–9, 311, 315–16, 323, 328–29, 333, 336, 340–43, 345–52, 355, 359–60, 365, 367–68, 370–73, 375, 378–82

Dhaka Central Jail, 160–61, 163

Dhaka University, xiv, 4–5, 28, 68, 84, 96, 108, 123, 346

Dhaka University Central, Students Union (DUCSU), 89, 91, 113

dialogue, 297, 311, 320, 324–25

diamond ring, 94, 98, 145, 261, 294, 361, 363, 365, 383, 385

dormitories, 5, 7, 10, 12, 16, 126, 279, 304, 329

DUCSU. *See* Dhaka University Central, Students Union (DUCSU)

E

East Pakistan, vii, xiii–xv, xviii, 1–3, 20–21, 29, 67–68, 84–85, 89, 92, 95, 108, 132, 154, 167, 172, 192, 200, 230, 234–35, 260, 267, 275–77, 283–84, 290, 295–96, 304, 314, 317–18, 323, 345, 362, 365

election, 2, 172, 175–76, 179, 281

exam results, 38, 86, 89, 98

exploitation, xi, 85, 118, 168, 230

F

Fulbaria Station, 27, 30, 109, 367

G

government, central, 2, 84, 282, 295–96, 317

governmental power. *See* power, governmental

H

Halim (Rokhi's uncle), 8–15, 17–19, 23, 47, 113, 116, 118–19, 143–44, 149–50, 157–58, 170–71, 175, 212–13, 227, 243, 248–49, 252, 256, 271, 274, 301–2, 306, 324, 337, 340, 349, 356–58, 361–64, 366–68, 372, 374–75, 382–83, 385

Harashpur, 22, 101–2, 105–6, 109, 111, 131, 135, 137, 139, 147, 184, 186,

National Assembly, 2–3, 172, 266

negotiations, 3, 5, 314, 320, 324, 328–29, 337

Nisar (Kabil's friend), 10, 12–13, 16–17, 24, 117, 122–26, 153–54, 158, 171, 173–76, 178, 180, 188–89, 199–203, 231–33, 243–45, 265, 267–71, 273–75, 305, 314–16, 325, 359, 363, 366, 374, 384

non-Bengalis, 19–20, 67, 100, 151, 183, 192, 230, 234, 261, 298, 304, 306–8, 312, 322–23, 358, 365, 367, 372

O

officers, 7, 87–88, 154, 366

oppression, 145, 230

P

Pakistan, vii, xiii–xiv, xviii–xix, 1–3, 14, 19–21, 67, 75, 92, 95, 134, 154, 230–31, 234–35, 259, 266, 276, 281, 289, 296–97, 312, 317, 319–20, 324, 332, 344, 348, 357–59, 362, 367, 374, 378

Pakistani military, xiv, xvii–xviii, 13, 19–20, 295–96, 345–49, 365–66, 368–69, 374, 383

Pakistanis, xiv, xviii, 3, 151, 295–96, 347, 351, 362

parliamentary seats, 2, 172, 260, 266, 274, 315, 319

People's Party, 2, 266, 274, 276, 315

police, 87–88, 91–93, 101, 109, 118, 120–22, 126, 128, 135–36, 141–42, 147, 153, 156, 241, 243, 245–46, 249–50

political prisoners, 154, 161–63, 167

politics, 16, 99, 123, 145, 151, 154, 156, 158, 160, 162, 168, 173, 176, 181–82, 191, 201–2, 207, 216–17, 228, 230, 232, 249, 251, 263, 272–73, 275, 278, 281, 286, 304–5, 307, 324, 330, 341, 351, 364, 373

power, governmental, 3, 21, 266, 275–76, 279, 281, 316

prime minister, 2–3, 266, 276, 297, 317, 319, 321

prisons, 161–62, 262, 346, 373

procession, 11, 84, 120, 155, 170, 233, 274, 297–300, 329

protest march, 5, 120, 122, 124, 136, 141, 168, 236

R

Rahman, Mujibur (Sheikh Mujib), xiv, xviii, 2–7, 11, 20–21, 84–85, 92, 95, 120, 167, 172, 196, 200, 228, 233–34, 243, 250, 266, 275, 281–82, 295, 309, 313, 318, 321, 324, 329, 346, 367

Rania (Kabil's aunt), 8–12, 14–17, 22, 25–26, 28, 31, 37–39, 42–44, 47, 49, 51, 66–68, 70–73, 75–76, 87–90, 92–94, 98, 101–10, 117, 127–32, 134, 138–40, 151, 153, 155, 157–59, 162–63, 166, 169–75, 177–80, 182–84, 190–93, 195–99, 211–12, 214, 219–21, 224, 227–29, 231, 234, 238, 242, 244–45, 248–53, 255–59, 261, 263, 270, 273–74, 280, 282–84, 286, 290, 293–94, 301, 306–10, 312, 323, 329, 338–40, 342, 348–49, 363, 366–67, 370–72, 374–75, 377, 379, 383

Printed in the United States
By Bookmasters